The Flame in the Mist

The

Flame in

the Mist

Kit Grindstaff

Delacorte Press

Text copyright © 2013 by Kit Grindstaff
Jacket art copyright © 2013 by Chris Rahn

Delacorte Press is a registered trademark and the colophon is a trademark of Random House, Inc.

Visit us on the Web! randomhouse.com/kids
Educators and librarians, for a variety of teaching tools,
visit us at RHTeachersLibrarians.com

Library of Congress Cataloging-in-Publication Data
Grindstaff, Kit.
The flame in the mist / Kit Grindstaff. — 1st ed.
p. cm.
Summary: Thirteen-year-old Jemma finds herself in a race for her life when she discovers an ancient prophecy that reveals the truth about her past and an unimaginably great and dangerous destiny—to defeat the evil Agromonds and restore peace and sunlight to Anglavia.
ISBN 978-0-385-74290-0 (hc) — ISBN 978-0-307-97914-8 (ebk) —
ISBN 978-0-375-99083-0 (glb)
[1. Magic—Fiction. 2. Prophecy—Fiction. 3. Fate and fatalism—Fiction.
4. Fantasy.] I. Title.
PZ7.G88448F1 2013   [Fic]—dc23   2012004546

The text of this book is set in 12-point Goudy Oldstyle.
Book design by Melissa A. Greenberg

Printed in the United States of America
10 9 8 7 6 5 4 3 2 1

First Edition

For Jemima and Oliver,
who make my world a brighter place

The Flame in the Mist

Prologue:
The Sometime Long Ago
Root of Revenge

"Help me—help!" A weary voice from outside. A fist, hammering on the door.

The boy turned from the fire and the potion he was stirring. Who would call at this hour, before dawn had yet dusted the town rooves? He ran to the door and flung it open.

A girl stood on the step. She was wild-haired and filthy, silken robes hanging in rags from her small frame. She could not have seen more than twelve winters, perhaps thirteen. The same as he.

"Help me, I beg of thee," said she, breathless as a hunted fawn, "for I know not where else to turn. . . ." In her black eyes, he saw the horrors she had witnessed: the killings, the terrors of her flight—

He clamped down his thoughts to prevent himself from seeing more, and reached out his hand. As she took it, he noticed the Stone hanging around her neck, its blue-green blaze promising magic. But the gold crest embroidered on the shoulder pouch she carried made his heart freeze.

The Agromond crest. The girl was an Agromond.

She saw him looking, and turned the pouch around to hide the crest. "I have no more use for my family's evil ways," she whispered. "That part of my life have I left at the castle. Would that thou believ'st me!"

1

Everything about the girl told him she spoke the truth. Her eyes. Her aura. The softness of her touch.

"I believe you," he said. "Come. Warm yourself by our hearth."

The instant she stepped over the threshold, Visions tumbled through his head. He saw all that her Gifts would now bring to the service of healing and Light, instead of to the Agromonds and their Darkness. And he also saw the terrible events that would unfold because of her betrayal of her family. Greater poverty. Greater misery. The Mist spreading, covering the sun. The Agromonds, meting out their fury on the Anglavian people for generations to come.

Then far, far in the future, another girl flickered into his mind's eye. One with fiery-colored hair like his own. One through whom the Agromonds would attempt to take out their greatest revenge, and achieve their greatest gain. Yet she would also be a danger to them—

His Vision clouded. He could not see the outcome. But he wished fervently that there was something he could do to help her. For he knew in his bones that she would be the only hope for peace and prosperity to reign once more.

"The Fire One," he murmured as he settled his beautiful, ragged guest by the hearth. "Thus shall this future one be known."

He glanced out of the window and saw tendrils of Mist snaking through the streets, contaminating the light of dawn.

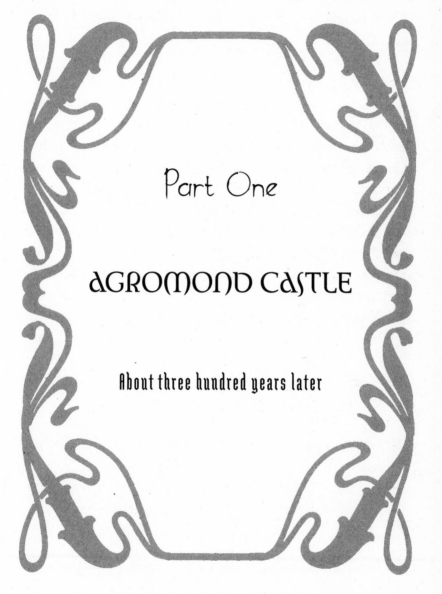

Part One

AGROMOND CASTLE

About three hundred years later

CHAPTER ONE

Mord Dawn

"No!" Jemma's eyelids sprang open. That dream again. Always the same urgency, the same terror, the children's voices calling her, *Jemma—help us, help!* This time, though, something had changed. She strained to remember what was different, but the fragmented details flew around her head like startled sparrows, too fast to catch.

Gradually, her heartbeat slowed, and she sat up, blinking her small, stone-walled room into focus. Though it wasn't yet light, she had eyesight like an owl's and could easily see the carved chest opposite her bed, the rickety chair under the window. On the wardrobe door hung the gray woolen dress, stiff and obedient, that Marsh had ironed the night before. Beneath it, a pair of black leather shoes sat on the floor like two lurking beetles. Her best clothes, reminding her: it was Mord-day, the day of her family's weekly Offerings to their dark Ancestors. As if that weren't bad enough, today's Ceremony was to be special, to prepare for her thirteenth birthday tomorrow. She groaned, and slid out of bed.

The air was colder than usual, and she went to the window to close it. "Vile Mist," she muttered, gazing out at the swirling gray. "I wish you would go away!" Wind swayed the pine tops. *Sweet thirteen,* it seemed to whisper. *Thirte-e-en . . .*

Something needled her memory, other whispers from her dream: *You're mine—all mine!* She slammed the window shut.

"I am a Fire Warrioress, the fiercest in the land!" she gasped. "Evil, evil, go away, cast out by my hand!" The secret incantation she'd made up when she was six and had first seen her flame-red hair in the mirror usually bolstered her, but today the words felt empty and powerless. She gulped down her unease, then noticed a scrabbling sound moving up the chair and onto the window-sill. Four ruby dots glinted at her; two whiskered snouts twitched in the dim, dawn light.

"Hello, Noodle, hello, Pie." Jemma picked up the rats and held them to her chest. "You're as nervous as I am today, aren't you?"

Noodle and Pie quivered, and Jemma held them tighter, feeling their tiny heartbeats flutter in her hands. She kissed their heads, remembering the first time they'd appeared two years ago, when she'd been feeling particularly gloomy. Golden-haired rats, unlike any she'd ever seen—they were special, that was obvious. They had cheered her up then, and had been cheering her up ever since.

Noodle licked her nose, his gaze flickering to the door. Footsteps approached.

"Marsh, already?" said Jemma. "That's odd. It can't be eight o'clock yet."

The rats scampered down Jemma's nightshirt, hopped to the floor, and skittered under the chest. The door creaked open and the lamp-lit face of a small, middle-aged woman peered in.

"Marsh!" Jemma's heart lifted as always to see her erstwhile nurse. "You're early!"

"Shhh!" Marsh shot a glance over her shoulder, then bustled into the room, closed the door, and put her lamp on the chest. She gave Jemma an uncharacteristically quick hug, her plump cheek warm against Jemma's, then took both her hands. "Listen, pet, careful-like. You must come to my room, tonight. No matter what."

"Tonight? But you know how tired the Ceremonies make me—"

"Jus' do it, Jem. It's important."

Nerves paddled Jemma's stomach. Normally, she loved sneaking up to Marsh's tower room after dark and listening to her stories, but clearly this was different. What could be so pressing? Outside, wind whistled through the pines. "Thirteen," she murmured. "It's something to do with my birthday, isn't it? Something— Oh!" All at once, images crashed into her head.

"What is it, Jem?" Marsh fixed Jemma's gaze. "That dream you keep havin'?"

"Yes. No. I mean, yes. There's the Mist as usual, and the screams, but there's more to it . . . a woman's voice, singing in the background . . . so beautiful! I've dreamed about it before, I think, but never remembered till today. Then . . . a man. Young. Dressed like in olden times, but ragged and desperate-looking, and . . . he's coming through the Mist to *get* me!" More images came, faster and clearer. "The screams are getting louder . . . everything's going dark—and the Mist! So thick, and sticky! It's sort of hissing, saying, *Sweet Thirteen! You're mine! Sweet Thirteen!* Marsh, it was horrible! I felt as though the Mist wanted to *swallow* me!"

Marsh paled. "Shush now, pet," she said, gathering Jemma

7

into her short arms. "Shush. It's all right. There's reasons this is happenin' now. . . . I'll explain tonight."

"What reasons? Tell me now—please!"

"T'ain't safe now, Jem." Marsh pulled back. "Walls have ears, remember? So later, when they's all in bed. An' more'n ever, don't let none of 'em know. I've noticed your words comin' looser an' more heated recently. You must mind your tongue, I mean it. Think before you speak, an' before you act."

Jemma nodded, her head swimming with Mist, the man, and screams.

Clang! The first toll of eight.

"I must be off." Marsh squeezed Jemma's hands. "Now, remember the Light Game. It can't help if you don't think of usin' it. I'll see you tonight. Without fail, mind—"

Clang!

"I'll be there, Marsh."

"Good girl." Marsh patted Jemma on the cheek and slipped from the room, closing the door behind her as the West Tower bell continued its doleful countdown to breakfast time.

As usual, Jemma was first to arrive in the Repast Room. On every other morning of the week she had the onerous task of helping Drudge in the kitchen. He was more ancient than anyone could remember, and Jemma found him revolting. But today, as on every Mord-day, she was spared from her duties, and so the long oak table was already laid, the candelabra lit, and a steaming tureen of porridge set by Jemma's place, next to a pot of mauve tea.

She walked to the table and sat with her back to the fire.

Across the room, beyond leaded window-panes, gray tree silhouettes hugged the crag outside. What would they look like, she wondered, if the Mist wasn't there, and the forest surrounding Agromond Castle was like the places that Marsh described in her stories? Places flooded with sunshine, where rivers sparkled with sky-blue reflections, and green fields shone in clear, golden light. Hundreds of years ago, Marsh said, even Anglavia had been like that. Before the Mist came and shrouded everything—

"Dreaming again, Jem-*mah*?" Jemma's older sister, Shade, strutted into the room. Her hair hung like curtains on either side of her face.

"Yes, dreaming again?" Feo loped in behind his twin. "Do share, Jemma."

"Thinking about her fantastic *Offering*, I expect," Shade sneered. She took her place opposite Jemma and flicked back her hair, revealing the red, diamond-shaped birthmark on her left cheek.

Jemma gritted her teeth. Shade and Feo, no doubt, had been practicing their Offerings as usual—unlike her. She'd have to face her mother's fury. Again. "I'll be fine," she muttered.

"Of course you will." Feo grinned, the birthmark on his face—like Shade's, but smaller—elongating. He slumped his long limbs into the chair next to his twin and shoved his cup toward Jemma. "Tea, sister, if you don't mind."

Jemma poured them each a cup of Drudge's special brew, and swigged hers in a single gulp. Usually, its citrus scent calmed her, but today it had no effect, and the caustic look Shade was giving her only made her anxiety worse. Then another scent invaded her nostrils: their mother's Eau de Magot perfume, gusting in through the door.

"Good morrow, children." Nocturna Agromond swept into the room, trailing her crimson Mord-day robes. Four black weasels slithered close behind. Her ever-present Rook was perched on her right shoulder, feathers fluttering. "And how are we all today?"

"Wonderful, Mama," said Shade and Feo.

"Yes. Wonderful," Jemma mumbled.

"Go-o-o-od." Nocturna settled into her carved chair at the end of the table, her black eyes flashing at Jemma. Jemma's stomach shrank. Over the past year or two she had felt increasingly as though her mother was watching her, waiting for some misstep. She forced a smile, and tried not to think of the Ceremony ahead.

The castle bell tolled once: eight-thirty.

"Good morrow, all." Nox Agromond strode in, sweeping his dark hair back with one hand, his Mord-day cloak breezing behind him. "I trust you slept well, Nocturna my dear?"

"Like the dead, Nox." Nocturna's familiar joke raised a titter from Shade and Feo.

"Splendid." Nox sat at his end of the table, and winked at Jemma. She winked back.

"So, let us begin." Nocturna said. "Jemma dear, do serve, if you would?"

Always me, Jemma thought as she ladled out the porridge. *Never the twins. It's not fair.*

The family munched in customary silence. Jemma ate her bowlful slowly, gradually uncovering the Agromond crest: a black Mordsprite, wings folded, ringed by hemlock and the family motto: *Agromondus Supremus.* Agromonds rule. She stared at the letters and reordered them in her head to see how many words she could make: *grand, groan, mouse, demons* . . .

"A groat for your thoughts, Jemma." Nocturna's deep velvet voice wafted down the table.

"I expect she's planning her Offering, Mama." Shade turned to Jemma. *Got you again,* her smirk seemed to say. "It had better not be like last week's, Jem-*mah.* I'm rather bored of you turning dust into butterflies and silly little things like that."

"And I'm rather bored of you needling me, Shade!"

"Well, never mind," Shade scoffed. "It won't matter after tomorrow."

"Shade!" Nox and Nocturna spoke together, their eyes snapping to Shade of one accord.

Jemma's nerves jangled. "After tomorrow?" she said. "Why won't it matter?"

"I . . . um . . ." Shade's birthmark darkened. "Nothing. Forget I said it."

"Apologize to your sister, Shade," Nox said, scowling at her. "Such tiresome jealousy!"

"Sorry, Jem-*mah.*" Shade looked daggers at her.

"Well," Nocturna said, rapping her fingernails on the table. "We still await our special delivery, do we not? Where is that, what's his name, Goodbellows?"

"Goodfellow, my dear. He's sending his boy. He should be here at any moment." Nox turned to the door. "Ah, here he is now. Enter, boy."

Digby? Here, on a Mord-day? Jemma's heart skipped a beat.

"Beggin' your pardons, sir, ma'am." Digby ambled in. "Mr. Drudge asked me to bring this up to you. Wolfsbane, cut fresh today, as requested." He placed a small packet next to Nox's elbow, and caught Jemma's eye. She looked down, trying not to smile. None of her family knew about her friendship with him. Like her nighttime visits to Marsh's room, it was her secret, and she looked forward to Tuesdays, when Digby and his father delivered groceries to the castle.

"Thank you, boy." Nox tucked the packet inside his waistcoat.

"Good day to you all." Digby glanced at Jemma again, his blue eyes making her heart skip, then tipped his cap, and left.

Nocturna blotted her mouth with her napkin. "Scruffy young ruffian! Imagine, dressing like a scarecrow to come here. He should have worn his Mord-day best."

"And the way he looked at Jemma!" Feo's birthmark darkened.

"What way?" Jemma said. "I didn't notice."

"I saw it too," said Shade, "as well as you, trying not to smile at him. Really, Jem-*mah*, you should know better. He's as common as muck."

"Come, come!" said Nox, slapping his palms on the table. "Today, our words should honor our Ancestors, not be wasted on petty quibbles. Now, the Ceremony. Let us adjourn."

"Quite." Nocturna rose from her chair. Rook flapped onto her right shoulder as she glided toward the door, Shade and Feo marching out behind her.

Jemma bit her bottom lip. Her father put his arm around her, his cloak draping her shoulders as they trooped behind the others across the hall toward their room of worship. It was some relief that, unlike them, he had always understood her dread of the weekly ritual. He stopped outside the Ceremony Chamber, then turned to face Jemma and took her hands in his.

"How the years have sped by!" he said, his eyes crinkling. "I can scarcely believe it. You, our little one, just one day from being thirteen. My sweet thirteen!"

Sweet thirteen! The words from her dream crashed into Jemma's mind. She gasped, and pulled her hands from her father's. He frowned slightly, a puzzled expression playing on his face, then ushered her through the great oak doors into the cavernous room.

CHAPTER TWO

Scaqavay

The Ceremony Chamber was already stifling, lit by a blazing fire and thirteen black candles ranged across the mantelpiece, which served as the altar. Shadows and light danced on the windowless walls and on the four enormous stone pillars that soared up to the ceiling. Sprigs of hemlock and deadly nightshade were strewn across the hearth and over the huge statues on either side of the fireplace: on the left, brandishing his scythe, was Mordrake, the great Agromond ancestor who had created the Mist some seven hundred years before; and on the right, draped with lizards and wielding a carved bolt of lightning, his wife, the beautiful ferocious-looking Mordana, for whom he'd had the castle built. Jemma had always found them alarming, partly because of their towering height—already small for her age, she felt dwarfed by them. But as much as that, it was because of their names. Only recently had she understood why: Mord, Marsh had explained, was the Frankish word for Death.

Nine tolls rang out from the Bell Tower as the family settled themselves in the pews. There were four rows in all, a reminder of the days when the Agromond family had been larger. Jemma sat in the second row next to Feo, with Shade on the other side of him. Her father sat in front of her, next to Nocturna, then looked over his shoulder.

"All right?" he whispered, eyebrows raised. "Don't you worry, Flamehead. You'll do splendidly, I know it."

Flamehead! He hadn't called her that in years. His pet name for her used to reassure her, and she wanted reassurance now, desperately. She smiled, but fear gnawed at her like a pack of wolves.

"That's my girl." Nox smiled back and turned away.

The last toll died down. Nocturna rose to her feet and walked to the fireplace, weasels circling her hemline. "All rise," she said, raising her hands above her head.

Jemma, Nox, and the twins stood. Rook fluttered to the altar and landed on a black globe set on one end of it. Nocturna began to turn counter-clockwise, the two pendants around her neck glinting in the firelight, one jet black, one aquamarine, as she chanted the Opening Invocation.

> *"South corner, East corner, North corner, West,*
> *Gathered here at Your behest*
> *We call upon thee, Lords of Night,*
> *To keep us ever safe from Light!"*

As always, Nocturna looked as energized by the Invocation as Jemma felt weakened by it. It was a relief to sit again as Nocturna launched into the Fealty: "We honor thee, O Mordrake and Mordana, whose blood flows through us to this great Time of Darkness . . ."

Her head bowed, Jemma counted the worm holes on the seat of the pew in front of her: last week, sixteen; this week, twenty-one. *Rotting, like everything else here,* she thought. Her mind wandered to Tuesday, and Digby's next visit. Only two days to go—

"O Mordrake, Mordana!" The family's rousing bleat snatched Jemma from her daydream. "Beloved founders of our dynasty! In everlasting thanks for the Mist and our continuing supremacy over this our land of Anglavia, accept our Offerings!"

"Come, Shade," said Nocturna. "You first."

Jemma's throat tightened as Shade rose from her pew and strutted to Mordana's statue, bowed and kissed its hand, then walked to her mother's side and turned to face the pews.

"All hail, Mordrake, Mordana!" she said. "Behold, the Extinguishing of the Light!"

Shade drew in her breath, billowing out her chest, and blew. A blast of ice-cold air streaked past the pews, leaving a trail of frost in its wake. It ricocheted off the back wall and returned to the fireplace. Rook, still perched on the black globe, shivered. Ten of the thirteen candles ranged beside him sputtered and died, their flames turned to beads of ice. The middle three remained lit. Shade's face fell.

"Suitably chilling, my dear." Nocturna said, stroking Shade's hair. "An impressive show."

"I wanted to put them *all* out!" Shade stomped back to her seat. "Just wait. Someday I shall freeze everything."

"Of course, dear," said Nocturna. "Your turn, Feo. Don't keep us waiting."

Feo leapt to his feet and shot Jemma a crooked grin as he loped to the front of the room. Jemma's dread thickened. Only last year, Feo could barely materialize a worm without it disappearing within seconds, but since his and Shade's thirteenth birthday Initiations eleven months ago—a secret Ceremony she had been too young to attend, her parents had said—something had changed. Feo's Offerings had gradually become more sinister. Like in last week's Ceremony, when at his command every fly in the room had simultaneously stopped buzzing, then dropped dead, pattering to the floor with the sound of a thousand raindrops.

Feo walked to Mordrake's statue and reached behind it for something, then stood beside Nocturna.

"All hail, Mordrake, Mordana!" he said, holding up the object for all to see: a glass jar, full of what appeared to be a tangle of wriggling black string. He unscrewed its lid, grabbed a strand, and extracted a large spider. Dangling it by one hairy leg, he tilted his head back, opened his mouth, and popped it in. Jemma heard the crunch of its body being ground between Feo's teeth, and the gulp as he swallowed. He took out another, its legs flailing, and repeated his performance. Then twice more, several spiders at once, until the jar was empty. Each time the pride in Nocturna's eyes intensified. Each time Jemma's heart shrank, imagining the spiders' struggle in Feo's throat, their pain as his teeth gnashed down on them.

"Suitably gruesome, Feo," Nocturna said, patting him on the back.

"Wait, Mama. There's more." Feo closed his eyes and screwed up his face. His diaphragm lurched three times, then he opened his mouth and stuck out his tongue. One by one, six spiders scurried out and fell to the floor. Relief flooded Jemma. They were alive! But just as the seventh was making its bid for freedom from between Feo's lips, he clamped his jaws around it, crunched again, gulped, and it was gone. He stamped his feet and squished the other six.

Nox rose to his feet. "Splendid, my boy!" he boomed, clapping his hands. "Splendid!"

Nocturna's eyes shone with delight. Rook cawed, swaying

from foot to foot. Shade picked at her fingernails, her face puckered with envy, as Feo swaggered back to his seat.

Nocturna turned to Jemma, her crimson robes haloed by the firelight behind her, and pulled herself to her full height. "Your turn, Jemma," she said.

Heat pressed into Jemma. Sweat dripped from her brow; her dress prickled, her shoes pinched. If only she'd practiced! But it felt so wrong, the things they wanted. It felt—

"Go on, my dearest," her father whispered as he sat down again. "I have faith in you."

Jemma's heart lifted slightly. She could do better than Shade, she knew she could! Surely it wouldn't hurt to call upon the Mord ancestors just this once, to help her summon some small, cloud-like Entity? Something mildly unpleasant, that she would command to tangle in Shade's hair? Feo would laugh . . . her parents would be proud of her. . . . No more of her mother's anger, her father's disappointment! And no real damage would be done, no creature injured; nothing but Shade's pride. What sweet revenge that would be! She could do it—she would!

Determined, Jemma walked to her mother's side, bowed to the statues, then turned her back to the fire and took a deep breath.

"All Hail, Mord—Mord—" The words stuck like knives in her throat.

"Yes, dear?" Nox leaned forward in his pew, his eyes ablaze with hope.

"I um, bring the Offering of . . . a . . ." It was no use. Fear had her in its grip.

"Speak up, Jemma," Nocturna said.

18

"I don't feel very well, Mama. Please, can't I . . . ?"

A chunk of plaster fell from the ceiling and shattered at her feet.

"You must do your part in honoring our Ancestors, my dear." Nocturna cracked a smile, but Jemma saw the danger lurking behind it. Her mother had lashed out at her before, and wouldn't hesitate to again if Jemma didn't deliver. Panic rising, she looked at her father.

"Just do your best, Jemma," he said softly.

Jemma's mind felt trapped in a vise. Shade and Feo's gazes bore into her, darkness surrounding their pale faces. The room began to fade. Materializing anything, even the merest ant, would be impossible with such anxiety rattling through her. She looked at her knees, willing them not to buckle. There at her feet, long tails twitching, were Noodle and Pie, come to her rescue, as they did every time she was at a loss during the Ceremonies. Raising her head to the ceiling, she waved her arms and squeaked twice. The rats hopped onto the hem of her dress and clambered up to sit on her shoulders, one on each side.

"Behold," Jemma croaked. "Rats, from thin air . . ."

Silence filled the room. The disapproval on Nocturna's face made her look as though she had just smelled something vile. The weasels edged out from under the front pew and hissed, baring needle-sharp teeth.

Shade was the first to speak. "Those disgusting rats again, Jem-*mah!*" she sneered. "Mama, Papa, make her do something different. She does the same thing every other week!"

"Yes, come on, Jemma," Feo urged. "You can do better than that!"

"I . . . I could make them fly. . . ." Jemma mumbled, desperate, and then immediately regretted it. She had tried to make things fly, often, but had only succeeded once, last Wednesday at dinner, when she'd spirited Shade's bread roll across the table and onto her own plate.

Nox stood, and strode toward her mother. "I think Jemma has done quite enough," he said. "We mustn't exhaust our daughter, Nocturna"—he lowered his voice—"*must* we?"

Nocturna inhaled. "Of course not." she said. "Jemma, sit."

Jemma staggered to the end of her pew, grateful for her father's intervention, and slumped down. Noodle and Pie nuzzled into her neck.

"Don't bring those revolting creatures *near* me," said Shade, her voice trembling as she shifted away.

"They're just *rats*, Shade," said Feo. "What are you so afraid of?"

Jemma stroked Noodle and Pie. She had never understood her sister's terror of them—there seemed to be nothing else Shade feared—but she was thankful for it. With the rats nearby, Shade kept her distance.

Clang!

Nine-thirty.

"And now, children," Nox said. "The time has come for your mother's and my Offering. Today, we have a surprise for you: the summoning of a new Entity. One that promises to be more inspiring than ever!"

Shade and Feo exchanged excited glances. Jemma began to tremble. The Entities: it was they that made her feel so drained, stirring a deep terror in her that she dreaded more than anything. *It's just fear getting the better of you,* her father always said. *You must learn to overcome it.* But his words never helped.

"This," Nox continued, "is a special event that, as decreed in our ancient Mord tradition, must take place shortly before the coming-of-age of the youngest Agromond. And as we all know, tomorrow our beloved Jemma will turn thirteen—"

"Yes, yes, Nox," Nocturna said. "The herbs, if you please."

Nox held Jemma's gaze as he tossed back his cloak and pulled the packet Digby had brought from inside his waist-coat. He untied it and gathered a fistful of foliage.

"*Wolfum malificarum!*" he said, throwing it onto the fire with a flourish. It fizzed and crackled, puffing out bile-green smoke. He and Nocturna closed their eyes, their faces in rapt concentration. They shook; their bodies stiffened. Then their eyes shot open and rolled back into their heads until only the whites were visible. The two pendants around Nocturna's neck pulsed in the firelight, blood-red, aquamarine, blood-red. . . .

Entranced, she and Nox began to chant, their voices low and ominous:

> "Morda-Morda-Morda-lay,
> You who keep'st the sun at bay,
> Send to us on this Your day
> Your favored phantom, Scagavay!"

Nocturna's pendants gleamed brighter. Waves of weari-ness washed through Jemma.

> "Morda-Morda-Morda-lay,
> You who keep'st the sun at bay,
> Send to us on this Your day
> Your favored phantom, Scagavay!"

The black globe on the mantel seemed to throb in time with the words, like a giant heart. Nocturna's pendants looked illuminated from within. Jemma's head spun.

"Morda-Morda-Morda-lay . . ."

The fire shimmered and flared, shimmered and flared again, then faded as if being inhaled by the grate. The room plunged into chill. Then the fire leapt up again, throwing her parents' shadows across the vaulted ceiling like enormous birds of prey. Smoke curled from the flames, stinking of rotten flesh. Suddenly, with an ear-splitting roar, a black mass spewed from the fireplace. Rook was propelled into the air, flapping frantically. Noodle and Pie scrambled inside the front of Jemma's dress. Feo, his face chalk-white, sat wide-eyed, biting his lips. The weasel on his lap fled under the pew next to its three companions; a yellow puddle appeared beneath them. Shade sat transfixed. Jemma felt the rest of her strength being sucked out of her.

This was worse than any Entity they'd summoned before. Far worse.

The black mass curled across the mantel and around each statue, then coalesced above Nox and Nocturna's heads. They fell to their knees, hands raised.

"Scagavay!" they said in unison. "Mord be praised! We have called, and you have come!"

Scagavay pulsed as if breathing, then suddenly sprang into the shape of a huge open-mouthed face. A sound like a thousand screams spilled from it into the room. Jemma felt as though her bones were ice, freezing her from inside. She knew that sound—had heard those screams before, in her dreams. Then they had been distant, echoey, as if from some long-ago time. But this was loud, and utterly soul-chilling, just like the Mist had been in this morning's dream, threatening to engulf her. . . .

"No," she whispered. "No . . ." She willed her words to the rats. *Noodle, Pie . . . Forgive me . . . if I could just borrow your strength . . . Just a spark, to get me moving . . .*

The two lumps in her bodice stirred, and Jemma felt the faintest glimmer of energy pulsing from the rats into her veins. She hauled herself to her feet and backed away from the black tendrils snaking toward her. *One step . . .* Now she knew what those flies struggling to peel themselves off the fly paper in the kitchen must feel like. She turned to the door. *Two steps, three . . .* The screams subsided. *Four, five, six . . .* Her bones felt warmer, lighter. *Seven, eight, nine . . .* Then she was running, and slammed into the huge carved door. Glancing over her shoulder, she was surprised to see that Scagavay had vanished. Her parents and the twins looked bewildered. Her mother's pendants had lost their luminosity and now lay against her chest, dull and ordinary.

"Jemma . . ." Nocturna's voice sounded almost pleading. "Wait . . ."

With one final burst of effort, Jemma pulled open the door and fled from the room.

CHAPTER THREE

Port in a Storm

Jemma ran across the hall and into the stairway leading to the kitchen below. Halfway down, she paused for breath, heart beating like the wings of a caged bird. Claws needled her chest—the rats, scrabbling beneath her bodice. She pulled them out and they hung from her hands, their golden fur sleek with her sweat, ruby eyes wild and unblinking.

"Noodle, Pie, thank you, thank you! You saved me again." Jemma pulsed what energy she could back into them, then placed them onto the stone step. They teetered into a nearby crevice and she hurtled down the remaining stairs, one thought blazing in her mind: to reach Marsh. She set off along the corridor toward the Vat Room, where she knew her trusted confidante would be, washing the laundry as she did on every Mord-day. Marsh would help her. She always did.

Jemma's footsteps echoed off the dank, torch-lit walls. The low ceiling, black with mold, glistened and blinked like spying eyes. Shelves lined with large jars of grotesque-looking pickles and preserves—huge limb-like gherkins, yellow peppers like twisted mandrakes—seemed to advance and recede. The horrific howl of moments ago still filled her head, and she imagined Scagavay pursuing her, seeping out of every crack in the walls, suffocating her. . . . She increased her stride.

How many times had she made an adventure of exploring

these corridors, imagining herself to be a rebel fleeing for her life, or a warrioress rescuing prisoners from years of captivity? Now, the peril felt all too real. She sped past herb hutches and hanging entrails, and into the kitchen, praying that the revolting Drudge wouldn't be there—that would be too much. But halfway across, his stooped shadow shuffled from the Corridor of Dungeons. He thrust out a spindly hand, his fingernails snagging the sleeve of her dress as she passed.

"Leave me *alone*," she muttered under her breath, her heartbeat galloping.

"Jmmaaagh!" His wheeze spat into the gloom behind her. "No afff . . . Help!"

Jemma picked up her pace and hurtled into the long West Passage, pulled as if by a magnet toward the Vat Room at the end.

"Marsh!" Jemma burst in. Steam belched from the sunken tub that practically filled the floor. Marsh was wrestling with a long pole, doing her best to stir a soggy mass of off-white sheets. "Marsh, help me!"

"Sprites, child!" Marsh dropped the pole and swept Jemma into her arms. "Whatever's the matter?"

"Everything! This place . . . the Ceremony . . ." Jemma sobbed onto Marsh's shoulder. "It was worse than ever! Why do they love it so much, when I hate it, hate it! I'm just not like them—I never have been! I've tried and tried, but I can't do what they want."

"Hush now." Marsh cradled Jemma, stroking her head. "Hush. There now."

"And that howling thing—I felt like it was sucking the life out of me!"

"Howlin' thing? Oh, no . . ." Marsh pulled away, the ruddiness draining from her cheeks. "Did you remember the Light Game?"

"No . . . I . . . But they would have seen it, wouldn't they? They would've known—"

"I've told you a thousand times, they can't *see* it, not if you use it the way I've taught you! You forgot, din't you? You *must* remember it, Jemma! T'aint a game no more—"

"Why, what's going on? Tell me!"

"Later, Jem. What've I told you about walls havin' ears? You mus' trust me, an' wait till tonight. Now go, back upstairs—"

"No, Marsh, no! I have to get away from here—I can't wait! I don't care if they say I'm too weak to go outside—I have to leave, now! Even if it kills me. I'd rather die than stay!"

"Pull yourself together, child! Breathe. . . . breathe. . . . That's it. . . . Good. Now listen to me, careful-like. There's things I've had to keep from you. Things too dangerous for you to know. Secrets. Lies. I know you're scared, Jem, but tonight, I promise you, everything will change. Till then, you got to be brave, and face 'em. So off you go. They'll come lookin' for you, an' they mustn't find you with me, 'specially not now. An' this time, remember the Light Game. It'll protect you. Above all, don't let none of 'em see how upset you are. Pretend, like we does sometimes—"

"But . . . secrets? Lies? What—?"

"Ssssh!" Marsh's eyes locked onto Jemma's and she whispered, "*Someone's comin',*" then snatched up her washing pole and poked at the sheets, admonishing Jemma in a loud monotone:

"Keep away from me, you stuck-up piece of vermin!"

Feigning coldness toward one another was a game Marsh and Jemma had played for as long as Jemma could remember to disguise their mutual fondness. Normally, at Marsh's cue, Jemma would shoot back some absurd insult. But now, words jammed in her mind.

"Burstin' in like you owned the place!" Marsh's voice was stern, but her eyes were full of softness. "Be off with you. Or did a harpy eat your legs?"

This grisly image always amused Jemma, and it snapped her to her senses. "What makes you think I'd want to stay around you, anyway?" she said. "You're fat, and barely bigger than a troll!" She turned to leave just as a bony form appeared in the doorway. Drudge stood there, swaying like a gnarled tree in a storm.

"Jmaaagh!" he said, his tongue lolling to one side. "No . . . afffr—"

"Out of my way," Jemma said, as firmly as she could.

"You, no aaaagh . . ." Drudge's sour breath cascaded over Jemma as his lips curled back, revealing a row of yellow-gray teeth. Jemma found him sinister at the best of times, but now he looked thoroughly alarming.

"Mr. Drudge," Marsh said. "No sense you keepin' this little so-and-so here. Best let her be on her way."

"You, no . . . Aagh . . . !"

"Let me past, if you *please*, Drudge." Jemma clenched her fists, her heart thumping.

"You—no . . . Aaagh . . . growm!" Drudge staggered toward her. "You, so . . . they. So they!"

Marsh gasped, then dropped the washing pole and shoved

between Jemma and the old man. "There there, Drudge," she said. "Don't say no more, eh?" She looked over her shoulder at Jemma and mouthed, *Go!* But Marsh looked as though she had seen a ghost, and Jemma stood rooted to the flagstones.

"Much!" Drudge's chest heaved with the effort of speaking. "Jmaaagh, so they! Go. Toniiigh!"

"Shush, Drudge!" Marsh smoothed the rumpled lapels of Drudge's jacket. "It's all under control. Let Jemma be on her way, now."

Jemma was stunned. Usually, Marsh was almost as sharp-tongued with Drudge as the rest of the family was. But now, she was being so civil to him—almost friendly. It's all under control? What did she mean? Whatever she knew, did Drudge know it too? Surely not! He'd been the Agromonds' servant for generations. He was one of them—

"Jem, *go!*" Marsh looked desperate.

"All right . . . I . . ."

"Jmmmaaah . . . no . . . aagh," Drudge wheezed. Suddenly, he looked at the door, his yellow eyes wide, and shook his grizzled head. Marsh let go of him and turned to Jemma.

"Go away this minute, Miss High-and-Mighty!" she said loudly, nudging her head toward the corridor. "Back upstairs where you belong!"

This time, Jemma caught on immediately. "You're one to talk, lard-woman. The cheek of it! Farewell to you. And to you, you old— Oh!" She looked at where Drudge had been standing, but he was gone. She glimpsed his silhouette backing into the steam until he was engulfed by it and no longer visible. A second later, a tall form emerged through the door, Rook on shoulder, musty-sweet perfume cutting through the warmth of wet laundry.

"Ah, Jemma, here you are." Nocturna cast a venomous glance in Marsh's direction as she reached her crimson-sheathed arms toward Jemma. "Come."

She clasped Jemma's shoulders and steered her out of the room on the first toll of ten.

CHAPTER FOUR

Deception

Nocturna's fingernails dug into Jemma's neck as she propelled her away from the Vat Room. Jemma felt as though an ax were hovering above her head—some threat, which would fall at any second. But no threat came, and silence accompanied them through the kitchen, along the Pickle Corridor, up the stairs into the hallway, past the Ceremony Chamber, its doors now closed, and into the Lush Chamber.

Rook flapped to the mantelpiece and perched there, wings hunched. Nox was languishing in one of two high-backed chairs on either side of the fireplace; the weasels were curled beneath the other. Shade and Feo sat side by side on the faded damask ottoman. All turned to look at Jemma as she and her mother entered.

Nocturna ushered Jemma to a tattered footstool and pushed her down onto it, then sat in her chair opposite Nox, a puff of dust rising up around her. Jemma tensed, waiting for sentence to be passed: being denied food for a week, or worse, locked in her room.

The fire blazed.

Nox coughed, and removed his cloak.

Shade tossed her hair.

Feo looked up at the minstrels' gallery.

As Jemma glanced from one to the other, she couldn't help

noticing how ragged all the tapestries and drapes were. Every day, it seemed, the castle was becoming more dilapidated. Threads stuck from the upholstery, as if some wild creature had been clawing at it. The picture frames were cracked. The portrait of Nocturna's mother above the fireplace had patches of paint missing, making her look diseased.

Jemma gazed at the motto carved into the mantelpiece: *Mordus Aderit.* Mord is present. Her mind flashed through the letters, re-ordering them: *dream . . . dead . . . murder . . .*

The weasels snuffled.

Rook ruffled.

Nocturna shuffled in her chair. "Jemma, my dear," she said, "we owe you an apology. Scagavay . . . I . . . we . . . misjudged. It . . . Nox, for Mord's sake, say something!" Jemma had never seen her mother awkward like this, her usual sleekness broken.

Jemma's father cleared his throat. "Jemma, what your mother is trying to say, is that we underestimated Scagavay's effect on you. Terrible . . . we had no idea. But you have nothing to fear. We all realize it was too much, do we not?"

Nocturna, Feo, and Shade spoke together: "Why, yes . . . Of course."

Jemma relaxed slightly, relieved that they weren't angry with her. But doubt prickled her skin. Her mother had hardly said a kind word to her in months, so why the concern now?

"So, my dear, please forget it ever happened." Her father raised one hand in the air and snapped his fingers. A pink rose appeared. He leaned forward with a smile and handed it to her. He had materialized roses before, red ones, and Jemma had always found their smell soothing. She buried her nose in its soft petals, allowing the intoxicating scent to waft over her.

"I think," Nox continued, "that this would be an apt moment for some good news. Dr. Graves will be here tomorrow, and from what he has told us of his recent tests on you, Jemma, your allergy to the Mist is much improved—in fact, you are practically cured! The lifelong threat to your health is over, and you will soon be strong enough to go outside, which means you may also accompany your mother, the twins, and me on our monthly ministrations. What do you think of that, my dear?"

"Really? You mean . . . go to the villages, and visit the people?" Outside! Oh, to actually ride in the carriage, instead of sitting in it in the stables, imagining! After all these years of begging to go out, pleading, protesting that she didn't *feel* unwell—far from it!—now, at last, she would see Hazebury, where Digby lived, and the other villages nearby. . . .

"Yes, really!" Nox beamed. "As early as next week, perhaps. We know how you have longed for this." He glanced at Nocturna. "Quite the birthday gift for our youngest, we hope."

"Quite." Nocturna turned to Jemma, an overly wide smile spreading across her face. "You will see how charming, how *delightful* our people are, my dear."

Jemma frowned. Charming? Delightful? Her mother had only ever referred to them as "dross." Something was wrong . . . Marsh's words gnawed into her head. *Secrets. Lies . . .*

"You'll like it, Jemma," said Feo. "I've been looking forward to you coming with us."

"Yes, Jemma," Shade trilled. "You will. Like it."

Shade, being nice to her? And saying her name normally, instead of making fun of it? That hadn't happened in years. Something was definitely wrong. Marsh's words weaseled deeper into her mind: *Secrets, lies . . . Things too dangerous for you to know . . .* She must play along. Pretend, like Marsh had said. She inhaled the rose's scent to calm herself.

"That's . . . wonderful. I, um, I can't wait." Jemma smiled, twirling the rose in her fingers. Its petals looked strange, seeming to fold in on each other. The room blurred: her post-Ceremony exhaustion was taking hold, more heavily than usual. Her limbs were as limp as wet rags. Everything was distorting—

"Jemma, Flamehead . . . are you all right?" Her father suddenly appeared huge, then shrank again.

"I . . . mmm . . ." Jemma's tongue felt thick. She gripped the rose, and a sharp pain shot up her arm as a thorn pricked her palm. The rose fell to the floor, its petals scattering. Weariness galloped through her.

"Worn out . . . poor dear . . . up to her room . . . not as strong as we thought, after all . . ." Her father's voice, distant. His face, looming large as he lifted her into his arms.

Jemma's mind sputtered like a candle, and went dark.

Sweet thirteen! hissed the Mist. My sweet thirte-e-e-n! You are mine! You bear my Mark . . . White chill turned black, then Scagavay was swirling and howling, squeezing the air from her. She heard Marsh yelling: "Wake up, Jemma, wake up! Before it's too late!" She tried shouting back, but her voice was silent. Marsh was nowhere, and Scagavay was everywhere, its stench making Jemma retch as she plummeted downward. Then Noodle and Pie were there too, pawing her, squealing. The castle bell boomed, one . . . two . . . three . . . four, and on and on . . . seven, eight . . . She was about to hit the ground—

Jemma woke in a cold sweat on the last stroke of nine, with the rats tangled in her bedclothes. The dream images pulsed through her, pressing her to the mattress. "I am *not* yours," she whispered to the Mist as she gulped down air, "and I don't bear your Mark! I am a Fire Warrioress, the fiercest in the land . . ." But she didn't feel fierce at all. She felt as though the wind could blow her away like a scrap of dust.

Two snouts nudged her cheek. Two squeaks. Rain, hissing outside.

"Noodle, Pie." Jemma turned her head and looked into their faces. "I'm scared. Really scared." Their snouts moved closer. Behind them, the room was pitch-dark; the whole day had passed. How had that happened? All she remembered was being with her family in the Lush Chamber. The rose. The room, spinning. Feeling faint. Nauseous. As if . . . had she been *drugged*? No, it wasn't possible! Agromonds couldn't be drugged or poisoned; her father was always saying so. Their magic detected it, making it smell noxious to them. She would have known. Besides, however unkind her mother could be sometimes, surely she wouldn't *harm* Jemma? And her father never would.

"Just the same old Mord-day tiredness, I suppose, Rattusses. But why is it so much worse than usual tonight?"

Outside, the rain picked up. Wind whistled through the pines. *Sweet thirteen . . .*

Suddenly, everything came back. The Ceremony. Scagavay. Running to Marsh—

"Marsh! I must go to her—but I can hardly move! What am I going to *do*?" What would Marsh say? *The Light Game, Jem!* Jemma recalled one of the ways Marsh had taught her to use it. *See yourself really small,* she'd said, *like a speck of sand, sailin' through your own blood to find whatever's ailin' you. . . .*

Jemma focused her intention, Noodle and Pie adding their energy to hers. And there it was, the dark cloud of weariness swimming through her. She imagined infusing it with light, watching it change, her blood turning red again. In the distance she heard the single *clang* of nine-thirty, and still she focused, and focused, until her mind cleared and she felt strong enough to sit. The rats lay next to her, panting with exhaustion.

"Noodle . . . Pie . . . Thank you! That's the second time today. What would I do without you?" She kissed their muzzles. "Now, I'm going to Marsh's room. Stay here and rest."

Jemma swung her legs off the bed, then tiptoed across the floor in her stockinged feet and opened her door just as the first strike of ten boomed out from the Bell Tower.

CHAPTER FIVE

The Conversation

Jemma peered along the corridor outside her room: all clear. But faint light flickered by the top of the stairs, emanating from below. Voices flared through the darkness. She crept to the banisters and looked down at the hall. The huge front door was heavily bolted, as was the Ceremony Chamber door to its right, but a sliver of light sliced across the flagstones from the Lush Chamber. Its door was ajar, an urgent-sounding murmur coming from within: her parents.

"I tell you, Nox, that woman knows something!"

"Shush, Nocturna, for Mord's sake!" Footsteps, then creaking as the door was closed. Jemma crept back along the corridor until she came to a hatch on her left. Very carefully, she eased it open, and inched into the minstrels' gallery. Her father's voice rose from below.

"Nocturna, my dear, please calm yourself—"

"Calm myself? Spare me your condescension, Nox!" Jemma heard a swishing sound and pictured her mother pacing up and down, the hem of her crimson dress sweeping the floor. "Marsh is a danger to us, I tell you. Jemma ran to her like a frightened pup to its mother."

"Come, Nocturna! Jemma always hides in the cellars. Why should she not, today? And if Marsh did happen to be there too, what could she possibly know? She's just a bumbling fool—"

"You're the fool, Nox! The woman didn't just *happen* to be there; she always does the laundry on Ceremony days. Jemma knew that, and went directly to her. And I saw the way Marsh looked at the child, as if—yes, I declare: she loves her, I'd swear to it!"

"So? I have a soft spot for Jemma myself, as you well know."

"Oh, yes, I know," Nocturna sneered. "How could I not, when you so obviously favor her over our own two?"

Jemma's heart punched into her throat. Their *own* two? What were they talking about?

"Nocturna—"

"Don't try to deny it, Nox. You and your sentimentality!"

"You know the reason for my affection, Nocturna." Nox's voice cracked. "Yet you torment me!"

The swishing stopped; the air bristled. Seconds marched by: one, two, three . . . Jemma heard what she guessed was Nocturna's heavy ruby ring, clinking several times on the stem of her wine goblet. Four, five . . .

"Well. Let us keep to the point, shall we, Nox? Marsh . . . Oh, I should have known, when she arrived so soon after Jemma, something was not right."

Arrived? So soon after . . . ?

"So soon? A whole year? Jemma was already two, Nocturna, if you remember. And as you yourself said at the time, Marsh was so gruff, so perfect for the children—"

"Well, what if she was pretending?" The swishing started again. Jemma crept toward the edge of the gallery. Her father was out of view; her mother paced furiously, Rook clinging to her shoulder, wings wafting like black sails. "Yes . . . the more I think, the more I'm sure of it: Marsh is not what we've thought for all these years. What if, Mord forbid, she was sent by Jemma's parents, to watch over her?"

Her *parents*? Jemma gasped.

Nocturna froze. "What was that?"

"What was what?"

Jemma held her breath, the words *Jemma's parents* hammering in her head.

"Shhh!" Nocturna raised her hand. The wind howled outside. "Just the wind. Now, where was I?" She started pacing again. "Ah, yes. Suppose Marsh was their emissary . . . sent here not only to watch over Jemma, but to help her escape before her Initiation? All our planning will have been in vain; generations of waiting to break the Prophecy and gain her Powers, wasted; the chance to destroy our family's old enemies and seal our supremacy once and for all, gone!"

"My dear, you are positively overreaching yourself!" Nox strode to the fireplace and stood with his back to the flames. "Emissary indeed! Why, if Marsh had been sent by Jemma's parents, the Mist would have seen her intention and stopped her, just as it stopped them!"

"*They*"—Nocturna's voice dripped with disdain—"were weakened by their grief, as we intended, and could not have masked their desire to save Jemma and destroy us. Besides, we have held their Powers in crystal captivity these past twelve years. But suppose there was somebody with strong Mind Control, well-trained enough to conceal their thoughts from the Mist and get through it? Do you not remember the reports of a woman, an ally of theirs, who single-mindedly quelled the Celdorian riots? Suppose it was *she*? A spy in our very midst, and we too blind to see it!"

"Preposterous! Marsh couldn't have hidden such a thing

from us for all this time. And, if it were so, why hasn't she told the child? It's obvious she has not. Jemma clearly has no real idea of her abilities, let alone who she really is—"

"You idiot!" Nocturna hurled her goblet to the floor. "A cunning spy would have kept the truth from the child so she wouldn't have to lie to us and risk slipping up, being discovered! In any case, Jemma would not have been ready before. Now would be the time to act: the night before her thirteenth birthday, just when her Powers are blossoming!"

Powers? What were they *talking* about?

"But we've kept draining her with the Ceremonies and Entities, precisely to prevent her awareness of her Powers, and weaken her! Why, I almost thought we'd gone too far today, with Scagavay. And as for that rose potion idea of yours, Nocturna—why, the poor child needs *some* strength for the Ceremony tomorrow!"

Rose potion? So they *had* drugged her! Jemma trembled as Nocturna stopped in her tracks and turned to face Nox, her crimson dress vivid in the firelight.

"You know Scagavay was a necessary test, Nox. Had Jemma been one of us, she would have been awed, not petrified. But you saw what happened. She fled. To Marsh. And do you think we managed to avert her suspicion afterward, telling her she can finally go outside? The child is no fool, Nox, though we've worked hard to keep her in ignorance. She grows more willful every day, and recovers her senses more quickly. It's a bad omen, I tell you, after she's been so dreamy-headed most of her life. Are you prepared to risk it all—*all*—so close to our goal? If Jemma escapes and lives to fulfill that Prophecy, we are doomed!"

"Nocturna, you surpass yourself! Why, even if she could

recover from the potion in time, how could she and Marsh survive the forest? Jemma's Powers will not fully come to her unless she has her Stone. As long as that is in our possession, we are safe."

"And what good is the Stone to us without Jemma? What if she was to *attempt* escape and was killed? Answer me that!"

Prophecy . . . Stone . . . killed . . . ? Jemma felt sick with confusion.

"I . . . well . . . but . . . but Jemma bears the Mark! Is that not the reason we kept her alive? She may yet come to our side!"

Nocturna stamped her foot. "You are grasping at straws, Nox! You know that I myself had high hopes that she would take to our ways when we found the Mark on her. And I continued to hope, until—well, you know what convinced me otherwise. For such a small thing to have upset her so! Jemma defies the Mark, she defies it!"

The Mark? Did they mean her diamond-shaped birthmark, like Shade's and Feo's? Jemma felt it hot on her back.

"Really, Nocturna! If you are referring to Jemma's eleventh birthday Ceremony, why, even if her cruel streak is not as developed as Shade's, that doesn't mean she couldn't change. Her gifts have always exceeded the twins'. And may I remind you what it would mean to us if she brought such strengths to our side. There is still time—"

"Enough of your pathetic hoping, Nox—enough! I'm sick of your endless defense of the girl, and your obsession with her. Just because she resembles your precious twin! But Jemma is not her, however alike she may look. Your twin is dead,

Nox, dead, and has been since you were four. You should have buried her memory thirty years ago, when your parents buried her body. But no. You have nursed it, with your self-pitying grief—"

"How dare you, Nocturna." Nox's voice was gravel. "How *dare* you!"

"I dare, Nox, because it makes you weak, and you are endangering our plans. I repeat: Jemma is not your twin. She is not like us. She never has been. Mord knows why the Mark has no effect on her, but it does not, and nothing has indicated the slightest inclination to come to our side, despite our efforts. Her parents' blood flows too thick in her veins, and is thickening even now, can you not feel it? But we can change its course forever. Forever, Nox! Strip the girl of her Powers, and gain them for ourselves! We cannot be stopped at this eleventh hour. So tell me, is Marsh worth the risk? No, I say, no! We must get rid of the woman. Tonight!"

"Very well." Nox sighed. "I will tell her to leave immediately."

"No, Nox. That is not what I mean. I mean, *rid* of her."

Terror shot through Jemma. Marsh was in danger too! They must flee—both of them!

"Nocturna, I will not have that on my conscience. Once was enough!"

"You and your conscience! You have the stomach of a mewling kitten!"

"I did what was required in order to increase Jemma's Powers, as the Lore decrees," Nox growled, slapping his hand on the mantel, "but I will not kill needlessly—"

"Needlessly? Oh, you lily-liver! You call yourself an Agromond?"

"I will order Marsh to leave!"

"Marsh must die!"

Their voices crashed around Jemma's brain. She must think clearly, run to Marsh—

"Tchah, woman! Let the forest do its work, if you will. What more could you want?"

"Kill her, I say! Or else I shall!"

No! They can't! Jemma's love for Marsh welled up in her like floodtide, overtaking her fear and all the other questions clamoring for answers. She bellied across the gallery floor and out of the hatch, closed it quietly, then pelted along the corridor toward the East Tower.

CHAPTER SIX

Goodbye, Marsh

Jemma had never run so fast up the stone spiral staircase to Marsh's room. By the time she reached the top, she was dizzy and nauseous, the newly revealed truth about her life whizzing around her head like runes on a spinning top. *Not my parents . . . I'm not their child . . . Not my parents . . .*

A candle flickered on the window-sill. Marsh leapt up from her bed. "Mother of Majem, child!" she said. "Where have you been? I been worried sick! I was about to come lookin'—"

"Marsh, I heard them talking—they know about you. I know about *them*, taking me—"

"Lawks, Jem—what a way for you to find out! I was goin' to tell you tonight—"

"Never mind that now! Mama—I mean, *she*—means to kill you. We must go!"

"Right." Marsh rummaged under her mattress and pulled out several small packages, which she handed to Jemma. "Food. I been gatherin'. Herbs, for unctions. An' a knife . . ."

Jemma was astounded by the deftness that infused Marsh's rotund body. "So you *were* planning our escape! And . . . I'm really *not* ill, then? No allergy to the Mist?"

"No, pet. There never was. That was a lie, drummed into you to keep you in, an' make you afraid of goin' outside, so's you wouldn't get no ideas about runnin' off." Marsh stood, holding a bundle wrapped in lilac-colored cloth that she placed on top of the other packages in Jemma's hands. "You're strong as an ox, Jem, an' don't you forget it."

"But Marsh, who are you? Did you know my real parents? *Did* they send you here? And what are these Powers I'm supposed to have—do you know about them?"

"Yes, yes! I'll tell you all about it on the way. But—your Stone! I was goin' to have you steal it before we left. . . . Now, even just one day away, your Powers may not be enough to get us through the forest without it!"

"Powers . . . ? Not enough . . . ?" Jemma gulped. "That's what Papa—what *he*—said!"

"Well, we got no choice. We'll have to leave it an' hope that between us, we can do enough—" Marsh froze. Footsteps, swift and deliberate, came echoing up from the bottom of the staircase. She leapt into action again, pushing Jemma toward the door. "Quick, up the tower."

Marsh shoved Jemma to the next flight of steps, then lowered her voice to an intense whisper. "Now, listen. You must get out of here before the hour you was born—nine tomorrow mornin'. That's when your Powers will come out, an' they plan to steal 'em—that's what your birthday Ceremony's really for. But first, you mus' get your Stone. That blue-green pendant Nocturna wears? It's yours. Take it, tonight, once everyone's asleep. Then run. Out the kitchen door will be safest. Drudge has the keys; you'll need the big silvery one—"

"But Marsh, what about you?"

"Don't you worry 'bout me. I got ways of protectin' myself—"

Clang! Ten-thirty. The footsteps were approaching rapidly. . . .

"One more thing." Marsh tapped the cloth-bound bundle. "This here's a book. It'll help. Ask, an' let it show you. Goodbye, my lovely, goodbye." She gave Jemma a quick hug, tears brimming in her hazel eyes. "Remember about courage. An' the Light Game. I'll wait for you outside, if I can. But whatever happens, never give up, never!"

Marsh turned away and hurried into her room. Jemma stepped back just far enough to be hidden, and peeked out as Nox swept into view. So he had won the argument! Thank goodness; Marsh would be safe.

"Marsh," he said, standing in the doorway, "you must leave. This instant."

"What? Sir—but why?"

"My wife wants you dead. I have locked her in the Lush Chamber, but it will not take her long to free herself. Go far, and swiftly, or she will track you and kill you, if only to spite me. But follow my directions exactly, and you will go in safety. Now, hasten." He blew out the candle. Rain lashed the window glass, and a flash of lightning illuminated his tall silhouette as it urged Marsh's squat one out of the room and down the stairs.

Marsh was gone.

Jemma staggered into Marsh's room. For as long as she could remember, it had been her refuge from the castle's cold gloom, so full of Marsh's warmth. Now it looked like a prison cell, furnished only by a rickety narrow bed with Marsh's trunk at the foot of it.

"At least she's alive," Jemma whispered to the darkness.

She threw the food packages, knife, and book bundle onto the bed, and slumped into the dip Marsh's body had worn into the mattress. Fear scoured through her. Her only ally had been ripped away. And it wouldn't be safe for Marsh to wait for Jemma outside—not now, with Nocturna determined to kill her.

Jemma was totally alone.

Lightning streaked across the room. Two small shadows skittered over the floor and onto her lap.

"Rattusses! Yes, thank goodness, I still have you."

The events of the day pounded through her head. The Ceremony, Scagavay, Drudge, her dreams. Her family not being her family. She'd always felt out of place, but it wasn't until two years ago that Nocturna and Shade had begun to turn against her. Now, remembering the eleventh birthday Ceremony that Nox had mentioned, she realized why. Nox had just finished reciting a rhyme he'd made up for her, when three bats flew in. Nocturna, irritated, had killed one with a deliberate shriek, which felled the other two. Shade and Feo had been delighted—but Jemma was distraught. She'd crept back later and found the two wounded ones fluttering weakly behind Mordana's statue, their wings in shreds, and had taken them to her room and nursed them back to health for a week before releasing them into the night. Her distress, and her empathy for the poor creatures, was obviously what had proven to Nocturna that she wasn't one of *Them*.

So what Powers could she possibly have, that they wanted? Was it something to do with the Prophecy that Nocturna had mentioned, not once, but twice? And what did Marsh mean, saying they'd stop at nothing to get it? Surely, however important it was, Nox wouldn't harm her. She was his favorite, even Nocturna had said so! And he'd refused to kill Marsh. But he *had* let Nocturna drug her; he himself gave her the rose. Even he couldn't be trusted. Despair speared through her. What would they do to her if they didn't get what they wanted? The words Nocturna had said not twenty minutes ago sprang to her mind: *Strip the girl of her Powers . . . gain them for ourselves . . .*

The truth was as sharp as Drudge's butchering cleaver.

"Rattusses," she whispered. "We have to get out of here. Tonight." Noodle and Pie trembled. Jemma's hands, too, were shaking. Like the princess in Marsh's stories, she was trapped. And terrified.

She has to find courage, see, Marsh had always said, *an' wear it like an armor of Light. That don't mean she wouldn't be afraid. Courage is doing what you must, even when fear is snappin' at your heart. . . .*

"Come on, you two." Jemma stood, gathered her packages, and spiraled down the stairs, the rats scurrying alongside. *Take the Stone, steal the keys from Drudge, leave . . . Take the Stone, steal the keys from Drudge, leave . . .* Perhaps it wouldn't be so hard. But when she reached the Bed-Chamber level, she heard loud thumping from below. The hall lamps were blazing. Then came Nocturna's voice, shrill as a banshee:

"You fool! You—let—her—go-o-o-o!"

Shade's and Feo's doors flew open. Jemma ducked into her room, Noodle and Pie skidding in behind her. She pinned her ear to her door, and listened as the twins' footsteps thundered toward the stairs, their voices merging with Nocturna and Nox's into one babble of hysteria: *"Let her go? Who? Not*

Jemma, surely?" *"No, Marsh!"* *"Shush, you'll wake Jemma! Do you want her to suspect?"* *"And what if she does? I just set the Alarm spell."* *"Still, go—check on her!"*

Jemma leapt into bed, shoving the packages under her pillow. The rats burrowed in beside her. Seconds later, her door creaked open. She lay still, her heart hammering, as she mimicked the deep breath of sleep. A corner of the sheet peeled back; the acid-and-brimstone smell of Shade's breath breezed across her cheek, then withdrew. *"Still out cold?"* Feo's voice, whispering. *"Shush, Feo, you idiot!"* The door closed, and their whispers became one with the now-muted voices drifting up from below.

They were all in it together. Even Nox and Feo had been watching her for months, she realized now, watching like demons. There was no way she could steal her Stone while they were awake—but no way either that she could linger another second in this sun-forsaken castle like a condemned prisoner awaiting her fate. She would have to risk leaving without the Stone.

Panic searing under her skin, Jemma threw off her bed-clothes, and began ripping the sheets into strips.

CHAPTER SEVEN

Alarm

Jemma tied one end of her sheet-and-blanket rope to the bedstead, then dropped its other end into the roiling darkness below, praying it was long enough to reach solid ground. Though her room was only on the second floor, the base of the castle below her window was built into a fissure in the crag, and the Mist made it impossible to see how far it was to the bottom.

She tore open the lilac-clothed bundle, shoved the food and knife on top of the book, then knotted the fabric on either side to secure it, leaving a length at both ends that she tied around her waist. Then, with one last tug of her makeshift rope, she jammed the bed against the wall under the window. Noodle and Pie were sitting on the sill, waiting, their fur whipping in the wind. "It's now or never, Rattusses," she gulped. "Into my pockets."

Hand over hand, she started down, counting the knots she'd made as she went. One, two . . . Rain stung her hands. Three knots, four . . . The sheets were soaked, but at least that made them easier to grip. A lightning flash revealed a misty-blue chasm with Mord-knew-what jagged rocks at the bottom, waiting to dash her to pieces. The thunder was practically overhead now. Wind whisked around her, buffeting her against the castle walls. *Jem-maaaah!* it seemed to moan. *My sweet thirte-e-een . . .*

Clang-ng-ng!

The first strike of eleven. Noodle and Pie peeked out of her pockets, then hastily dived down again.

Five knots. Only two to go. Jemma shivered with cold and fear. Her hands were frozen, her fingers raw from scraping hard granite. *Jem-maaaAAH!* The wind rose to a howl, mingling with the tolls booming from the Bell Tower. Six knots . . . The last two strips of sheet flapped below her, and the ground was still nowhere in sight. She would have to reach for one of the treetops swaying below—

A blast of wind slammed her against the wall. Her right bootlace caught on a shard of stone. Its hastily tied knot unraveled. The boot hung perilously from her foot, and she wriggled her toes to try and stop it from falling, but it slipped off and plummeted. With a chilling *scree!* two thick prongs shot out of the wall several feet below her, a net suspended between them. The net caught her boot and bound it up like a fly in a spider's web, then retracted into the wall with a low rumble, its leather prey hanging limp and helpless.

"Mother of Majem, Rattusses—that would have been us if we'd gone much farther!"

Suddenly, a high-pitched siren split the night air. Candlelight flared from Nocturna's Bed-Chamber, then moved rapidly from window to window toward Jemma's room. . . . Terror jarred through her. As fast as her hands could grab, she shimmied up the torn sheets and blankets, and tumbled onto the bed, spilling Noodle and Pie from her pockets. They darted under the chest as she yanked up the soaked sheets and blankets and tore off her sodden dress, which she'd thrown over her night robe. Hiding the lilac bundle under the mattress, she piled her dress, sheets, and blankets onto the bed, then shoved the bed back into place and jumped onto the windowsill just as her door was hurled open.

"What are you doing?" Nocturna streaked across the room and grabbed Jemma's arm. "You're soaked to the bone!"

Jemma opened her mouth, but no words would come out.

"Well?" Nocturna yelled, thrusting her head forward. Two pendants swung out from under her night robe, almost hitting Jemma on the chin. Nocturna's black amulet. And the aquamarine Stone.

Mine! Jemma thought. *I mustn't let her know that I know. . . .* She fixed Nocturna's gaze, trying not to shake. "I . . . I was just . . ."

Nocturna's grip tightened. "Explain yourself, Jemma. This instant!"

Nox strode into the room. "What in Mord's name is happening? Nocturna?"

"Ask that of this child!"

A lightning bolt struck a tree outside, setting it alight. Jemma's Stone shone in the flames; then a trail of aqua light shot from it into her chest, so fine that she wasn't sure if she'd imagined it. Energy jolted through her, and she found her tongue.

"I . . . I was sitting with my feet out, Mama, Papa, watching the storm. It was cold, so I'd put my boots on. One of them fell off. Then I heard this horrible scraping sound, and my boot disappeared into the wall. Then that . . . *noise* started. What in Mord's name is it?"

"Just an alarm, Jemma," Nox said, stepping forward, "to warn us of intruders. No doubt your boot set it off." He pried

Nocturna's grip from Jemma's arm. "There's no need to worry, Nocturna, my dear. All is well."

Nocturna frowned, and dropped her hand.

Shade and Feo appeared at the door. Lightning threw shadows of alarm across Feo's face. Even Shade looked ruffled. It steeled Jemma's nerve.

"Isn't the storm beautiful, Mama?" she said, smiling. Thunder ripped the sky.

"Yes, beautiful . . ." Nocturna turned her gaze outside. The Stone pulsed against her throat, a pulse that Jemma felt under her skin.

It's as if it knows I've recognized it, she thought, forcing herself to look away. But the pulse energized her, and her mind was crystal clear. Secrets and lies? Two could play at that.

"The thunder woke me," she said. "I felt so weary, Mama, but the storm made me feel strong again. I don't know why. As if . . . as if something's happened to me. I can't explain it, but I'm . . . I'm *different,* somehow."

Nox inhaled sharply. Nocturna peered at Jemma, her eyes reflecting the tree still blazing outside. Jemma held her gaze. And held it. Finally, Nocturna's face relaxed. "Well, then," she said, "put on some dry clothes and into bed with you. But—what in Mord's name? Why are your bedclothes piled up like that?"

Oh, no! Jemma thought. *They're all torn, and sopping wet! They'll find the food, the book. . . .* She glanced at her Stone to give herself courage. "I had a bad dream," she said, her thoughts coming as swift as bats' flight. "I woke feeling furious, and took it out on my blankets. But the storm comforted me. May I watch a little longer? I do love it. Just as you do."

"No harm in that, I suppose," Nocturna said. She looked slightly confused, and scratched absently at the skin beneath Jemma's Stone, where a faint rash was spreading. "But keep warm. We don't want you catching a chill."

Of course you don't, Jemma thought, *so I'll be strong for whatever you have planned for me tomorrow. . . .* "Thank you, Mama," she said.

"You see, Nocturna!" Nox whispered, a smile spreading across his face "The storm. Jemma feeling changed. I was not wrong to hope!"

"Perhaps. . . ." Nocturna tilted her head to one side and searched Jemma's eyes for a moment, then planted a kiss on her cheek. "Good night, Jemma dear," she said. "I shall see you tomorrow. Nox, go and put an end to that tiresome noise; I forget the spell. Come, you two."

She swept the twins out of the room.

Nox beamed. "So like your mama, loving the storm!" he said. "I can't tell you how happy this makes me. Don't stay up too late now, Flamehead. And don't forget dry clothes, hmm?"

"Of course not, Papa. Good night."

"Sweet dreams, my child." Nox closed the door behind him.

Jemma sat on the sill, trembling. The storm raged; the alarm wailed. *To keep intruders out,* Nox had said. But it was all too obvious: like the locks, chains, and bolts, the alarm was not intended to keep others out, but to keep her in. Slowly, her trembling subsided, the thunder became more distant, and at last, the wailing stopped. Jemma slid off the window-sill, put on dry clothes, and sat on the bed. Noodle and Pie crawled out from under the chest, then snuggled into her lap.

"I don't know what to do, Rattusses," she sighed. "Even if we steal the keys from Drudge, the alarm is bound to go off, no matter which door we try."

Eleven-thirty struck. Despair edged into her bones. The swift clarity she'd felt seemed to have been washed away by the relentless storm outside. But it had been real—and it was her Stone that had given it to her. That flash of aqua blue . . .

"Pull yourself together, Jemma," she whispered, imagining what Marsh might say. "First things first. Wait till midnight to make sure they're all asleep. Then get the Stone. Maybe I'll be able to think more clearly again once I have it." But for now, her mind felt as blank as a dead sheep's face.

Pie nudged Jemma's hand with her snout, then hopped off her lap and nosed under the wet bedclothes. A corner of the lilac fabric was peeking out from underneath the mattress: her makeshift pouch, with the book inside it. It was probably ruined, soaked by the rain. But Marsh had said it could help. . . .

Jemma's throat tightened. How was Marsh faring, out in the wild night? *Please, please, let her be all right.* . . . She gulped back tears and picked up the bundle.

It was bone-dry.

"Strange," she whispered. She fingered the fabric, noticing for the first time how soft it was—softer, even, than Pie's belly fur. Her hands began to tingle, and she lifted the bundle to her face. The fabric smelled musty, but there was another scent floating through too, delicate and eerily familiar, making her slightly dizzy. She put the bundle down and untied it. The fabric was a shawl, warm to the touch, and the book and food packages wrapped inside it were also dry.

"*Really* strange . . ." Her heart beating faster, Jemma picked up the book. It was bound in scuffed brown leather, its spine cracked. There was a faint indent of a title, so worn that it was illegible. "This must be as ancient as Drudge! How can it possibly help?"

The book shimmered in her hands.

"Look, Noodle, Pie . . . It's changing! It looks as though it's lit from inside." Sure enough, a title began shining out from the battered cover. "*From Darknesse to Light,*" she said. "And look at the date—almost three hundred years ago!" She flipped it open to the frontispiece, where the title was written again. Beneath it was the author's name: Majem Solvay. "Majem? I thought 'Mother of Majem' was just an expression. I never knew there was an actual person with that name."

The rats' tails whisked across her thighs. Her fingers were heating up. What was it Marsh had said? *Ask . . . Let it show you. . . .*

"All right, then," she said, taking a deep breath. "How can I get out of here?"

Jemma opened the book. Her hands felt as though they were on fire.

CHAPTER EIGHT

Birthright

The book flopped open at page thirty-seven, a chapter headed "Hystory."

"*Thousandes were taken as slaves for the building of the Castle upon Mordwin's Crag,*" Jemma whispered. "*All did perish under their toil, but for one Zacharias Bartholomew, who every night for thirty yeares did in secret digge him a Tunnelle from the Dungeons. Thence he did escape, sealing his exitway so that none may discover it.*"

"Noodle, Pie, look—a prisoner escaped, after he helped build the castle! Zacharias Bartholomew . . . He dug a secret tunnel from the dungeons . . . But where?" She racked her brain for the most likely place. "There are two locked doors in the South Passage. And that other one, through the Vat Room. They're the only ones Drudge has never let me into." Whenever she had asked him, he had frowned and shaken his head and said, "Keys, losssst!" Obviously, he'd been lying; the tunnel must be through one of them.

Jemma snapped the book shut and placed it onto the lilac shawl with the food packages and knife, once again fashioning a pouch she could tie around her waist.

"There," she said. "My survival belt." It felt hot in her hands. She eyed the wet, torn-up sheets and blankets. "I wonder . . ." She held the pouch close to them. "Get dry," she whispered, only half-believing they would. Nothing happened. "Dry!" she said, mustering more conviction. "*Dry!*"

With a slow *pssshht!* a cloud of steam rose up.

"Sprites! It worked!" Amazed, she tucked the pouch under the mattress for safekeeping. Her fingers touched something else hidden there—a small notebook Digby had given her a year ago, in which she'd written all her secrets and fears. *I mustn't forget to take this,* she thought.

A deep sound reverberated through the room: the first toll of midnight.

It was time.

"You wait here, Rattusses. I don't want the weasels attacking you."

Slowly, she opened her bedroom door and stepped into the corridor. The bell continued its clanging through the storm, announcing the new day. Then it struck her. Today was her birthday. What better moment to take back her Stone—her birthright.

Darkness billowed out of Nocturna's Bed-Chamber and into the corridor. Even with her night vision, Jemma could barely make out the shape of the huge bed, and Rook's domed cage next to it. She closed the door and tiptoed in. One step, two . . . She heard rustling from Rook's cage, and stopped. Silence. Three steps, four, five . . . Jemma could see her Stone's faint aqua glow, beckoning from the bed. Her hip brushed the edge of Nocturna's dressing table. The vials and bottles on top of it rattled; she stopped again, and held her breath. More rustling, this time from the bed. Two weasel shapes turned around, then settled again.

But something else had caught Jemma's attention.

In the middle of the dressing table was a glass jar, in which two cylindrical crystals were immersed in dark liquid. In all the times Jemma had brought Nocturna's breakfast tray to her, she'd never noticed them before. *Take the crystals out! Take them with you!* a voice in her head urged. No—she mustn't falter now. Not for anything. But the voice insisted: *Do it! Take them!*

Jemma reached for the jar and hastily removed the crystals. They were cloudy and gray, about three inches long, and pointed at each end. She slipped them into her pockets, and quietly replaced the jar. Just steps away from the bed, she crept toward it again.

Nocturna lay sprawled across her four-poster island, satin sheets in twisted disarray as if they'd been besieged. Her face, illuminated by the soft aqua of Jemma's Stone, was beautiful, but her chest was now covered with a livid rash. *It's as if the Stone is attacking her skin,* Jemma thought, *now that I've realized it's mine.*

More rustling, as the other two weasels stirred. They started snoring, gently at first, then louder, like the saw Drudge used to cut up carcasses. No wonder Nox slept in his own room.

Nocturna groaned and turned over, then started thrashing her arms and legs. Jemma stiffened, but Nocturna rolled onto her back, arms splayed, revealing her own amulet lying on her chest, next to Jemma's. The weasels snuffled, stirred, and continued their rattling snores.

Jemma stood beside the bed, and leaned in. Her Stone's clasp lay on Nocturna's shoulder, tangled in her hair. As

Jemma inched her hands toward it, her Stone's light began to pulse. But so did Nocturna's, blood-red glowing from deep within its blackness.

Jemma found the clasp, her fingers working fast. The blood-red pulse grew stronger, its heat burning her hands. Suddenly, Nocturna's eyes shot open. She sat upright, arms and torso stiff, and stared straight ahead of her.

"*Jem*-maaah!" she hissed, her eyes like glass. She was still fast asleep.

Jemma held her breath, petrified, while her fingers kept working. But now Rook had woken, and fluttered frantically under his blanket.

"*Caw! Caw!*"

Nocturna began to shake as if possessed.

"*CAW!*"

With one last frantic scramble, Jemma's fingers freed the chain's clasp. Her fist closed around her Stone. Nocturna keeled backward in a dead sleep, her face reflecting the fierce, red glow of her own amulet, which throbbed under her chin like a warning signal.

Jemma dashed from Nocturna's room and leaned against the cold wall of the corridor, clutching her precious Stone in her left hand. Waves of euphoria flowed through her. After a few gulps of air, she hastened toward her Bed-Chamber. Lightning flashed through the hall windows below, illuminating the upstairs landing.

Someone was outside her door, holding a candle. Nox. He turned, and saw her.

"Jemma—you're up!"

Jemma's mind leapt into action. She glazed her eyes, stiffened, and glided past him.

"Jemma?"

She continued along the East Corridor toward Marsh's tower.

"Jemma!" Footsteps hurried behind her. "Flamehead, are you asleep? It's me, Papa!"

Nox touched her shoulder and gently turned her to face him. Jemma widened her eyes and gripped her Stone harder.

"Flamehead, wake up!"

"Mmmm?" Jemma blinked. "Oh, Papa!" She looked around. "Why—what—?"

"You were sleepwalking," he chuckled.

"In Mord's name! *Really?*"

"Yes, really!" Nox smiled. "And with your eyes wide open! You should see how they're glowing—like beautiful blue-green lamps. Now, to sleep with you, my little storm lover. Come. I'll tuck you in." He took Jemma's right hand and led her toward her Bed-Chamber, candle sputtering.

Oh, no—he would see that her sheets were all ripped up. . . .

Just as they reached her door, Jemma feigned a sneeze and blew his candle out.

"My poor child, have you caught chill? Quickly, into bed. Keep your clothes on; you'll be warmer." Nox fumbled into the room. Jemma leapt under the blankets and hastily straightened them over her, hoping he wouldn't notice the two furry shapes that nestled in behind her.

"My dear Flamehead." Nox leaned down and kissed her on the forehead. "You remind me so much of someone I knew, long ago. When you were little—around the same age she was when she died—I used to watch you while you slept, wondering what you were dreaming."

"Oh." Jemma's heart squeezed a little, remembering the twin sister Nocturna had mentioned. Then, thinking it might be suspicious if she didn't show curiosity, she asked, "Who was she, Papa?"

"Someone very dear to me. But it doesn't matter now; it's all in the past. Sleep tight, Flamehead. And happy birthday! Midnight has struck, you know."

"Oh? I didn't hear it." Jemma clutched her Stone. "Thank you, Papa."

Sometimes, she thought as Nox closed the door, *he seems so ordinary. It's hard to think that he could possibly do anything to harm me.* But he *had* harmed her. Had torn her away from her real family. She steeled her heart and closed her eyes, knowing that she must wait yet again for a safe amount of time, until he was asleep. Then she could make her move.

Never had she imagined it could be so easy to escape the castle. Being Outside felt completely natural, as if she had been there her whole life. The air was part of her; the breeze defined the edges of her skin, the sound of it in the trees invigorated her bones. Golden light dappled everywhere, and danced in her veins. She was free! Free at last to twirl and swirl, to run from the forest and out under the Mistless sky, the sky Marsh had described so often. Then she was standing on a cliff, looking down at a sparkling expanse of water the color of her Stone, the color of her eyes. . . .

"Jemma . . . Jemma!" A voice lilted from behind her. She wheeled around. A woman was running toward her, arms

outstretched, auburn hair streaming like a sunlit flag. The woman began to sing, the song beautifully familiar, lilting like a lullaby: "Jemma—my darling angel!" Jemma was flying then, over a field of flaxen waves, cloud shadows racing her, and then everything turned lilac-colored, the lilac of the shawl the woman was wearing—the same shawl Marsh had wrapped the books in! Jemma felt its softness on her cheek, breathed in its fragrance as strong arms held her, safe at last. . . . But—how could this be? Wasn't the shawl at the castle, under her mattress with the books . . . ?

The sky blackened. Clouds, playful only moments ago, menaced and lowered. A bell tolled. One . . . Wind whipped up, pulling her away. Two . . . The woman's arms were letting go. . . .

Jemma woke on the last strike of three, clutching her Stone. Pie was tugging at her clothes. Noodle, tangled in her hair, was nipping her ears. Neither the storm outside nor the rats' attempts to wake her had broken into her sleep.

"Oh, no! The night's half over—we must fly!"

Jemma leapt out of bed, tied her Stone around her neck, and yanked on her weekday boots. Then she grabbed the lilac pouch from under her mattress, knotted it around her waist, and fled from her room, with Noodle in one pocket, Pie in the other. The Stone dangled from her neck, like an aquamarine beacon lighting her way to a new life.

CHAPTER NINE

Behind the Third Door

Monday, early hours

Jemma crept up to Drudge's sleeping alcove just inside the Corridor of the Dungeons. A wire was strung across it, on which his tattered velvet jacket and doublet hung like a make-shift curtain. She winced as she pulled them aside, imagining decades of filth swarming onto her hand.

Drudge lay on his pallet as if someone had dropped him from the ceiling, a skeletal mound whose snores ricocheted around the granite walls. Jemma peeked under a corner of his worn blanket. The keys were on a large ring tied to a thin, leather strap around his waist. Noodle and Pie hopped from Jemma's pockets and quickly gnawed through it. She grabbed the keys. They clanked loudly.

Drudge opened one yellow eye. "Jmaaaagh! Help—"

Jemma spotted an edge of white porcelain under his pallet: his chamber pot. "Sorry, old man," she said, grabbing it. "I can't risk you sounding the alarm." For a second, his eyes met hers, and he seemed suddenly meek; just very old and tired, and not sinister at all. She felt a pang of guilt. Then panic took over, and she swung the pot onto his head. Foul-smelling liquid spattered her dress. He groaned and fell back onto his straw pillow.

"Sorry," she whispered again, then took off across the kitchen, her pouch banging against her hip as she ran. The book, food, and knife inside it were heavy, but she was glad she had them. Halfway down the South Corridor, she remembered something else: the two crystals. She checked her pockets: empty. "Oh, no! They must have fallen out while I was asleep. . . ." For some reason, she felt sad about leaving the crystals behind, but it was too late to go back for them now.

She stopped at the first of the three locked doors. Noodle and Pie ran to and fro across its threshold as Jemma fumbled with the keys. Most were shiny and smooth from recent use, but three were lumpy and covered with rust—the three, Jemma guessed, that she needed. The first was too big; the second, too small. The third slipped into the lock, and turned with surprising ease. She looked down at the rats, who stared up at her, unblinking.

"What is it?" she whispered, pushing the door open.

A faint sound began echoing in her head: high, distant squeals. As she stepped inside, her boots crunched onto something brittle. She looked down. Thousands of small bones were strewn everywhere—tiny mouse- and rat-sized rib cages and skulls—and whole skeletons nailed to the walls in tortured positions: bats and birds, their wings tattered by years of decay.

Jemma reeled back in dismay. "Ugh! You were trying to warn me, Rattusses, weren't you?" She covered her mouth with her hand. "Oh, the poor things . . ."

She and the rats ran along the corridor to the second door. Her hand shook as she tried the first, then the second of the remaining keys. Neither worked. She tried the first again, using both hands to turn it. The lock gave slightly, then shot back. Noodle and Pie started dashing across the threshold again.

"You know there's something bad, don't you?" Jemma whispered. "But what if the escape tunnel is in here?" She pushed the door, but something behind it prevented it from opening. The rats nipped at her feet, squealing. The echoes in her head began again, closer now, and lower in pitch. She leaned harder against the door. Slowly, it scraped open.

What met her eyes was more horrific than she could have imagined. Countless small human skeletons were grouped together in twos and threes, some whose arm bones embraced another; others with finger bones entwined. Several behind the door looked as though they'd been trying to claw their way out.

"Oh, no . . . *No!*" Jemma leaned against the door frame as the horror sank into her, and she held her head to stop the voices. The screams that had haunted her dreams for so long. Children, calling for help. Were these their remains? How long had they been here? Her stomach heaved.

Noodle and Pie clawed at her ankles. But Jemma's legs felt leaden, and she couldn't move. Pie clambered up to her shoulders, leaned around her neck, and nudged the Stone. Jemma closed her hand around it. Its energy infused her. Pie jumped back down to the ground, and the three of them set off again. Through the kitchen. Along the West Passage. Into the Vat Room. Across it was the third and last locked door. The final key slid easily into the lock as if it was well-oiled and ready for her, and the door swayed open into a long corridor, curtained with cobwebs. At the far end, she could just make out another door.

"Thank goodness—that must be it!" Jemma slipped the

key ring around her wrist, leather strap dangling, and ran, the rats bounding alongside. The walls on their right were interspersed with glassless, barred windows through which rain teemed from outside, puddling at intervals along the floor. She slashed through the cobwebs as she passed the first three windows, then the fourth, the fifth, the sixth. . . .

A swooshing sound swept up from behind her. Black wings swooped at her and swiped at her cheeks. Noodle and Pie clambered to her shoulders and struck out at the creature as Jemma grabbed it and wrenched it away from her face. A gray beak jabbed at her hands, drawing blood. Jet eyes blazed at her, full of malice.

"Rook!" Jemma stopped and tore at his feathers. He screeched in pain but kept beating his wings, trying to peck her neck. "You foul creature! I don't want to kill you, but you give me no choice!" She reached for the knife in her pouch, but Drudge's keys, clanking on her wrist, gave her another idea. In one deft motion, she slipped her hand free of the key ring and whipped its leather strap around Rook's legs, then tied it to the bars of the seventh window. Rook flapped furiously, wings slapping the stone walls as rain sheeted onto him from behind. "Struggle all you like, wretched bird!" she said, knotting the strap securely. "You won't get free. Now, hang on, Rattusses."

The rats clung to Jemma's shoulders as she took off, Rook's caws fading behind them. But his presence meant Nocturna wouldn't be far behind. Jemma ran as never before, past the eighth window . . . the ninth, tenth. . . . The opening at the end of the passageway was getting closer. They were only seconds from it. . . .

Wham! A portcullis slammed down in front of them.

"No!" Jemma hammered at the iron bars with her fists. "Not now! Mother of *Majem!*"

A deafening boom rang out: the single stroke of three-thirty.

Light flickered behind them. Footsteps and rustling silk approached. Jemma clasped her Stone and tugged, breaking the fine chain holding it around her neck, then turned. Nocturna was speeding toward them, lamp in hand, the angles of her face sharp in its light. Her four black weasels trailed her like malevolent shadows. Jemma backed into the portcullis, Noodle and Pie quivering into her neck.

Nocturna flicked the rats to the ground and grabbed Jemma by the collar. "So, you thought you could escape, did you, my sly vixen? Oh, you put on a fine show earlier—changed, indeed!" She fingered Jemma's throat. "Where is the Stone? Tell me!"

"I'll never give it to you. Never!"

"Yes, you will, Mord take you," Nocturna said, gripping her harder, "if I have to kill you to get it."

"Much good it'll do you if I'm dead!"

Nocturna's grip loosened slightly. Seizing her chance, Jemma grabbed Nocturna's wrist with her free hand, pulled it to her mouth, and gnashed into it. Nocturna screamed, pulled away, and dropped the lamp. Glass shattered. The light flared, then burned out.

"Why, you—"

Jemma and the rats pelted back along the corridor toward Rook's caws. He was soaked, and flapped with less fervor now, but four dark shapes slithered in front of Jemma, crashing her to the ground. The Stone was jolted from her hand and slid across the floor, out of reach. Two of the weasels clamped their jaws around her ankles; the other two made a beeline for the rats.

"Noodle, Pie, run!"

"*Caw! Caw!*" Rook beat his wings with renewed vigor from the next window.

"Rattusses, *run!*"

One of the weasels had Noodle by the leg. Noodle whipped around, bit its nose, and wriggled free. But Pie was caught, squealing in agony. Noodle clawed the weasel's face, but it held fast.

"*No-o-o!*" Jemma grabbed the two weasels at her ankles and squeezed their necks. They hissed, their mouths falling open. She hurled them against the wall and leapt onto Pie's attacker, pressing her fingers into its jaws and forcing them apart. Pie plopped to the ground.

"Quickly, Noodle, Pie, *go!*" The weasel snapped its needle-like teeth, shredding Jemma's fingers. She held on to it—but the other three were snaking toward the rats. Jemma kicked them, giving Pie just enough time to drag her blood-soaked body into a crevice, pulling one limp leg behind her, with Noodle nosing her on.

Jemma's Stone glowed from a dark rain puddle on the floor, several feet from her. She crawled toward it, fingers and ankles raw from weasel bites.

"*Jem*-mah! Don't think you can be victorious over me."

Jemma looked up. Nocturna, lampless, was stumbling along the corridor. Had she seen the Stone? The weasels had, and were slinking toward it. Jemma sprawled forward and slapped her palm onto it. But Nocturna's foot crunched down on her knuckles, just where the weasel had bitten. Pain leapt up her arm. Rook cackled and flapped.

Nocturna towered over Jemma and stretched down one hand, palm upward.

"Now," she said. "I want it, *now*."

"You'll have to fight me for it!"

"Then fight we shall—"

"*CAW!*"

Nocturna turned. "Oh, my poor Rook!" She stepped toward him.

Jemma's fingers closed around her Stone. The pain in her hands and ankles ebbed slightly.

"You cruel witch!" Nocturna grabbed her by the hair and yanked her to her feet. "How could you do this to my helpless bird?"

"*I'm* cruel? What about all those skeletons? Those children!"

"Untie him!"

"*You* untie him—"

"Untie him, I said!" Nocturna shoved Jemma toward the window. "No—wait! First, give me my Stone."

"My Stone, you mean!" Jemma clenched both her fists, the Stone hot in her right hand. The pain subsided a little more. Energy inched through her. She tried to wrench free, but Nocturna's hand was twisted in her hair, holding fast.

"Mord take you, Jemma!" Her face purple with rage, Nocturna plunged her free hand into Jemma's pockets. "Where is it? Give . . . it . . . to . . . me!"

"Never!"

Nocturna's groping hand found the knotted fabric around Jemma's waist.

"*Aha!* And what do we have there, my wicked one? Some rag left for you by that Marsh woman, no doubt." She yanked the pouch around to Jemma's front with one hand, still clutching her hair in the other. "Hidden the Stone in there, have you?" Jemma kicked and bit, but Nocturna kicked back as she ripped at the pouch's knots with her nails. The knots loosened, spilling the food packages and knife onto the floor. "So, you planned your escape well, Jemma. And what's this?"

She pulled out the book, then dropped it with a yell of pain. Her hand rose up in livid blisters: the book had burned her. Furious, she kicked it into the shadows.

Jemma clutched her Stone. Its Power inched through her.

"What evil have you done to me, you ingrate?" Nocturna snarled. "I'll make you pay!" She twisted Jemma's hair more tightly and thrust her blistered hand into the now-empty pouch. "Where *is* it? It must be here!"

"It's *mine*, and you'll never lay your hands on it again!" Jemma's scalp felt as if it was about to be ripped from her head. But her Stone's Power was building in her. It was almost enough to wrench Nocturna's fingers from her hair—

Nocturna's nails tore at the lilac fabric, shredding it.

"No—don't!" Jemma said, trying to push Nocturna's hand away.

"And why not?" A sneer spread across Nocturna's mouth, then she wrenched the shawl from Jemma's waist, held it out of her reach, and let it fall. It fluttered to the flagstones like a mortally wounded butterfly. Nocturna ground it with her heel. Jemma gripped the Stone as hard as she could, but her attention was caught, and her strength dwindled with every twist of Nocturna's foot on the shawl. *It's just a bit of fabric!* she thought, frantically trying to regain control. *Why should it matter so much?*

"I'm losing my patience, *Jem*-mah." Nocturna moved her face up to Jemma's, her sneer folding back into a snarl, like a hyena about to devour its prey. "Do I have to call upon a little help, perhaps, for you to be persuaded?" She threw her head back and laughed, then said, slowly, *"Morda-morda-mordalay . . ."* The stone around her neck began to glow blood-red, and as it did, Jemma's Stone cooled in her hand.

No, don't desert me now, please! she begged silently. *Please . . . help. . . .* But her faith was draining, and all help seemed to have gone. The book was splayed open on the ground, ordinary and old. She was lost. Defeated.

"Nocturna, Jemma!" Nox's voice boomed through the shadows. "What in Mord's name is going on?" Lamplight flickered. Nocturna turned toward it, and Jemma saw her chance. She thrust a fisted hand past Rook and out of the window, hurling her Stone into the stormy morning air.

CHAPTER TEN

The Littlest Dungeon

Monday, early hours

Nocturna and Nox marched Jemma down the Corridor of Dungeons. At the end they stopped. Nocturna shoved her through an iron-barred door, clanged it shut, and locked it.

"You have little more than five hours to tell us where the Stone is, my fine wench," Nocturna snarled, nursing her wounded hand, "else things will be the worse for you. And don't think you can get the better of Drudge again. I shall be keeping the keys from now on." She turned and stormed away.

Nox gripped the bars of the door, his face haggard. "Jemma," he sighed. "I don't want to see you in here, but you give us no option. Just tell us where the Stone is—come join us! We can have fun again, be a truly happy family, with no more secrets—just your Powers, combined with ours—"

"Never!"

"Please, think about it. Please! Pretend, even, and at least continue to live with us as you have been—"

"Pretend? Like you, you mean, pretending I was weak and sickly to keep me inside, and imagining I'm your twin sister?"

Nox's face turned ashen. "Oh, Jemma, Jemma," he said,

"if you knew what a cruel thing you say! Yes, it's true that you remind me of my twin. Malaena . . . But she died when we were four. It's you—*you*, Jemma—whom I care for now." A tear glinted in the corner of his left eye.

Jemma felt a stab of guilt, then fury took over again. "And do you expect me to believe that your lovely birthday Ceremony wouldn't kill me if I wasn't really on your side? Just like all those others you murdered! I saw their bones. I know what you've done, you and Nocturna—"

"No, no! We haven't . . . not for years—"

"Why? Because you were afraid I'd find out, and be so disgusted with you all that you'd lose the chance of . . . of *converting* me?"

"Yes—no . . . I mean, I would never hurt you, Flamehead! You belong here, you do! Why—the Mark . . . your birthmark . . . It shows you *are* one of us!"

Jemma's words stuck in her mouth; her head spun. The Mark? He and Nocturna had mentioned that earlier. It couldn't mean she was one of them, could it? Surely it was just a coincidence! Cruelty felt wrong to her. Helping those bats—that was what had felt right. Yet she had been unkind to Nox, just seconds ago. Did that mean—?

"I see you are wavering," Nox said. "I knew it! My dear Jemma . . ."

Rage seized her again. *His* dear Jemma? Whoever she really was, he and Nocturna had ended that life. Ripped her from it. And for what?

Nox was smiling now. "Oh, Flamehead, think of how marvelous everything will be when you are truly one of us. . . ."

"Ruling over all of Anglavia?" Jemma clenched her fists.

"And . . . and . . . with just the occasional sacrifice of some insignificant little creature or other?"

"Yes—yes! It's not too late! Come to our side. Nocturna would not harm an Agromond ally!"

"And that," Jemma said slowly, "is something I can never be."

Nox's eyes hardened, and his expression twisted, sending chills through Jemma's bones. "After all these years of my love, my nurturance!" he said. "Very well, Jemma. Have it your way. But know that you have just sealed your fate." He turned and stalked away.

Jemma shook like syrupwater jelly. Fear brought pain back into her weasel-bitten fingers and ankles. What did he mean, she had sealed her fate? Then it hit her: without her Stone and her Powers, they had no reason to keep her alive. She had let her tongue run away with her—just what Marsh always warned her against!—and the Ceremony tomorrow would probably be the death of her. What if she *had* pretended, as Nox suggested, in order to save herself? No, no—she couldn't live here, in this dismal, evil place! Not now. Not without Marsh. She would rather die.

She looked around the stone cell, less than six feet square, with its mildewed walls and single wooden bench. How often had she played in the dungeons with Digby—in this very cell, even, pretending to be imprisoned, and he her rescuer? What a cruel irony that was now! She kicked at the door, and shook the bars.

Clang!

The bell sounded deeper in the bowels of the castle. Another toll followed, then two more. Four in the morning. Only five hours until the Ceremony. Jemma slumped onto the bench and buried her face in her hands. Remember courage? The Light Game? Marsh's advice was powerless to ease the terror gripping her bones, let alone dissolve solid walls and steel.

"I'm sorry, Marsh," she whispered, tears trickling between her fingers. "I tried." She lay on the bench and closed her eyes, and felt her life dribbling away like the damp on the dungeon walls.

Black swirled around her. "I am not your sweet thirteen!" she screamed. "I hate you! I hate your Mark! May the Sun burn you up!" Then came a dim light, and a woman shimmered through it, draped in the lilac shawl—the same woman Jemma had dreamed earlier, her face now full of sorrow. "Don't give up!" the woman pleaded. "Please . . ."

Darkness closed in again.

"Jmmmaaaagh!" A voice wheezed through the gloom. She was suffocating, cold water splashing over her—

Jemma woke, gasping for breath. Fabric filled her nostrils. Fabric, and dust, and a faint floral scent . . . The lilac shawl! She snatched it off her face, sneezed, and opened her eyes. The shawl was in her hand, tattered after Nocturna's assault on it, and Noodle was lying on her chest. He was dusty and covered in scratches.

"My poor Noodle! That horrid weasel . . . Thank goodness you're all right. And you brought the shawl . . . but where's Pie?"

More water splashed onto her. "Jmmmaaaagh!"

Jemma jumped. Drudge was standing outside the dungeon, wearing a long cloak she had never seen before. He held a half-empty tumbler in one hand, Pie in the other.

"Drudge! Don't hurt her!" She leapt to her feet and went to the bars.

Pie sat quietly in Drudge's palm. The vicious wounds inflicted on her by the weasel in the corridor were now mere scabs. Drudge placed the tumbler on the cross-bars of the door, then ran his free hand over Pie, inches from her fur.

The scabs vanished.

Pie leapt onto Jemma's shoulders, nudged her cheek, then scampered to the ground and onto the bench next to Noodle, who was scrabbling at the wall.

"Drudge . . . you just healed her!"

Drudge nodded, then stretched his hand toward Noodle. Noodle's fur shimmered; his scratches closed over. Amazed, Jemma turned back and looked at the old man. He was wheezing heavily.

"Efff . . . fort," he explained. His eyes were watery and clouded over, with a faraway look in them that made Jemma feel strange, as if he, like her, dreamed of distant places. A large bump was peeking through his wispy hair, like a mountaintop through clouds.

"Drudge, I'm sorry about hitting you with the chamber pot," she said, remorse prickling her skin.

"Guilt, baaad." He looked at Jemma's torn fingers and shook his head. "Weazzl baaad!"

"How did you know the weasels did that?"

Drudge smiled and tapped his forehead. Then he took her hands in his. At any time before, Jemma would have pulled away, but now she was transfixed. Warmth spread through her body; the soreness in her fingers subsided. He released them. The wounds had completely healed, and the weasel bites on her ankles were also free of pain.

"Drudge! How did you *do* that?"

"You . . . let me," he said.

Jemma thought of all the times she had been disgusted by the old man, and felt ashamed. Perhaps she really *was* bad, having such horrid thoughts about him.

"Gnaaa!" Drudge frowned and shook his head. "Bad thought . . . not make you . . . bad. Shhhame . . . not good. Make weak!"

"And now you're reading my thoughts? Drudge, I've been so wrong about you—who *are* you?"

"Me, good. Red. Here . . . For you. Now, time." He delved into his pocket and pulled out two shiny, cylindrical objects, pointed at each end.

"The crystals! You knew where they were. . . . You *see* things too, don't you?"

Drudge nodded and handed Jemma the crystals. She gasped. Their former cloudiness had faded to a silvery gray.

"Maaaa . . . paaaa . . . Ssso . . . they," he sputtered. "Free! You . . . Sssso they!"

"'*You, so they.*' You said that yesterday, in the Vat Room." For the first time, Jemma realized how frustrating it must be for him not to be able to speak coherently. "I'm sorry, Drudge. I never could understand you very well. I've been too impatient—"

"You . . . SSSSO-they! Mussst . . . sstrong! Essscep. Tunlll—"

"Tunnel?" Jemma's heart flipped. "Do you know where it is?"

"Gnnnnaaa. But . . . Trusssst," he said, tapping his forehead again. "I sssee. You—free! Go, sssooon!"

"But how? I've no idea where the tunnel is either."

77

"Gnnnnn—*trusssst!* L-l-look!" Drudge pointed to the back of the cell. Noodle and Pie were still scratching away, a pile of mortar lying on the bench between them.

"Rattusses, what are you up to?" Jemma went to the bench, put the crystals down, and scraped around the stones with her fingers. Chunks of mortar fell away, revealing a small crevice. Noodle hopped into it and disappeared. Heart pounding, Jemma pushed on the stone. It thudded to the ground on the other side of the wall, and she knelt on the bench and peered into darkness. Noodle's ruby eyes met hers, then he ducked and disappeared again. Seconds later, a loud squeak echoed out of the hole.

It was more than just a small space.

"Mother of Majem—can it be . . . ?" Jemma shoved away the surrounding stones until she had made an opening large enough to climb through. "A cave! This must be where that prisoner Majem wrote about hid to do his digging!" she said. "Thank you, Zacharias Bartholomew! He made a wall within the walls . . . and over there—there's a hole in the ground!" She turned to Drudge, hope surging through her.

"Sssseee!" he said. "Ratssses know too!"

Noodle scurried back out into the dungeon, and he and Pie ran in excited circles.

"This is really it? Oh, Drudge!"

A smile cracked across the old man's face, then he pointed to the floor. "Fffood." At his feet was a wineskin, several packages, and a loaf of bread with a knife sticking out of it.

"You've thought of everything!" Jemma picked up the wineskin, took out its stopper and sniffed. Sour milk! With hope came hunger, and she swigged it back, then poured a little onto the floor for Noodle and Pie. They lapped it up as Jemma tore off a chunk of bread for them, then chomped into the loaf herself. Drudge looked on, chuckling.

Jemma tucked the knife into her boot top, then made a new pouch out of the shawl, into which she put the crystals, the new food packages—cheese in one, by the smell of it, and sausages in the other—and the rest of the loaf. She tied it around her waist, threw the wineskin's strap over one shoulder, then turned to bid Drudge farewell. But he was not done yet. He pulled off his cloak and stuffed it through the bars.

"Ssstorm, ssstopped," he sputtered. "But cold, outsssssd."

"Where did this come from?" she said, wrapping it around herself. Its thick maroon velvet looked as though it had been torn and mended many times, but it was warm, lined with silk, and better yet, had a hood. It also had a pocket, in which she found a vial of purple liquid.

"Mauve . . . ," he wheezed, "esssssnnce. Make strrrrong. Use wise . . . l-ly."

"Thank you, Drudge. For everything. How can I ever repay you?"

"Be ffffreee . . ." His eyes misted, and he rubbed the velvet on Jemma's shoulder, then touched his palm to her face, murmuring her name in a strangely jumbled way. She looked at him, puzzled. A blue aura seemed to shimmer around him, then disappear, so she wasn't even sure she'd seen it at all.

Clang! The deep toll snapped Drudge out of his momentary dreaminess.

"Fffour-thrrrty—go, now!" he said. "Fffind. Big cave.

Nothrrr . . . tunnll. Way ffrrm caaaasssll. No alaaa . . . alaaam . . ."

"A big cave. Then another tunnel, which will lead away from the castle, where there's no alarm. I understand." Jemma squeezed his hands. "I wish I wasn't leaving you here! But—"

"Go!" Drudge pulled his hands away. "Mussst, now! Gbye, Jmmmaaah."

"Goodbye. And please say goodbye to Digby for me, will you? Tell him . . . tell him I'll look for him in Hazebury, when I get there."

Drudge nodded, wiping one eye with the back of his sleeve. "Trusssst," he said again, softly.

Jemma turned and squeezed through the gap, arms first, then head, shoulders, and torso. Noodle and Pie hopped in after her. She took one last look across the tiny dungeon. Drudge waved, then was gone. A fragment of her heart tore off and followed the old man up the dark corridor as he shuffled back to his lonely alcove.

CHAPTER ELEVEN

Rite of Passage

Monday, early hours

Jemma burrowed down a steady slope, Noodle and Pie dashing ahead and back again like two scouts as she hacked at the insect-littered cobwebs stretched across the tunnel. It had become narrower a while ago, and she'd had to wriggle out of Drudge's cloak and roll it up beneath her to prevent it becoming any more tattered. Thank goodness she could see in the dark—carrying a candle as well as everything else would have been next to impossible.

"It's all very well for you, Rattusses!" she said, spitting out another half-eaten cockroach. "Your favorite food. Not mine!"

The air was beginning to smell stale. Where was the cave Drudge had mentioned? Not much farther, she hoped. The muted tolls of five and five-thirty had come and gone: It must be almost six by now—the time when, every weekday for the past five years, Marsh had woken her for kitchen duties. In little more than two hours, the family would wake and begin searching for her. . . . She wriggled on with renewed fervor.

The air became suffocating; the cobwebs got thicker. Where *was* that cave?

Suddenly, the ground pitched sharply away, and Jemma was sliding headfirst down a steep incline, the rats tumbling with her. Her heart seemed to fly up to her boots as dark liquid rushed to meet them. They landed in a pool of ice-cold water in the middle of a cave.

"Help!" Jemma gasped with the shock of cold. "I c-c-can't s-s-wim!"

Noodle and Pie rat-paddled to the edge and scrambled out. They shook themselves, then sat, spiky-furred, squealing encouragement as Jemma flailed toward them. Her hands hit rock, and she clambered from the water, still clutching the knife in her right fist. She tucked it into the top of her boot, pulled the cloak from the pool, wrung out the skirt of her dress, and then began rubbing her arms and legs vigorously.

"S-s-sprites! I've never been s-so c-c-cold in my l-l-life!" She jumped up and down, scanning the cave as the rats licked their fur dry. Crescent-shaped, its shorter wall was made of rock, its longer wall hewn from the same granite as the castle. A few cracks shed faint slivers of light into the cave. Overhead was nothing but blackness.

"I think we're at the b-bottom of one of the t-towers, Rattuss-usses," she said, her teeth chattering. The cloak was rumpled on the ground, and she picked it up.

It was bone-dry.

"How weird. Just like Majem's book . . ." She wrapped it around herself and it warmed her through. "I wish I still had the book," she murmured. "I hate the idea of leaving it behind." Then she remembered something else she'd left: the notebook Digby had given her, hidden under her mattress. The thought of any Agromond eyes reading her innermost feelings over the past year felt like an invasion, but it couldn't be helped now. She sighed resignedly.

"Come on, you two," she said. "Let's find that last tunnel."
Noodle and Pie scampered up to her shoulders and plopped
into the cloak's hood.

The hollowness above seemed to move. Unease stirred in
Jemma's stomach. More movement, and a fluttering sound.
Suddenly, from directly overhead, came a deafening

Clang!

The first strike of six. The sheer force of it pressed Jemma
into the ground.

Clang!

She blocked her ears, but the thundering toll surrounded
her in a thick, throbbing ring.

Clang!

The ring began to spin, closing in, darker than the darkness itself, sucking the air from her lungs. It wasn't just the
sound of the bell. It was something else.

Clang!

Jemma tried to move, but the ring pressed in, holding
her fast.

Clang!

The spinning was now so rapid that she couldn't see
beyond it, couldn't breathe. There was only one thing that
could do that—

Clang!

Mordsprites!

Faster and faster they spun, tighter and tighter. Jemma
choked and gagged, trying to beat off the swirling, diaphanous blackness. She couldn't draw breath; her lungs felt on
the verge of collapse. Where were Noodle and Pie? A tiny
claw scraped her neck.

Then came another sound from above: whirring, getting rapidly louder, like mighty wings in a rush of wind. It whipped through the Mordsprites, fragmenting their mass into individual wraiths that fled upward as fast as they'd come. The wind dropped; the wings' beating softened into gentler flapping, punctuated by synchronized breaths. Jemma blinked, and saw: bats. Thousands of them, surrounding her, openmouthed, teeth glistening like tiny white needles.

Even if she could have moved, there was nowhere to run.

In one motion, the bats closed in and whooshed around her, the air from their wings lifting her from the ground. Tiny fanged faces swooped in and out of her vision; tiny black eyes locked onto hers, then disappeared again. She was propelled toward the outer edge of the cave, and up a pile of rubble. The bats deposited her next to a hole at the top of it, then moved back and continued their flapping and rhythmic breathing until the fear pumping through her veins had subsided; the spinning in her head had slowed; and the rats, who had clambered from the hood and up to her shoulders, had stopped panting.

"Thank you," she whispered. "You weren't attacking us at all! You saved us."

Two of the larger bats flew up to Jemma's face, their black eyes fixing on hers. An image of her eleventh birthday Ceremony flashed into her mind—the distress she had felt for the bat Nocturna had killed, and for its two companions that she had later rescued. She recognized the wings of the two in front of her now, scarred and jagged—wings she had tended until they had been healed enough to fly again.

The two bats moved back into the hovering throng. For a

split second they all held her gaze; then, with one unanimous blink, they were gone.

Jemma sat with her back against the hard granite, awed by what had just happened. To think of the bats' protection of her, compared to the treachery of the people she had believed were her family . . . How she hated this castle, hated every cold, hard, dark corner of it!

Noodle slid to the ground and stretched up the wall just to the right of the hole, his front paws tracing the indent of something. He squeaked, and Jemma leaned over to see. The letters ZB were carved into the wall.

"ZB . . . Zacharias Bartholomew! The prisoner who escaped."

Jemma looked into the dark space. From somewhere beyond it, the Outside beckoned. She tightened the shawl around her waist, then crawled with the rats into the opening that only one man had ever entered before, seven hundred years ago.

The tunnel was larger than the one leading from the dungeons, and she could belly through it without having to flatten herself like a mouse. It sloped gently uphill, snaking around large boulders. In several places the earth had fallen in, making progress laborious. Soon, she heard a distant boom, and felt the low rumble of the huge bell reverberating through the ground. Six-thirty. One-and-a-half hours until the family awoke.

Weariness set in. Drudge's cloak seemed to lose some of its warmth, and she began to shiver. Soon, cold and exhaustion were creeping through every muscle, clouding her reason. Her bones begged for rest, but Noodle and Pie's nips and squeals cut into her dulled mind, spurring her on. So on she went until her bones gave up, and she barely cared about the seven tolls she heard in the distance, driving the dawn hours dangerously onward.

"I can't, Rattusses, I can't . . ." She lay her head on her arms. But the rats were having none of it. Pie nudged her face, keeping her awake, while Noodle nosed under Jemma's hip, then bit, hard.

"Ow!" She jerked up, bumping her head, and then felt the lump in the cloak's pocket: the vial of mauve essence Drudge had put there. Noodle wriggled up to Jemma's face with the vial clamped between his teeth, then held it fast while Pie pulled out its cork stopper. Jemma took the vial and swigged it back. The essence's sharp tang kicked through her body, a shot of instant energy. She crawled on. Within moments, fresh air breezed against her face, bringing a scent she had never experienced before: sweet, with a refreshing, slightly sharp edge.

"The Outside! We must be close. . . ."

Noodle and Pie scuttled ahead, disappeared around another boulder, then squeaked loudly. Jemma followed. Mere feet away, the tunnel sloped sharply upward, a faint trace of dawn filtering down from the top of it.

"We're here! At last!" Jemma reached toward the slice of light above her head, her hands ripping away bundles of prickles and twigs still drenched from last night's rain. The slice of light became larger, and larger. Beyond it, Mist-white and waiting, was the Outside.

Noodle and Pie scrambled onto Jemma's shoulders and hopped through the hole. She untied the pouch from around her waist and threw it out to join them.

Now it was her turn.

How many times had she fantasized about this moment, and the elation she would feel to be Outside, able to go where she pleased? Instead, all the fears instilled in her by the Agromonds rose up like an army, trying to block her way. But she knew they were lies, and steeled herself with Marsh's words: *Courage is doin' what you must, even when fear is snappin' at your heart.*

With the rats squeaking their encouragement, Jemma wriggled out onto the hillside.

She lay on the soaked ground, half-expecting the shriek of the Wailing Alarm to wake her and for this to be a cruel dream; or to faint, felled by her supposed allergy to the Mist. But no Alarm came. This was real, as real as the soft earth beneath her. And she was alive and well.

"Rattusses," she whispered. "We're free."

Free, for the first time she could remember. Free to find Marsh, her real family, and the world beyond Agromond Castle. . . . The possibilities were wonderfully, terrifyingly endless. Noodle and Pie stood on their hind legs and sniffed at the dawn air, then began nosing into fallen branches and nibbling gleefully on dead bugs as though life Outside was nothing new to them. She wished she could feel their ease. But Jemma felt the trees edge toward her, tendrils of Mist thicken around her. The place where she had longed to be did not feel the least bit friendly. All she knew was that within an hour, the Agromonds would wake. She must flee, as fast and as far as she could, before then. But first, there was her Stone to find, caught somewhere in the shadows of the castle walls.

Part Two

AGROMOND FOREST

CHAPTER TWELVE

In the Shadows

Monday

The dawn breeze chilled Jemma's earth-caked clothes. She brushed herself off and wrapped Drudge's cloak around her, pulling its hood over her head and hugging herself for warmth. Then, tying her shawl bundle around her waist, she stood and faced the castle.

The only home she knew loomed through the Mist like a massive beast of prey. For twelve years, it had hoarded her in its belly, and now it crouched as if plotting its revenge on her for daring to break out. Her skin bristled, every instinct telling her to turn and run—run, into the forest, despite the dangers it held, and come back tonight—not go searching for her Stone now! Surely that was madness? It would be safer to wait, at least until after the hour of her planned Ceremony had passed, so that the Agromonds wouldn't be so intent on finding her.

"Stop it, Jemma," she muttered, gritting her teeth. "It's almost a whole hour until they'll wake up. Whatever happens, you'll be stronger with your Stone. So calm yourself! Breathe. Now, where are we?"

Directly in front of her was the Bell Tower, which meant the kitchen and Vat Room, and the corridor from which she'd thrown her Stone, must be around the back of it. Noodle and Pie scampered alongside as she set off, her footfall soft in the silence. The sodden ground felt strange to walk on after a lifetime of flagstones, and she teetered a little, off balance, but soon got used to the rise and fall of the grass-tufted earth.

To the left, ranks of trees sloped away into the forest, pale silhouettes in a sea of gray. Mist swirled around her like damp fingers, suspicious, searching her out. She shuddered, focusing her intention: the Stone, its aqua glow . . . The Mist seemed to edge back, and she relaxed a little.

Keeping her distance from the castle, she rounded the Tower, expecting to see a long expanse of wall stretching away toward the kitchen. What met her eyes took her aback. Built into the side of the castle, as if swarming its base, was a mass of ramshackle huts. Of varying heights and sizes, they leaned every which way, looking desolate and desperate. Most had no rooves. A few had tumbled down completely, leaving their stone chimney stacks to point accusingly up the castle walls.

"The Dwellings, Rattusses," she whispered. "That's where the servants used to live, till they went away." She had all but forgotten, but now it dredged up from the depths of her childhood, the hushed talk she'd overheard: kitchen-maids, and footmen, spooked by the cries they heard late at night from the forest. The hauntings, they'd called them—most likely the same cries that had plagued her, she now realized. It was no longer worth staying, all the servants had said, even for food and shelter. The last to go, when Jemma was seven, had been the cook. Apart from the fact that Jemma then had to start helping Drudge with the cooking and cleaning, she hadn't cared—in fact, had been glad to be rid of them, as most of them were dour and unfriendly. *If only Drudge would go too*, she'd thought at the time; but she'd been wrong about him, and she'd probably been wrong about them, as well. Living under a shroud of fear, no wonder they'd been so surly.

Noodle and Pie skittered onto a furrowed, pebbly track running parallel to the castle walls—the track that must lead to Hazebury. She imagined Digby and his father trundling along it in their cart on delivery days. What would they think when they came tomorrow and found she had gone? Would Digby be worried? Would he miss her? Then she imagined the Agromonds in their coach, leaving for one of their "visits" to the villages. What did they really do on those trips? Terrify the life out of people, no doubt. Certainly nothing benevolent, as they'd always pretended.

The track was easier going than the rough ground, and Jemma picked up her pace. Above the huts and occasional leafless tree, she could just make out the slit windows of the corridor where Nocturna had caught her. Soon she was parallel to the one from which she'd hurled her Stone—the seventh. The hut beneath it looked sturdier than most, and had a tree growing in front of it.

"Let's get closer, Rattusses. I couldn't have thrown it this far out."

The rats hopped ahead as Jemma crept along, scanning the ground. Brambles and briars unfurled as if awakening from slumber and snagged her cloak, slithering around her ankles, slowing her down. Noodle and Pie were also being assaulted, their gnawing barely keeping ahead of the unrelenting undergrowth. Finally, she and the rats reached the huts. But there was still no sign of her Stone.

"Sprites! Where *is* it?" *Breathe, Jemma, breathe,* she told herself. *Keep calm. . . .* But it was hard to keep calm while precious minutes marched by like soldiers with swords raised, ready to strike. Maybe she should come back later after all, and run for cover while she still could.

Her foot hit something large and pale, lying on a low thicket of brambles. A book, splayed open, pages downward, the faint indent of its title shining from its wet, leather cover.

"*From Darknesse to Light!* How did that get here?" Jemma bent to pick it up.

The instant she touched it, a story unfolded in her mind: Nocturna, going back to the corridor after locking Jemma in the dungeon, intending to destroy the book for having the audacity to wound her . . . protecting her hand with the hem of her dress . . . the fabric searing . . . the book sailing through the air, hurled from the window in a rage. Jemma hugged it to her chest. It felt like an old friend.

"I'm glad to have found you," she whispered. "Perhaps you can help me find my Stone."

She was about to open it when a tiny bead of turquoise light appeared in front of her eyes, then grew brighter, and brighter still. It floated upward, leading Jemma's gaze through the branches of the tree, then stopped several feet above the roof of the hut. Its light intensified and expanded, then flared and disappeared, leaving a faint aqua glow through the Mist. Her heart leapt.

"There it is, at the end of that branch! I'll have to climb up to get it." Slipping the cloak off her shoulders, she piled it with the book, wineskin, and pouch at the base of the trunk next to the rats. As she touched the tree, its bark seemed to expand a little into her hand as if welcoming her, but the roughness of it surprised her. She had expected it to be soft, the way firs looked. But such large beings needed to be sturdy to hold themselves up and root themselves into the earth, she reasoned, remembering Marsh's explanation of how they grew.

The lowest branches were within easy reach. Smoother than the trunk, they were slippery, still damp from rain. Carefully, Jemma hoisted herself up, keeping her eyes fixed on the glow. From beyond it, up the castle wall, a light flickered through the Mist. Tensing, she stopped climbing. It was coming from the kitchen window. Drudge! He must be preparing the breakfast trays. She felt a pang of regret for having judged the old man as she thought of his entreaty to her: *Trusssst . . .* The words warmed her, and she wished him warmth too, hoping that somehow, he would feel it.

Moments later, she was lying on the branch that held her Stone. Its thin chain was wrapped around a twig at the end, and it swung slightly as she inched toward it. The branch bent under her weight. She clung on with one hand, reaching the other toward the precious aqua glow. Just a hare's whisker more . . .

Her fingers closed around her quarry. Energy surged through her. Mist recoiled from her hand, leaving a clear halo around it in which she could see every nub of the twig, every thread of her woolen cuff.

"Well, Mother of—"

Clang!

Seven-thirty.

Jemma started. Her hands and legs slipped, and she swiveled around the branch. Hanging upside down from it, she felt the branch shake and dip. Then, with a loud *snap*, it broke, and fell to the roof of the hut below, with her still clinging to it. The drop was only a few feet, but the roof splintered under the impact, and she crashed through it onto the earthen floor inside. The Stone was jolted from her palm; her right foot twisted beneath her. Yelping in pain, she rolled on the floor and clutched her ankle. It swelled under her hands.

Noodle and Pie wriggled in through a gap in the door, and scampered to her side.

Stone! Stone will heal you! The words flew into her head, though not exactly as words, more as impressions that formed as words.

Jemma looked at the rats. "Was . . . was that *you?*"

A dazzle of aqua caught the corner of her eye. She turned, and there it was: her Stone. The instant she picked it up, a tingling sensation shimmered from the top of her head to her wounded ankle. The pain subsided, and was gone.

"Sprites! How did that happen? When I was fighting Nocturna, it worked so slowly. Perhaps she had a bad effect on it."

That's right. Very bad.

"Rattusses . . . you just did it again!" Jemma looked at them, amazed, then stood and tied the amulet around her neck by the two ends of its broken chain. "Right. Let's get out of here."

As she stepped toward the door, her foot clanged against a half-empty pail of water. Two cups hung on metal hooks over its lip. Then it occurred to her that the hut was warm. Embers were burning in the grate. A pot hung in the fireplace; another sat to the right of it.

Someone lived here.

Clothes—or rags, more like—were piled on a three-legged chair. At the back of the hut, two filthy mattresses lay end to end, one large, one small, blankets strewn across them. On the smaller one, propped against the wall, was a cloth animal—a rabbit, barely bigger than the rats. Glassy-eyed, its ears flopped over its shoulders, one hanging from its head by a thread. It was wearing a patched leather waistcoat, much like the one Digby wore, and was missing an arm.

An eerie recognition clawed at Jemma's chest. "I've seen that before," she said, "but how could I have?" She wanted to look at it closely, touch it, hold it—and yet, angst fizzled under her skin. Why? Why be afraid of something that attracted her like a magnet?

Jemma turned, ran out of the hut, grabbed her belongings from the base of the tree, and pelted away as fast as she could. This time, the brambles and shrubs held back their grasp, and within seconds she was on the track. She stopped, out of breath, and turned to see Noodle and Pie leaping over tuffets and brambles, trying to catch her up.

"Sorry, Rattusses—I didn't mean . . . to leave you behind. It was . . . just . . . so . . . so *spooky*." She tied the pouch around her waist and stuffed the book into it, then looked back at the hut. Who lived there? A mother and child, evidently. Did anybody else know about them? And why had that toy rabbit alarmed her so much?

Jemma slipped the wineskin over her shoulder, pulled on the cloak, and picked up the rats. Then she noticed the clear air around her hands again: Noodle and Pie's fur looked as well-defined as if they were indoors, every golden strand of it clearly visible.

"Look at that, Rattusses! If the Stone can do that, and heal my ankle, perhaps it'll help us on our way. Quickly, let's be off, before they find out I've gone."

She looked down the track. It would be easier to navigate than the steep slope leading into the trees, but she knew from Digby's descriptions it meandered around the crag's flatter side before leveling off into Hazebury. That meant it was a longer route. It was also the way anybody searching for her on horseback would take. She decided to run along it for five or ten minutes to put some distance between her and the castle, then head into the trees, where it would be harder to follow her and there would surely be more places to hide.

She slipped the rats into her pockets and broke into a trot. But she had barely taken ten strides, when the air was split by a blood-chilling scream coming from the castle. Nocturna! She must have woken early. . . . Jemma imagined her hastening to the dungeons, eager to carry out her torturous Rites, and now, staring at the empty cell.

"The Wrath of Mord be upon her!" The rage in Nocturna's voice sliced through the early morning Mist and into Jemma's nerves, promising revenge. She pictured Nox urging his black stallion, Mephisto, along the track, the horse's hooves thundering behind her as he bore down on his target, so easily visible out in the open—

Jemma veered to her right and hurtled down the steep incline into the forest.

And then the storm began.

CHAPTER THIRTEEN

The Hollow

Jemma sped over rocks and rotting branches, through sheeting rain that pounded the earth, pounded her. Thunder roared overhead, a great beast whose lightning talons raked through the air again and again, stripping trees of their limbs and striking the ground around her. Her Stone thumped against her chest as she ran and she clasped it, willing its help. But it had no effect on the storm, and seemed powerless in the thick of the forest.

And now the forest, too, was assailing her. Tree limbs stretched out, whipping her face as she passed. Roots rose from the earth like skeletons from the grave, tripping her. Again and again she slammed to the ground, terrified she'd squashed Noodle and Pie. Again and again their nips and squeals told her they were all right, and she struggled to her feet, picked up the increasingly battered book, and pressed on.

Finally she stopped and fell to her knees. The mauve tea essence had completely worn off; she was exhausted, and felt as though her pounding chest would tear open, baring her heart to the vengeful Wrath of Mord, which surely this was, unleashed by the furious Nocturna.

"Must . . . find somewhere to hide," she gasped. "Can't . . . keep going . . ."

Between the firs, through a curtain of rain, a shadow moved. And another, darting into view, then disappearing. Fear shot into Jemma's veins and she took off again, stumbling over the uneven ground yet managing, somehow, not to fall. Her clothes were heavy, soaked through. And still thunder roared, and lightning speared down. In its brief flashes, she could see more shadows gathering. They looked like pale Mordsprites, small, bedraggled, skeletal. She lengthened her stride, but the ground was slick, and she slipped, slamming facedown in black mud. Hauling herself to her feet yet again, she came face to face with one of the shadows.

It was not a Mordsprite at all, but the gray silhouette of a child, a sunken-cheeked, hollow-eyed boy of no more than five, his ragged arms reaching out to her through the Mist.

Jemma stood petrified, her heart hammering as he swayed closer, oblivious to the chaos crashing down around him. Others closed in behind him, a straggling band of waifs, all moving in the same direction.

Toward her.

"What do you want?" she rasped. He opened his mouth and emitted a hissing sound, his words, if there were any, inaudible in the storm. The others joined in with strangled moans and wails. Noodle and Pie turned frantically in her pockets, urging her to flee, but her muscles felt as slack as chicken giblets, and she couldn't move. The boy was a mere arm's length away, almost touching her—

And then, he walked through her.

For a split second, a freezing shudder seemed to separate Jemma's mind from her body. It brought her to her senses, and she took off down the hill again, past the ghostly herd whose grabbing hands were as insubstantial as chilly gusts of wind.

But there was one more ahead, staggering out from behind a tangle of brambles. A girl . . . no, a stooped woman, carrying a long stick in one hand. Her face was haggard, hair plastered over it by the rain, lips curled back in a gap-toothed snarl. *Just keep running—straight through it, like the others,* Jemma told herself. The phantom-woman stepped aside, but Jemma felt a slap on her arm as she passed, as real as any slap Shade had ever given her. She stopped, then turned to see the woman scurrying away up the hill, cackling like a maniac as she disappeared into Mist. The muted tolls of eight o'clock began thrumming out from on top of the crag. Jemma staggered on, the thought of the Agromonds coming after her shooting through her like acid.

"Noodle . . . Pie . . . ," she stammered. "I don't know how much more I can take. We have to find somewhere to hide." But the Wrath of Mord was not about to show any mercy. Raindrops turned to beads of ice that stung her face and hands, and she could barely see a few feet in front of her, let alone spot any cave or overhang that might give shelter. And now she became aware of something new stalking her. Something low to the ground, scuttling alongside. Two of them, three, and more—she didn't stop to count. Then several scudded across her path.

Spiders. Enormous, hairy wolf spiders. Nox had taught her and the twins about them, and the particularly venomous variety that inhabited Agromond Forest. One bite could easily kill a grown man. And they were hemming her in, forcing her along a path of their choosing.

"Oh, no, *no* . . ." Jemma broke into a run; the spiders ran faster too. She tried to veer in another direction, to jump over them, but they reared up and waved their forelegs, keeping her moving, driving her on to Mord knew where as ice pellets the size of pebbles hurled down on her.

"I can't . . . go . . . on . . ." She was on the verge of giving up, stopping, sinking to the ground, letting the spiders, the forest, the storm, the Agromonds, have their victory—

The ground fell away, and she tumbled into a deep hollow, over sodden leaves and pine needles. Noodle and Pie spilled from her pockets. Her pouch came untied and tumbled in next to her. She looked up. Spiders were crouched leg to leg around the rim, like spectators at a stoning, eager to watch her being battered to death by ice pellets, or simply gazing into this large bowl in the ground at their prey—Jemma and the rats—before devouring it.

Terror and weariness turned to fury. If she was going to die, she would die fighting. She leapt to her feet, throwing off the rain-drenched cloak and the wineskin, then yanked her knife from her boot top and waved its blade up at the spiders.

"All right!" she yelled, her face pummeled by the relentless ice. "Come and get me—but I'll slice the legs off of every one of you first!" She was taut, ready for the onslaught. But the spiders turned their backs, and in quick succession, each shot a thick, glistening thread from their underbelly. The threads blew across the hollow, carried by the wind, and caught on roots on the other side. Then, circling over the net they had created above Jemma's head, the spiders began spinning. She sliced and slashed with her knife, but it glanced off the threads, as ineffective as a feather trying to cut through steel. Soon, the spiders were no longer visible between the thick webbing. Their pattering footsteps faded to silence; the pounding of ice pellets was reduced to a steady hiss; the thunder outside became muted. In no more than a minute, the spiders had sealed Jemma and the rats under a glistening white canopy.

"Mord take you!" she shrieked, stamping her foot on the soggy leaves. "Why didn't you just kill us, and be done with it? Why leave us to rot down here?" She looked around frantically for Noodle and Pie. They were sitting in the center of the hollow, licking each other's fur, evidently completely unruffled. "Rattusses—you're not scared? Didn't you *see* those beasts? We're going to make a fine feast for them!"

Something rustled behind her. She wheeled around. Nothing. But there was a dip in the ground at the rim of the web, forming a hole that looked big enough for her to crawl through. She peered out of it. An enormous fanged jaw moved into view, and eight jet-black eyes peered back.

"Aaagh!" Jemma recoiled. "Keep away! If you come any closer, I'll . . . I'll . . ."

The spider remained motionless. Then Noodle scrambled onto Jemma's feet, clambered up to her shoulder, and took a flying leap out of the hole.

"Noodle—stop! It'll eat you alive!"

Noodle snuffled at the spider's jaws, then hopped back onto Jemma's shoulder and squeaked softly in her ear.

Friend. Because of yesterday. Feo's Offering.

Jemma remembered the pain she had felt for Feo's eight-legged victims. "You mean . . . somehow it knows what happened?"

The black eyes moved closer. Calm washed over her. And

then came the same sense of wordless words she had felt earlier from Noodle and Pie, only this time, they came from the giant arachnid bathing her in its gaze: *Safe here. Rest. Storm will pass.*

Just like the bats, they had been protecting her.

She blinked, and the spider was gone.

Rest, it had said. Suddenly, she realized how badly she needed to. Fight and flight drained from her; she sank to her knees and crawled to where the cloak lay next to her shawl pouch and the book. Just as they had done earlier, the book and cloak had worked their magic: they, and the leaves around them, were dry. So was her pouch. She curled up under the cloak, Noodle and Pie nesting in beside her.

In seconds, she too was dry and warm. For a moment, she looked up at the white canopy above her, marveling at how shiny it was. Then, to block its brightness, she pulled the cloak over her head and closed her eyes. Thoughts of Marsh and Digby sputtered through her mind, before fading, with everything else, into sleep.

CHAPTER FOURTEEN

Thirteen

She was flying like the wind down the crag, the skirts of her dress trailing in silken threads behind her. Voices screamed from the castle, calling her name in a strange, muddled way—"Ma-Jemmajemjamem!" The bell began its fiendish toll, once, twice, thrice, and on and on. Something was chasing her through the Mist—a monster, attacking—its jaws about to snap her in two. . . . She grasped her Stone, and an immense force filled her, propelling the monster backward in a blaze of aqua just as the bell sounded out for the ninth time. Nine o'clock. Nine . . . nine . . .

Jemma woke with a gasp and heard the last toll fading into the distance. Was it real, or had she just dreamed it? Nine . . . her birth time . . . Her body tingled, her head swam with murky images from her dream. Blue-green light surrounded her—or was that, too, in her head? And where was she? The hollow. The spiders. The forest, Mist, and gray shadows. She wanted to run from them, run from it all—the nightmare she was waking from, and the one she was waking to. But where would she run? To her family? She didn't even know who she was, let alone who they were. *Jemma, I'm Jemma! I must go . . . far, far from the castle, from the Mist. . . .* The blue-green pulsed like a gentle heartbeat, lulling her. Weariness washed through her bones. Everything blurred into oblivion, and sleep folded her back into its heavy arms.

* * *

Jemma peered out from under the cloak. Colors sparkled in front of her: blue, red, golden and green pindots, which shimmered across her vision, and then merged into two golden shapes, with four red dots shining out of two small, furry faces.

"Hello, Rattusses. What time is it?"

Hello. Afternoon.

"Afternoon! I've slept for hours." Jemma pulled the cloak around her. For a split second, the rats' faces seemed to separate again into myriad colors before reconfiguring into snouts and whiskers. Puzzled by her shifting vision, she sat up. Her stomach growled. "Ouff, I'm hungry. That must be why I'm seeing things. Thank goodness for Drudge's food packages!"

She reached for her pouch and unwrapped it. The two crystals lay on top, their grayness almost completely gone today. She set them aside. The scent of bread and cheese made her mouth water, and she, Noodle, and Pie tore into their meal. The bread, flattened from her falling on it, was deliciously stale, and the cheese was perfect—runny with age and reeking of feet. Only after she and the rats had devoured most of it did she think to ration their supplies.

"Oh, well," she sighed, taking a more restrained swig of sour milk from the wineskin. "Let's call it my birthday treat. We'll have to be more careful, though, and make the rest last. Now, I suppose we'd better think about moving on." But although the thought of the castle still being so close chilled through her, the idea of having to face the forest again, and the storm, sank like mud into her bones. "Some birthday," she muttered.

Thirteen.

With every passing year, Jemma's birthday had become less fun and more pompous. But the one person who had always celebrated it with enthusiasm was Marsh. She would hug Jemma, smuggle treats for her from the kitchen, and tell her some special new story. Marsh's absence seared through her now. To think of her, cast into the forest with all its dangers . . . How would she survive? *I got ways of protectin' myself,* she'd said. With all her heart, Jemma hoped so. And she still had those dangers to face herself.

Noodle and Pie wriggled onto her lap.

"I'm scared, Rattusses," she said. "I don't know what these Powers are that Marsh said would come out at my birth time, but that was hours ago now, and I don't feel any different." Powers. The hour she was born. All at once, Jemma's dream came back to her. Being chased. The voices, calling. But something about it had felt odd. What was it? Then she realized: the person in her dream had been wearing a long silk dress, nothing like her shorter, woolen one.

"It was almost as if I was someone else," she murmured. "Someone from long ago. She was being attacked, then she felt this jolt of energy—*I* felt it—just as the clock struck nine. . . ." And the jolt she'd felt—was that her Powers coming into her? If so, what form were they supposed to take? The book had Power, and her Stone; but *her?* She felt weak and afraid. Perhaps being Initiated was a way of sealing Powers in, and would have given her courage. But it was too late for that now. Even if dreaming strange dreams and thinking she heard rats and spiders speaking to her counted as Powers, they were surely no defense against Mist and monsters.

Jemma sighed, then forced herself to her feet and went to the opening to look outside.

Pale gray, everywhere. The Mist, swirling over rocks and tufts of grass. Daylight dwindling. But at least the storm was over, and a fine pins-and-needles sensation spattered her face: freezing drizzle. That was better than ice pellets, but still cold and miserable. It was so tempting to stay in the warmth of the hollow. Even if the Agromonds were still searching for her, she'd be well hidden. But would they even bother, now that it was too late for them to steal her Powers?

"How about it, Rattusses?" she said, settling next to them again. "One more night in here, nice and snug? Then I can read more of this." She picked up the book and opened it at the front. "Written by Majem Solvay . . . Was that a man or a woman, do you think?"

A woman. Noodle and Pie hopped onto her knees and peered at the pages.

"I think so too, for some reason. 'Solvay . . .' Why does that sound so familiar?" She squinted at the name again. "Wait a minute—'Majem' is an anagram . . . of Jemma!"

The rats looked at her, cocking their heads to one side as if to say *We knew that.*

"Sprites, Rattusses! In all the years I've heard Marsh saying 'Mother of Majem,' it never occurred to me!" Jemma thought of the way Majem's book had dried her. The cloak had, as well. Had it, too, been Majem's? If so, how did Drudge come to have it? Mystery thickened. There was some connection between her and Majem that went deeper than names; she could feel it, like a secret path winding from some ancient, dark place. And somehow Drudge was tied into it too—

Pie nipped her knuckles. "Ouch, Rattus! What is it?"

The rats flattened their ears against their heads. Jemma held her breath and listened. Outside, a branch cracked in the distance. Then another. Then the sound of sticks beating the undergrowth, and voices—a lot of them—heading toward the hollow.

Panic ripping through her, Jemma wriggled under the cloak. Soon the voices became distinguishable, and she could make out their words between the blood pounding in her ears.

"Anything over there?"

"Naaa. You wannus to keep looking, m'lady?"

Then a voice that struck horror in Jemma's heart—

"*Yes*, keep looking!"

—Shade!

"But it's almos' dark—"

"You'll cease when I say so, and not a moment sooner, else we'll not pay you a single groat! D'you hear me, you pack of lily-livers?"

Muttering, and cursing. The search party was getting closer. Footsteps, firm on the ground nearby. Jemma bit into her forearm, hard, to stop herself from trembling, so that the rustle of leaves underneath wouldn't give away her whereabouts.

"I don't know why we're still looking." Feo's voice. "The time for the Ceremony is long gone." They were practically at the rim of the hollow. Either he or Shade was sure to see the web, so pale against the dark ground! The footsteps stopped.

"Why?" Shade said. "Because I say so, idiot! And because Mama says so."

"Sh . . . ugh . . . gnnn . . ." Jemma heard choking from above, then gasping. "You didn't have to strangle me like that, Shade!" Feo croaked. "Whose side do you think I'm on, for Mord's sake?"

"The side of the addle-headed, evidently! If you'd been listening when Mama explained, instead of gazing out of the window, you'd know. We still have until nine next Mord-day morning to carry out the Ceremony and take Jemma's Powers. But she also has until then to get Initiated by her blood parents, and Mord help us if *that* was to happen! You know the consequences."

Feo snorted. "And how could she possibly find her parents? She doesn't even know who *she* is, let alone them!"

"Oh, do stop wittering, Feo!" A foot stamped on the earth, its impact juddering through Jemma's bones. "Obviously, that Marsh woman told her! Why else would Jemma have taken the two crystals as well as her Stone? With the crystals in her possession, Mord forbid her parents start to guide her!"

The two crystals? What did her parents have to do with them? Jemma peeked from under her cloak, and saw them glinting at her.

"So like it or not, brother dear, we're going to search every day, and we *shall* find her. Alive, if we can, but dead, if needs be. Anything to stop her. She must not leave the forest!"

The footsteps resumed. At any second now, Feo and Shade would fall through and find her! Jemma bit harder into her arm. Leaves shushed; the ground shuddered. The twins walked within inches of the web, then passed by. Her nerves unwound with relief. She was safe!

"Wait!" said Shade. "What's that smell?"

Two sets of ankles, clad in heavy-looking leather boots, stopped just outside the opening. Jemma held her breath.

"What smell?" Sounds of sniffing. "Mmm, yes—sort of . . . sharp, like old socks."

Oh, no—the cheese packet was still lying open! Jemma's teeth were about to break skin.

"Really, Feo," said Shade, "you might wash your feet once in a while. You know that cleanliness is next to Mordliness."

"I washed them yesterday, if you must know. As I do every Mord-day—"

"Hrmph. So you say. Well, darkness is almost upon us. Call off the search. Your voice is more of a foghorn than mine."

"Better that than a banshee scream," Feo retorted. Then he yelled, "All in for the night!"

The two pairs of ankles turned and walked away.

"Of course, you can keep looking if you want, Shade," said Feo, his voice fading with the snapping underfoot, "since you're evidently so unfraid of being out here in the dark."

"Ha! I need my beauty sleep," came the reply. "Besides, Jemma won't get far. She doesn't know her destination, so she'll just keep going in circles. The Mist will see to that."

Jemma counted each rapid thump of her heart as the sounds of voices, breaking twigs, and stick-beaters passed by again. By the time she'd reached three hundred and fifty, the thumps had slowed and the last voice had gone.

She sat up and wrapped the remains of bread and cheese in the shawl with the book and crystals. It had never occurred to her that it was not just the Agromonds she had to fear, but others they would recruit to look for her. But whoever those others were—Mord allies, or merely Agromond underlings—they were evidently afraid to be in the forest at night. Which meant night was the safest time for her to travel. And whatever Shade had said about the Mist making her go in circles if she didn't know her destination, she *did* know it: Hazebury. As long as she kept heading downhill, she reasoned, she'd get there sooner or later. No Mist would stop her. For something was pulling at her even more strongly than the village. Something Shade had said: *We have until nine next Mord-day morning . . . but she also has until then to get Initiated into her Powers by her blood parents. . . .*

She could still be Initiated. She had six more days. Why, she didn't know. She didn't care. But her Initiation was something the Agromonds feared. And that suddenly made it important to her. No, vital. Although Feo was right, she didn't know who or where her real parents were, she was determined to find them. Once she got to Hazebury, she would look. Perhaps Digby would help her. The crystals might, too; from what Shade had said, there was some connection between them and her mother and father.

"I'll look at them more closely tomorrow, when we find our next hiding place, Rattusses," she said, plopping Noodle and Pie into her pockets and tying her shawl pouch around her waist. "And the book. I want to know more about this Majem Solvay too. Right. Let's go."

Whatever the night was to hold, Jemma felt a new sense of purpose. It lit in her mind like the tiniest lantern, giving her a flicker of hope as she bid goodbye to her brief haven and braced herself to face the drizzling darkness of Agromond Forest.

CHAPTER FIFTEEN

Wild Woman

Monday night/Tuesday, early hours

Jemma picked herself up from the wet ground. From the outside, the hole through which she'd just crawled looked like nothing more than the entrance to some small creature's home—a rabbit, perhaps, or a fox. The web was covered in leaves and debris, with no sign of the bright hollow beneath it. Smiling at the spiders' ingenuity—and grateful to them for saving her life—she pulled up her hood and set off down the slope.

"Hazebury," she muttered, holding the name in her mind like a signpost. "Here we come."

As before, roots rose up from the ground to trip her, but by walking at an even pace, Jemma was able to anticipate and avoid most of them. Eight o'clock came and went. Now that she was rested, any dangers the forest might throw at her didn't feel nearly as daunting as before. Even the prospect of the ghost children finding her again didn't seem so scary: she could simply walk through them. With no search parties out at night, the only thing she really had to be wary of was the Mist, and her Stone would help with that. A wave of optimism spread through her. This was going to be easier than she'd expected.

Eight-thirty clanged from on top of the crag. Just ahead, Jemma saw movement through the trees. She ducked behind a bramble bush and peered over it. The madwoman she had seen that morning was creeping up the hill, her stick raised over one shoulder, its front end whittled like a spear. Suddenly, the woman thrust her arm forward. The stick shot from her hand, impaling a rabbit not three paces from Jemma and pinning it to the ground. Horrified, Jemma looked on as the poor creature thrashed about, squealing, then, with a final thump of its hind legs, lay still.

The woman stepped up to the rabbit and yanked it off her stick.

"Come, me bonny bunny. Come to Rue." Her voice grated like a knife on a whetstone. Then she began to sing, rocking the slain rabbit in her arms.

"Rue, rue, rue the day
They took me bonny babe away . . ."

Despite her worn features, the woman was not nearly as old as Jemma had at first thought—around Nocturna's age, possibly younger—and her face was really quite pretty when she wasn't grimacing. She lilted on, her voice becoming soft with sorrow.

"They took me babe, so fair and red,
I loved me laddie, but now he's dead.
His sea-green eyes will see no more,
Like so many babes before. . . ."

Chills fingered Jemma's spine.

"Ah, me pretty, me fluffy one." The woman cradled her bob-tailed victim. "Rue is sorry fer killin' yer, truly she is, but she and her son has to eat." She slung the rabbit over one shoulder and continued her way up the hill, crooning as she went.

"She really is barking mad," Jemma whispered as Noodle and Pie crawled from her pockets up to her neck and nestled into the folds of her hood. She turned down the hill. In what seemed like no time, nine o'clock pealed out from the castle. But the bell sounded no farther away than it had half an hour earlier. A *trick of the Mist*, Jemma thought, looking up the crag. *It must be. We left the hollow an hour ago.*

She padded on. The drizzle had almost stopped, but the night was getting colder. To her right, she saw a faint orange glow between the trees. Firelight. Someone was limping toward it—a small boy, slightly stooped, a blanket wrapped around him. Was he the son the madwoman had referred to? Perhaps they were the ones who lived in the hut, and it was his stuffed toy that had unsettled her so much.

On she walked, roots and rocks barely bothering her now. Her footsteps were hypnotic, and she fell into a rhythm, chanting "Hazebury" in time with it. Minutes melted into hours. Through the trees to her left, she saw fireglow again. Eleven o'clock struck. The bell sounded as close as ever. *Must be the Mist,* Jemma thought, *trying to fool me.* Eleven-thirty. More fireglow, with the smell of something roasting.

"How many people are out here, Rattusses?" She glanced at the tempting orange light. A fireside would be warm, and her stomach was growling again. She stopped for some sour milk. The wineskin had given it a more pungeant flavor than usual, and she drank thirstily.

"That's almost the last of it," she said, holding the spout for Noodle and Pie. "We'll need to find water soon."

She trudged on. Six times more the bell tolled; three times more she saw fireglow. Over the hours, cold sank deeper into her bones, and by three in the morning, when the seventh fire crackled through the Mist, its promise of warmth was hard to resist. Maybe whoever was tending it would let her rest for a while, even give her a bite to eat—

A twig snapped behind her. Jemma wheeled around, and came face to face with the stooped boy she'd seen earlier. Except that he wasn't a boy at all. He looked about Digby's age, or even a little older, but was at least a head smaller than Jemma, his body twisted, his back hunched. Without a word, he grabbed Jemma's arm and dragged her toward the fire.

"Hey—let me go!" Jemma tried to wrench away. "Who are you, anyway, and how did you get here? I saw you hours ago, up the hill."

"Caleb's the name," the boy said in a hoarse whisper. "Me, I ain't gone nowhere all night. You, though, you been walkin' in circles, that's how *you* got to be here."

"Walking in circles? Oh, no!" Jemma remembered Shade's words from earlier: the Mist had done just as she said it would. "Please, I have to go. . . ."

The boy stopped, his dark eyes piercing hers. "You want some roast bunny or not? Me ma's offerin'." He tightened his grip and listed toward the fire, pulling Jemma with him. Inside her hood, Noodle and Pie dug their claws into her shoulders, and she felt their soundless warning—*No! No!*—but between hunger, curiosity, and confusion, found herself stumbling along beside Caleb and ignoring the rats' agitation.

They approached a small clearing and Jemma saw the madwoman through the Mist, turning a small carcass on a spit. On a rock beside her, the rabbit's skin was spread fur-side up, its glassy eyes reflecting the fire's orange glow. Jemma gulped. Noodle and Pie ducked behind her head and clung to her hair, quivering.

"Sit," the woman rasped, patting the rock next to her. "Rue's been waitin'." She stroked the rabbit's head. "You shouldn't mind dead things, girlie, bein' as where *you're* from."

Caleb shoved Jemma toward Rue. Jemma's stomach knotted and she backed up a step, but Rue snatched her hand and yanked her down beside her. Her eyes sharp in the firelight, Rue lifted a grimy finger to Jemma's face and scraped its long nail down her jawline.

"Pretty little thing, in't yer. An' look at yer hands, it's all clear around 'em."

Jemma stuffed her hands beneath her cloak, keeping her gaze fixed on Rue.

"Why d'you s'pose she'd want to run away from the castle, eh, Caleb?" Rue tucked a lock of brown frizz beneath her filthy scarf.

Caleb grunted, and kicked at the fire.

Jemma shifted on her rock. "What makes you think I came from there?"

"Been watchin' yer fer years, haven't I, while you was doin' yer fetchin' an' carryin' in the kitchen an' stables. You never saw me, 'cause I kep' hid to make sure you wouldn't. But I know who you is, oh, yes. I can sense yer from a hundred paces. Knew it was you as soon you ran by me this mornin'. Fast as a fox bein' hunted by hounds, you was. An' don't think I din't see yer behind that bush, neither, when I caught Mr. Rabbit 'ere. Caleb, why don't you slice off a little piece for our guest, eh? A nice leg for a nice lass." Rue smiled, revealing a row of tombstone-like teeth alternating with dark gaps.

Caleb handed Jemma a charred rabbit leg and she munched into it, as much to quell the eeriness of Rue having spied on her and claiming she could sense her as from hunger. The meat was overcooked and dry, killing her appetite, but Rue's eyes narrowed, and Jemma had the feeling that to stop eating would be taken as an insult.

"So . . . is it you two that live in the hut next to the castle?" she ventured, desperately trying to swallow.

Rue moved her face closer, the ripples between her eyebrows knitting into a frown. "What do *you* think, eh? Pretendin' like you don't know!"

"Oh." Jemma pulled back, feeling herself blush. "Yes. Um . . . sorry about your roof—"

"Find wot you was snoopin' for, did yer?"

"Snooping? No—I didn't even know the huts were there. I mean, I'd forgotten—"

"She'd fergotten!" Rue spat into the flames. "D'you hear that, Caleb?"

"Easy, Ma." Caleb stood across the fire from his mother and huddled into his blanket. "Maybe she don't remember. She was jus' little—"

"Remember *what*?" Jemma said, not sure that she wanted to know.

"Me . . . *me!* Your Rue! Nursed you, I did, from the night you arrived, an' looked after yer fer a whole year—I'd even take yer to me own hut now an' then! That is, till that Marsh woman come along." She ground her teeth. "Then you din't need me no more."

So that was why Jemma had recognized the toy rabbit! She must have seen it there, when she was a baby. . . . "So, you knew Marsh," she said, her heart squeezing as she spoke Marsh's name. "You . . . haven't seen her, I suppose?"

Rue sneered. "She couldn't take them ghosts neither, eh? Hrmph. An' wot about that vile old loon Drudge, is he still there? Kep' me distance from him, I did."

So did I, Jemma thought, ashamed of her old judgments. "He's still there."

"Hrmph. Last *man,* if you can call him that, wot stuck around. Unlike me rotten husband. Caleb's pa." Rue's mouth twitched between a smile and a grimace. "Worked at the quarry, he did, then ran off after it was shut down. An' you know why?"

"No," Jemma murmured, puzzled about the quarry. She knew it had existed long ago—the castle was built out of rock from the crag—but had no idea it had still been mined so recently.

"He left 'cause of *this*!" Rue pointed at Caleb. "His bent-up boy! Shamed by him, is wot he said. An' shall I tell yer how Caleb got to be that way, eh?"

Caleb bowed his head. "Ma, don't—"

"He got that way 'cause when he were a toddler—afore you was here, mind; them twins wasn't even born yet—he ran into the stable yard one evenin', just as that Nox Agromond was ridin' out, an' startled his horse. Horse reared up, throwin' the Lord an' Master to the ground. When I come runnin', he said his leg was broke, an' we'd have to pay. We can't pay, sir, I told him, we ain't got two beans to rub together, so he snarls at me like a raddled bear, says that's not what he meant, an' he'd take payment in kind. Next thing I know, my Caleb's writhin' about in agony, screamin' blue murder all night long. Weren't nothin' I could do to comfort him. By mornin' he was like this—a human corkscrew!"

"Ma, please!" Caleb shrugged into his blanket, making his hump look bigger.

Jemma felt the blood drain to her feet. "Nox did that?"

Rue nodded, bitterness galloping back across her features. "To punish him, he says. Evil man, puttin' such a twistin' spell on my Caleb, an' him not yet two years old!"

"Why did you stay? Why not leave?"

"An' where would a girl find work, saddled with a deformed son, an' nought but her milk to offer? You don't *think* much, do yer?" Rue shoved her face up to Jemma's, her eyes as hard as flints. "The very next day, them twins was born. Shade and Feo. I was needed to feed 'em, 'cause that black-hearted mama of theirs couldn't. Her milk dried up, jus' like a witch's does." She pulled back from Jemma, her top lip twitching into a snarl. "My blood curdled, havin' to suckle 'em, Marked as they was, when my own boy was so fair-skinned. An' bonny too, afore Nox Agromond crippled him!"

"Marked . . ." Jemma gulped. The Mark, again. She thought of the livid red diamond on each of Shade's and Feo's faces. The one on her back itched.

"Yes, Marked! The Mark of Mord!" Rue seemed to melt into the darkness behind her. "Won't find any ordinary folks wot have it. It's a sign that a child will follow their evil ways, see. It's said that any Agromond babe born without it is done away with sooner or later, so it's lucky for them two that they both had it. An' lucky for me they needed my milk. At least it bought me shelter."

The Mark of Mord? Jemma remembered Nox's words: *The Mark . . . your birthmark . . . It shows you are one of us. . . .* She gulped.

"Ah, but then . . ." Rue's features suddenly relaxed, and she looked almost pretty again. "Then they brought the new babe. . . ."

Jemma tensed, expecting to hear her own story being woven into the tragedy.

"Such a sweet boy . . . Fair-skinned as me own Caleb he was, only he weren't all gnarled up. Me little bunny. *Rue, rue, rue the day they took me bonny babe away. . . .*"

"Boy?" said Jemma, surprised. "What boy?" She glanced at Caleb, who quickly averted his eyes. Noodle and Pie scratched at the back of Jemma's head. *Go, we must go. . . .*

"*They took me babe, so fair and red, I loved me laddie but now he's dead. . . .*"

Rue's gaze darkened, and Jemma inched away.

"*His sea-green eyes will see no more, like so many babes before. . . .*"

Jemma turned, ready to run, but a jerk at her neck slammed her onto her back.

"Not so fast, my pretty!" Rue yanked her spear from the hem of Jemma's cloak, then crouched over her and pulled back the hood. "What boy, she asks!" She grabbed Jemma's hair, and laughed. "Why, the boy they took before you—the one whose stuffed rabbit you was lookin' to steal! And him dead, dead, because of you, yer flame-headed wretch!"

"Because of *me*? Why?"

"Because it wasn't him they wanted!" Rue banged Jemma's head on the ground. "It was you, you! 'Cause you had the Mark, an' he didn't! Once they'd took yer, t'weren't

long before they got rid of him. Gone, me bonny bunny!"
She began to wail. "An' it's *your* doin'! You're evil, you
are—evil!"

"Ma, that's enough." Caleb shuffled toward them.

Noodle and Pie squirmed from inside the folds of Jemma's
hood and dug their teeth into Rue's fingers. But she was swift,
and yanked them away with her free hand.

"Here, Caleb—a snack for the pot!" The rats flew through
the air, and Caleb caught them.

"Nooooo!" Jemma tried to wriggle free, but Rue held fast.

"Ma," said Caleb. "Enough!" The rats writhed in his fists,
squealing.

"Shut up, yer Mordforsaken gimpy-leg! Put them nice
morsels in the pot and do something useful for a change!
As for you, Miss Red, I daresay they'd like to see yer back
at the castle, wouldn't they? Thinkin' you could run off an'
keep yer Powers all to yerself. They'll reward me finely, oh,
yes! Haaahahahahaaaa!"

Jemma grabbed her Stone and shoved Rue away with her
feet. Rue careened backward, looking as though she'd been
struck by lightning, then began dancing in wild circles.

"Hahahahaha! Get away, she thinks, get away! Oh, me
bonny boy, get away, it's time to die, me bunny laddie-O! Yer
fire's gone, for she's the One!"

"Here." Caleb shoved Noodle and Pie into Jemma's hands.
"Run, while she's possessed."

"Thank you! But what about you? I mean—" Jemma
glanced at his wild-eyed mother.

"Her? I'm used to it. Happens all the time. An' don't mind
her callin' you evil. Says that to me almost every day. Yer all

right, Jemma, I can tell. Jus' go. But hurry! Her fits don't last long."

"Which way, though? I was walking in circles all night."

Caleb shrugged. "If I knew that, I'd have gone long ago. 'Cept I couldn't, 'cause of my legs. An' the rest of me. 'Sides, she is my ma."

Jemma looked into his dark, lost eyes and her heart went out to him. "Thank you," she said again, then fled from the clearing and back into the forest, clutching the rats, whose hearts beat like tiny hammers against her palms.

CHAPTER SIXTEEN

The Dead of Night

Tuesday, early hours

Jemma ran until she felt her lungs would explode, then staggered to the nearest tree and slumped at its base, gasping for breath. Noodle and Pie squirmed from her fists and lay in her lap, trembling.

"Rattusses! Are . . . you all . . . right? Almost thrown . . . into the fire! I should have listened to you . . . kept away. I'm so sorry. . . ." Rue's stories clawed at her stomach, and she unstoppered the wineskin to try and drown the feeling with sour milk. Only a few drops remained, and she gave a sip to the rats, then swigged the rest.

Clang!

Three-thirty. It was over seven hours since they'd left the hollow. The rats curled up, clearly exhausted. Soon, their tiny snores joined the sound of the breeze rustling through the pines, ruffling the edge of Jemma's hood. She closed her eyes. . . .

Wispy figures lurched through twilight Mist, reaching, grasping. Smoky black tendrils wound around them with a stench just like the stench from yesterday's Ceremony. "No," she screamed, "no!" Then a flare of aqua, and a soft voice, soothing: "They are only phantoms, Jemma, but to get past them, you must face them. . . ." Jemma heard herself yelling back, "But who are they? Who was the boy? Did he die because I was Marked and he wasn't? Am I evil, then? Please, I don't want to be!" A tiny shadow floated toward her between moaning pines, a shadow shot through with flame. Chubby, gray baby fingers stretched out and touched her face—

Jemma screamed, waking herself, then jumped to her feet, spilling Noodle and Pie to the ground. "Who's there?"

Nothing. Nobody.

To her left, the bushes trembled. Every nerve on edge, she crept over to them. A gust of wind rippled through fallen brush. Was that something to her right—a phantom, slipping behind the trees? And another to her left, rustling the undergrowth? Jemma held her breath, then, convincing herself that the shadows had gone—if they had been there at all—she hastened back to the rats, her brief dream still rattling in her head.

Squeak. *Not your fault the boy died. You were just a baby too.*

Jemma nodded, trying to swallow the doubt gnawing at her.

Clang!

A single toll. She had slept for almost an hour, and was thirsty. But the wineskin was empty. All around, trees dripped from yesterday morning's torrents. Jemma walked beneath them, letting pearls of water fall into her mouth, but they only whet her thirst.

"We need to find a stream, Rattusses—hey, where are you going?"

Noodle and Pie were scurrying up a ridge. They disappeared over the top of it.

"Wait! We should be going downhill, not up! Stop!" Jemma took off after them, following their squeaks down a small dip, then up between huge tree roots. At the top of the next incline, she saw what they had been leading her to: water, gushing from a gully. They were already crouched at the brink, drinking to their hearts' content. Jemma fell to her knees next to them and shoved her face into the cool liquid.

"Thank you, Rattusses!" She wiped her sleeve across her mouth. "Thank you!"

Don't mention it.

As Jemma filled the wineskin, a thought struck her. "Water only flows downhill . . . so this will lead us away from the castle! Come on, you two." She slung the wineskin around her neck, and scrambled alongside the stream, energized by new hope. Finally, they were getting somewhere.

Clang!

Five in the morning. At last, the bell sounded more distant.

Clang!

A breeze shushed through the pines.

Clang!

The stream dropped away between two rocks, and disappeared into the earth.

Clang!

The rats sat stock-still, ears alert. Something moved in Jemma's peripheral vision: a silhouette, darting through the Mist. Then another, and another.

Clang!

The ghosts. This time, there was no doubt about it. They had found her again. And they were gathering fast, ranging down the slope in ever-paler shades of gray, eyes blank, mouths open. *Remember, they're not solid,* Jemma muttered under her breath, *not real.* But then the hissing began, growing into a thin, wordless keening. Her earlier bravado about simply walking through them seemed to slide off her like mud from a greased pig. She picked up the rats and dropped them into her pockets, then turned and clambered back up the rocks.

Her legs quickly grew weak. She felt dizzy from hunger. Glancing over her shoulder, she saw the phantoms gaining on her, their moans and wails growing louder every second, along with Noodle's and Pie's squeals. The ground leveled out again, and she picked up speed. But so did the phantoms. She veered to the left; they followed. To the right; still, they kept closing in. A gust of wind blew through the canopy of trees above, their leaves rustling a familiar refrain: *Sweet thirteen . . .* And still the gray figures were gaining on her, their cries filling the misty air.

Stop! The rats scrabbled in her pockets. Stop? Surely they weren't serious! Her limbs felt liquid. She tried pushing forward, but it was all she could do to stop her knees from buckling her to the ground at the mercy of the clamoring mass.

Stop! They mean no harm!

"No harm? What are you *saying?* They're *chasing* us!"

To get past them, you must face them, remember?

Jemma remembered the voice from her earlier dream. Then another voice came to mind, saying one word:

Trusssst . . . Her teeth chattered as the silhouettes advanced, and she laid her hand over her Stone. "Help me, p-please. . . ."

Blue-green light pulsed from the Stone. Light . . . light . . . The Light Game! How often had Marsh told her? *You got to imagine a great golden ball, all around you. See it, Jemma, see it!* Jemma focused and saw: the brightness surrounding her, growing larger, until she was standing in a luminous golden sphere. And in its light, she could see every detail of the phantoms as clearly as if the Mist wasn't there. Each small figure, with its harrowed face and eyes full of longing, was perfectly visible. Every hand, outstretched as if starved and reaching for a crumb—any morsel at all—was perfectly outlined. Noodle and Pie had been right: they meant no harm. They were just ghosts, after all. Child ghosts. Hundreds of them. Lost, and desperate.

The wind dropped, and they stopped at the edge of the light sphere.

"You . . . you're the ones whose cries I used to hear at the castle," Jemma said. "The ones who frightened all the Dwellers away. But I thought you were inside, not out."

One of the phantoms—a girl of no more than six years old—opened her mouth. Her words sighed out like a mournful breeze: *"I want my brother."* Then other voices joined hers in echoing whispers: *"I want my brother. . . . I want my sister. . . . Help us. . . . Help. . . ."*

"Help you?" Jemma said, sorrow welling up in her. "But how? What can I do?" Did these children not know they were dead, their bones rotting in the dungeons?

"I want my brother. . . . Trapped in the castle. They can't reach the Light. . . ."

"What do you mean?"

The phantom girl pushed one hand into the golden sphere and brushed Jemma's arm.

"Dead, but still there," she whispered. "Their souls was swallowed by the monster."

The monster. Yesterday's Ceremony. The screams Jemma had heard pouring from the Entity's mouth. . . . She tried not to think of its name, but couldn't stop herself. Scagavay.

"Yes," she muttered. "Yes, they're all trapped. . . ."

The luminous sphere shimmered and began breaking apart. Fragments of its golden light faded away as the ghosts dulled into silhouettes and melted into Mist and emptiness.

Jemma stared down the hill. "Come back!" she shouted. "Tell me your story!" But all that answered was the hooting of a lone owl high in the trees.

Six in the morning struck, then half past. Jemma wandered aimlessly, not caring if she went uphill or down. She felt haunted by those hollow beings, and by their lost brothers and sisters. But why, why had they been murdered? Had killing them given the Agromonds some kind of Power? It must have. Why else would they have done such a thing?

Dawn filtered through the trees; the Mist was getting paler. Jemma's own plight hit her: before long, the search parties would be out again. And she had nowhere to hide.

Hollow! Noodle's and Pie's thoughts streaked into her. *Warm hollow!*

"But how will I find it again?

Ask the book.

She pulled it halfheartedly from her pouch, opened it,

and read aloud: *"If thou know'st not where thou goest, how cans't find the place? The starting-pointe remains too stronge in the Mynd, and pulleth thee backe. Only keep a cleare picture of thy Destination in thy heade, and it will be as though it come to you. . . ."*

"But I *did* know where I was going," Jemma groaned. "Hazebury!" She pondered the words further. *A cleare picture* . . . Perhaps a name wasn't enough. And she'd also kept worrying about the castle—the "starting pointe." As the book said, it had felt like an anchor, pulling her back. Making her walk in circles. But if she'd been walking in circles, that meant the hollow couldn't be far.

A clear picture. Jemma closed her eyes and recalled as much detail of the spiders' hollow as she could: its luminosity; its warmth; the soft, dry leaves beneath her. . . . Her legs began to walk, and she opened her eyes again, letting her feet carry her. A left turn here, down the slope, uphill there. None of it was the way she would consciously have chosen, but she felt magnetized, as if an invisible force pulled her onward. Before long, she heard voices coming from behind her: hunters, no doubt, looking for her. Her heart skipped; thoughts pushed into her mind—*This way, surely? Not that!*—but she ignored them, running as if in a trance.

"Oy, Axe—look over 'ere! The ferns are flatter, like someone's bin walkin'."

The voices were getting closer. And closer. Suddenly, with a familiar pattering sound, seven or eight wolf spiders sped up the path toward her, then passed her by, heading in the direction of her pursuers. Yelps cut through the Mist. *"Look at the size of them things!" "Don't let 'em bite you, whatever you do, or you'll be done for!" "Aagh—get away!"*

Just ahead, Jemma felt the web pulling on her, revealing its whereabouts.

"Watch out—run! Gus—behind yer!"

She threw herself into the hollow's earthy entrance, and sank into soft leaves.

"Don't be such cowards!" Shade's voice. "Just kill the monsters!"

Sounds of swiping, then "Missed! They won't keep still."

"Mord take them!" said Shade. "This way, then."

The sounds of the search party faded. The enemy was gone—for the moment. But now Jemma had the key to getting out of the forest. A clear destination. Digby had described it to her often enough: the edge of the forest, the moat, the river, the village . . . She needed to actually see it all in her mind's eye, not just say a name. Then, once she was there, she would find Digby, and—

First things first, she thought, curling up with Noodle and Pie in the crook of her arm. *Now, we need rest. Later, before we leave, I'll read some more, and take a good look at those crystals.*

But rest evaded her, and for several tolls of the castle bell she was plagued by images of wraiths and rabbit heads, babies and black shadows. Finally, long after nine, she fell asleep.

When Jemma woke, it was already dark, and she'd lost precious travel time. The crystals, and the book's secrets, would have to wait. Hastily gathering her belongings, she pulled herself out of the hollow for the second time. But this time, she felt sure, there'd be no coming back.

It was time to move on. She was ready.

CHAPTER SEVENTEEN

Lair

Tuesday night

Noodle's and Pie's squeals cut through the night. *Stop, stop!*

Jemma dug her heels into the ground, teetering at a precipice. Her feet slid from under her and she grabbed a shrub, clinging to it for dear life. A large stone, dislodged by her boot, rolled off the edge. It cracked against rock as it plummeted, then landed with a splash several seconds later, somewhere far below.

The rats scuttled up behind her.

"Rattusses, thank you! One step more, and . . ." Jemma pulled herself to sit. Beyond her feet, the sheer face of Mordwin's Crag fell away into a sea of white. The Mist, waiting to swallow her whole.

Not safe to walk.

They were right. She would have to crawl.

According to Digby's description of the crag, at some point its sheer face met a perpendicular arm of equally sheer rock that sloped downward, eventually leading to the road into Hazebury. By her reckoning, that was to the right of where they now were.

"This way, Rattusses." Jemma dropped to her hands and knees.

We'll go first.

Noodle and Pie slithered along the edge of the precipice, stopping every few feet to wait for Jemma, then moving ahead again and disappearing into the Mist. *If they hadn't warned me,* she thought, *I'd be nothing but a broken heap at the bottom of the crag. I can't afford to let my focus waver, not for one second.*

Another hour passed, then two. Occasionally, the three of them stopped to rest, gobbling down a bite of sausage and sipping a little water. Eleven o'clock clanged out from on top of the crag. At least the bell sounded farther away now. But every inch of progress was perilous and exhausting. The shawl pouch around Jemma's waist felt increasingly heavy, and the snail's pace drove the night's chill deeper into her bones as warmth from the book and cloak ebbed. It seemed that they too needed rest occasionally.

At last, the dark shadow of a tree line loomed through the Mist. Jemma scrambled to her feet and trotted after the rats into the forest, welcoming the softer ground and the cover of pines and firs. A lone mountain cow grazed nearby. She'd only ever seen one before, delivered to the castle two Mordmases ago by Digby and his father. Shy creatures, Digby had said, as they'd hung the shaggy red carcass in the scullery. Jemma had been impressed by its horns, but hadn't liked the taste of its meat; it was too thick, somehow, as if it was full of mud.

"So have no fear of me, cow," she whispered. "I'm not looking for beef tonight. Though I wouldn't mind your coat."

The cow raised its head and lumbered away as soon as it saw her. But its motion made something flutter in its wake: a triangle of fabric, snagged on a bramble. Jemma's heart leapt. That brown, woolen weave . . . She ran and picked it off the thorns.

"A piece of Marsh's dress, Rattusses! So she was here." Jemma shoved the ragged scrap into one pocket, uttering a fervent wish for Marsh's safety before walking on.

Branches rustled. Owls screeched, trees creaked. The ground became steeper. Jemma kept her eyes on it to avoid roots, rocks, and rabbit burrows. The Mist was thinning slightly, and she relaxed a little, able to fix her destination more clearly in her mind: the row of thatched, stone houses Digby had so often described, in the middle of which was Goodfellows Grocery, where he lived with his parents and younger brothers and sister—the triplets, whose antics she loved hearing about. The thought of his face—vivid blue eyes, sandy-colored hair, lopsided grin—made her smile, and now Marsh's face joined in her imaginings, doubling her optimism. Perhaps Marsh would be there too, waiting for her.

The single toll of eleven-thirty drifted down the crag.

"The bell is definitely farther away now," Jemma said. "Definitely! By this time tomorrow, we could be in Hazebury—"

Snap!

Jemma stopped in her tracks and looked up. Light beams darted around ahead of her, and she saw four burly, long-coated silhouettes attached by thin cords to smaller silhouettes closer to the ground. She ducked behind a tree. Then came a series of strange sounds, something between Feo belching and a gruff groan, only ten times as loud.

"Shut up, Fang!" A man's voice, low and gravelly. "Stupid hound!" He yanked the cord he held, and the creature at the end of it let out a sharp yelp. " 'Ere, Zeb, give 'im another whiff of the girl's dress."

"Right you are, Lok."

Rustling, mumbling, cursing, then another yelp, this one sounding eager and hungry. Noodle and Pie clawed their way into Jemma's pockets and lay there quivering. Jemma felt as though worms were crawling around her belly. Unlike yesterday's posse, these men weren't afraid of the forest at night. They must be really tough, or mean, or both. . . .

The men moved away. But one of the hounds lifted its snout into the air and sniffed, then broke from the pack, snapping its leash. It headed straight toward Jemma.

"Oy, over there—Fang's got the scent! Gimme a hand up, Zeb, you idiot."

Jemma took off down the hill, begging her Stone for help. Brambles and branches reached out to snag her as she passed; others pulled back to let her through. But the snorting and growling behind her was getting closer, and closer, until it was practically at her heels.

She turned and swiveled her pouch around to the front, then snatched the remaining sausages from it and threw them at the hound. It caught them in its jaws and chomped them down in one mouthful. She lunged for her knife. But before she could grab it, the creature leapt. Jemma dodged to one side, but too late. Its teeth sliced through her shawl bundle, tearing it from her waist. It thrashed the fabric from side to side as if it were a dead duck. The crystals flew in opposite directions; the book plopped to the ground. She seized it and ran.

"There she is!"

Snarls and thumping feet behind her. Snapping twigs, snapping jaws. Shouting, getting closer. Her limbs fired with terror. At any second now, the hounds would be upon her—

Suddenly, the ground beneath her collapsed, and Jemma plummeted down a narrow shaft. Her arm scraped rock; her sleeve ripped, her skin seared. She felt the cloak catch, jolting her; then it too ripped, and she fell through empty space, landing on her back onto something soft and furry. The book bounced off her stomach and landed on the floor beside her. Noodle and Pie wriggled out of her pockets and lay flat on her chest, their teeth chattering.

Five silhouetted heads and shoulders peered down at her. One of the hounds had evidently fallen in after her and hung by its leash, thrashing against the sides of the shaft. It yelped as the man holding it yanked it back out and onto solid ground.

"I ain't goin' down there," the man said. "We'd never get out!"

"Aukron's lair, by the looks of it," said another.

"An' how do we get our reward, without proof she's a gonner?"

"That bit o' scarf Fang's been gnawin' on is as good a proof as any. Let 'em try'n' deny *me* my cash!"

"Wait a mo', Lok—over 'ere. Look—a hand! Someone else the Aukron had fer dinner, I s'pect. We can use it to fool them Agromonds. It's small enough to be a nipper's, so if we strip the rest o' the flesh off of it . . . like this . . . there! They'll never know it's not the girl's. *Sorry, sir, ma'am; the dogs got 'er—we couldn't stop 'em in time—but 'ere, let us give you a hand!*" The men broke into demonic laughter and walked away amidst the sound of howls and breaking branches.

Jemma felt nauseous. A hand . . . ? She fingered the piece of Marsh's dress in her pocket, grief searing through her. *Stop it!* she said to herself, biting back tears. *Maybe it's not Marsh's hand. Even if it is, that doesn't mean she's dead.* She breathed deeply to calm herself.

"Ugh!" The air smelled foul, and she hastily pushed herself up to sit. Her hands were resting on thick, matted fur. A mountain cow lay beneath her, slit from belly to throat, innards spilling onto the ground. The cow was still warm; freshly dead—so that couldn't be where the stench was coming from. As her eyesight adjusted, Jemma saw that the cow wasn't the only unfortunate creature to have fallen into the cave; the ground was strewn with carcasses. Hanks of rotting hide lay all around, crawling with maggots. Beneath them was a carpet of bones, some intact, others splintered as if they'd been subjected to furious attack.

Dread seethed through her. "Oh, no," she whispered, suppressing the urge to throw up. "Maybe those thugs were right, and this really *is* the Aukron's lair. . . ."

She had always scoffed at stories of the Aukron, laughing off Nox's gory enactments of its ferocity, which had delighted her and the twins when they were little. She'd even doubted its existence, though Feo insisted it was real.

"*Oh, yes, Jemma,*" he'd said. "*It roams the forest at night. Cunning it is, and loves to make its prey as afraid as possible. It won't eat whole humans, though—just their guts. They're its favorite snack!*"

"*And how could anybody possibly know that, silly?*" she'd

always retorted, laughing. *"If it ate your guts, you'd be dead, and it would be a bit difficult to tell anyone, wouldn't it?"*

But now, it was obvious: the Aukron was the Agromonds' creation, its tastes determined by them, so of course Feo would know. The intestines that coiled at her feet and oozed blood onto her boots were nothing to laugh at.

Her own stomach tightened. "We've got to get out of here, Rattusses," she said, standing up. "Fast."

Jemma looked up the shaft. It was about twice her height, and just wide enough for the cow to have fallen through. Jutting across the bottom of it was a large, pointed rock—no doubt the one that had grazed her, and caused the cow's grisly death. If she could grab hold of it, perhaps she could hoist herself up. She stepped onto the cow's flank and bounced on it to see if she could spring high enough, but her hand batted thin air. Next, she took off her cloak, and managed to hook it around the rock, but when she pulled on it, she heard its fragile velvet rip.

"Think, Jemma, think!" Frantically, she looked around the cave. From about halfway up its earthen walls, what appeared to be branches were jutting out in every direction—tree roots, she realized: a mass of them, tangled across the roof of the cave. That might be a way to climb to the shaft. But even the lowest one was several feet out of reach. She looked around again. The book. Bones. Hide. Rotten flesh. Roots. Bones. Roots. Bones. The words beat through her head in time with her thumping heart, churning up an idea. She found a long femur, splintered at one end, rounded at the other. Using a skull as a hammer, she drove its sharp end into the wall at knee height, leaving about a foot of its rounded end sticking out. She stood on it and stretched her arm up. The roots were still out of reach, so she hammered a second femur into the wall. It wouldn't hold. She tried in several other places, but all around the cave, the earth crumbled above waist level.

"Mord take it!" Jemma hurled the bone to the ground. It somersaulted, then embedded itself between coils of intestine, a taunting reminder of the Aukron's favorite delicacy. Panic rising, she looked around again. Skulls. Hide. Cow guts. Cow guts . . . *Strong as wire*, Digby used to say about them. Once, he'd made a skipping rope for her out of them. Skipping rope . . .

Rope! Jemma eyed the shaft, estimating the distance of the jutting rock. Then, taking her knife from her boot top, she sliced off a length of the cow's innards, amazed by how much fit into one animal. Folding the coil in two, she threw the looped end up toward the rock. It flopped down just short of its mark. Again she tried, and failed.

"Patience, Jemma, patience," she said. "See it happening." She took a deep breath and tried a third time. The loop hooked over the rock, leaving two lengths of intestines dangling down. But they were slippery, and impossible to hold on to. She picked up the book, held it to the glistening tubes, and concentrated. *Dry . . . Dry . . .* Steam exuded from them, and within moments, their surface was tacky: perfect to grip.

"Come on, Rattusses," she said, tucking the knife back into her boot

Noodle and Pie clambered up to her shoulders, ears flat against their heads. Jemma stuffed the book into one pocket, shoving her stone inside the front of her dress. She was about to start her climb when she spotted something brown sticking out from beneath the cow's horns.

A boot.

She picked it up, instantly recognizing its scuffs and tattered laces: it was one of Marsh's. "Oh, no. . . ." She sank to her knees. The thought of Marsh meeting her end down here, with the goats and cattle . . .

Noodle nuzzled her face. *Bones. Wrong size. Look around.*

Jemma looked. "You're right. They're all too big or too small. A shoe doesn't prove anything." She dropped it, and with heavy determination stood, then hauled herself up the sticky gut-crafted rope onto the rock. Below her, Marsh's shoe lay among the bones. "It doesn't prove anything," she said again, wiping her hands on her dress. "Nor does the hand." But her heart weighed like lead in her stomach as she wedged her back into one side of the shaft and her heels into the other, and began shuffling herself upward.

From up on the crag, the twelve tolls of midnight started booming into the night. Two sets of claws dug deeper into her shoulders as the dim circle of light at the top got closer. And closer. Finally, on the eleventh toll, Jemma heaved herself out and lay facedown on the damp grass, taking deep sobs of breath as Noodle and Pie panted into her neck.

Clang!

The last strike of midnight shuddered through her. Wednesday. Four days left to escape the forest and find her parents in time to be Initiated by them. Four days . . . but what would become of her and of her Powers if she failed? *I can't let that happen,* she thought. *I have to succeed. I have to.* And at least she'd be safer now: with the hand that the thugs had taken as proof of her death, the Agromonds would surely call off the search.

Jemma pushed herself to her feet. Then she felt it: the low growl reverberating through her, the hot gust of breath at her back. Whatever was there, she could sense, was enormous. Without so much as a glance behind her, she grabbed the rats and ran.

CHAPTER EIGHTEEN

The dukron

Wednesday, early hours

Branches crashed behind her, low grunts belching out in time with her pursuer's pounding feet. Jemma felt as though she was flying down the crag, her feet barely touching ground, her cloak trailing in her wake. The forest seemed to open before her like a clear tunnel, showing her the way as she hurtled over rocks and ferns, until she came to the middle of a clearing.

The racket behind her stopped. Jemma stopped too. Trees shivered. The air was still, as if holding its breath. She stepped forward. To her right, a branch cracked. She halted, scalp tingling. Silence. Another step, another crack, this one closer, coming from behind; then another, to her left. Down the slope, a shadow hulked between the trees. Dropping Noodle and Pie into her free pocket, she changed direction. The shadow was there, ahead of her. Each way she turned, it anticipated her, hemming her in.

She was trapped.

A low rumble vibrated from the earth and up through Jemma's bones. It seemed to come from all directions at once. She spun around, terrified, as a huge black form leapt in front of her. Sinewy and muscular, its hind knees bent forward like a human's. Its forelegs were long and triple-jointed, its fingers tapering into thick, curled talons. Raw flesh hung from its belly. Hatred blazed from its narrow, orange eyes.

The Aukron. And here, in the clearing, Jemma was at its mercy.

It circled around her, once, twice, its gaze fixed on her. Then it reared onto its hind legs and stomped toward her, talons raised to strike. She turned and ran for the trees, but a swipe to her back slammed her to the ground. Hot breath blasted her as she scrambled to her feet; her hair sizzled and singed. A gigantic hand caught her left leg, and she was dragged along the forest floor, rocks and twigs slashing into her skin. Her cloak was torn from her, and Pie and the book were jolted from her pockets. Noodle squealed, and she felt his claws dig into her hip as the Aukron hoisted her upside down into the air. It held her level with its giant jaws, then opened its mouth and flipped its black tongue from side to side, drawing her closer, its fangs ready to impale her with one fatal chomp. A scream froze in her throat. The world beyond the forest flashed through her head. She would never see it now. Never know what life was like beyond the Mist—

Noodle let out a rat screech of terror. Like a mother fox protecting its kits, Jemma felt ferocity surge through her and forgot all else.

"Leave him alone, you Agromond monstrosity!" She snatched the knife from her boot top and struck out, slicing the Aukron's top lip. Bile-green liquid spurted out, and the monster drew its free hand to the wound, snarling with pain. But still its huge leathery fist was clamped around her, its talons digging into her skin. She jabbed and slashed at the gnarled fingers, which only clamped tighter until she could barely breathe. Its mouth widened in what looked like a cruel smirk, full of the delight of an imminent meal.

The Light Game, Jem! Marsh's voice wove into her head. *Remember . . .*

Jemma imagined gold Light filling her, surrounding her, expanding outward. The Aukron hesitated, its eyes narrowing. She intensified the Light, vaguely aware of Noodle clawing his way to her neck. He tugged her Stone from inside her dress, and she grasped it with her free hand and thrust it toward the Aukron's face.

Bright aqua light saturated its eyes. For a split second, they turned icy white, and she felt the purest evil looking at her. Then, with a roar, its grip released and she plummeted, crumpling to the ground. Noodle landed on top of her and dashed to Pie. Jemma stood and grabbed her Stone, then held it out in front of her as she limped toward the beast. It lumbered backward, howling, clamping its fingers over its eyes. She kept advancing, Stone in hand, the Aukron cowering from its light. Near the edge of the clearing, it sank onto its haunches and groaned. She turned and ran.

But the Aukron was not done with her yet. It struck out and slammed her facedown on top of the book, knocking the knife from her hand. Four massive limbs surrounded her. Its hot diaphragm pressed forcefully into her back, squeezing the air from her. Its roar rattled through her; its huge heart hammered against her back. The book pressed painfully into her hip; her Stone was crushing her sternum. She thought she would break. From beyond the beast's belly, she could hear Noodle's and Pie's frantic squeals. Desperate, she reached for the knife, and felt a tiny muzzle nudging its handle into her hand. But the Aukron had her arm pinned, and she couldn't move a muscle.

A name sprang into her head, and she called out to it.

"Majem! Help me, please! I don't want to die. . . ."

The earth beneath her shivered, and she felt as though she was melting into it. Then the book and her Stone seemed to dissolve and float up through her, as if the molecules of her body were dissolving too, flooding her with heat. She heard a hissing sound where her back met the Aukron's stomach. With a loud bellow, the Aukron recoiled, its flesh burning.

Jemma and her cloak were unscathed.

Her focus pulled together. Every fiber in her body fired into action. She flipped over and stabbed the Aukron's thick hide. The beast pulled back, the knife's hilt sticking from its gut. Jemma grabbed the weapon with both hands and sliced upward. Black flesh ripped open, and there, beating right in front of her and webbed with dark veins, was its monstrous heart. She glimpsed her face reflected in its glistening sur-face, hair flame-red, teeth bared, aqua eyes fired with deter-mination. With one final thrust, she punctured the beating balloon.

Jemma scrambled clear as the Aukron fell to its side, wheezing and groaning. Green liquid spurted from the gash, searing the grass and spattering her hands. The spurts slowed, and lessened, and slowed more, until finally, the Aukron lay still.

"Oh, my—oh, my—" Jemma dropped the knife. Her hands stung from the creature's blood and she wiped them on the grass, looking around for the rats. They were huddled next to her cloak several feet away, shaking, but unharmed. They teetered toward her. She picked them up and hugged them fiercely. The horror of having almost lost her life—and theirs—flooded through her, washing away the force that had infused her moments ago. She had killed the beast, saving herself, and Noodle and Pie. She should be triumphant, but all she felt was weak, and sick to her stomach.

Pie nudged Jemma's hand. *Us, or it . . .*

"I know, Pie, I know. But even so . . ." She buried her face in the rats' fur. She craved rest, but couldn't stop here—not with that Mord monster lying mere feet away. She would have to find shelter, just until she could catch her breath.

"Let's move on, Rattusses." Jemma picked up the knife and tucked it into her boot top, then crawled over to the crumpled cloak and wrapped it around her.

Crystals. We must get them.

She groaned. Of course, she couldn't go without the crystals. Stuffing the book back into her left pocket, she and the rats began the long trudge uphill toward the Aukron's lair.

Noodle and Pie perched on Jemma's shoulders as she stumbled down the hill again. One o'clock had passed, and now a second single toll marked the passing night. One-thirty. She had soon found the place where the hound had caught her. The remains of her shawl had gone—part of the men's proof of her death, she supposed—but after a mercifully short search, she had found the crystals. She checked them again now, one in each pocket.

Approaching the Aukron's corpse, Jemma noticed that it had become smaller, not much bigger than a cow—and it was shrinking with every step she took toward it, disintegrating before her eyes. She stopped and stared as the monstrous head deflated, then separated into thousands of black maggots that slithered away beneath the leaves. The last shadow of its legs slowly disappeared, then its arms, and finally its torso. All that remained were the burst shreds of its heart, like a large black bowl containing the last pool of the monster's green blood.

In the middle of it, something moved.

Jemma leaned in closer. There, in the liquid, she saw a tiny but unmistakable image, which expanded to meet her gaze. Two people—Nocturna and Nox—were running; then they were standing before Mordrake and Mordana's statues, arms raised in a gesture of worship. The image expanded again. From beneath his night robes, Nox pulled out a bundle and unwrapped it: the remains of Jemma's shawl, with the skeletal hand—the hand that the thugs had given them as evidence of her death. He placed it on the altar, then he and Nocturna waved their arms above it. Jemma remembered Nox teaching her that this was a way to track who, or what, a limb or fragment of clothing had belonged to. "A *piece of their essence remains,*" he had explained, "*and we can see who they are, or were.*" Jemma held her breath as she watched a shadow form rising up.

Marsh. So it *had* been her hand.

Grief jolted through Jemma. *It still doesn't prove she's dead,* she told herself, but a tear rolled down her cheek and into the Aukron's blood. The image rippled, obscured for a moment. When it cleared, Nox and Nocturna were looking over their shoulders, appearing puzzled, then angry. Nox snatched something from the end of the mantel: the black globe. He placed it in the middle of the altar, and waved his arms again. A dark shape appeared: a small version of the Aukron, which then shriveled and collapsed. Nocturna's mouth formed an enraged O, sending the soundless scream of her fury jarring into Jemma's bones.

They knew. They knew that she had killed the Aukron. That she was still alive. The hand in their possession was Marsh's, not hers. And from the look on Nocturna's face, Jemma had a feeling that the Wrath of Mord was about to be unleashed on her again.

The night darkened. A violent wind tore through the trees from the top of the crag. Thunder roared. The forest seemed to expand around her, dwarfing her. Grabbing the rats, she took off into blinding rain, which turned to needle-sharp sleet, then eyeball-sized hailstones that rolled beneath her feet, crashing her to the ground. She slid downhill under the heaving canopy of the forest, past firs bent almost horizontal by the wind, over ferns that cowered close to the earth, battered by the elements. Her cloak snagged on roots and rocks, jerking her every which way as she was blown down and down and sideways, and she realized with horror that the wind was propelling her straight toward the sheer edge of Mordwin's Crag. She thrust out her arms in an attempt to hold onto passing trees, brambles, anything—but she was falling too fast, in a cascade of leaves, stones, and branches.

Her head cracked against something hard. She felt a brief sensation of flying, of being caught by the wind. Then blackness closed around her.

CHAPTER NINETEEN

Bryn

Friday morning

Pain shot through Jemma's limbs. Her hands felt as though they were on fire, but she was holding something in each palm, cool, cylindrical, and soothing. Her Stone was hot on her chest, and some kind of hide covered her, yet shivers racked her body.

"Rattusses," she managed to whisper. "Are you there?" She couldn't turn her head to look, could only see rock several feet above her, dark and jagged. A cave, she must be in a cave. She was lying on something soft, and could smell leather and straw and smoke, as well as something pungent. She remembered vaguely her head being lifted, and hot, bitter liquid being poured down her throat. Above and to her left, orange tinged the ceiling; her left side was warm. Fire, crackling gently. Where were Noodle and Pie? Were they all right?

"*Rattusses,*" she wheezed, a little louder.

No answer. A bead of sweat dribbled into her hair. Jemma closed her eyes and sank into blankness again.

Garbled words began swimming through her mind: *Leth gith bal celde . . . Leth gith bal celde . . .* Were they anagrams? She was too confused to tell, too lost in the fog of fever.

"Miss. Miss." A mournful whisper. Echoey, distant, yet

right in her head. She opened her eyes. A gray figure hovered over her, small, ragged. A girl. Was she dreaming, or was one of the phantom children here in the cave with her?

Who are you?

"I'm Cora," the figure said. "Me and my bruvver was taken when we was six. They killed 'im. Left me to die in the dungeons, wiv 'is body tossed in beside me."

No, no! I don't want to hear this—not now. . . .

"Help us, please, help!" Cora's hand passed like a breeze through Jemma's shoulder. "Please, you got to free my bruvver. 'E's my twin. Like my uvver half. I can't move on wivout 'im. 'S the same for all of us out 'ere. You's our only hope."

Me? Why? How can I help? Your brother's dead—you're dead! Maybe I am too. . . .

"Please! They's all trapped in the castle. . . . You can help. You's the One. . . ."

The One? I don't know who I am. I'm just me. Just Jemma.

Clang!

One lone toll, from far, far away. *Leave me alone, Cora, please. . . .*

Cora dissolved into the granite ceiling, and disappeared with a long drawn-out sigh as the strange words began circling Jemma's head again: *Leth gith bal celde . . .*

Two cold dots nudged Jemma's chin. She opened her eyes.

"Noodle, Pie!" The rats were lying on her chest. They blinked, and hopped to the ground. Without thinking, Jemma sat up. "Ouch!"

Her back was sore, her head ached, but otherwise most of her earlier pain had subsided. The Stone felt warm on her chest, and energy seemed to be snapping between it and her hands, in which she was clutching the crystals. Who had placed them there? The same person who had lit the fire, no doubt, and had recently piled wood onto it. Evidently, this was their home. Three pots sat by the fire, and a shelf of rock held several roughly hewn wooden bowls and cups. Next to them, a tall cup held a bunch of yellow and white flowers. Dried herbs hung by ribbons of sacking from the cave's roof. On the earthen floor beside her, Jemma now noticed her cloak, neatly folded by whoever lived here, with the book, the wineskin, and her knife stacked on top of it. Her boots sat side by side on the floor. She stretched, grateful for the fire's warmth, then placed the crystals beside the knife. They were completely clear, no trace of cloudiness remaining.

Outside the cave was a mass of swirling white.

"Where are we, Rattusses? Where have you been?"

Pie scuttled to the fire and nosed a pile of round white objects next to a smaller pile of pale creamy-colored ones, and finally, clusters of small purple berries.

Food. For you.

"Mushrooms and nuts!" Jemma grabbed them. The mushrooms were cool and plump, and the nuts—hazel and pine—crunchy and fresh. "Mmmm, thank you! And what are these berries—not nightshade, surely?"

No, silly.

The rats' feast was surprisingly filling. Her hunger satisfied, memories of the past few days filtered back into her head, and as they did, her spirits sank. She remembered the strange words she'd heard when she'd woken earlier; but more vividly, she remembered the girl ghost, Cora, with her plea for help.

For her, and her twin, and all the others in the forest. Their earnestness and sorrow felt like a mission Jemma had been handed—a mission she was not sure she wanted.

She sighed, pulling back the long, red-haired hide covering her, then saw her legs.

"Mother of Majem!" she said. Her stockings were torn to shreds, and her thighs were streaked with scabs and bruises that glistened with a greenish ointment. Her right ankle was bound between two rough splints of wood, her bare foot sticking out of the end. "What on earth happened?"

Noodle hopped into Jemma's lap and lay there, stockstill. A picture flickered in her mind, a memory of falling, of intense pain as she whomped onto white-covered treetops, branches giving way beneath her one after another, until she crashed onto the ground in a shower of cold wetness. Then her vision shifted, and she seemed to be outside herself, watching from ground level as she was lifted by sturdy arms attached to a thickset form that was roughly clad in animal skins, with sacking bundled around the feet and ankles for shoes. Dark hair flowed over broad shoulders, on one of which perched a tiny bird. It wasn't her own eyes she was seeing through, Jemma realized, but ones close to the snow-covered earth, darting this way and that, following behind and watching as she was carried across a white, powdery landscape and through the Misty forest as though she were the most fragile china. Then she saw what she guessed was the bottom of Mordwin's Crag, and several feet up it, the mouth of a cave.

In the far distance, a bell tolled. The vision imploded, scattering into tiny fragments. Jemma looked at Noodle, lying as still as a rat statue, his ruby eyes staring. He blinked, then shook himself, golden spikes of fur sticking up from his body.

"Noodle . . . that was . . . you just showed me . . . ?"

He twitched his whiskers. *Easier than words.*

"Who was carrying me?"

"Me," said a husky voice behind her. Jemma wheeled around, and saw a large shadow at the back of the cave. Instinctively, she shrank back.

"Who are you?"

"Me Bryn. Look after you till you well. Bryn like to do that." Something chirruped. As her eyes adjusted to the darkness, Jemma saw a bird huddled in Bryn's hand. He lifted it level with his lips and chirruped back at it. "Soon well, Sparrow. Soon mend wing. Girl land in tree, hurt you." He looked up at Jemma. "You hurt too."

Bryn sat cross-legged, stroking the bird. His face looked as though it had been flattened by an anvil. His nostrils spread almost halfway across his cheeks, which were pitted with what Jemma knew to be pockmarks—the remnants of smallpox, described many times by Nox, who had a horror of disease. Bushy brows sprouted from a bony shelf jutting above Bryn's small eyes, and he peered at her through a curtain of greasy-looking hair. But as alarming as his appearance was, Jemma felt safe under his gaze. He emanated kindness and calm.

The bird fluttered to Jemma's lap and rubbed its head on her fingers.

"Sorry I hurt you, Sparrow," she said, then looked at Bryn. "Hello, Bryn. Thank you for rescuing me."

"Hello." Bryn crawled to a pot next to the fire and scooped

some liquid from it into a wooden bowl, which he handed to Jemma. "Drink. Help heal."

The brew smelled like a combination of Drudge's breath and rotting potatoes, and Jemma screwed up her face as she sipped. "How long have you lived here, Bryn?"

Bryn's eyes disappeared beneath a frown. "Don't know," he said. His voice was as low and resonant as the tone from the empty syrupwater flagons Jemma used to blow into. "Long ago, me, boy. Live up hill. In hut, by castle." He pulled one of his hides around him. "My ma wash clothes there. But Bryn get sick. Bad man in cloak, he say no can stay—"

"Nox? Nox Agromond?" Jemma gritted her teeth.

Bryn shook his head. "No! Nox boy, like me. Bad man in cloak his pa. My ma, she bring me to forest, make well with plants, berries. Then she take me back to hut. But Nox's pa scared. See my face, say Bryn still sick, must stay away. Nox cry, say he want me to stay and play, he lonely now without his sister—"

"His twin sister! Yes, they were just little when she died."

"Mmmm." Bryn smiled, revealing a row of startlingly white teeth. "She pretty. Hair red, but not like yours. Hers dark, like blood."

"You mean . . . you actually *saw* her—Malaena—alive?"

"Oh, yes. We play. She nice. But one night, my ma say she hear screams. After, no more Malaena."

"How awful." Jemma shuddered, and felt a pang of pity for the boy Nox had been, and for his twin sister. "What happened to her?"

Bryn picked up a twig and drew patterns in the earth with it. "Ma says they kill Malaena because her skin white as snow. She got no Mark. Nox, he got Mark."

Jemma gasped, remembering Rue's words: *The Mark of Mord . . . Any Agromond born without it . . . done away with . . .* "Oh, no," she croaked. "Go on, Bryn. What happened after you were sent away again?"

"We come here. Here, home. Many winters pass. Ma do good work, heal men who hurt at quarry. Me help too, she teach me. Then quarry shut down because crag lose its magic."

"Magic? What magic?"

"Rock from crag give Power. Give Agroms Power. And they sell rock to men from far away, to give them Power too. Pay a lot. Make Agroms rich."

"So the rock's magic—the Power it gave—was bad? Evil?"

"No, no! Ma say, not good or bad. Magic is what men make it. Ask for bad, get bad. Ask for good, get good. But must use with *respect*." He scratched his head. "She say, when you take from earth, you must give back, or earth die. Crag need something called sun. But Agroms not know. Hate sun. Love Mist. So they no feed crag, and rock die. Magic die. Power, gone."

"So that's why everything was decaying! The crag needs sunlight—the very thing the Agromonds have been keeping away. Poor crag . . ."

"After quarry shut, just Ma and me. We happy. Better than at hut." Bryn's eyes softened; he sighed, his eyebrows knitting into a single furry line. "One day," he said, "Ma's breath stop. She gone to the wind, to the stars. Me plant her body in earth."

"Oh, Bryn . . ." Jemma reached for his hand, wondering how anybody could bear such a lonely life. She couldn't imagine how hers would have been without Marsh and Digby.

"No sad!" Bryn said. "Ma grow into pretty flowers. See?" He looked up at the blooms on the shelf, and smiled. "Bryn not alone. Ma with me. Birds, animals too. Trees. Earth. All teach me, how make things better, make animals better, make you better. Me happy! Me make medicine, like Ma show me, like plants show me. But shiny things"—Bryn pointed at the two crystals—"*they* magic. Me hold them, get strange words in head. Like voice, but not. Say they want to be in girl's hands. Me put them there. And then—you heal, fast, fast!"

Jemma glanced at the rats, who were busy licking each other's fur. Had they found a way to communicate with Bryn, as they did with her? Or had the crystals somehow spoken to him?

"Me never seen that," Bryn continued. "Just two days, two nights, you almost well! You got the magic too. You good, like my ma!"

Jemma looked at him. She could feel his honesty, his wholesomeness. Could feel it in *her*, vibrating like the hum of a spinning top.

"I hope you're right, Bryn," she said softly, pushing down thoughts of her Mark. Then his other words hit her. "Wait— I've been here two days and nights? Sprites! That means it's Friday morning . . . which leaves only two days to find my parents—Noodle, Pie, we must go!" She pulled her hand away from Bryn's. Sparrow, startled, flapped from her lap onto the ground.

Bryn shook his head. "No! Not ready—"

His warning came too late. Jemma tried to kneel. Pain seared through her splinted calf, and she fell back onto her bed of straw.

"Oooowww!"

"Bone, broke," Bryn said apologetically. "Need more time to mend. Me go now, find more horsetail, more mugwort. Water too. Come, Sparrow." He picked up several wineskins, including Jemma's, then scooped the small bird into his hand.

"Wait, wait!" Jemma grabbed Bryn's sacking-clad foot. "I can't just stay here! Can't you heal me faster? I have to find my parents!"

A shocked expression widened Bryn's eyes. "Faster? You crazy! Anyway," he added more gently, prying Jemma's fingers from his makeshift bootee, "not me who heal you. Plants do that. And shiny things. Me just help. But you mend fast. Go soon."

"Tonight, then. I'll go tonight."

Bryn shook his head. "Bird wing take days to mend," he said. "Leg maybe take"—he frowned, counting slowly on his fingers—"five days or . . . six."

"Six days!" Jemma groaned, slumping back onto the straw. Finding her parents in time to be Initiated would be impossible now.

"Me sorry," Bryn said.

From outside came the faintest strike of a distant bell. *The castle is still plaguing me,* Jemma thought, counting the tolls. Eleven. How much longer before she would be free of that dark sound? She crossed her arms and glared at the roof of the cave, vaguely aware of Bryn throwing another log onto the fire before he lolloped outside and into the Mist.

CHAPTER TWENTY

Identity

Friday

Noodle and Pie sat on top of the book, behind the crystals, staring at Jemma.

You're rude.

Guilt prickled her skin. They were right. It was unfair of her to have been short with Bryn. The delay wasn't his fault, and besides, he had rescued her, salved her legs, given her healing potions. She should be thankful. She would be, if she could feel some sense of purpose, but now that she was bound to miss her Initiation, she felt as though all determination had just drained from her, leaving a heavy hollow in her stomach.

Don't give up. Crystals. Look at them.

"But what's the point, Rattusses? I'm stuck here!" Jemma's body began to ache again, as if her growing despondency was spreading like poison through her blood, bringing worse thoughts to her head. What if not being Initiated meant she lost her Powers? Without them, who would she be? Just an ordinary girl, no threat to the Agromonds at all. "And Marsh is probably dead." She sniffed. "I may as well face it."

But you're alive. We're alive.

True. She had survived the forest's ferocity, and falling off

Mordwin's Crag. So had Noodle and Pie, without suffering a single scratch. A spark of gratitude lit in her heart.

Crystals. Look!

Jemma sighed. "Maybe later, Rattusses."

Something small and weighty fell onto her arm: one of the crystals. It had two wet smudges on it. Noodle and Pie twitched their snouts.

"You really want me to look at this, don't you?" She picked it up and wiped off the rats' nose marks, then peered into it. Its facets gleamed, throwing rainbow colors around the cave. So pretty . . . and so different from how gray it and its companion had looked when she'd first taken them from the jar in Nocturna's room! Perhaps they *were* magical, like Bryn said. They had helped heal her, after all. She peered more deeply into the one she was holding. *All right*, she thought halfheartedly, *show me*. Nothing happened.

"I don't know, Rattusses. . . ."

Noodle and Pie hopped onto her lap. Their furry faces appeared through the crystal, looking grossly enlarged by it. Jemma chuckled and sat up, then tried again. Still, nothing.

Breathe!

Jemma took several deep breaths. The bitter wormwood scent of Bryn's concoction filled her head, calming her. Then she narrowed her eyes the way she imagined Marsh might have, and bored her gaze into the crystal. It glowed slightly. Curiosity nibbled at her, and she took another breath, relaxing her eyes. The glow expanded, then shrank again. Her eagerness growing, she focused on what the crystals supposedly represented, sharpening her intent.

"What can you tell me about my parents?"

The crystal glowed more strongly; Jemma peered more closely.

"Show me. Please!"

Faint blue-green spindles, like minute fronds of lightning, sparked back and forth along the crystal. Then slowly, the spindles spread like mauve tea across a tablecloth, joining together to form one solid glow—the same color as was shining from her Stone. The color of her eyes. She felt a tugging at her heart, as if a cord was attached to it, pulling her vision farther into the clear quartz. The light in the crystal changed, taking on hints of other colors, forming a pinkish-brown blur, with a darker brown outline. . . .

"Sprites!" she gasped. "It's making a picture . . . a face . . . a woman's face!"

Two darker areas appeared, two sapphire-blue eyes, blazing at her. Jemma willed the face to become clearer, to reveal itself completely, and for a second, it did—beautiful, and clear. But then, like a flare whose light is suddenly spent, the eyes disappeared and the crystal went dim.

"No!" she said, desperate to hold on to the image. "Don't go!"

She grabbed the second crystal and peered into it, searching for another face—a man's. The crystal twinkled faintly, then showed a hazy hint of eyes and mouth that quickly shrank as if retreating. "Mord take it!" She slammed it onto the hide blanket, making the rats jump. "Oh, sorry, Rattusses! It's just . . . I saw . . . I think it might have been . . ."

Jemma snatched up the book next to her and opened it, desperate for any clue. On impulse, she flipped to the back cover. Close to the spine was a razor-neat slit, with a corner of paper sticking out of it. She pulled it out, hands trembling, and unfolded three thin sheets, yellowed with age and frayed along the creases.

At the top of the first one, inked in capital letters, was written: ANGLAVIAN BULLETIN. Just beneath that, in small print, was a date.

"Eight days after my first birthday," she murmured. Her eyes grazed the heading:

SOLVAY CHILD STILL MISSING

"Solvay! But . . . that's Majem's other name. . . ." An eerie feeling seeped into her veins, and, at the next words, seemed to leap out through her skin.

> The disappearance of one-year-old Jemma Solvay is still causing much consternation throughout the land. Two days after the abduction, the ANGLAVIAN BULLETIN has learned fuller details of the dreadful event.

"Jemma Solvay!" Jemma yelped. "Noodle, Pie—that . . . that's *me*! That's who I am—Jemma *Solvay*!" Her gaze sped down the page.

> Beloved healers Lumo and Sapphire Solvay were traversing the Heathshire Moors en route to Yarville, at the edge of the Mist, where they were to minister to its smallpox-smitten townsfolk. As night approached, their coach was ambushed by a cloaked horseman who snatched the infant from her mother's arms. A furious chase ensued, continuing over many miles. At one point, the horseman turned, felling the Solvays' coachman, Julius Sharm, with his sword.

Mr. Solvay unharnessed one of their four steeds and set off in pursuit, but the kidnapper fled into the thick of the Mist, and the unfortunate infant's father was forced to turn back, unable even to summon a Luminal to go to her aid. He found his wife in much distress, although she had succeeded in bringing Mr. Sharm back from death's door.

"There's no doubt who the kidnapper is," a family spokesperson told us, pointing out the effect the Mist had had on Mr. Solvay. "Everyone knows it only attacks those who are after Them."

"Them," of course, means the Solvays' longtime adversaries, the Agromonds, whose ancestor Mordrake created the Mist hundreds of years ago, giving it the power to confuse and render insane any who intend harm to the Agromond family.

"Oh, my . . . Oh, my . . ." Jemma gulped down air, trying to take the story in. Her parents—Lumo and Sapphire Solvay—were healers. Like Bryn and his mother. People who helped others, not destroyed them. And they were *her* people; this was her story too. It had flung her into a world beyond the castle, beyond the forest and Mist; a world primed for her by Marsh that felt deeply familiar. At last, she had found out who she was. Jemma Solvay. Moreover, Majem Solvay must be her ancestor—the magical Majem, not Mordrake or Mordana! Any trace of worry about being evil vanished as she fumbled for the next sheet of paper. It was dated two days later.

HOPE FADING
Mist Thwarts Solvay Attempts at Rescue

Jemma Solvay's grieving parents admitted today that their attempts to penetrate the Mist and rescue their daughter have been in vain. As Mr. Trufold, a family friend, told us, "Their desire to save her is too great. The Mist reads their minds, and they cannot venture in."

He went on to say that the mission to Yarville had been unnecessary, since no smallpox outbreak has occurred there. The call for help must therefore have been a lie, plotted by the Agromonds to ambush the Solvays and carry out their dastardly plan.

When asked how the abduction could have happened so soon after

Here the ink was smudged and unreadable. Jemma skipped to the next sentence.

The Solvays, exhausted by their terrible loss, have now returned to their home in Oakstead, where they will likely remain.

"Oakstead," Jemma murmured. "That's where they are." She branded the name onto her mind. It was hard to focus on the passages that followed.

MISSING CHILD STILL ALIVE!
A Different Kind of Abduction?

. . . Initiation Stone taken with her . . . under normal circumstances, used on her thirteenth birthday to bring her fully into the realm of the Solvays' healing legacy . . . believed that instead of killing her, the Agromonds are planning to usurp her Powers . . . Stone's Power directed by whoever has the strongest will . . .

The strongest will . . . Jemma's mind reeled through the ways Nox and Nocturna had controlled her. Not only had they drained her at the Ceremonies to make her believe she was weak and unwell, but they'd put her to work every weekday morning—cooking, cleaning, taking the family's breakfasts to their rooms, feeding the horses, mucking out the stables. "All to keep me feeling like the underdog. Oh, Rattusses, how could I not have realized I wasn't sickly, let alone deathly ill, when I was doing all that? How blind can you be!"

Made you strong, though. Helped you survive now.

"Yes. You're right." *Strong as an ox,* as Marsh had said. With growing resolve, Jemma scanned the final article, dated ten days later.

SOLVAY POWERS WANING
Skirmishes Break Out As Mist Spreads

Centuries-long vendetta between the two ruling families . . . hopes of Anglavia coming back to a time of peace and prosperity dashed . . . fears that without the Solvays' healing influence, the evil Agromonds will now prevail . . . Jemma's Powers as well as their own demonic strength could give them everlasting supremacy . . .

. . . Solvays suffering severe exhaustion . . . Bad enough when their son disappeared . . . they have now lost their only remaining child . . .

Here, the page was torn off.

"Only remaining child!" Jemma's throat tightened. "Look, Rattusses: They had a son—I had a brother!" An older brother . . . but what had happened to him? Had her parents ever found him? Were they still weak, after all these years? Were they even *alive*?

An insistent *chirrup* interrupted Jemma's thoughts, and

Sparrow fluttered around her hair, landing on her head just as Bryn appeared at the mouth of the cave.

"Me find herbs! Fill wineskins too." He handed Jemma's to her, which she took with thanks.

Soon, the cave was full of pungent steam. As Bryn stirred the pot, he talked about the coming winter, and the spring that would follow, with its high river waters, and the new growth that even the Mist couldn't stop. Jemma listened to his stilted words with half an ear, while her mind chewed on all she'd just read. Feeling a renewed determination to heal as fast as she could, she sipped Bryn's revolting concoction as soon as it was brewed. Thankfully, he'd also gathered roots, mushrooms, nuts, and berries, which, along with some venison he had stored at the back of his cave ("Me no kill," he said, "only find what fall off crag"), made a delicious stew. For Noodle and Pie, he'd brought back a selection of nuts and dead bugs, which they crunched on with glee. Over the course of the afternoon, Jemma dozed, crystals in hand, while Bryn hummed softly, alternately tending the fire and Sparrow's broken wing. Eventually, he too fell into a doze, with the full-bellied rats curled on his stomach.

Sapphire-blue eyes pierced the Mist. . . . She ran and ran, trying to reach them, but they kept receding. Water was rising, pressing on her from inside. . . .

Jemma woke, the strange triangle of energy tingling between her hands and the Stone again. She needed to relieve herself. Still half-asleep, she untied the straps around her right ankle. Then, being careful not to disturb Bryn and the rats, she put down the crystals and crawled out of the cave to find a private spot. The cold bit into her skin, and the snow was strange to walk on—crunchy, yet it melted when touched.

When she returned to the cave, Bryn was sitting up. "You walk!" he said, gaping at her. "Leg, all better!"

She hadn't even thought of it. But now she saw the splints lying by her straw bed; it was them whose straps she had untied moments ago without realizing it. All that remained of her fall was a dull ache in her ankle.

Excitement crackled through her.

She could leave, tonight.

No. She could leave this afternoon. Now.

Bryn sat in silence while Jemma gathered her things. As she replaced the old bulletins into the book, a scrap of paper fluttered to the ground—one she hadn't seen before; it must have been stuck between the others. An orb of light surrounded it, illuminating the black-and-white sketch of a face: a woman in tears, hair cascading over shawl-clad shoulders.

She picked it up. The orb around it stretched toward her, enveloping her. Air stuck in her throat. She could almost feel the woman's warmth, hear her voice, smell her fragrance. Even before she read the caption beneath the picture, Jemma knew what it would say.

MISSING CHILD'S MOTHER

It was the same face she had seen in the crystal. Her mother's face. The image of it slid into a hollow in her that she hadn't even known was there, like a puzzle piece that she had never before realized was missing. It resonated deep inside her, as if it were a pebble dropped into water, whose ripples reached to where Jemma sat now. She turned the picture over. Tiny writing was scrawled with obvious effort across the back.

My darling child. We are waiting.

Jemma felt her destination sharpen in her mind, as clearly as etching on glass. For somehow, something in her knew that her mother, at least, was still in Oakstead—and alive.

CHAPTER TWENTY-ONE

At the Edge

Friday night/Saturday, early hours

Bryn waved from the mouth of his cave. He still looked a little abashed after the long hug Jemma had given him as she thanked him for making her well. "*Happy, me help,*" he'd said, blushing.

Jemma waved back at him one last time, then walked away, wishing she could have told him that she'd return to visit someday, but his cave was too close to Agromond Castle for her to consider making such a promise.

Noodle and Pie settled into the hood of her cloak as she trod along in the tracks Bryn had made in the snow. "*Go to tree where you fall,* he'd said, *then straight, to river. Bridge to village this way.*" (He'd pointed with his right hand.) "*Not far.*" To her right, she could dimly see the crag's descending slope running alongside her, a vague form through the Mist.

Snow squeaked underfoot. Thank goodness for the deer hides that Bryn had tied around her own flimsy boots; they'd prevent her toes from freezing, and make the going easier. He had also bound her legs in strips of sacking—which prickled, but helped fend off the cold—and given her an extra hide for her shoulders, as well as making her a shoulder pouch from a burlap sack he'd found at the back of his cave. She felt it now at her back, holding a chunk of roast venison he'd given her, as well as some pine nuts for the rats, her knife, and the book, whose warmth spread through her with the warmth of her thoughts about him.

Jemma gripped the crystals in her pockets, her breath puffing into the night. The forest was blanketed in silence, the fir branches weighed down by white. Occasionally a branch tipped its load onto the ground with a *shush,* as if whispering a warning, but she felt safe, held by the stillness around her, despite the dark rock of the crag brooding to her right. From behind her, muffled by Mist and distance, came seven tolls. Moments later, Bryn's footprints ended by a fir tree, beneath which a pile of snow was scattered with broken twigs and branches.

"This is where we landed, Rattusses. It's a wonder Bryn found us."

Noodle and Pie peered out of the hood, and the three of them looked up. Even the top of the tree wasn't visible, let alone the edge of the crag from which the wind had hurled her. At least the Agromonds would now believe she was dead—who could possibly have survived that fall? It was a miracle that she had.

Cloak. Like wings. It saved you. Saved us.

The cloak billowed slightly as if confirming the rats' thoughts, and Jemma wrapped it more tightly around her as they snuggled back into its hood. Soon the ground became flatter, the snow covering thinner, and Jemma could feel pine and fir cones under her feet. As the hours passed, she could no longer hear the bell tolling from the castle. The trees became sparser, but more varied. Interspersed with firs and pines were others she didn't recognize—trees without leaves, whose branches stretched out at awkward angles. Hummocks, like hunchbacks huddled under white cloaks, crouched between them.

To her right, the descending slope of the crag was closer, and Jemma could make out piles of rock through the Mist, hewn into blocks of various sizes. Large, metal wheels creaked in the wind, rust on rust, and several huge chutes leaned against the rock face as though they were propping it up. *That must be the quarry*, she thought as she trudged by, leaving its ghostly shapes and the silent echoes of centuries of workers behind her. She wondered about the crag's magic, and what Bryn's mother had said about its effect depending on how men used it. Whatever it had once been able to do, it now seemed sad and wasted.

Finally, the slope leveled out. *"When ground flat, river not far,"* Bryn had said. Encouraged, Jemma pressed on. Puddles squished underfoot, soaking through the skins around her feet. Her toes and ankles numbed. A white flake floated down from the sky and landed on her nose, melting into a chilly dribble. Others began falling, gently at first, then thicker and faster, blowing into her face, creating dots of cold on her skin. The wind picked up, blowing head-on through the trees, turning the dots to ice. White drifts piled around her feet, making it hard to walk. Ice gathered in clumps around the rim of her hood. Even Majem's book was no match for the cold, and soon the only warmth Jemma could feel was from Noodle and Pie, who nestled into her neck, their thoughts seemingly as frozen as their shivering bodies.

Her ankle felt sore, making her limp. Bryn had tried to

persuade her to rest it for one more night, and she began to worry that she had been too impatient and made the wrong decision. The snow fell in a thick veil, and without the rock face to her right, Jemma had no landmarks. If she headed into the wind, she reasoned, she'd get to the river. But the wind kept shifting, confusing her. It was impossible to tell which direction she was going. She held her Stone. It infused her with a faint wave of warmth, but gave her no sense of where the river was.

She was lost. Lost, in a swirl of blinding white. Was this another of Nocturna's storms? If so, did that mean the Agromonds knew she was still alive?

"Oh, no . . . no . . . They can't know. Please, no . . ." Despair dripped into her veins, and she pulled the cloak closer around her, but the wind whipped it from her grasp. The pain in her ankle worsened. She tried thinking of Hazebury and Digby, and of Oakstead and her parents, to no avail. Shoving her left hand into her pocket, she closed her fingers around the crystal in which she'd seen the glimmer of her mother. *Help me,* she entreated, *if there's anyone there.*

Snow whirled furiously around her, sticking to her lashes, making it harder to see. She gripped the crystal harder. *Help me. . . . Mother—please, help!*

Her palm buzzed. Pins and needles prickled through her hand and up her arm. Then a lightning-bolt sensation snapped to her chest, where her Stone lay. Its aqua light pulsed out, illuminating whorls of snow ahead of her, which then spun in a vortex, forming a tunnel. Jemma stumbled into it, her feet in automatic motion. The tunnel was eerily silent, as if the world had disappeared, leaving nothing but darkness.

Then, at the end of it, two points of blue began glimmering faintly, then more strongly—just like those she'd seen earlier in the crystal. Brilliant, sapphire blue. Sapphire . . . *Sapphire Solvay* . . .

"Mother . . . ," Jemma whispered, then shouted out, "Mother!"

The wind's howl faded behind walls of whirling snow-flakes. The points of blue became more vivid, pulling her forward. Jemma blundered toward them through the silence, picking up speed. Blue light flooded the tunnel, then she could see eyes at the end, sapphire eyes in a face framed by brown hair. Then a distant voice was calling her, as if through a wall of water: *Jemma, my child, come! We are waiting. . . .* Jemma ran toward it, her heart on the verge of exploding—

Suddenly, the face disappeared, taking the vortex, snow, and wind with it. Jemma found herself teetering at the bank of a river. On the other side of its rushing waters, a faint light glimmered through the Mist, then went out.

"Look, Rattusses," she said, "that must be Hazebury." But the face had gone.

Jemma's heart emptied, and she stood for several moments in the still, white night, gazing blankly at the ice floes speeding by. Noodle and Pie nuzzled her face.

They're waiting for you. She said so. Trust.

Trust . . . she wished she could. But it was hard to have faith out in the biting cold, with still so far to go. She stroked the rats' heads with one hand, wiping away a tear with the other. Then, turning to her right, she started clumping along the river's edge toward the north, where the bridge to Haze-bury lay.

* * *

The Mist paled in the dawn light. After walking all night, Jemma was exhausted. With every step, pain flared from her ankle. Her Stone had helped for a while, but now, it seemed exhausted too. She was hungry, and pulled the venison Bryn had given her from her pouch, chewing on it while she fed the handful of nuts to Noodle and Pie, who ate them voraciously. Rain started spitting down, but she was beyond caring.

The river babbled to Jemma's left, a dark stripe in the snowy ground. An unwelcome memory punched into her thoughts: a geography lesson in which Nox had taught her and the twins that between Agromond Forest and Hazebury, the Stoat River formed part of a moat that surrounded the base of Mordwin's Crag—and the moat was stocked with deadly, long-jawed Aquadyles, which wouldn't hesitate to make a meal of her.

"We'd better stay away from the water, Rattusses, and keep our eyes peeled," she said, shivering. Her hunger evaporated. Thrusting the rest of the venison back into her pouch, she pressed on. To her right, beyond an expanse of white, the forest gloomed in the background.

The snow was melting, becoming slushier as the rain increased, and the ground was now patched with mud. It was slippery, slowing her down. Between her and the forest line, the bog was spiked with long-dead skeletal trees. They towered over her like spies whose bare limbs might somehow send a signal up the crag to the Agromonds: *She's alive . . . alive . . .* No. They mustn't catch her. Not now. Not after all she'd been through.

Rain stung Jemma's face. Her cloak was soaked; her feet

felt like blocks of ice; her ankle kept giving way. She muttered her old incantation under her breath to bolster herself—*I am a Fire Warrioress, the fiercest in the land*—then sighed at the innocence of the girl who had made up that rhyme. But it did seem to energize her, and she limped a little faster.

To her left, the river waters lapped the shore. Ice floes prodded the bank, as if trying to climb. Then, with a loud *crack*, one lifted and broke. A shadow emerged from under it. Jemma heard the splish of large feet on wet ground. A long, low shape slithered into view ahead of her, like a huge lizard padding on sharp-clawed feet, swishing its tail.

An Aquadyle. Its long jaws parted slightly in what looked like a grisly grin. Evidently, it had marked Jemma as breakfast.

Fear fired her bones. Veering to her right, she sloshed toward the forest; she would be able to move faster on drier ground. But mud weighed her down; rain lashed into her. The Aquadyle's squelching footsteps were catching her up, punctuated by rhythmic snorts that drowned out her own gasps for breath. She reached for the knife in her pouch, but before she could grab it, she felt a tug at her recently healed ankle and splatted facedown in the mud. Pain shot up her leg. Her foot was in the Aquadyle's mouth.

"Let me go!" Looking over her shoulder, Jemma aimed her free foot at the creature's snout, ripping a nostril. It snarled, and bit harder. Noodle and Pie dashed from her hood and down her leg, then began gnawing through the straps holding the deer hide around her boot.

"Rattusses, be careful!" Jemma screamed. They were right next to the Aquadyle's mouth. But they chewed through the straps swiftly, then clambered onto the Aquadyle's head and clawed at its eyes. Jemma wriggled her ankle, gritting her teeth in agony, but the Aquadyle's jaws remained clamped around it. The rats clung on and continued clawing as it thrashed Jemma from side to side. Her ankle felt on the verge of breaking again; the pain was unbearable.

"Leave . . . me . . . a-LONE!" she shrieked. For a split second, the Aquadyle stopped, looking startled. Noodle and Pie seized their chance. With a final scratch, they sliced open its eyeballs. Clear, gelatinous fluid burst out and oozed down its knobbly snout. It opened its jaws in an agonized roar, and Jemma pulled her foot free. The rats leapt clear. She grabbed one in each hand and scrambled to her feet, then hobbled away as fast as she could. The Aquadyle continued flailing its head blindly.

But now a second Aquadyle was weaving toward them through the bog. Remembering the venison in her pocket, Jemma whisked it out and hurled it at the beast, but it landed in the mud and the Aquadyle passed it by, apparently more interested in a bigger meal. Noodle and Pie's squeals urged her on, but she was flagging, the Stone of little help. The tree line was just ahead—but so was a third Aquadyle, joining the hunt.

As her feet hit the solid forest floor, Jemma plopped the rats into her pockets and tried to increase her stride, but the spasms in her ankle were too excruciating. In no time, the two Aquadyles had flanked her, hemming her in.

Terror ripped through her. Wind buffeted her from left to right, whipping the extra hide from her shoulders. Ahead of her, in a small clearing, treetops crashed into one another in the wind. Another of Nox's lessons sprang to mind.

"*Aquadyles are like sharks,*" he'd said. "*Once their jaws start snapping for the kill, there's no stopping them until they've torn their prey to pieces.*"

Inspiration struck. Jemma pelted into the middle of the clearing, then stopped abruptly. On either side of her, the Aquadyles also stopped, and turned to face her, teeth chomping. She stood stock-still, heart pounding, sensing them in her peripheral vision as they lumbered toward her. Suddenly, they lunged. At the last split second, she sprang forward. Guttural roars broke out behind her. Glancing over her shoulder, she saw the Aquadyles tearing into one another, shreds of flesh and leathery hide flying everywhere. Stomach lurching, she turned and ran.

Mist thickened again. Branches whipped her face as she passed. Shrubs and hummocks seemed to move in front of her, making her falter. The sickly orb of sun was hidden behind trees; she'd lost her bearings. The ground began sloping upward, and felt as though it was undulating beneath her. Her ankle burned. Her limbs were as limp as mops. All she had learned, every device she might call upon for help, jammed in her head.

"Rattusses, I don't know which way to turn. . . ." The slope became steeper; the trees more dense. The road . . . she must find the road to the bridge. . . .

"Jemma, over here!"

A voice, soothing, through the Mist.

"Jemma!" A woman's voice, sweetly familiar, calling from up the hill. "Come, Jemma, it's me! Over here."

It couldn't be, could it? The fragment of dress . . . the shoe . . . the hand . . . She'd been so sure! But that voice, lilting like music, full of stories, safety, and love—it *sounded* like—

"*Jemma!*"

Relief filled Jemma's chest. "Marsh!" she cried. "Marsh, where are you?"

"To your right, Jemma. Follow me!"

Through the firs, Marsh's familiar form moved away, disappearing up the crag.

"Marsh, I can't see you!" Jemma's yells were absorbed into Mist. "Where are you?"

"Here—up here!"

Branches eased back, clearing her way. Jemma limped onward, the pain in her ankle now searing. "Marsh, wait, please! I can't keep up—" Noodle and Pie scratched and clawed in her pockets as she staggered up the hill. Then Noodle bit through her dress, his tiny teeth sinking into her leg.

"Ouch, Noodle—what are you *doing*?"

Stop! Noodle bit again, hard.

"Stop? Noodle, you're hurting me!" Jemma yanked him out of her pocket and shook him. "Why should I stop? Can't you *see*? It's Marsh!" Noodle squirmed, clawing her fingers, and she dropped him. He clambered back up to her pocket, and he and Pie kept nipping and scratching at her leg. "Rattusses, *please*! We're so close—"

Then came a sound she hadn't heard for days.

Clang.

So close . . . The castle bell. But how could it be? She was miles from the castle, wasn't she . . . ?

"Jemma . . . !"

Jemma's heart punched into her ribcage. Marsh only ever

called her Jemma when she was cross, or had something urgent to tell her. It sounded like Marsh's voice, but—

"*Jem*-mah!"

That was Nocturna's way of saying her name. Which could only mean one thing: the image wasn't Marsh at all.

"Oh no—an Approjection! I should have known!" It was an illusion. A trick. And she'd fallen for it, had followed it uphill, back toward the castle, and the Agromonds. A few more steps, and she'd be in its sphere, and the Agromonds would know it, and hold her there. She already felt magnetized by it, and couldn't stop.

Hooves thundered up behind her. A vision of Nox bearing down on her swam into her mind. The hooves galloped closer. She buried her head in her hands and howled. Outrunning Mephisto was impossible. She should have listened to Bryn, and stayed another night—should have listened to the rats, telling her to stop! But it was too late. Nox had found her. And still, she crashed toward the Approjection, unable to prevent her legs from moving.

The hooves stopped.

"Jem, behind you!"

Her life was over. She would be the Agromonds' prisoner, powerless, destined to die—

"Stop, Jem, stop!"

Footsteps now, and strong arms, grabbing her, pulling her back, wrapping her in a warm, leathery smell . . .

"Got you!" Digby's voice, whispering in her ear . . . Jemma opened her eyes, and saw his freckled face and blue eyes, strong and earnest, as she collapsed into his arms. And there, just yards away, was Pepper, the Goodfellows' horse, tossing her head and stomping the ground. "Dig . . . Digby!" Jemma sobbed. "Is it really you?"

"Yes, yes, it's me. It's all right. You're with me. That thing can't get you now." Digby lifted her onto Pepper's back and jumped up behind her. She was vaguely aware of being held by him, vaguely aware of his garbled words murmuring through the pounding of Pepper's gallop. For the first time in months, it seemed, she felt warm, and she leaned into him as they sped past the dark trees. They had made it, she, Noodle, and Pie. It was over—her long ordeal was over.

But as she began to drift into sleep, foreboding rippled through her bones. She still didn't know for sure what Marsh's fate was, and her own was far from certain. She might be free of Agromond Castle, and the forest, but the Agromonds were still there. And as long as they were, their evil would spill over the edges of Mordwin's Crag and seep, like the Mist, across the land. And nothing would stop it from finding her.

This was not over. Not at all.

Part Three

ROOTS

CHAPTER TWENTY-TWO

The Storehouse

Saturday morning

"Ma—warm water, Carbolic, quick!"

A low ceiling blurred above Jemma as Digby carried her into a small room.

"Digby, thank heavens!" A woman's voice, lilting, low. "You're home, safe and sound! Oh, my—jus' look at this poor child. Take her into the parlor, love. I'll be there in a trice."

Digby set Jemma down in an armchair by a fire. Weariness drained from her, and she drifted in and out of restless slumber, sounds and images weaving through her mind.

"Poor mite!" Something soft and warm dabbed her skin. ". . . like she been dragged through a thistle patch backward." The smell of coal tar, stinging pain, dulling into darkness again . . . *She was flying into thick gray, the Aukron close behind.* . . . "Look, the Stone—she got it!" *Ghosts, floating around her* . . . "Ugh—rats!" " 'Sall right, Ma, them's her friends. Noodle an' Pie." "Well, really! Digby, Gordo, look away, now." Kind hands, undressing her, then pulling on clean clothes. " 'Tain't safe here . . . away from the village . . ." *A small boy, toddling toward her, his hair the color of fire, his eyes sea-green* . . . "What about Mowser, with them rats?" Jemma was lifted again, leaning back into strong arms. More hooves, pounding through her dreams, then she was laid onto what felt like a bed of leaves, wrapped in warmth. And, at last, heavy sleep.

Jemma inhaled the sweet scent of hay, and felt the softness of it beneath her. Through the haze of sleep in her eyes, she saw Digby gazing out of a small window. Was she dreaming? *Blink.* He was still there, haloed by dusty light. Her head spun, trying to make sense of her surroundings. To Digby's right, a door. Next to it, stacks of crates, the words *Eurovian Sunshine* stamped on them. To his left, hay bales piled to the beams. About halfway up them, Noodle and Pie were snuggled into what looked like a large ginger-colored fur pillow. They were surrounded by apple cores, their bellies swollen like small balloons.

Jemma heaved herself onto one elbow and pushed back the woolen blanket covering her. The rough sleeves of a serge shirt at least three sizes too big for her flopped over her wrists, and the trousers she was wearing felt baggy and strange. But they—and she—felt warm and clean.

Digby turned. "Hey, Jem! You awake already?" He walked over and sat on the edge of the hay bales she was lying on. "It's only jus' past eleven. I was goin' to let you sleep another hour or so. How're you doin'?"

"I'm all right. I think." She ached all over, and her ankle throbbed. "Where are we?"

"Our storehouse, 'bout a mile north of Hazebury. Ma, Pa, an' me, we decided to bring you here las' night, after Ma patched you up an' dressed you in some of my old togs."

"I can't say I'll miss my stinky old dress. . . . But why here? Why not your house?"

"First, the storehouse is a mile farther from the castle. Second, it's best that no village folk see you. What they don't know, they can't tell. So if anyone comes lookin' . . ." He swept a lock of sandy hair from his face. "Well, we can't have them Agromonds findin' you, can we. Not now."

"Agromonds!" The name jolted Jemma fully awake and brought the last few days crashing back into her head. Would they still be searching for her? "I have a feeling," she said, hoping she was right, "that they think I'm dead."

"Really? Why'd they send that Approjection, then? A few seconds more, and you'd've walked smack into it. Then they'd've known exactly where you was. They was lookin' for you, Jem. It was a trap."

"But I didn't walk into it, thanks to you. They really might think I'm dead."

"Maybe. Not worth the risk, though, is it?"

"I suppose not." Jemma sighed, the closeness of her escape shuddering through her. How had Digby known where to look for her? She was about to ask, when he took her hand.

Her breath caught in her throat.

"I can't imagine what you been through, Jem, gettin' out of that forest," he said. "You want to talk about it, jus' let me know, all right?"

Jemma exhaled. Any lesser drama, and she knew she'd be talking about it non-stop. But this felt too recent, and too huge, to relive just yet. "Thanks," she said. "Maybe another time."

"Well, you're safe now. Long as we keep you out of sight."

"Safe," she murmured. She'd felt that way with Digby from the moment she'd met him four years ago, when his father, Gordo, had first brought him to the castle to help with deliveries. Though he was more than two years older than she, they'd taken to each other immediately, and Gordo always hung around for an extra half hour, chatting to Marsh so that Jemma and Digby could be together, exploring the cellars or just talking. *Salt of the earth, them two,* Marsh always said about Digby and Gordo, and Jemma was sure the rest of the Goodfellow family would be just like them. She felt a stab of sorrow at the thought of Marsh, then a stab of disappointment at not being in the cozy cottage she'd so often imagined, and then a stab of shame for her fleeting ingratitude.

"What you thinkin', Jem?"

"Oh . . . just . . . I'd have liked to meet your ma. And the triplets. That's all."

Digby grinned. "Well, if we wanted to let the world know you'd escaped, an' where to find you, that'd be the way to do it. Them triplets can't keep their mouths shut, not for a moment. 'Specially Tiny. He might as well be the village crier, that one. Now . . ." He let go of Jemma's hand and pulled a puffy crust of bread from a leather bag on the floor. "You hungry?"

The fresh-baked smell dispelled all of Jemma's questions, and she grabbed the bread and chomped into it.

"Hey, easy, Jem!" Digby chuckled. "Here's some cheese too, an' your wineskin. I filled it with milk. Sorry—it's a bit fresh for your likin'."

"Thank you!" She took a swig. It wasn't sour, but it would do.

"You an' them rats!" Digby said. "I never seen any critters eat so fast. Now, since you're up, we might as well get movin'—"

"Mmmvpm? Wrrto?"

"You know, where your ma and pa is. Oakstead. I'm goin' to take you. If we leave soon an' push our pace a bit, there's a good chance we can get there by tomorrow breakfast."

Jemma stopped in mid-chew. Her parents. Tomorrow. Mord-day. The last day she could be Initiated.

"Anyways," Digby continued, "the farther you is from that castle, the better. Good thing we got that Stone of yours. It helped protect you in the forest, an' it'll help protect us on our way, I'll be bound—"

"Digby, wait—my parents . . . Oakstead . . . the Stone . . . How do you know about all that? And how did you know where to find me?"

"I told you last night, on the way to Hazebury. I— Oh, Jem, I'm sorry. I should've realized you was too tired to take it in. Well, the other night, see—Tuesday, it was—"

A loud whinny from outside interrupted him.

"Oh, rotten rhubarb—Pepper!" He leapt to his feet. "Forgot her bran mash. I'll go an' feed her, an' saddle her up. You put those on." He pointed at some boots and socks on the floor, then walked toward the door. "They're some old 'uns of mine, they should fit. I'll explain everythin' once we're on our way, all right?"

Jemma gulped down the last of the bread and cheese, then swung her legs off the hay and dangled her feet onto the floorboards. Her cloak, book, wineskin, and knife were piled next to her hay bed, with the crystals on top. She picked them up, and instantly felt the same triangle of energy that she'd felt in Bryn's cave, snapping between them and her Stone. Her ankle tingled, and the throb subsided a little. She looked into the crystals. They were as clear as water.

"Are you there?" she whispered. A bluish tinge appeared

in one of them—and then her mother's face began shimmering through. "Show yourself—please!" she said, louder.

"Here I am!" A child's voice lilted across the room.

Jemma snapped her head up, swiftly pocketing the crystals. "Who's there?"

"Me." From behind a pile of crates, eyes the color of forget-me-nots peered at her. Then one foot appeared, followed by the rest of a girl's slight form, topped by a tangle of honey-colored hair. "You said, 'Show yourself,'" she said. "So I did." She broke into a broad grin the image of Digby's. "Your hair! It's brighter than they say, even. You really are the Fire One!"

"Fire One?" Jemma felt a little uneasy. "What . . . ? No, I—I'm just me. Jemma. And let me guess: you're Digby's little sister, Flora."

Flora nodded and skittered over to the pallet. "I'm seven," she announced, as if that explained everything about her. She sat next to Jemma and gazed intently at her. "Was it hard to escape from the castle?"

"Yes, it was," said Jemma. "But how do you know about it?"

"Well, I— Oh! What's that?" Flora pointed at the Stone hanging from Jemma's neck. "It's lovely."

"It's . . . something I found."

"Where, at the castle? Did you *steal* it?" Flora's tone of voice suggested she hoped that were the case.

"Yes. No. Well, not exactly. You see—"

But Flora didn't wait for an answer. "What was it like livin' there? Were you scared? Was they really horrid to you? What was the forest like? Was there *lots* of monsters? Hey, d'you know the nursery rhyme about them Agromonds?"

"*Nursery* rhyme? About *them*? No, I—"

"It goes like this: *All little children had better beware. Hide in the attic or under a chair. There's evil a-comin' from up on the hill. If the Mist doesn't get you, the Agromonds will!* But you"— Flora paused for breath—"*you're* not evil, I can tell. Even though you jus' came from up there. You're nice! An' pretty too. *You* could never be a Agromond. But that's 'cause you in't. I know who you is! I heard that lady tellin' Ma, Pa, an' Digby, jus' the other night."

"Lady? What lady?"

"Tuesday, it was. We was s'posed to be in bed, me an' Simon an' Tiny, but there was this loud thumpin' at the door, see, an'— Oh! How sweet." Flora looked at Jemma's feet, where Noodle and Pie, having evidently woken, were now attempting to heave themselves up her legs. "Yellow rats! I ain't never seen yellow rats before. Are they yours?"

"My friends, yes." Jemma picked up the rats and plopped them onto her lap. "Flora—"

"Good thing Mowser didn't get 'em. He's the cat. Over there." Flora pointed to the hay bale where the ginger fur pillow had now grown, revealing four legs and a confused-looking face, its green eyes fixed on the rats.

"Flora," said Jemma, hope glimmering under her skin, "that lady you mentioned—"

"Mowser usually hunts rats, but yours must've scared him!" Flora laughed. "Can I stroke 'em?" She reached for Pie's head without waiting for a reply.

"The *lady*, Flora. Who was she?"

"I don't know." Flora shrugged and tickled Noodle and Pie's heads. "After the knockin', we creeps to the top of the stairs, me, Simon, an'—"

The storehouse door burst open. "Flora!" Digby marched over and yanked Flora to her feet. "What in Mord's name are you doin' here?"

"I jus' wanted to see her—"

"Flora, the lady—?" Jemma tried to grab Flora's sleeve, but Digby pulled her away.

"You know you're s'posed to stay home!" he said. "Mord sakes, I don't have time to take you back, I got to get Jemma out of here—"

"I don't care! I came on my own, din't I? I'll go home on my own. It's *her*, I know—the one you was talkin' about the other night—"

"I can't let you go alone! T'aint safe. Oh, you . . . ," Digby growled. "Jus' when we had the chance to get a head start. Jem, give me half an hour. I'll be back." He dragged Flora outside.

Jemma hastily shoved her feet into Digby's old socks and boots and tied the laces. The breeches she was wearing—also old ones of his, she guessed—almost fell off as she stood, and she cinched the belt to its last notch, stuffed Noodle and Pie into her pockets, then stumbled out of the door. Flora was wriggling in Digby's grasp as he attempted to lift her onto Pepper's back.

"But *why* can't I tell Tiny and Simon?"

"For Mord's sake, Flora!" Digby's face was red with anger. "Nobody means nobody! *'Specially* not Tiny. His tongue's the loosest of all of you. You got to promise me—"

"Ow! You're hurtin' me, you pig."

"Well, if you'd jus' keep still—"

At that moment, Gordo emerged through the Mist, red-faced and running. "Flora!" he yelled. "Thanks be, you're here! Your ma an' me, we been worried sick."

"Sorry, Pa." Flora stopped wriggling. Digby put her down with a sigh of relief.

"You're safe, is all that matters." Gordo took her hand. "Mornin', you two. Jemma, lass, good to see you lookin' a little lively again." He mopped his brow, reddening more, then bit his lips. "I . . . I still don't know, Digby lad, about you goin' along," he said. "Your ma, she keeps frettin' 'bout what could happen to us if them Agromonds find out you're helpin'—"

"Why would they find out? Pa, I told you. They got no idea I know her, do they, Jem?"

Jemma thought of Digby's arrival at last Mord-day's breakfast, and shook her head.

"So please, don't you an' Ma worry. I'll be back by Tuesday, in time for deliv'ries. 'Sides, I couldn't let her go on her own. Wouldn't be what you'd raised me to do."

"I s'pose not." Gordo sighed. "Come on then, little 'un, home with you."

"Remember, Flor," said Digby. "Not a word, you understand? Promise me!"

"All right, all right. I promise." Flora broke away from Gordo, then ran over to Jemma and threw her arms around her. "Bye, Jemma," she said. "You *are* the Fire One, I knows it! I bet you're magic too, jus' like they say. Come back an' see me one day, won't you, please, please?"

"I'd like that," said Jemma, wondering how that would ever be possible, with Flora living so close to Agromond Castle. She walked Flora back to Gordo, ruffling her hair. "You keep out of mischief, mmm? And Gordo, I'm very happy that Digby will be with me. Thank you."

Gordo hugged her, then Digby. "Jus' take care of each other, eh?" he said. "Blessin's be with you."

Jemma smiled as she watched him lead Flora away into the Mist. She'd been right, thinking that the triplets would be like Digby—Flora was, anyway, both to look at, and with her unabashed cheek.

"Right, Jem," said Digby, tightening Pepper's girth. "Get your things, an' let's get crackin'. Sooner we go, sooner we'll be there."

Jemma fetched her belongings from inside the storehouse. Throwing the wineskin over one shoulder, she packed the cloak, book, and knife into the saddlebags slung across Pepper's back, then pulled the crystals from her pocket and placed them on top. Only as she was closing the saddlebags did she realize that the pain in her ankle had gone. Once again, the crystals had healed her.

"One more thing," Digby said, pulling something from his pocket: a square of sacking. "Here. Wrap this around your head. Can't have folks seein' your hair an' guessin' who you is. You never know where spies is lurkin'."

Jemma took the sacking and tied it on. Her hair marked her, she realized, but even so, the idea of having to hide it annoyed her. Besides, the burlap stank of parsnips—her least favorite food. "Ugh! You might have rinsed it out, Dig. And it's so scratchy!"

"Sorry, m'lady." He tucked a stray lock into her makeshift scarf.

"I forgive you, I suppose." Jemma glowered at him.

"I sup-*pose*," he mimicked, making a face. She smiled, despite her momentary irritation.

"All right, all right, you win!"

"Course I do." Digby gave her a leg up into the broad saddle and sprang up to sit behind her. "Why, Jem—look at that! There's no Mist around your hands!"

"It's been that way since Monday," she said. "My birthday."

"Really? Well, well. P'raps Flora was right, an' you is magic."

"It doesn't exactly *do* anything though, does it? I mean, it's just a clear space."

"We'll see," he said, shortening the reins and kicking Pepper forward. "Time will tell."

CHAPTER TWENTY-THREE

Fire-Branded

Saturday morning/afternoon

The world looked different from Pepper's back: larger, and wider, giving Jemma a sense of invincibility. Digby held his left arm around her as the path meandered between gorse and hawthorn brush, and she soon got the feel of balancing in the saddle. She marveled at the scene unfolding to her: shadow bushes, crouched in the Mist; the odd shack, looming from the white, then being absorbed into it again; the pale orb of sun, low in the sky. In the distance, the Stoat River lapped gently. Digby urged Pepper into a trot, and held Jemma more tightly. She closed her eyes, amazed by how so simple a thing could ease so much of the past few days' terror. Even the distant clang of the castle bell tolling the noon hour didn't ruffle her contentment. But it didn't last long; a few minutes later, she felt Digby tense up.

"Mord's spit!" he said. "Up ahead . . ."

Jemma opened her eyes. At the top of an incline, a group of twelve or fifteen people—men, women, and three children—were milling across the path. They looked cowed and nervous, their clothes ragged, and seemed to be haloed by gray, which disappeared when Jemma blinked.

"Who are they?" she asked, her stomach knotting.

"Hazebury folk."

"But . . . they can't be!" This were not at all how she had pictured them.

"'Fraid so. Flora must've told Tiny and Simon she was goin' to come an' see you. They prob'ly want to get a peek at you too, Jem, jus' like Flora did. Say nothin' an' jus' play along, all right?" Digby pulled Pepper to a halt. "Mornin', Mrs. Jenkin, Mr. Scragg. Mornin', all."

Jemma looked at the eyes staring at her from sallow, drawn faces.

"We come to see the Fire One," a young boy said. "'Tis her, in't it, Digby? Tiny said—"

"No, Ned. Tiny got it wrong. This is . . . my cousin. I'm jus' takin' her home to Yarville."

The crowd shuffled from foot to foot, making Jemma nervous. Then one pointed at her. "Look, her hair . . ."

A long strand of red blew across Jemma's face. She hastily tucked it back into her scarf.

"It's her. . . . It's her. . . . The one from the Prophecy. . . ." Their voices reminded Jemma of a mournful wind blowing around the castle towers. Several hands reached out and clutched at her breeches with desperate fingers. She recoiled inwardly.

"Easy, everyone, easy," said Digby. "Look, I'm sorry, I din't want to lie. But them Agromonds will be out huntin' for her. Them, or their spies. So listen, careful-like. Any strangers come to the village, you mustn't tell 'em you seen us, all right? 'Specially not any Inquisitors."

"No worries, lad," said an elderly man at the back, who had a shred more spark in his voice. "We won't say nothin'. Will us, eh?" A dreary chorus of "no's" murmured around him.

"Thanks, Mr. Higgs. Much obliged. Be seein' you, then." Digby kicked Pepper onward and the gathering parted to let them through. As they passed, the boy named Ned grasped the cuff of Jemma's breeches, then held on as he trotted alongside, his brown eyes staring up at her.

"Bring us back the sun, won't you, Miss? Please . . ."

Pepper crested the incline, and Ned let go. Jemma peered back at him, silhouetted in the Mist. He looked almost as bedraggled as the phantoms. *Yet another*, she thought, *asking me to help.* She turned away, her unease growing.

"Too bad they seen us close up like that," Digby said as they reached a furrowed track at the bottom of the slope. "Tongues wag, no matter what they promise."

"Digby, what did Ned mean, 'Bring back the sun'? And . . . who's the Fire One? Flora mentioned that too."

"Ah. Right." Digby cleared his throat. "There's this Prophecy, see, hundreds of years old, sayin' how someone with hair the color of fire is goin' to come an' free Anglavia from the Agromonds' rule, an' make the Mist go away. People want to see the sun, like in olden times, only they're not even sure what it looks like."

Jemma thought of her own longing. "I know how they feel."

"This person," Digby continued, "they call the Fire One. Or sometimes Fire Warrior. Only in your case, I s'pose it'd be Fire Warrioress, eh, Jem?"

Jemma felt as though snakes were curling around her innards. She had never told anyone about her private incantation, not even Marsh. "But why me?" she muttered. "It can't be me! Dig . . . *you* don't think it's me, do you?"

"Well, I can't say as I ever believed in the Prophecy before. Just some musty old story, I thought, never bein' one for superstition. But now . . . I mean, your hair . . . an' that clear air around your hands . . . You got to admit, Jem, it's weird."

"But . . . a Prophecy? Freeing Anglavia?" She thought of Nocturna's words to Nox last Mord-day night, expressing her fears that Jemma might "fulfil the Prophecy," and about what Shade had said to Feo about the danger to them if Jemma were to be Initiated by her real parents.

"They didn't just take me to get my Powers," she murmured, realization dawning on her. "They took me to stop me from making the Prophecy come true." Freeing Anglavia . . . bringing back the sun . . . It weighed in her gut, like entrail stew. Had a part of her always known, somehow? She'd hated the Mist for as long as she could remember, after all, and had made up her Fire Warrioress incantation when she was only six. And just yesterday, finding her parents in time to be Initiated had felt like a mission that wouldn't wait. But now that others seemed to expect something of her too, it was overwhelming. She looked up at the wan orb of sun, and sighed.

From nowhere, words floated into her head: *Leth gith bal celde* . . . The same words she'd heard in Bryn's cave. Was it some kind of message? An anagram, as she'd thought back then? She tried reordering their letters, but they made no sense. It must be a foreign language.

"Look, Jem," said Digby, "here's the moors. Now we can put some distance between us and them Agromonds. Hold on!" He kicked Pepper into a gallop.

Jemma fell back against him with a gasp of surprise. The momentum whisked all apprehension from her, and she let out a whoop, loving the feel of wind buffeting her face, the sound of Pepper's hooves pounding the ground, and the way the trees appeared out of the Mist, then receded as they sped past. Her heart soared as she leaned into Digby, losing herself in thoughts of daring rescues in vividly colored landscapes until he pulled back in the saddle and slowed Pepper to a brisk walk.

The Mist was slightly thinner now, revealing more of the countryside: rising hillocks, broken fences, barren trees. The Stoat's babble was gone. Noodle and Pie, having climbed from Jemma's pockets, were twined in Pepper's mane on either side of the pommel, noses twitching. Digby eased Pepper off the track and onto a path winding between heather and gorse. He pulled up near a cluster of derelict stone cottages, then slid to the ground.

"Time for a quick leg stretch an' some lunch," he said, helping Jemma down and untangling the rats. She was surprised how wobbly she felt after no more than an hour of riding—and how hungry. Soon they were sitting under a tree, tucking into Digby's mother's ox-dripping sandwiches, and swigging milk—which Digby's family evidently preferred fresh—while Noodle and Pie snoozed, their bellies still round as pomegranates from breakfast. Jemma untied her burlap scarf and pulled it off, shaking her hair loose.

"Just while we're here," she said, before Digby could protest.

"An' you think you in't the Fire One!" He chuckled. "Look jus' like a fox, you do."

"Didn't you tell me once that people hunt foxes, though? I don't want to be hunted, thank you very much. Unless it's by you . . ." She glanced at him, and smiled. "How *did* you find me, anyway?"

"Oh. Right." Digby chomped into an apple, talking as he ate. "Well, Pa an' me went up to the castle as usual las' Tuesday, an' you, of course, wasn't there. Mr. Drudge, he kep' sayin' you'd gone, an' how I had to find you. On no account was I to go far into the forest, he said, but I was to wait for you near the road. I'd find you there sometime after Friday evenin'—by Saturday mornin' at the latest."

"Dear old Drudge." Jemma's heart warmed, thinking about the old man.

"Dear ol' Drudge? But you always hated him!"

"I was blind, Dig." Jemma felt herself blush. "He . . . he's amazing. He helped me, gave me food and drink, and this cloak. . . . But how on earth did you understand him?"

"I always was a tad more patient than you, Jem." Digby took another bite of apple. "Anyways, at first I thought he was jus' bein' his usual weird self, spoutin' off like that, but I soon realized he was serious, an' as the hours went by, it ate into me more an' more. By the end of the day I was that worked up with worry, the thought of waitin' three whole days till Friday . . . I jus' couldn't. So I decided to start lookin' for you that night, Tuesday, no matter what Drudge had said. Ma an' Pa tried to talk me out of it—fretted as cats about to lose a kitten, they was—but I told 'em, I couldn't let you down, an' I'd go with or without their blessin'. I was all set to leave— jus' before midnight, it was—when someone starts bashin' on our door—"

"Tuesday night! The lady Flora mentioned . . . was it—"

"Marsh? Yes, Jem, it was."

"She's alive!" Jemma threw her arms around him. "Thank goodness!"

"Whoa, Jem!" Digby laughed, and Jemma sat back, listening intently as he continued. "So there she was at our door. Pa an' me, we barely recognized her, she was so tore up. An' Jem, I should tell you . . . she had a bad fight with somethin', an' . . . an' she lost. . . ."

"Her hand; I know—but she's alive! *Alive!* Is she all right? Where is she?"

"Yes, she's all right. We bandaged her up, an' next day she left for Oakstead to find your folks an' tell 'em what had happened. She's got a lot of Power, that one, recoverin' as fast as she did." He shook his head in admiration. "Told Ma, Pa, an' me all about it, how she trained for years under your pa's parents—your grandparents—long before you was born. Could've knocked me over with a feather, Jem. . . . We'd heard of the Prophecy—most folks has—but we had no idea that it was *you!* She said you had no clue neither, an' I should break it to you gentle-like, if it came up."

Digby went on to relate the story Marsh had told that night, adding to the one Jemma herself had so recently learned about her abduction and the Agromonds' plot to steal her Powers. At first, her parents and Marsh had been afraid that the Agromonds had killed her. But then word came that she was still alive. ("The fella wot used to deliver to the castle before Pa," Digby said, "he was told by one o' the servants, an' told his missus. Word gets about, y'know.") Still, her parents had been powerless to do anything: not only did the Mist prevent them from rescuing her, but the Agromonds had put a spell on them, weakening them further. They'd no longer had the strength even to leave Oakstead. They'd been desperate. So Marsh insisted she'd go instead.

"She loved you more'n anythin', see, next to her husband," Digby said. "So since the Agromonds had killed him, she had nothin' to stay in Oakstead for—"

"Wait—her *husband*? They killed him? But . . . she never said she was married!"

"Course not, Jem. She couldn't tell you anythin' that might give away who she really was. Her husband, he was drivin' your parents' carriage the night you was taken."

Jemma's mind flicked back to the newspaper articles: *Felled coachman, grieving widow* . . . "Julius, that was the coachman's name. Julius Sharm. But that's awful! Poor Marsh . . . Oh!"

"What?"

"Sharm . . . Marsh . . . They're anagrams. But go on." Jemma picked up her fifth sandwich.

"Ana—what? Well, once they'd agreed that she'd go . . ."

Already expertly trained in Mind Control, Marsh had trained for months more to make sure she could outwit the Mist, then went to watch over Jemma and eventually help her escape. For this, though, the timing had to be exact: just when Jemma's Powers were stirring strongly enough for her to overcome Nocturna's hold on her Stone, as well as to survive the forest. But there was another thing: Jemma had to want freedom for herself—*really* want it, not just dream of it, as she had for so long. Only then would her Stone recognize its true owner.

"But then," Digby said, "Marsh was found out, as you know. An' here we are."

"So my parents knew it would be years before they saw

me again . . . and Marsh waited all that time, just for that one night. . . ." Jemma felt humbled by the depth of Marsh's love, and appalled by the danger of her mission and how tiny the window for their escape had been. "I've been half-asleep, just grumbling about how I didn't belong there, but doing nothing about it—and not seeing the truth about the Agromonds until it almost killed me, and Marsh as well!" She tugged at a tuft of grass, ripping it up from the roots. "What an addlehead I've been!"

"Jem, you can't blame yourself! There was nothin' you or Marsh could've done sooner. You had to wait till you was strong enough, remember? Besides, you thought that lot was your *family*, for goodness' sake! How was you to know different?"

"I suppose you're right."

Family. What would her real parents be like? Did seeing her mother in the crystal mean that they had recovered and were now strong again? The thought of them began to feel more real, and she felt a frisson of excitement. Her *family*! Then she remembered her missing brother. Had her parents ever found him? Perhaps he'd been in Oakstead all these years . . . perhaps . . .

"Dig, did Marsh . . . did she say anything else? About my real family, I mean . . ."

Digby shook his head. "No, Jem, I told you everythin' she told us."

"Oh. Right." A shadow moved across Jemma's heart, and somehow she knew that her brother was still lost. She picked up a pebble and tossed it against one of the cottages. It ricocheted off the stone, landing with a *shush* in a drift of fallen leaves. Then she heard another sound, a slight rustle, coming from within the cottage.

"What was that?"

Digby stopped chewing, and listened. A small brown creature scuttled out of the door, and away into a pile of rotten logs.

"Just a weasel, Jem. Nowt to worry about."

Jemma shuddered, thinking of Nocturna's four pets. "So Marsh has gone to Oakstead, to find my parents."

Digby nodded. "She was dreadful cut up about leavin' you at the castle, Jem, but she couldn't go back. She'd hid her intentions from the Mist all them years ago, but this time it'd be expectin' her, an' would attack her, jus' like it attacked your folks—'specially since she was still weak from bein' in the forest. But she refused to give up hope that you'd get out. I told her what Mr. Drudge had told me, an' that I'd find you, an' we'd follow her up north.

"So she borrowed a horse—quite the horsewoman she is, even with one hand—an' off she went. An' though Drudge had said I wouldn't find you till Friday, me an' Pepper started lookin' for you from then on, whenever Pa could spare us. Like Drudge, Marsh had said to stick near the road, so that's what I did. Then, come Friday evenin', me an' this old nag was pacin' that road non-stop from dusk till dawn, wasn't we, Pepper? I was beginnin' to despair of findin' you, thinkin' maybe you hadn't made it—but finally, there you was. What a relief, I got to say."

"Oh, Dig . . ." Jemma felt her cheeks flush. "You spent all that time out there! You . . . you could've been caught. . . ."

"Rotten bloody Agromonds." Digby chomped off a piece

of crust. "The thought of you bein' stuck there, after everythin' Marsh told us . . . well, I didn't care about the risk. I was doin' it for you, Jem. Not for Good against Evil. For you."

"Thank you. Really. You saved me." Without thinking, Jemma took his hand.

Digby stopped chewing and grinned. "Maybe it was worth it," he said. Their eyes locked for a moment, his grin widening. Then he jumped to his feet. "Time to get movin'. Marsh told me 'bout somewhere we can stay the night, but it's still a good few hours from here."

Digby shoved the remains of their picnic into his leather bag. Jemma plopped Noodle and Pie into her pockets, where they lay like two leaden balls. Digby was about to help her onto Pepper's back when something caught her eye: a large bird, landing in the tree under which they'd just been sitting.

"A falcon," said Digby. "Good hunters. Used for sendin' messages too, by them that can tame 'em. I hope that don't mean . . ." He frowned, looking around. Then he froze.

A shadow pulled back from one of the windows.

"There, Jem . . . Did you see?"

Jemma nodded, her heart racing. She hastily tied on her scarf, then realized it was too late. Obviously, they'd already been spotted, Jemma's blaze of hair and all.

"What if it's an Agromond spy?" she whispered. "Should we confront them?"

"No point, Jem. Whoever it is, no sense in givin' 'em a better look at you. Come on, let's get out of here."

As they galloped away, Jemma looked behind at the cottages. An old woman, small and stooped, hobbled out of one of them. Jemma felt the woman's gaze pierce her, and for a moment, thought she saw a black shadow outlining the wizened form. Then it disappeared, leaving the woman shrouded in Mist.

Just a harmless passer-by, Jemma told herself. *A vagrant. Perhaps she's deaf, and didn't hear anything.* In any case, an old hag like that probably couldn't read, much less write messages for falcons to carry. Besides, where would she get paper and ink? Jemma turned away, her mind working at calming her, while her stomach felt like a nest of writhing vipers.

CHAPTER TWENTY-FOUR

Darkness Gathering

Saturday afternoon/evening

Jemma's heart was in her throat as they galloped through the gray countryside. Would they have to be suspicious of everyone who crossed their path? Her fantasies of the Outside dwindled into dust as a horrible realization sank into her: The miles between her and her lifelong prison didn't make her safe. People out here could be just as treacherous as they were at Agromond Castle.

The moorlands ended, and they slowed past hills and fields. Rows of people—men, women, and children—were stooped in some kind of hard-looking toil. Land workers, Jemma guessed, remembering Marsh's descriptions of how potatoes and turnips were grown and harvested. Soon the farmlands turned into more rugged, wooded terrain, and Digby pulled Pepper to an abrupt halt at a bushy copse, then jumped to the ground.

"Hop on down," he said. "We're goin' blackberryin'."

Food? Noodle and Pie nosed out of Jemma's pockets.

"But why? We only ate a short while ago." Jemma took Digby's hand and slid from the saddle, then followed him into the copse. She plucked a few berries and fed them to the rats, popping one into her mouth. It was sweet, but she was surprised to find she quite liked the taste.

"It in't for food, Jem." He tramped through the under-growth, grabbing clumps of the fruit as if his life depended on it. "It's for your hair. We're goin' to dye it, an' cut it short. Come on, use your scarf to collect 'em in."

"What? No! You can't just decide that without asking me—it's *my* hair!"

"An' it's like a flag, in't it, tellin' everyone who you is."

"But . . . but . . . all right, so we'll dye it." Jemma whisked off her scarf and snatched a few berries. "But you are *not* going to cut it off— Ow!" A thorn pricked her. "Mord take it!"

"Jem." Digby stopped, and turned to her. "You saw what happened back there. First the villagers, then that woman. Your hair is what folks notice about you, soon as they see you. You got to understand how dangerous it is out here. We don't know who we might meet."

Jemma looked into the turbulent blue of his eyes. He was worried—and with good reason. "Sorry, Dig. You're right."

Before long, she was shorn, and Digby had made a paste of the berries crushed with mud from a brackish puddle—a mixture his mother had used recently, he said, to dye an old shirt of his. He packed the paste onto her head.

"You look like a boy," he said, grinning, as he tied the bur-lap scarf around her mud-caked tufts. "Put your cloak on too, an' keep the hood up. That'll keep your head warm until the mush dries. Then we'll crumble the lumps out, an' your hair won't be reco'nizable."

"I should think not, after being covered in this muck," Jemma grumbled, wiping her berry-stained hands on her trou-sers. "But it's still going to stick out like a sore thumb."

Digby shrugged. "It won't be flame red, though," he said. "That's the main thing."

By the time they set off again, the pale sun had dipped toward the horizon. This was the first day she could remember, Jemma realized, whose hours had not been marked by the gloomy sound of the castle bell. She tried not to think about the hacked-off locks they'd left buried in the copse ("Don't want anyone findin' 'em," Digby had said), but the berries-and-mud concoction was like a heavy helmet, reminding her, and her head and shoulders felt strangely bare, even with Noodle and Pie nestled around her neck. She felt a tweak of annoyance at Digby. *Grow up, Jemma,* she told herself. *Think of all he's risked for you. Is still risking.*

"Jem. Up ahead."

Jemma looked up to see four silhouettes shuffling from behind a clump of bushes. Digby slowed Pepper to a walk to let them pass: a man, a woman, and two small children. They looked even more cowed than the Hazebury folk earlier. One of the children—whether a boy or girl, it was impossible to tell—stopped and stared at Jemma. She had never seen such a mournful face on a living soul.

"Don' look at strangers!" The woman pushed the child on. "They might steal yer away."

The family shambled into the Mist.

"They look half dead!" Jemma said. "Why are they like that?"

"Why d'you think?" Digby said, kicking Pepper into a trot. "Them Agromonds. This Mist. Everyone's poor, an' half-starved, like the spirit's been sucked out of 'em. Most don't have any fight left. Not since your folks . . ." He trailed off.

"Not since they lost their Powers, you mean, and became too weak to help." Jemma gripped the saddle, her knuckles whitening. How could she have wondered? The Agromond blight was everywhere. "So why aren't you like that? You and your family seem full of life."

"Hmph. We're lucky, you might say, bein' the grocers an' all. They need us to deliver their food to 'em, so we get extra supplies to keep us happy. But it's a sham, to suit them. We give what we can to our neighbors, but it ain't never enough. An' there's still the rest of Anglavia. Like them poor beggars jus' now, their little 'uns barely more'n shadows."

Jemma was chilled to the bone. Was there anyone, anywhere, that the Agromond evil didn't touch? "You know what they used to tell me, when they went out visiting the villages?" she said. "They said they were ministering to the poor. And to think I believed them!"

"Ministerin', my eye!" Digby said. "Oh, they do their rounds once a month, all right, grantin' their so-called favors to this one and that—extra rations, that kind of thing—makin' everyone hanker after it, hopin' it'll be their turn this time. But I see what it does. It hardens folk against each other, makes 'em compete for crumbs, givin' 'em just enough to keep 'em under control, but not enough that they dare rebel."

Jemma gulped, remembering the way she'd been similarly manipulated by Nox's affection. It had been just enough to keep her compliant, hoping for more.

"Sometimes I think it's like most of 'em's under some kind of sick spell," Digby went on. "But I s'pose we ought to be thankful that children ain't disappearin' no more. Used to happen twice a year or so, Pa said, some little 'uns would be took. Always twins or triplets, it was. It's even said them Agromonds put a spell on married folks so's they'd give birth to more twins an' triplets than normal, an' to keep up the supply."

"Ugh. That wouldn't surprise me. . . . But why did they want twins and triplets?"

"For some kind of . . . sacrifice, it's said. Something to do with some kind of bond between twins that breaks when one of 'em dies. S'posedly the Agromonds got Power from it, don't ask me how. Went on for hundreds of years, But all that stopped jus' before they took you, thank goodness, or no doubt we'd be worryin' about our Flora, Simon, an' Tiny."

Jemma thought of Cora, the little girl ghost in Bryn's cave, and all the other small ghosts who had been wandering the forest for eons in search of their lost brothers and sisters. "All that suffering," she murmured. "It's a wonder you ever gave me a second look, Dig," she murmured, "since you must've thought I was one of *Them*."

"You? Y'know . . . funny thing is, now that I think of it, it never occurred to me. All Pa said, before he first took me up there, was that he thought you was lonely an' could use a bit of comp'ny. Then when I met you . . . well, I liked you, is all." He laid his chin on Jemma's shoulder.

Jemma took a deep breath. "Dig . . . I'm sorry I lost my temper back there."

" 'S'alright, Jem. I understand. Your hair is kind of your crownin' glory. But you still look pretty good without it."

Jemma smiled, her stomach flipping.

"Does stink a bit, though," he added.

Twilight fell. They had passed a few stragglers on the path, and several more tumbledown hamlets, stopping occasionally for Pepper to snatch a mouthful or two of grass. Now, the mare was lagging, and she stumbled increasingly on the stony path. They would rest soon, Digby said; he knew of the perfect place, described to him by Marsh, where Jemma's still-damp head would dry in no time, and they could sleep for a while. From there, Oakstead was a mere four hours' ride, and they should be able to arrive soon after dawn. Jemma felt a thrill of anticipation. *Not long now,* she thought, hoping, somehow, that her parents could pick up her words on the ether.

A chill breeze nipped through the air, and she reached behind Digby into the saddlebags, pulled out the book, and hugged it. Noodle and Pie rested on her forearms, close to its warmth.

Jemma peered over Pepper's ears into the dusk, hearing a distant rush of water, punctuated by a rhythmic *whomp, whomp.* She saw a faint glow off to the right, which became brighter as they approached, and the whomping grew louder.

"Digby, what's that noise? And that light?"

"We're gettin' close to the Elm River. The noise is a water-wheel. An' the light . . . well, you'll see."

The glow took on a rectangular form. Digby drew Pepper behind a large bush nearby, then slid to the ground and tethered her reins to a branch.

"Wait here a mo'," he said. "I'll check there's nobody around." He ran off, leaving Jemma and the rats alone with the sound of paddles working through the water. She tucked the book back into the saddlebags, then patted Pepper's neck nervously. The mare seemed bigger without Digby there. Although Jemma had often lingered in the castle stables after mucking them out, and imagined riding Stag, Nox's old stallion, to be actually sitting astride a horse on her own was another matter.

"All clear." Digby reappeared through the Mist. "So, here we are, Jem—our palace for the night: Blackwater Greenhouses."

"Greenhouses?" Jemma slid to the ground, then plopped Noodle and Pie into her pockets and followed Digby along a muddy path toward several long, low, luminous buildings with strange-looking shadows inside. She tapped one of the walls. It was glass, whitewashed on the inside. "Why greenhouses? They're white."

"You'll see." Digby strode ahead of her, opened a door, and stood aside. "Enter, m'lady."

Jemma was hit by a wave of warmth. Lamplight glared from the ceiling. Rows of trestle tables held pots of all sizes, containing all manner of plants. She recognized herbs— basil, rosemary, tarragon—and cucumbers, fennel, and as- paragus, but there was a host of other fruits and vegetables in other shapes and colors that were unknown to her.

"Mother of Majem! What . . . How . . . ?" Already, she felt hot, and tore off her cloak and burlap scarf, dropping them to the floor. Several clumps of purple mud fell from her head. Digby snorted, suppressing a laugh, and Jemma whacked him playfully. "Thank *you*, warthog!"

"You're welcome, ma'am. Things can't grow proper-like in the Mist, see," he went on to explain, "so there's green- houses. Mos' towns an' villages by rivers have 'em. The light's made by the waterwheel, goodness knows how— some kind of Agromond sorcery, usin' the water. Makes the warmth too."

Jemma noticed small stoves placed along the aisles, pump- ing out blue-red heat.

"All this food!" she said. "So why are so many people starving?"

"Mos' greenhouses jus' grow a few basics—them rations I was tellin' you about, remember? The only other place that has this many is Hazebury. For them Agromonds."

"Hazebury. For the Agromonds," Jemma repeated, unease bristling under her skin. "Why here, then? Digby, what are you not telling me?"

"Well . . . these greenhouses belong to Blackwater, an', thing is, Blackwater . . ." He took a deep breath. "It's rife with Agromond followers an' henchmen who get special treatment. But don't worry, Jem. The town's a mile or two away, an' Marsh said as long as we steer clear of it, we'll be fine. We jus' got to be careful, is all, an' if we run into any Inquisitors, act half-dead, so's they won't suspect nothin'. Anyways, there's very few around these days since the protests petered out, an' them what's left is more interested in drink than anythin'."

"But . . . Agromond henchmen? Inquisitors? What *are* Inquisitors, anyway?"

"Jus' . . . them that enforce Agromond law."

"What? No! Digby, you should have told me before now!"

"An' worry you ahead of time? Why would I do that? If you'd been anticipatin' the worst all day, you'd've been miserable!"

"But I have a right to know, Dig! It's me they want, not you. Why did we come this way if it's so dangerous?" She stuffed her hands into her pockets, forgetting that the rats were there. They squealed with surprise.

"Don't get huffy with me, Jem! Look, maybe I should've said, but I'm doin' my best, all right? An' I'm doin' it for you. It ain't like there's another road north. I'm jus' followin' Marsh's directions." Digby sighed, and pulled something from his bag. "Here, have a turnip. I'll go an' settle Pepper, an' bring the saddlebags in. These lights should go out soon, then we can get us a bit of shut-eye. Do us all good, I reckon." He paused by the door. "Sorry I upset you," he said, and walked out.

Jemma glowered at the turnip in her hand, feeling a twinge of guilt at losing her temper with Digby again. But it was his fault, making decisions without telling her! She wasn't helpless, after all. Hadn't she managed to escape from the castle and through the forest?

He saved you. Two heads peeked from her pockets.

"Oh, Rattusses. I know. But . . . but . . ." But nothing. "I'm just not used to having someone else around all the time, I suppose. You're right, though. If Digby hadn't found me . . ."

Jemma bit into the turnip and strolled along one of the aisles, her footsteps in time with the *whomp, whomp* of the waterwheel outside. Munching as she went, she took in the variety of leaves and odd-shaped objects poking from under them, some bulbous and green, others long and yellow. Such an assortment of food! If the Agromonds could grow all this for their own kind, why not for everyone? Come to that, why not make light for everybody too, and heat?

"Hoarding it for themselves and their followers, and keeping everybody else starved," she muttered between gritted teeth. She took another chomp of turnip and stuffed the rest of it into her pocket. "Oh, sorry, Rattus." Noodle wriggled out, sniffed, and then he and Pie hopped onto the trestle and began munching on some round, red objects growing on tall stems nearby.

"Trust you two!" Jemma chuckled. "Go on—eat them out of house and castle!" She took a swig of milk from her wineskin. It had soured over the course of the day, and was just right—though Digby, no doubt, wouldn't like it. Where was he, anyway?

Her scalp prickled from the warmth, and she scratched her head. More clumps of dried mud fell from her hair, which felt stubbly and granular, like matted fur.

"Dig-*by* . . . ," she growled, then stopped herself, and thought instead of what she liked best about him. Warm, kind, dependable . . . her irritation turned to concern. Dependable. Surely he should be back by now? Perturbed, she started toward the door.

Suddenly, the greenhouse plunged into darkness. The stoves went out. A dark fear crawled up Jemma's spine. Between the *whomp* of the waterwheel and the rush of the river, she heard sounds from outside: growling, barking, shouting.

"'Ere—got 'im!"

Lamps threw long shadows across the white walls. Jemma dropped to a crouch, then crawled to the door and peered through a broken pane of glass. Two men were yanking Digby from a shrub. A wiry boy stood behind them, pulling back on a leash attached to a snarling barrel of hate: a hound, just like the one that had pursued her that night in Agromond Forest.

"I wasn't doin' nothin'!" Digby yelled. "Let me go!"

"This the bloke wot you seen prowlin' around earlier, Sharky?" said one of the men, picking up a large bag and throwing it over one shoulder.

That voice—so grating, cold, callous . . . And the long coat the man was wearing . . .

"Yes, sir, it was, sir. I come as soon as I seen 'im, sir, like you said I should."

"You done good, boy" said the second man. "Now, let's get this piece of dross back to town. What should we do with 'im, eh, Lok—put 'im in the stocks?"

Lok! The thug whose hound had almost caught her—

"Stocks is too good fer the likes of 'im," Lok growled. He dragged Digby, wriggling and cursing, toward a thicket of trees. "I'll think of somethin', Zeb, don't you worry. Somethin' tonight's rabble will like. Come on, Fang, you useless mutt!" He kicked the dog, which yelped. Lok laughed. The same, chilling laugh Jemma had heard from the Aukron's lair.

The boy led three horses from behind the trees. He leapt onto one of them, Zeb onto another, then Jemma watched, dismayed, as Digby was bound and gagged, and thrown like a sack of potatoes onto the third. Lok tied him down and climbed up in front of him. Then men and boy lurched into the night, with Lok's vicious hound on their heels, baying like a banshee.

CHAPTER TWENTY-FIVE

A Dark Place

Saturday

Jemma slumped against the greenhouse door, its handle rattling in her trembling hand. What punishment would Lok dream up for Digby? Possibilities swarmed her head—Fang, dungeons, torture. . . . She must find him, and quickly, before those men could hurt him.

She grabbed her cloak and raced outside, Noodle and Pie skittering behind her. Pepper, still tethered to the bush where Digby had left her, tossed her head and pawed the ground as they approached.

"Pepper, thank goodness they didn't find you! Sorry, girl . . . Can't rest . . . Those men took Digby . . ." Jemma whipped the reins free and pulled Pepper toward a nearby tree stump. "Quick, Rattusses, into the saddlebags— Oh, no!"

The saddlebags had gone. Of course—Digby was going to bring them into the greenhouse; that must have been what Lok was throwing over his shoulder. Which meant that he also had the precious items stowed inside them: her book and crystals, as well as her knife. Seething, she scooped Noodle and Pie into her pockets, then gathered Pepper's reins.

"Go easy on me, girl, all right? I've never ridden on my own." She clambered onto the stump, jumped into the saddle, and shoved her feet into the stirrups. Now what? Stomach churning, she took a deep breath and kicked, the way Digby had earlier.

Pepper took off. Jemma clung to her mane, frantically trying to think of how Digby had used the reins to steer, but Pepper needed no guidance, and sped along the track the men had taken. Noodle and Pie's claws dug into Jemma's legs. They were managing to hold on—but she was losing her foothold. The stirrup slipped from her left boot and flapped against Pepper's flank, making the mare veer off track. Seconds later, Jemma's right stirrup came loose. Now both were flying into Pepper's sides, driving her faster, hooves snapping through heather, mane whipping into Jemma's face.

"Easy, girl—easy!" Terrified, Jemma gripped with her legs as she lay over Pepper's withers, her arms wrapped around the mare's outstretched neck. The ground rushed by. She could feel her cloak streaming behind her like wings. Wings that had saved her, breaking her fall from Mordwin's Crag. . . . She began to feel as though she was flying, and melted into Pepper's thundering gallop, remembering the thrill of speed she'd felt earlier with Digby's arm around her. All fear vanished. Her mind merged with the mare's, envisioning where to go: *Over there, to the right— Yes! That's it.* . . .

Pepper galloped back onto the track. Moments later, they came to a fork in the road, and Jemma pulled to a halt. Which way had Lok taken?

The crystals. They were in the saddlebags he'd stolen. . . . Jemma grabbed her Stone and thought of the triangle of power she'd felt between it and the crystals, back in Bryn's cave. *Show me where you are,* she muttered. *Please! Show me.*

The Stone warmed. An odd sensation welled up inside

her, as though air was expanding her from within and ballooning out to the right, pulling her in that direction.

"This way, girl!" Jemma tugged the right rein, and Pepper took off again. This time, riding fast felt as easy as it had ever been in her imagination.

Clusters of shacks appeared by the roadside. Ahead, dots of light hazed through the Mist, seeming to dip and sway. As Pepper galloped closer, Jemma could see that the dots were lamps held by people—men, women, and children, in groups of eight or ten, some on horseback, a few in carts, but mostly on foot, straggling in the direction she was headed. She eased back on the reins; flying by at arrow-speed might attract unwanted attention. Pepper slowed to a walk, her flanks heaving after her sprint, breath snorting from her nostrils.

"Good girl," Jemma said. "Now, let's find Digby. He can't be far ahead now." She pulled up her hood and trotted past each group as fast as she dared. Was this the rabble Lok had referred to? Why were they going to Blackwater, tonight of all nights? She huddled into her cloak, glancing cautiously at a few of them as she passed by. They looked hardened and more fierce than any of the villagers she'd seen earlier that day, though better fed and dressed less raggedly. But these people, she remembered with a shudder, were on the Agromonds' side. She wondered whether they too liked the Mist, and hoped none of them would notice the clear air around her hands. At least at night it was less obvious.

Snatches of their murmurs caught her ears: "A big 'un, this time . . . Mus' be important. Mord be praised!" A sense of doom crept into her belly, and Noodle and Pie burrowed deeper into her pockets.

The shacks flanking the road became more numerous,

built in denser groups. The crowd was more dense too, their murmuring louder, excitement bristling. Ahead, a dark form took shape, gradually revealing itself as a long, wooden wall, at least twenty feet high. It stretched away in each direction as far as the eye could see, before disappearing into Mist. There was a gap in it, about three times the width of the main door to Agromond Castle.

The gateway to Blackwater.

The pulling sensation became stronger, balling in the center of Jemma's sternum, and she craned her neck, scanning the sea of heads and horse buttocks in front of her. The crowd jostled. Jemma's nerves wound tighter, the specter of Digby's fate growing larger in her imagination with every second. Where was he? She clutched her Stone. It tingled under her fingers. Then she saw something through the Mist: two beads of blue, blinking faintly from close to the gateway. Sapphire blue, just like her mother's eyes in the vortex of the snowstorm—

"There—the crystals!" Jemma kicked Pepper on. Noodle and Pie nosed from her pockets, their gazes fixed as intently as Jemma's on the beads of light ahead. Suddenly, a cord of luminous blue leapt from the crystals and crackled into her fist. She gasped in amazement, then panicked, willing the cord to disappear—people would see it, would see her, would find her out! But nobody looked. Nobody reacted.

The sapphire light sparking between her Stone and the crystals was visible only to her—and, apparently, to the rats, who were blinking with surprise. Elation washed through her. The crystals shone more intensely, drawing her on. For a split second, she saw the group of three horses, one with Digby hanging over the back. They entered the gateway into Black-water, and the cord of light dissolved.

"Oh, no, we've lost them!" Jemma steered Pepper forward, ignoring the irate glares aimed at her. The crowd shoved and pressed, their murmurs growing in pitch. Children cried louder; people yelled to one another: "*Save me a place, Kal-las!*" "*What d'you s'pose 'e's called us for, eh? In't ration time yet.*" "*Oy, Lila—meet me outside the Strangler's Arms after, will yer?*"

Pepper tossed her mane and ground her teeth, her ears flat on her head. Jemma could feel the panic rising in the mass of muscle beneath her; though used to seeing people on the Goodfellows' delivery rounds, Pepper had probably never seen a mob like this. Praying that the mare wouldn't kick or bite and draw attention to herself, Jemma kept talking softly to her. Finally, they funneled through the gates, and poured with the rest of the crowd into a small square of ramshackle wooden buildings, lit by a blaze of torchlight.

The hubbub grew: other horses, neighing; carts, their wheels squealing; voices, yelling; babies, screaming; hounds, barking. The air was thick with smoke, and stank of rotten eggs and charred meat. Around the square's perimeter, chil-dren juggled sheeps' eyes, men pulled rabbits out of tall hats, and women turned small animals on spits above open fires that glowed with coals. Beside them were piles of cages full of the next victims: birds, rabbits, and creatures that looked sim-ilar to Noodle and Pie, but with thicker coats and bushy tails.

"Squirrel! Three farthin's for a luvverly roast squirrel!"

Jemma felt the blood drain from her face. "Hide your-selves, Rattusses," she whispered, "or you might be next."

221

Noodle and Pie dived into her pockets and lay there, still as stones.

She urged Pepper across the square into a torchlit street along which the crowd was surging. Several times, she saw a flicker of blue ahead, only to lose sight of it in a wisp of smoke, or behind a silhouetted rider. It was getting harder to push through the jostle and crush. She'd have to find another way.

"Over there—up that alley. Easy, girl. That's it." They broke into a dank, narrow street, then Jemma steered into another alleyway to the right. At the next intersection, she spied a narrow corridor running parallel to the main artery, and trotted Pepper into it. But Pepper was flagging, her hooves sliding on the carpet of mud and garbage, her neck hanging with exhaustion.

"Come on, girl—please!" Jemma tried directing energy from her Stone into the mare, but tonight's sprint had obviously proven too much after the long day's ride. Pepper plodded to a halt and refused to take another step.

"Oh, Pepper . . . What am I to *do* with you? I don't feel safe leaving you here!" But there was no alternative. Jemma slid from the saddle and dragged Pepper farther into the corridor, where the shadows were darker and she was less likely to be found, and then held the mare's face between her hands. "If anyone comes," she said, "run. Use your hooves and kick, if you have to. Just don't get caught. I'll be back soon with Digby." *I hope*, she thought. Pepper whickered as if in answer, though Jemma doubted that she'd understood. Checking her pockets for the rats, she found the rest of the turnip Digby had given her and fed it to the mare. Then she ran to the next corner and pelted in the direction of the crowd. Noodle and Pie bounced in her pockets, squeaking in time with her pounding feet.

The noise increased. Sweat beaded on her face. Blood thumped through her veins. She'd lost so much time! How would she find Digby now?

Suddenly, she felt the crystals' pull again, this time to her left, from another alley. She raced into it. The pull grew stronger, as if she was being hauled along by some force outside herself. She hurtled out into a street, and slammed into a horse and rider. The impact sent her pitching into the mud, the rats tumbling from her pockets.

"Oy, watch it, you!" A gruff voice. Impatient hooves, stamping. Jemma rolled out of the way and lay facedown in the gutter, peering through her fingers as three horses walked by, away from the crowd.

Away from the crowd . . . ?

Three horses. One black, one bay, and bringing up the rear, a roan. Slung across its back was Digby, wrists and ankles trussed up like a Mordmas turkey. He was looking straight at her, his eyes wide with astonishment that turned rapidly to alarm.

"Mmmm—mmmm!"

Off to her left, Noodle and Pie squealed. From behind her, Jemma heard a guttural snarl. Something heavy landed on her back—something solidly muscular, every fiber of its body rigid.

Fang. Fang, intent with revenge for the prey he'd been denied on Mordwin's Crag.

In a flash, she felt the hound's jaws opening, the heat of his breath as he was about to sink his teeth into her neck, and forced herself to kneel in an attempt to throw him off. But Fang hung on, his claws digging through her cloak, raking down her back. She stifled a scream, but couldn't help a high squeak escaping her. Lok turned his head to look over his shoulder—

Jemma hurled herself and her assailant into the alley, then tossed off her cloak. She bundled it around the gnashing creature and hauled it farther into the shadows. The bundle heaved and snapped. She had to act fast, before Lok came looking. . . . Yanking back the cloak, she twisted her fist into Fang's collar and fixed his venomous gaze. "Now listen, you," she hissed, clutching one of his drooling jowls with her free hand, "it's like this. . . ."

Gory images snapped through her head, and she propelled them into Fang's pus-colored eyes: *Mordwin's Crag . . . the Aukron . . . So huge! I killed it . . . Me! Killed it, dead . . .* "The choice is yours, Fang. I kill you, just like I killed that monster, or I let you live. But if you show your master where I am, or hurt my friend, I'll get you. Wherever you are, I'll be coming for you."

Fang whimpered, cowering. *Want . . . live . . .*

"Oy, Fang—where yer got to, stupid animal?"

Jemma released the hound and pressed herself against the wall just as a black horse appeared at the end of the alley. Two small shadows scurried through the mud and launched themselves onto her boots, a peep of air escaping them as they landed.

"Huntin' rats, are yer?" Lok's voice grated from the street. "Heel, yer little beggar!"

Fang ran toward his master, tail tucked between his legs,

and the two of them disappeared. Jemma leaned against the wall, heart hammering as she gulped down air. Fang's claw marks stung on her back, but there was no time to dwell on that now. Noodle and Pie clambered up into her pockets, their golden fur black with mud. She picked up the cloak and wrapped it around her. Then, pulling up its hood, she trotted to the corner and peeked around it.

Lok stopped at the next alley, outside a stone building not thirty feet away.

"Right, young Sharky, we're done with yer." He jumped off his horse and threw a coin at the boy. "Here's a ha'penny for yer trouble. Now, get lost, yer little toad."

The boy scurried away, and Lok turned to his companion. "Bring this thievin' good-fer-nothin' inside an' get 'im locked up. A good stonin' after the rally oughta teach 'im a lesson, don't yer reckon, Zeb? A nice treat for the crowd." He swaggered into the building, carrying the saddlebags, which pulsed sapphire blue into the night, like beacons warning of jagged rocks in a storm.

CHAPTER TWENTY-SIX

Rally

Saturday night

Jemma crept to the window of the stone jail and peered in. Flame flared: Lok, lighting a lamp on the table. Digby, held from behind by Zeb, gnashed into his gag, his body tense with restrained fight as Lok tipped out the saddlebags' contents: book, leftover sandwiches, two apples, Jemma's knife, and last of all, the two crystals.

"'Allo, 'allo, what do we 'ave 'ere?" Lok picked up the crystals; Jemma cringed as he turned them in his filthy hands. "Looks like they might be worth a bit. Somethin' you thieved, eh, boy?" He turned to Digby and spat at his feet. "Well, it don't matter how you came by 'em. They're mine now!" He laughed, and pocketed them. Jemma's stomach clenched. How dare he!

Zeb shoved Digby into a cage in the corner of the room, slammed and locked the door, then hung the key on a hook nearby. Lok blew out the lamp. Jemma ducked into the alley as the two men swaggered out, and waited until their horses' hoofsteps had splattered away.

Noodle and Pie crawled onto her shoulders, and she stepped cautiously back into the empty street. Suddenly, from an alley opposite, she heard a jumble of voices, and the sound of feet running through mud. A herd of urchins burst into view. Jemma froze, unsure whether to dart into the jail, stand her ground, or run. Then they were upon her. She dodged aside, but one of them grabbed her cloak as he passed. Her hood fell back, and the rats plopped into it.

The boy laughed. "Come on, spiky-head!" he said, pulling her into their midst. "Better hurry or you'll be late fer the rally!"

He let go and ran on. Jemma tried to turn back, but boys crammed her on both sides, sweeping her into their stampede. Then a small hand pressed into hers. A girl, a little shorter and more slight than she, was running beside her, dragging her along.

"Wait—no!" Jemma tugged at the girl's hand, but the girl's grasp was like iron

"What's the matter, boy?"

Boy? Of course . . . her shorn head. Digby had said she looked like a boy.

"Won't do not to go," the girl said. "You know the punishment if they find you been skivin' off." She nipped between other runners. She was as fast as she was strong, and Jemma was panting by the time they reached the main street. They slowed down as they flowed into the gathering tide of Blackwater folk. "Ain't seen you around here before." The girl tossed a hank of black hair from her face. "What's yer name?"

Jemma's mind scrambled. What if her accent gave her away? "I . . . it's . . . um . . ."

"Um! Odd name, innit? Mine's Talon." She made a face. "My pa's idea. Stupid git."

Talon. The name fit, if her grip was anything to go by. Jemma's anxiety intensified as the squeeze of the mob increased, then eased slightly as they spilled into a square much larger than the one at the town's entrance. It was packed, the yelling and whooping almost deafening now.

Talon pulled Jemma toward one of the houses bordering the square. Next to it was a tiny alleyway—an escape route, if only Jemma could break away. . . .

" 'Ere, let go of me!" Jemma imitated Digby's accent, imagining him in a grumpy mood, and tried to prize her hand from Talon's. "I got to find a good view."

"That's jus' where I'm takin' yer—best seats in the house!" Talon stopped outside a door and pulled a huge bunch of keys from her skirt pocket. "Here we are . . . this one." The door creaked open, and she yanked Jemma into a dusty hall, holding her hand tighter as she took the rickety steps two at a time up three flights. At the top was a small trapdoor, which she pushed open with one hand. "Up you go," she said, shoving Jemma through it and onto a shingle roof. Talon hauled herself up to sit beside her. "My favorite place, this," she said. "I always watch from up 'ere."

Jemma could see why. Below was a swirl of color. Torches burned in brackets placed on the walls around the square at regular intervals, sending up thin trails of black smoke. The crowd teemed toward the far end of the square, where a platform had been erected. The sheer mass of people was breathtaking; Jemma had never imagined, much less seen, so many at once.

"Good, innit?" Talon said, wrapping her arms around her knees. "We in't the only ones, though. See?" She pointed to the rooves surrounding the square, dotted with other onlookers.

Jemma tensed. She couldn't help liking Talon; she seemed to be a bit of a loner. Even so, she had to get away from her and back to Digby—but how? Talon seemed determined to cling to her, and would outrun her in seconds. Noodle and Pie turned around in her hood, their nervousness as palpable as her own. She felt for her wineskin; perhaps a swig of sour milk would help. It didn't.

"Yer lookin' a bit peaky, Um," said Talon. "You afraid of heights?" She looked at Jemma sideways.

"I'm fine," Jemma muttered.

"Grisly goblins—look at them Inquisitors!" Talon squeaked. "Five of 'em, round the stage."

Jemma looked down and saw five men in long black coats, flanking the platform. Coats like Lok's—so he was an Inquisitor! She squinted, but couldn't see him among them.

"How d'you like 'im, then?" Talon asked. "The Master, I mean."

"The Master?" Jemma felt faint. The Master . . . Surely, it couldn't be . . . ?

The crowd broke into a roar. She held her breath and looked down. A black steed pulled up next to the platform; a cloaked rider dismounted. He strode onto the stage, his back to his audience, then raised his arms. Jemma's fists tightened, her knuckles grazing the rough shingles.

"It's like he's got 'em all under a spell," said Talon, her voice full of awe.

A spell . . . That was what Digby had said earlier. Jemma's belly felt like a thousand leaves in a hurricane, and she wished she could blow away, to anywhere but here. Anywhere but near that man below . . .

Very slowly, Nox Agromond turned around.

Jemma snatched her Stone. Her head spun. After all she'd been through—he couldn't find her now! She felt Talon's stare boring into her. *Must calm down. . . . Don't let her see what I'm feeling. . . .* The Stone's pulse took the edge off her panic. The crowd's roar died down. A fierce drizzle began to fall, needles of wet through the misty glow.

And then Nox spoke.

He spoke of the Agromonds' tireless championing of their followers, and his words were answered with cheers. He spoke of the mindless rabble that made up the rest of Anglavia, the idiocy and superstition that was rife among the villages—everywhere, in fact, other than Blackwater—and his words were answered with jeers. He spoke of the rebels who even now refused to recognize the Agromonds' supremacy, and his words were answered with louder jeers. Even so, he said, the Agromond influence was spreading fast.

"But, friends, Blackwatermen, countrymen!" he boomed. "Heed me well! I come tonight to warn you: there is one at large who threatens our supremacy, and our very existence!"

A deathly hush fell over the square, leaving nothing but the hiss of rain.

"Yes! It is true. I had thought to be telling you tonight of our success in obliterating this danger, and to be celebrating with you, for just this morning we had evidence, or so we believed, that our adversary was dead"—*When I wasn't snared by your Approjection*, Jemma thought—"but, my friends, we were misled! For on my way here, I happened upon a trusted ally,

230

the Widow Strickner, who was on her way to bring me the dread news: She had seen our adversary not an hour before, taking luncheon on the moors, as merrily as you please!"

The crowd booed. Sweat beaded on Jemma's forehead. So the old woman at the cottages *had* been a spy! Jemma clutched her Stone harder. It burned in her fist.

"What's that, Um?" Talon pointed at the turquoise light glowing between Jemma's fingers. "An' why's the air around yer hands all clear?"

Jemma quickly tucked the Stone down her shirt and stuffed her fists into her pockets. Talon's gaze drilled through her. Fang's claw tracks throbbed on her back.

"And who, you may ask, is this adversary of whom I speak?" Nox continued. "Why, none other than the One I have spoken of before—Jemma, the girl we have been nurturing since she was a babe, giving her succor! The child of our sworn enemies, who, Marked as she was, we believed to be one of us! And oh, dear friends, I cared for her as my own—" His voice cracked, and sympathetic murmurs rippled across the square. "Yet she turned against me. Against us. Against *you*, my friends, you! And now, to add insult to injury, she is set on destroying us! You must keep your eyes as keen as a hawk's and your wits as sharp as a razor's edge, for she is close by, even as I speak. You will recognize her by her flame-red hair—"

Jemma gulped. Thank goodness Digby had shorn her, and dyed her stubble!

"—which she may, however, have thought to disguise. She also has an accomplice—a youth of around fifteen or sixteen years—and may be traveling with two yellow rats, as well—"

"Two *rats?*" said Talon incredulously. "*Yellow* ones?" Titters drifted up from the square.

That's not nice! Noodle and Pie stirred in Jemma's hood.

"—and, we are certain, is en route to Oakstead to find her parents, our sworn enemies—"

"Mord's revenge upon 'em!" someone yelled. Others took up the cry: "Mord's revenge! Mord's revenge!"

Nox raised his arms, hushing the hecklers, then continued. "At all costs, she must be prevented from reaching Oakstead before nine tomorrow morning. For up until that time, she can still gather great Powers unto herself with which to carry out her mission!" He paused, letting his words sink in. *My Initiation,* Jemma thought, more determined than ever to make it in time.

"How do we know she in't already there?"

"Excellent question, my good man! But fear not. The Widow Strickner sent falcons to all our allies between here and Oakstead, bearing stones whose message they well know: that the girl is loose and must be stopped. Besides, she could not yet have gone that far, for remember I was but an hour behind her, and my steed is as swift as lightning"—he gestured to Mephisto—"whereas she and her cohort, I am told, have naught to ride but an old nag, barely even fit for a dog's dinner!" More jeers, and laughter.

"And so, my friends, I bid you join the hunt! The boy is of no consequence, do with him what you will. But the girl . . ." He cleared his throat. "If you catch her before nine, and then bring her to me—unharmed, mind—you shall be richly rewarded. At the very least, stop her. We already have spies and Inquisitors posted along the main road to Oakstead, and with your help, we shall surely achieve our goal."

"An' after nine, then what?"

"Why, the spies and Inquisitors will go home, and you may all rejoice! For as long as she does not reach Oakstead by nine and receive her Initiation, she will no longer be a danger to us. No, my friends! As history has shown us, those with such Powers who are not properly Initiated lose their Powers. Moreover, any she already has will dry up like a rotting carcass, rendering her harmless to us—a paltry dreg, like the rest of Anglavian peasantry, and no longer able to disintegrate the merest fly! Then let her wither away with her own kind, within Oakstead's walls—or better yet, go where she pleases, for she will be nothing but a laughing-stock, a public disgrace to those who have believed in her! Let their noses be rubbed in it! For then, what effect can she have on us, my friends? What effect can a gnat have on a lion? I tell you, only prevent her from entering Oakstead, and after nine on the morrow, the danger will be over—victory will be ours, with nothing to oppose us any longer! And then, oh, then, how we shall celebrate! Mord be praised!"

Cheers erupted amidst cries of "Mord be praised! Victory! Nine tomorrow—victory!"

Jemma trembled with rage and disappointment. So what she had feared in Bryn's cave was true—her Powers really would be gone! Her dreams of helping to end the Agromond reign of Mist and terror shattered like eggs hurled from a high tower. There was no hope of reaching Oakstead in time, not with every Blackwater eye looking for her—including Talon, whose gaze continued to spear into her. The girl suspected her, Jemma could feel it. Under Talon's scrutiny, even rescuing Digby and hiding out until after the danger was passed were impossible tasks now—let alone reaching Oakstead by morning. Rain and sweat dribbled down her forehead, and she wiped it with her hand, then looked at her hand in horror.

It was purple. The rain was washing the berry dye from her hair. Without thinking, she pulled her hood over her head. Noodle and Pie flew out of it, and thudded onto the roof. Rain streaked the mud on their coats, revealing patches of golden fur.

"Two yellow rats, eh?" Talon snatched Jemma's hand. "It *is* you, innit? You in't a boy at all!"

Jemma tried to pull away, but Talon held fast.

"You best come with me," she said, opening the trapdoor, "or there'll be Mord to pay."

"Please, no . . . ," Jemma said, but it was hopeless. She was caught, like a mouse in a maze.

"Hurry!" Talon jumped down. "An' tell yer rats to look lively too."

"What?"

"Quick, I said! Let's get you out of 'ere, afore they start huntin' for yer."

Noodle and Pie leapt onto Jemma's shoulders, then Talon turned and raced down the stairs, with Jemma on her heels. They crashed out into the square just as an enormous image appeared above the platform. An Approjection. Of Jemma. Her red hair and aqua eyes were illuminated giant-sized in the Misty rain for all to see.

"This is she, my friends," Nox said. "Do not be fooled by her air of innocence. . . ."

"Grisly goblins, look at that!" Talon said. "Amazin' what they can do. Come on—this way." She dashed into the tiny alley that Jemma had spied earlier.

"Talon—" Jemma was puffing, trying to keep up. "Why are you helping me?"

"I hate 'em," Talon said. "Every one of 'em. An' I know all about you, Jemma Solvay. Been hearin' tales 'bout you all my life. My ma an' pa used to work at the castle, see, an' Ma told me 'bout the terrible goin's-on there, an' how this new baby arrived one night. We left when I was two—you was four, I think—an' came here, but Ma never forgot you. Said you wasn't like *them*, even when you was little. Later, she heard 'bout some Prophecy, an' jus' *knew* you was the Fire One it talked about. Her an' me always said we hoped you'd escape someday—an' to think now, it's me as is helpin' yer!" She zigzagged along tiny alleys, and in what seemed like no time had led Jemma back to the street where the jail was. Even from here, they could hear Nox's voice echoing across the ramshackle rooves.

" . . . a special event tomorrow, to celebrate—a stoning, arranged by my good man Lok."

"Good man Lok, my big toe!" Talon snarled as she stomped toward the jail, pulling her keys from her pocket. "Let's get yer friend out of that cage."

Jemma trotted after her. "How do you know it's him in there?"

"Saw 'im from the alley when Lok and Zeb brought 'im in, then saw you lurkin'. I din't know who you was, though, or that you was tryin' to save 'im. Thought you was jus' lookin' to thieve what you could from their swag, same as I was. Then I 'eard what Lok said 'bout the stonin'. Typical of 'im. Look." She stopped, and yanked up one sleeve, revealing a large bruise on her upper arm.

Jemma gasped. "Lok *hit* you?"

"Hits. Whenever 'e can." Talon wiped a sodden strand of hair from her face. "In't that what a pa does to his daughter? Bein' the Chief Inquisitor's kid has some uses, though." She grinned and jangled her keys, then marched into the jail. Jemma stood for a second, horrified by what Talon had just revealed, then ran inside. Talon unlocked the cage, and the door swung open. Digby was slumped on the floor, looking worn out.

"Dig! Digby—wake up!" Jemma ran over to him.

"Mmmm?" His eyes shot open. "Mmmm mmm mmm!"

Jemma grabbed her knife from the table and slashed through his gag, while Noodle and Pie started chewing through the ropes binding his ankles, and Talon untied his wrists.

"Ag-ro-mond! Ag-ro-mond!" The cry rose into the night.

"Jem! How . . . Where . . . Who's this?"

"Digby, meet Talon. Talon, Digby. Dig, we've got to hurry. Nox is here. That's him they're cheering." She stood, and shoved the book and sandwiches into the saddlebags, heartsore at the loss of her crystals.

"Where's Pepper?" Digby said, leaping to his feet and rubbing his wrists.

"An' who in Mord's name is Pepper?" asked Talon.

"Digby's horse. Dig, I'm sorry, I had to leave her in an alley."

"Oh, no!" Digby hoisted the saddlebags over his shoulder. "Fat chance we have of findin' her in a place like this!"

"Yer prob'ly right," said Talon, "but let's go an' see. Show us where, Jemma."

With Noodle and Pie in her pockets, Jemma wove through

the muddy alleys, retracing the way she had come. Her mind burned with Pepper's image, calling to her—*Be there, girl!* But when they reached the corridor, the mare was nowhere to be seen.

"Mother of Majem!" Jemma said. "We've got to find her!"

"Got to leave 'er, more like," Talon said. "Can't waste time lookin'."

"But she's my family's livelihood!" Digby said. "Pa will never forgive me—"

"Dig," Jemma said, "it'll be worse for them if they stone you to death!"

A distant roar rose above the rooves.

"Listen," Talon said, "any minute, they'll be startin' to look for yer. You got to go—"

"But where?" Jemma said. "There's already spies and Inquisitors out there—you heard what Nox said!"

Talon frowned, then broke into a grin. "I know—come to my house! It's the last place anyone'll think of lookin'. Pa's never home, an' it'd never occur to 'im you'd be hidin' under our roof. Don't worry, Ma can't stand 'im any more'n I can. We both felt 'is fist a bit too often. 'Sides, she'd be dead chuffed to meet yer. So come on, let's be off!"

It was their best chance, Jemma and Digby agreed. Jemma pulled up her hood against the gathering rain, wiping more dribbles of purple from her face as they followed Talon back to the smaller square by the town gates. It was eerily deserted, all evidence of the earlier mayhem reduced to garbage and half-eaten skewers of burned meat strewn in the mud. Only the cages remained, stuffed with birds and rodents that sat like statues, awaiting their inevitable fate.

"We must free them!" Jemma ran to a pile of cages and

lifted the latches. A few animals darted out, but most sat gazing at the open doors as if restrained by some invisible chain.

"Come on, Jem." Digby pulled her away. "There's no time for that. You done what you could."

Talon was waiting by the gates. Her face fell as Jemma and Digby approached, and she pointed wildly at the main street. Jemma turned. A darkly cloaked rider was emerging through the Mist and galloping full tilt into the square, straight toward them. Digby and Talon grabbed her, hauled her through the gateway and pushed her into a watery ditch, throwing themselves and the saddlebags beside her. Her hood fell back, and she stayed still, praying that the rapidly approaching rider wouldn't glance to the side and see the girl with purple rain streaming down her face, and two golden rats on her shoulders. . . .

The hooves galloped closer, and closer, then passed by, and faded. Jemma looked up and saw Mephisto speeding away into the night, the black cloak of his master streaming behind like the tail of a dark comet.

CHAPTER TWENTY-SEVEN

The Final Hours

Mord-day, wee hours/dawn

They walked past the shacks in silence. There was no point avoiding the main road, Talon had said: Who would expect fugitives to be in plain view? In any case, nobody would dare suspect the Chief Inquisitor's daughter. She was right, it seemed. Several packs of youths rode by, laughing and yelling; then a few girls about Digby's age rattled past in an old cart, chattering wildly. Nobody stopped to question Talon or her companions, but Jemma kept her hood up, just in case.

Soon, the rain let up, and Jemma told Digby about Nox's speech, and how at nine the following morning—the last moment she could be Initiated by her true parents—the Agromonds would declare victory. He nodded, purse-lipped, looking strained under the weight of the saddlebags. She could tell he was still upset about Pepper, though he was trying not to show it, even pointing out that they'd have been more noticeable on horseback.

As they walked, the truth of her situation sank in. It was one thing to wonder whether her Powers would be gone if she wasn't Initiated, but knowing for sure was far worse. It was all over. Anglavia would never be free of the Agromonds and their Mist now. Gloom gnawed into her bones. She wished

Digby would say something. Didn't he realize how serious things were?

He knows. Pie crawled to Jemma's shoulder and nuzzled her ear. *Feels he let you down.*

Oh.

The shacks behind them, they came to the fork in the road, and trudged on. Another band of marauders rode by on ragged-looking ponies, jeering as they passed—at least ten or twelve of them, including two girls. A stench of stale beer trailed in their wake, turning Jemma's stomach.

"Wicked lot," Talon mumbled, wringing out her soaked skirt. "Good thing you're with me, or they'd attack yer jus' for the fun of it."

Digby shifted the saddlebags to his other shoulder. "How much farther, Talon?"

"Just up 'ere, then left by the yew tree." She sighed. "Home sweet bleedin' home."

"Why not leave?" Jemma asked, then immediately felt foolish. *It's not so easy,* she thought. *I should know.*

"Leave?" Talon said. "Wish I could. But Ma's sick. Nothin' infectious, mind," she added hurriedly, "jus' . . . well, sick in her spirit, is what I think. It's been years. She can't hardly move any more. Married to my pa, an' havin' six other bairns, each one of 'em dead before a year old, it's took its toll. I'm all she's got. So I in't goin' nowhere without her."

"Oh, Talon . . ." Jemma took Talon's hand, her own problems seeming to shrink slightly. "And to think you have to deal with Lok, as well."

Talon shrugged. "Don't see that much of 'im these days. Keeps 'im away, Ma bein' like she is. Somethin' to be thankful for, I s'pose. Look, here's the yew. This way."

She turned along a narrow path, which led through a grassy marsh. The three of them walked in single file, their footsteps falling into a rhythm. Jemma's cloak had already dried her, and she lent it to the others, who soon dried as well. Before long, the air began to stink of stagnant water, and tall reeds swayed in the breeze. Then, at the far edge of the marsh, a shack came into view. It was larger than most they'd seen—probably because of Lok's status—but just as run down. Its walls pitched in every direction, and looked as though they were being devoured by the black mold and toadstools clinging to them. A cow was tethered to a fence nearby and looked up lazily as they approached. ("She's called Horn," Talon said. "Another of Pa's stupid ideas, like my name, and Fang's.") The only other sign of anything faintly wholesome was the candlelight sputtering in one of the crooked windows.

"Won't your mother be asleep?" Jemma said, putting her cloak on again.

"Nah. She hardly ever sleeps. Her dreams is too scary. She jus' naps." Talon opened the door gently. "Ma, I'm home. I brought some friends. . . ."

"Friends?" a thin voice wheezed. "Bring 'em in, love. Make 'em some nettle tea."

Jemma and Digby followed Talon into the shack. The floors sloped, gaping with holes from which Jemma heard rustling and pattering footsteps. Mice and rats, probably. *Stay hidden,* she thought to Noodle and Pie. *They might not be very friendly around here.* Pie dropped from Jemma's shoulder and burrowed into her pocket next to Noodle.

In the corner, a woman lay under a heap of blankets, looking barely more than skin and bone. Talon walked over to her and squatted down. "Ma," she said, "you remember at the castle, the baby they took? The One we figured was from that ol' Prophecy?"

"Course I do," came the weak reply. "'Ow could I forget a thing like that? Poor l'il mite."

"Well, guess what? She's here! Jemma—she's here, Ma!" Talon beckoned to Jemma, who walked over and knelt beside her while Digby stoked the coals in the hob and poured some water into a pan.

Talon's mother looked at Jemma. "This can't be her, love. Her hair's too dark."

"She dyed it, to disguise herself, but look—there's a few bits as bright as flame, see? It's her, all right, Ma. Nox Agromond was in the square t'night, sayin' as she had to be found, an' now, folks is out huntin' for her. I said she could stay here, with her friend."

A wan smile spread over Talon's mother's face. "Any time," she murmured.

"Thank you, Mrs. . . ." Mrs. Lok? Jemma couldn't bring herself to call her that.

"Alyss. Call me Alyss." Alyss lay a damp hand on Jemma's, then closed her eyes. Instantly, Jemma sensed the blackness twining through the ailing woman. It resonated in her own body, sapping her strength, reminding her of the terrible Entity she'd experienced last Mord-day. It was as though threads of Scagavay's evil were here, in Alyss. Jemma pulled her hand away, imagining light inside her to ward off the darkness. No wonder Alyss's dreams kept her awake. Then a strange thought came to her, as if from somewhere outside her own head.

"Talon," she whispered. "I think your mother has been cursed."

"I *knew* it! This all started when Pa started workin' for

that Nox. The wretch! Poor Ma. . . . Is she jus' gonna keep fadin'?"

Not if I can help it, Jemma thought. "If only I had the crystals," she muttered. They had healed her, in Bryn's cave, and somehow, she knew that they could have helped now.

"Crystals?" Talon said. "What crystals?"

"Your dear pa took 'em." Digby said from over by the hob. "I watched him."

Talon dug into her pockets. "You mean these?" Two clear quartz cylinders lay in her palms.

"Talon . . . Yes! But how?"

"Told you I was watchin' the jail to see what I could thieve, din't I?" Talon blushed slightly. "When Pa an' Zeb rode away, I saw somethin' drop from Pa's pockets. Found these on the ground. Sort of smokin', they was. Sorry. Din't know they was yours."

Jemma took the crystals. As soon as she held them, energy crackled between them and her Stone, then jolted through her.

"Alyss," she said, "do you mind if I try something to help you? I can't promise anything, but . . ." Alyss nodded, her eyes still closed, and Jemma settled herself cross-legged on the floor, wondering what on earth she was about to do. But if her Powers were going to drain as Nox said, then this might be her last chance to bring about some good, and at that moment, nothing felt more important. Especially if it could erase an act of Agromond evil. "Dig, would you pass me the book?"

Digby pulled the book from the saddlebags and handed it to her. She placed it on the floor between her and the mattress, took a deep breath, and improvised an invocation.

"Calling on Majem," she said, "and all my healer ancestors, to come and help this woman." Noodle and Pie crept from her pockets, and sat on the book. "Trust," she whispered, imagining Drudge by her side, as well as Bryn, with his simple, earthy goodness. Then she thought of her parents. *You too*, she murmured, as she slipped the crystals into Alyss's upturned palms. *If you can* . . . Alyss drew in a sharp breath and winced.

What happened next, Jemma couldn't have anticipated. A pale stream of smoky light began curling up from the book, surrounding the rats, and enveloping her. Then a clear, airy force seemed to take her over, flowing through the top of her head and pulling her into a kind of trance, guiding her movements. Her hands danced above Alyss's torso, fingers unwinding what appeared to be thick, tarry strands of blackness from Alyss's bones and sinews. A story unwound with them, filling the room with a flow of images—or were they in Jemma's head? Alyss at the castle, daring to defend five-year-old Feo from Nocturna's cruel tongue after he'd wet his bed again . . . Lok's rage about their ensuing banishment, and hers toward him, for taking it out on two-year-old Talon . . . Talon, bruised and crying . . . Lok swearing loyalty to Nox . . . A contract being signed in blood between the two men, followed by Lok being given his black Inquisitor's coat . . . Then Alyss's first collapse in the small garden she tended outside their Blackwater shack, and the six more babies she bore to Lok, every one sickly, buried before its first birthday. Each image burst like a bubble, scattering fragments that turned into gold light and drifted back into Alyss as though she were transparent, filling the spaces that the darkness had occupied. And all the while, the crystals

sparkled with luminous blue, like lightning across two minia-
ture night skies, as Noodle and Pie sat stock-still, watching.

The smoky light shrank as if it were being sucked back
into the book. It hovered for a moment around the rats, then
disappeared. The images stopped, and Jemma's mind snapped
back into the room. She was exhausted. The crystals' glow in
Alyss's palms began to fade.

"Jem!" Digby's amazed voice came from behind her.
"What the . . . ?"

"Look at Ma!" Talon said. "She's sleepin' like a babe! I
don't know what you done, Jemma, but you done somethin'.
Her breathin's easier too."

Jemma was vaguely aware that the soreness on her own
back from Fang's scratches had subsided as well. She mumbled
thanks to whatever or whoever had guided her, then crumpled onto the floor next to Alyss. The image of a face—her
mother's—floated from one of the crystals and hung in the
air. Another, a man's, hovered beside it. Her father? It wasn't
clear, just a dark blur.

The faces diffused, and she fell into a deep sleep.

*A cord of light pulled her toward a man. Behind him, a small
town appeared, walled, on a hill. The man became clearer—the
one from her dream last week, cloaked, coming for her through
the Mist! She tried to scream, and resisted with all her might,
but the cord of light kept pulling, pulling. . . . Then she saw his
face. It was Nox Agromond—she was being pulled toward Nox
Agromond! "You have the Power to call her back," he said. "The
mare. Call her back!" Who, Pepper? Why, why was he telling her
this, him of all people?*

245

＊ ＊ ＊

Jemma woke, terrified. Noodle and Pie were sitting in front
of her face, their ruby eyes blinking at her in the gray dawn
light.

Another dream?

Yes, another dream, and she didn't want to think of it.
She sat up and looked around. Alyss, on the mattress, was
still sleeping peacefully, with Talon beside her. Over by the
hob, Digby was snoring on the floor, the saddlebags under his
head as a pillow.

Last night's events rolled through Jemma's head: her hunt
for Digby, the rally, Nox's words. . . . A dull ache spread across
her chest. What time was it? About six, judging by the light.
Three more hours to go. Then they would stop looking for
her. She'd be safe. But Powerless.

Even if Pepper was to turn up at that very moment, it was
too late to reach Oakstead in time. And anyway, far too dangerous, with people out hunting for her.

Call her back. Noodle nudged Jemma's hand with his
snout. *The horse. Call her back.*

"Are you reading my dreams now, Rattus?" Jemma whispered. *Call her back.* . . . Well, she may as well try. Closing
her eyes, she thought of Pepper's velvety muzzle, her brown
eyes, her dappled coat—every detail she could. *Pepper,* she
called in her head, picturing the route they'd taken from
Blackwater. *Come on, girl. Past the fork. Left at the yew . . .*
She crawled to the window to look outside. Nothing but Mist,
of course. She crawled back to the rats and nestled with them
under her mud-caked cloak. What was it going to feel like to
lose her connection with it, and the book and the crystals?

Would she no longer be able to hear Noodle and Pie either? The thought was unbearable. It was all unbearable. Even the prospect of meeting her real parents did nothing to lighten her mood. Anglavia was doomed. And she would be nothing but a laughing-stock for the Agromonds and their followers to crow about, just as Nox had said.

Jemma opened one eye. The mattress next to her was empty.

"Hey, Jem." Digby was squatting next to her. Behind him, Talon was sitting at a small table, Alyss opposite her, both tucking into something and finger feeding morsels of it to Noodle and Pie, who were perched one at each bowl.

"What time is it?" Jemma's voice rasped. Her heart felt as heavy as an anvil.

"Around noon. We thought we'd let you sleep. Here, I'll help you up." He held out his hand and pulled her to her feet. "There's some nice bread an' milk. You must be hungry."

Hungry? She ought to be; she'd hardly eaten a thing for almost a day. But she had no appetite. The world had changed. All her dreams, come to nothing. She slumped onto an up-turned pail at the table.

Alyss took her hand. Her fingers were skeletal, but this morning, energy bristled through them. "I can't thank you enough, child," she said. "I been out of bed for more'n an hour. It's at least two years since I was strong enough to do that."

Jemma tried to smile.

"Jem," said Digby, putting a bowl of milk-soaked bread in front of her. "I know this is hard on you. Your Powers gone, an' all. But life don't end here. Your folks is waitin' for you in Oakstead. Marsh too. You still got family. An' me."

"Us too," added Talon. "Me an' Ma, we're gonna leave Blackwater as soon as she's strong enough, in't we, Ma? You done that, Jemma. You healed 'er. You changed our lives."

Jemma nodded and picked up a piece of the soaking bread. It smelled nice and stale, and she nibbled at it, hunger inching into her. "Any sign of hunters?" she said.

"No," said Talon, shaking her head. "I heard yellin' earlier, though. Hollerin' like lunatics they was. Sayin'—" She clamped her lips together.

"Saying what?"

"Victory." Talon whispered. "Sorry, Jemma. I should've kept me trap shut."

"Victory." Jemma sighed. "It doesn't matter. It's the truth; I may as well face it. At least Digby and I can go to Oakstead now, with nobody to stop us. How long do you reckon, Dig, to get there on foot?"

"On foot?" Digby's face lit up. "We in't goin' on foot, Jem! While you was asleep— Well, come an' see!" He jumped to his feet, pulled Jemma to the door, and threw it open. "Look who turned up a couple of hours ago!"

Pepper lifted her head from a patch of chickweed, tossed her mane, and snorted.

"Don't know how she found us, but find us she did. All ready to go, she is."

Hope dribbled into Jemma's veins. The last acts of her short-lived Powers were here in front of her eyes: Alyss's recovery and Pepper's return. At least that was something.

"Well then," she said. "Oakstead, here we come."

Before long, she and Digby had packed up their few belongings, filled her wineskin with milk, and were back in

Pepper's saddle, having made Talon and Alyss promise that they'd come to Oakstead as soon as Alyss was strong enough to travel.

"Thanks again for savin' Ma," Talon said, patting Pepper's shoulder. "I'm awful sorry 'bout you losin' yer Powers, though. Here, let's make a friends' knot. Like this . . ." She reached for Jemma's hand and interlocked their fingers. "Now, say, 'Friends forever, friends forever—'" She stopped, her eyes widening. "Well, grisly goblins . . . Look—around yer hands!"

Jemma looked. The air around them was still free of Mist—even though her Initiation time had passed.

"Cor, yes," said Digby, peering over Jemma's shoulder. "It's still clear around 'em!"

"What d'you s'pose it means?" Talon said.

"I'm not sure," Jemma said, her spirits lifting, "but I think it might be a good thing."

Digby kicked Pepper into a gentle canter. Jemma looked over her shoulder and waved at her new friends until they were no longer visible in the midday Mist, then turned her gaze forward. Nine o'clock was long gone; yet around her hands, every strand of Pepper's mane was crystal clear. Perhaps she had not lost her Powers after all, back there among the couch grass and reeds.

CHAPTER TWENTY-EIGHT

Light Games

Jemma wrapped her cloak around her and leaned against Digby to give him some of its warmth. Soon after leaving Talon and Alyss, they'd been deluged by rain that had washed the remaining berry dye from her hair before she'd had a chance to cover it. Now, a steady drizzle was falling. Noodle and Pie burrowed into her pockets, and Pepper's initial zest after leaving the shack was replaced by a solid, soggy stomp. But despite the cold and damp, she felt content. Every muddy hoofstep was bringing them closer to Oakstead and meeting her parents. And rain or not, being close to Digby was not such a bad place to be.

"Your hair's red again, Jem," Digby said, stretching. "All but a few bits. Hey, look down there in the valley—you can just see the river. This must be the Elm River Pass."

Jemma wiped her face dry with her cloak and looked at the faint ribbon of water below. "We couldn't have seen anything from so far away, yesterday. The Mist is definitely getting thinner."

"Mmm. But not much. An' Marsh said that by an hour north of Blackwater, it'd be nothin' more'n a wisp. Which means it's spread quite a bit since she last came this way, twelve years ago."

Jemma gripped Pepper's mane. The Agromond evil was

everywhere, even this far from the castle. Well, if the clearing around her hands meant anything, and Nox had been wrong about her losing her Powers, then she would show them, somehow! Them, and their accursed Mist—

"Jem!" Digby gasped. "What's happenin'?"

A bubble of clear air shot out to several yards beyond Pepper's ears. Within it, every raindrop and blade of grass was sharply visible.

"I didn't do that, did I?" Jemma said. The Mist sprang in, engulfing them again.

"You tell me!" Digby sat up straighter. "Try it again, an' let's see."

Jemma focused, and prayed, and muttered under her breath—*Mist, be gone!* Nothing happened. She held her Stone, and the Mist rolled a few inches up Pepper's neck, then swirled into the space again. "Sorry, Dig," Jemma said. "It must've been a coincidence." Her momentary hope deflated like an overcooked soufflé. Nox must have been right, after all. It probably just took time until her Powers drained completely. And besides, merely having a halo around her hands wasn't much use to anyone, and certainly couldn't bring down an empire.

Digby walked Pepper at a steady clip. They'd seen no sign of Inquisitors, and had passed barely a soul; the moorlands were almost devoid of any shack or cottage. Mid-afternoon, the road turned west, and Jemma spotted two shadowy figures lurking between the trees, then slinking away. Digby and the rats tucked into the rest of the previous day's sandwiches as they rode, but all Jemma could manage was a few swigs of milk. The closer they came to Oakstead, the faster her heart beat in anticipation of meeting her parents, and the harder her stomach churned. Eight miles to go, Digby said. Then seven. Then six—

"Stand an' deliver!" The gang was upon them before Jemma or Digby realized it, lashing their ponies into attack from behind the trees, screeching with gleeful triumph, and wielding whips and knotted ropes.

"Get 'em!" A boy pulled alongside—the ringleader, Jemma guessed. His face was scarred, his nose pierced with a small bone. The others moved closer, the alcoholic stench of their breath filling the air. With a start, Jemma realized who they were: the last herd to careen past them last night on the road from Blackwater—the ones Talon said would attack just for sport.

One of the girls reached for the saddlebags. "Let's see wot they got 'ere!"

"No you don't!" Jemma slapped the girl's hand away. The ringleader reached out and grabbed Jemma's arm, leering at her with a rotten-toothed grin.

"An' who are *you* to be tellin' *her* what to do?"

"Careful, Jem," Digby hissed into Jemma's ear. "Pretend to be a boy—"

"Let us go!" Jemma jerked her arm away. "We've got nothing—"

"Yeh, but *we* got *you*!" The girl fingered Jemma's cloak. "Nice . . ."

"Leave it *alone*!" Jemma tugged the cloak away.

"Wait a minute, wait a minute!" The ringleader held up his hand, quieting the others, then looked Jemma up and down. "Them eyes," he said, "an' the purple all over yer ugly mug—" He darted out his hand and yanked her hood back. A slow smile oozed across his face. "Well, well . . . looky here! If it in't that girl wot Nox Agromond is wantin' . . . she in't a boy at all!"

The girl laughed. "Yer right, Rizzle. Jus' like that Approjection las' night!"

Jemma felt Noodle and Pie tensing in her pockets, and willed them to lie low. If they tried to help, they'd be dead in seconds. "You heard what Nox said," she croaked, trying to quell the tremble in her voice. "I'm no use to him now. My Powers have gone. Don't you remember?"

Rizzle glared at her, then clasped a clump of her hair.

"Hands off her!" Digby kicked him, and made a grab for him.

"Digby, don't!" Jemma screamed as a rope slammed down on Digby's shoulder. Several more hands restrained him.

"Well, Little Miss Betrayer," Rizzle said, pulling Jemma's head back, "'ow's it feel to be without yer Powers? An' don't you look a sight, nothin' more'n a grubby little red hedgehog!" His cronies cackled and jeered. Then his expression hardened and he shoved his face up to hers. "An' jus' for the record," he sneered, "I don't give a rat's crap what Nox Agromond said. You done us *all* wrong, thinkin' you could beat us. We're gonna make yer pay! Whad'you say, gang? Should we take 'er, or should we do as she asks, since she asks so *nice*-like, an' let 'er go?"

"Take 'er! Take 'er!"

"No!" Jemma grasped at her Stone, but hands grabbed her from either side, pulling in both directions. As she struggled to stay in the saddle, the saddlebags were whipped off Pepper's haunches. Digby was dragged to the ground. Several of the gang leapt from their ponies and pummeled him with their fists, yelling "Get 'im! Get 'im!" Jemma wriggled and bit, as Pepper, panicked, pounded her hooves perilously close to Digby. He was lashing out in fury, but was no match for the four boys pinning him down.

"Stop!" Jemma yelled, trying to pull from their grasp. "Don't hurt him! No—STOP!"

A tide of determination swept through her. Suddenly, her mind seemed to leap outward in all directions at once. The Mist shot back, creating a large, clear sphere around them all. Light poured into it—light so bright that it obliterated everything in Jemma's vision: the gang, the horses, even Digby. She heard voices, yelling—"*Where'd she go?*" "*I can't see nothin'!*" "*Rizzle, where is you?*" "*Help!*"—followed by screams, and shrieks of terror—"*Ow, somethin' burned me!*" "*It's comin' fer us—run!*" "*She's a witch—Ruuuun!*"—then frantic whinnying, and stamping hooves. . . . With a final burst of light, the sphere collapsed, and the band of attackers galloped pell-mell into the darkening Mist.

"Digby!" Jemma jumped off Pepper. Digby lay on his back, groaning, with the saddlebags next to him. The crystals had been thrown out of them and lay in the mud nearby, smoldering. She picked them up and pressed them into his palms.

"I'm all right." He winced, and closed his eyes tight. "Jus' give me a mo' . . ."

All right? Jemma bit her lips. His hands and face were covered in scratches, a bump rising up on his cheek. She imagined Light pulsing from her heart into his. Noodle and Pie nosed out of her pockets and sat on his chest.

Digby opened one eye. "I really *am* all right, Jem. Honest." He grinned. "Gave them thugs quite a turn, you did."

"Why, what happened? All I remember is wanting to stop them beating you. Everything else was a blur."

"Well, you . . . you jus' sort of burst into flames, Jem. Only it wasn't flames. It was light. You burst into light, Jem."

"I *did*?" She'd never realized the Light Game could be so powerful. "Burst into light . . ."

"Yup. A bit like las' night, when you was helpin' Alyss." He let go of her hands and heaved himself up to sit, causing Noodle and Pie to roll onto his lap. Then he looked at his fists. He was still holding the crystals. "Well, rotten rhubarb! Look, Jem—my hands!"

His scratches had already healed over.

"The crystals did that," said Jemma. "They healed me too, in the forest. They probably helped make the light too, just then."

Digby looked at the crystals, then at her. "Maybe that was true last night. But they was nowhere near where that ball of light started, Jem. That was *you*. You realize what this means?" He looked at her squarely. "I reckon you ain't lost your Powers after all. I'd stake my life on it."

The harsh moorlands gave way to gentler, rolling hills. The drizzle had stopped soon after the attack, and now the milky orb of sun dipped behind the treetops.

Noodle and Pie lay between Pepper's ears, peering into the distance. Jemma gazed over their heads into the graying twilight, wondering for the hundredth time about her parents. Would they be like the heroes and heroines in Marsh's tales, bold and fearless? Magical, mysterious? Her mother had looked beautiful in the crystal. But what did her father look like? He'd only been a vague image. Why hadn't she been able to see him? Perhaps showing themselves took effort, more than he could muster, for some reason. For example, what if he was still weak, even after twelve years? Whatever the case, it wouldn't matter to her. She just wanted to meet them.

"Jem, listen . . . D'you hear that?"

Hooves thundered toward them. Jemma's heart lifted. Someone was coming to meet her! She strained to see as a pony emerged from the Mist. Its rider was short, one arm raised in a welcoming gesture, an arm with a bandaged stump where a hand should be—

"Marsh!" Jemma vaulted to the ground and pelted toward her. "Marsh! Marsh!"

"Jem! My precious pet!" Marsh swung from the saddle and folded Jemma into a bear hug. "Thank goodness—you're here! You're really here—safe, at last!"

"Marsh, Marsh—it's so good to see you!" Overjoyed as Jemma was, she peered over Marsh's shoulder into the Mist. No one else was there. Disappointment flared through her. But Marsh was here, holding her, just as she'd held her during all those years at the castle.

"Jem, my Jem . . ." Marsh swayed her from side to side, humming gently, then pulled away and held her at arm's length. "Let me look at you. Oh, my, your hair! It's all gone! An' your face—it's all streaky an' purple! Well, that's some disguise, pet, I must say!"

"It was Digby's idea. He's been amazing, Marsh. I'd never have managed without him." Jemma took a breath, plucking up the courage to ask about her parents. "Marsh, where are—"

"Digby, lad!" Marsh said as Digby pulled up beside them. "Thank you for bringin' her!"

"Told you I would," he said, grinning.

"An' look—them rats of yours, Jem, perched on Pepper's head! I never was gladder to see a rodent, I don't mind tellin' you." Marsh's gaze softened. "I can't tell you how we been hopin' an' prayin', your folks an' me," she said. "Then, just a short while ago, your ma had this feelin' in her bones, an' she says to me, 'Ida,' she says—"

"Ida? That's your real name? Ida Sharm . . . That's going to take some getting used to!"

"I'll always be Marsh to you, Jem. Long as you want. Anyway, your ma says she just had a Vision—a Vision, Jem, her first full one in twelve years! She saw you in a great ball of Light, an' knew you was near. Sent me to come an' meet you—oh, she wanted to come herself so bad, but she couldn't—the Mist still holds her back. So here I am. But hush my mouth! We mustn't waste time gabbin'—plenty of time for that! Your ma's waitin' back at the inn. She's been *livin'* to meet you!"

"And . . . and my father?"

"Of course—he's there too. But . . ." Marsh's eyes clouded. "Thing is, Jem, there's somethin' you need to know about your pa before you meet him. Your ma will tell you, though."

So I was right, Jemma thought. *He's still weak. That must be why he was just a blur.* "It's all right, Marsh," she said. "I know. I have these two crystals and saw, in one of them—"

"You saw *him*—your *pa?*" Marsh looked shocked, then

puzzled. "He didn't want you to, not till your ma had warned you—but . . . well . . . that's good, good! No nasty surprises, then. Come on, let's be off. Your ma's orderin' the inn's finest fare. Looks like you two could use it!"

She jumped onto her pony, and Digby pulled Jemma back into the saddle. Noodle and Pie clambered down Pepper's neck and hopped into Jemma's lap.

"Marsh. Your hand," said Jemma. "I'm so sorry."

"Ah, Jem. Reckon you an' me knows a thing or two about that forest, don't we?" Marsh's expression darkened for a moment, then she smiled. "But here we both is, alive an' well. An' as for this"—she waved her bandaged stump—"long as I can still ride, an' shoo away the odd sprite or two, I'll be fine. Now, let's get goin', eh? It's gettin' dark an' chilly out here. Giddyap, Flashwing—back to Oakstead!" Holding the reins in one hand, she kicked her pony and took off into the Mist. It was all Pepper could do to keep up.

They galloped past sweeping fields, where cattle and ponies were grazing, and soon Oakstead loomed into view. Jemma instantly recognized it: the small town on a hill that she had dreamed of just last night. She remembered the cord of light she'd felt pulling her, and the man it was attached to. Nox. Her stomach clenched. *It was just a dream*, she reminded herself.

Marsh pulled up outside the gates. "Your family's stronghold, pet," she said. "Centuries of Solvays have lived within these walls. Them, and their followers. Full o' good folk, it is, wot have kept it protected these past twelve years. Not with arrows and cannons, mind," she added, registering Jemma's surprise. "They create a sort of force around it, like a shield.

You won't find a bad soul within a league of here nowadays, you mark my words."

They rode side by side through the arched entrance and continued slowly across the town square. It was bordered by half-timbered houses with worn whitewash and cracked windows, their rooves sagging as if under an invisible burden. Candlelight flickered from behind drawn curtains. Along the pavements, wooden poles held lanterns—mostly unlit—and in the center of the square was a circular pool of dark water. A stone clock tower stood on one side of it, the clock's pale face barely visible through the dusky Mist.

"Used to be grander, all this." said Marsh. "The fountain hasn't worked in years. An' the clock stopped the instant they took you, Jem. In mid-chime, so it's said. Six-thirty on the dot."

Both hands were pointing downward as if frozen in perpetual defeat.

"Yep," Marsh murmured. "It's like time's stood still here." *While for the Agromonds,* Jemma thought, *it's kept booming out from the Bell Tower like a death knell.*

"Marsh," she said, steeling herself to ask the question she'd pushed back from her mind. "My brother . . . They never found him, did they?"

"No, pet, they didn't. I'm sorry."

They rode in silence toward an inn at the far end of the square. It was a larger building than the rest, with broken stone steps leading up to its entrance. Above the doorway, haloed by a large lantern, swung a sign: THE HEATHSHIRE ARMS. As they approached, Marsh leaned over and nudged Jemma with her stump. "You ready for this, love?"

Jemma bit her bottom lip and nodded. Her heart felt as though it was stuck in her throat.

"Good luck," Digby whispered.

Every nerve and fiber of Jemma's body jangled. In a ground-floor window, a curtain pulled back, and a face pressed against the glass. The curtain fell; a shadow hastened out of view. The inn's door opened, and a woman stood silhouetted against the warm light inside. She swayed slightly and clutched the door frame, her flowing robe billowing in the breeze like a silken flag. A flag of hope. Of triumph.

"Jemma," she said, her blue eyes piercing the twilight. "My child . . ."

"Mother," Jemma whispered. The air between them seemed to spark into life, throwing golden beams around the square, and all at once Sapphire Solvay was running down the steps and Jemma was on the ground, speeding toward her mother's outstretched arms, arms that enfolded her as if they would never let go, as if they never had.

At last, she was home.

CHAPTER TWENTY-NINE

The Clock

The murmur around the low-beamed dining room fell as Jemma, her mother, Marsh, and Digby entered. Beer tankards were placed onto tabletops, cutlery onto plates. Men and women with their youngsters nodded a greeting at Sapphire, then fixed their eyes on Jemma, whispering as she passed— *"It's her! Look . . . her hair!"*—then nudging each other and digging back into their dinners as if to stuff down the impulse to gossip.

Jemma's mother walked to a far corner of the room, seeming to float through the smoke and lamplight. She was slight, like Jemma, yet she commanded attention, as if a core of fire ran through her. She ushered Jemma into an alcove and slid in beside her. Digby and Marsh sat at the other side of the table. Jemma was glad they were there. The emotional moments of reunion over, she felt a little shy, and in awe of this longed-for stranger next to her.

Sapphire took Jemma's hands, her eyes almost luminous as they searched her face. "My darling child," she said. "Ida— Marsh—has told us so much about you during these past few days. And now I see for myself how strong your spirit is, and how full of Light and color. How I've longed for this moment, hoping and praying for your safe return. And at last, here you are!"

Jemma looked at the suffering etched on her mother's face, and the silver mane of hair cascading over her shoulders. "I've longed for it too," she said, her awkwardness ebbing slightly. "I used to hear your voice in my dreams, singing, only I didn't know it was you."

"How were you to know I even existed? Those monsters! I can hardly bear to think of what you've been through, living with them."

"What *I've* been through? What about you and Father? Losing me, so soon after my bro—" Jemma clamped her lips shut.

"Ah." Her mother drew out a long breath. "So you know about him. You found the articles Ida left hidden for you in the book, then, and read about his . . . his disappearance?"

Jemma nodded, noticing flecks of gray flit across her mother's eyes. Stupid, stupid! Why did she have to go and mention something so painful, so soon?

"Don't feel badly, Jemma." Sapphire said. "It's normal that you'd be curious about him. We shall tell you all, in due course. But . . . not today, all right?" She smiled, and squeezed Jemma's hands. "How much of the book did you read?"

"Just bits and pieces," Jemma said, surprised at how her guilt lifted under her mother's touch, and how rapidly her shyness was passing. "It helped me a lot, though. It gave me clues when I asked it questions, like Marsh said it would. It kept me warm and dry. Oh, and I also realized that Majem is my ancestor, and that her name and mine are anagrams. I feel such a connection to her, somehow—more than just our names and being related, I mean."

"Those anagrams are no accident, Jemma. They are

sacred, giving power to your very name. But there's another reason you would feel the connection with Majem. Your Stone came from her."

"Really?" Jemma felt the Stone's mysterious Power fluttering through her.

Her mother nodded. "We shall talk more of all this another time. But now, let us sup! Digby looks as though he could eat a horse."

"Oh no, ma'am," said Digby, looking shocked, "I'd never do that."

"It's just an expression," Marsh whispered to him. Digby's face turned red.

"Well, horse or not, Digby," said Sapphire, "I trust you will eat well after your long journey. I can't thank you enough for bringing our daughter home! What a friend you are to her."

"An' she is to me," he said, reddening more.

Sapphire let go of Jemma's hands, then turned toward the back of the room and beckoned to a stout, balding man. "Pedrus! We're ready when you are, please!"

"Isn't Father going to join us?"

"Your father? He's . . . a little weary, and before you meet him, I need to warn you—"

"She knows, Sapphire," said Marsh softly. "She saw, in the crystal."

"What? After all his efforts—how could that be? Jemma, were you not alarmed?"

"Alarmed?" Jemma said, wondering why she should have been. Was her father weaker than she'd imagined? Unwell, even? "No, I wasn't. But—"

"What a wonder! He went to great pains to conceal

himself. That is why he's so weary now. But by tomorrow, I am sure he will have recovered. Then you will meet him."

Jemma's mind whirled. Her father was tired—that was all? Then why had her mother and Marsh been so afraid that she'd be alarmed by seeing him? She was about to ask, when two girls appeared carrying bowls, spoons, and bread, and a flagon of water with four tumblers, all of which they hastily placed around the table while stealing curious glances at Jemma.

"Grub's up!" Pedrus walked up behind them, plunked down a pot, and lifted the lid. A meaty puff of steam wafted up. "Special stew, for a special day!"

"Thank you," said Jemma. The stew smelled delicious, even though she couldn't detect any spleen or pancreas in it.

"Yer most welcome," he said. "It's good to 'ave you back, lass. Come along now, Bethany, Moll. Let's leave 'em be." Pedrus walked away, the two girls scuttling off behind him. His daughters, Jemma guessed. They looked just like him.

As Marsh ladeled out the stew, Noodle and Pie clambered out of Jemma's pockets and onto the table. They perched by the pot, snouts twitching.

"Mother of Majem!" Sapphire exclaimed. "Rats!"

"Oh, dear . . . I . . ." Jemma felt herself blush. "Um . . ."

Sapphire smiled. "You must be Noodle and Pie. Ida's told me about you two, with your lovely golden coats." She stroked them under the chin, and they fluffed with pride.

As they all tucked in, Jemma fielded a barrage of questions from her mother and Marsh about the perils she'd faced at the castle after Marsh's banishment. The revelation that Drudge was not only an ally, but also had visionary and healing powers, surprised them all. Marsh had realized that he was not who he pretended to be last Mord-day in the Vat Room—but why, if he had the Sight, had he not seen through her own subterfuge? Then Marsh pondered ruefully that perhaps he had, but, like Jemma, her disgust of him had blinded *her* to *his* true being. Digby reassured her that he'd never have guessed either, and what was more, the Agromonds obviously didn't know, so for whatever reason, the old fellow was doing a good job of hiding who he really was.

"I wonder whether he knows I've arrived here," Jemma said, suddenly sad about him. "I wish he wasn't stuck in that awful place. When did he first go there, anyway, and why did he stay? All *they* ever said about him was that he'd served 'generations of Agromonds,' or something pompous like that. He does look ancient, though—at least a hundred."

"A hundred?" said Digby, mopping his bowl with a chunk of bread. "More like two!"

"We may never know about him," said Sapphire. "Some mysteries remain mysteries."

"I wish I'd realized about him sooner, though," Jemma said.

Second helpings of Pedrus's stew took them through the horrors that Jemma and Marsh had endured in the forest. Marsh told them of the terrible loss of her hand, which she'd cut off herself and tossed at the Aukron to divert it—to no avail, it turned out, since the Aukron had kept pursuing her anyway, until she eventually managed to stun it with Light. Listening to Marsh's trials tore at Jemma's heart and brought back the shadows of her own ordeal. They ebbed slightly in the telling, and in the healing warmth she felt from her mother. Thank goodness for Bryn and the crystals, Sapphire said, and for Majem's cloak, book, and Stone—and of course, the rats and Digby. They had all played a vital part in Jemma getting out of Agromond Forest alive.

"But without you, Mother," Jemma said, "I don't know if I'd have made it through the snowstorm that night. You saved me."

"We helped, it's true. But *you* saved *us*, Jemma."

"What do you mean?" Jemma bit into a chunk of meat. "How?"

"By taking those crystals that night. You released us. You see, it's an ancient sorcerer's spell to capture a part of an enemy's soul and seal it in clear crystal, which they then submerge in a tincture of *aqua furva*—a very dark substance—to keep it hidden. The Agromonds did this to us shortly after they took you, while we were weakened by grief. Otherwise, they would never have been able to manage it. We guessed what had happened when our healing abilities vanished, and we felt so utterly drained. The Mist's effect on us worsened too, so that we could barely venture beyond the gates of Oakstead. Worst of all, with our Vision clouded, we were unable to See you for all that time. Twelve years . . ." She shook her head. "We have been a fine laughing-stock for the Agromonds and their followers—more so than if we had been dead."

"That's what Nox said he wanted me to be too," Jemma said with a shudder. "So why didn't you ask Marsh to look for the crystals when she arrived at the castle?"

"Why, Jem," Marsh said, "even if I'd found 'em, them Agromonds would've seen they'd gone in no time, an' who but me would be guilty of takin' 'em, eh? They'd have had my guts for garters, an' then where would you have been for all them years, with nobody to help you when the time came? Not that I did much," she added, "in the end."

"I'd have been lost without you, though." Jemma smiled at Marsh, thinking of all that Marsh had risked. For her. For her parents. Eleven years of her life gone in that bleak place.

"I wouldn't 'ave had it any other way, pet," Marsh said.

"It's true though, Ida," said Sapphire. "We owe everything to you."

"And all that time," Jemma said to her mother, "the crystals held a part of your spirit? That's terrible!"

"Yes. Until, shortly after midnight on your birthday, I felt a jolt of awakening, like quicksilver running through my very being. Your father felt it too. We knew there could be only one cause: somebody—you—had removed the crystals from the liquid. We immediately tried to communicate with you through them, but could not; the Mist still prevented us from Seeing. But little by little, our Powers began returning, and on Thursday, we felt a pull on our energy—you, being healed in Bryn's cave, no doubt—and from then on, whenever you connected with the crystals, we were able to see you, and guide you when you asked." Sapphire took a sip of water.

"Like when Lok took them with Digby into Blackwater," Jemma said. "I saw their blue light, and could follow them."

"Rotten rhubarb!" Digby gulped. "I din't realize that's how you an' them crystals found me."

"Indeed," said Sapphire, "we sensed the danger. But finally, when I felt you call upon my help with a healing in the early hours of this morning, Jemma . . . well, what a relief!"

"That was Alyss—a woman we met. Thank you for helping, Mother."

"Oh, but I did nothing, Jemma! I merely glimpsed a few

images of what was happening, and tried to visualize a good outcome for her. It was you who did the healing."

"It was amazin' to watch," said Digby. "Them's some Powers you got, Jem!"

Or had, Jemma thought. Her nerves rankled. Hearing first-hand about her parents' suffering, the idea of the Agromonds' victory began gnawing at her again. If only she and Digby had arrived in time for her Initiation, she could have sought justice, revenge—

"Do not concern yourself with your Initiation, Jemma," Sapphire said. "You will see—"

"How did you know what I was thinking?"

"When your thoughts are loud, I can hear them. Perhaps you will develop that gift someday, as well as any others that I, or your father, possess."

"But how?" Jemma thumped her fist on the table. "I missed my Initiation! There's nothing to stop the Agromonds now. They'll get away with everything they've done—to you, to me, to all of Anglavia. They've won!"

"Jemma, they have not won!" Sapphire said. "For one thing, they no longer have you, and . . . well, there is more to it, but . . ." She wrung her hands, her eyes flecking with gray again.

"Try to let it go for now, Jem," said Marsh, patting her hand. "Things'll look better in a day or two, I promise. Jus' give your ma time to explain why."

"Anyways, Jem," Digby chimed in, "like I said, I don't think your Powers is gone at all. I told you, after you scared them hooligans off earlier—"

"*I* didn't scare them, Dig. That was the Light Game. All I did was think of it."

"An' d'you s'pose if I'd thought of it, the same thing would've happened?"

"I don't know." Jemma crossed her arms and slumped into the bench. The talk in the room fell to a hum, then to silence, as if everyone had been infected by her growing gloom. The truth was undeniable: she, their only hope, had failed them.

Noodle and Pie stopped eating, and looked at her with their heads cocked.

Don't give up. Wait. You'll see.

Just then, through the stillness, a single chime, silvery but insistent, rang from the square outside. It reverberated from wall to wall, between the beams, the cubicles. The room froze. Then slouching bodies pulled themselves upright, faces turning to one another, and then to Jemma. Her mother's and Marsh's eyes widened. Noodle and Pie scampered onto Jemma's shoulders. Digby looked as puzzled as she felt.

"The clock!" Sapphire said. "It's started again! Twelve years to the day—to the minute!"

Marsh was the first to leave her seat. She bustled to the window and pulled back the curtain. "Majem be praised!" she said. "It's true—the minute hand is at six thirty-one!"

A murmur started from table to table, then chatter broke out, echoing Sapphire's words: "The clock! Twelve years to the day—to the hour—to the very minute!"

"Six thirty-one!" Pedrus shouted. "Look—six thirty-one!"

All around the room, people leapt to their feet and tumbled out of the door shouting, "Look—six thirty-two, six thirty-two!"

"Come," said Sapphire, "let's all go and see." She took Jemma's hand and led her outside. Marsh and Digby followed, and the four of them stood facing the square. From every house, men, women, and children emerged carrying lamps and candles and staring in wonder as the clock's minute hand ticked forward to the next moment. Their murmurs grew, and as the minute hand clicked to six thirty-four, hundreds of voices raised in a cheer.

Then one voice rose above the rest: "The Fire One—look, the Fire One has returned!"

A hush fell over the crowd. Everyone turned to where Jemma stood flanked by her mother and Marsh. Hope emanated from every one of them—hope that flared in her too. Her entire body buzzed as an image flooded her mind: Anglavia, bathed in sunlight, free of Mist and starvation—free of Agromond oppression! There was nothing she wanted more, and it felt wildly, insanely possible. Initiation or not.

All at once, energy surged through her like water released from a dam, breaking out of every pore of her skin and across the square. She reeled backward with the force of it, sending Noodle and Pie flying from her shoulders. Digby grabbed her arms to steady her.

The crowd gasped. The entire square was clear of Mist.

"Mother of Majem!" whispered Marsh.

Sapphire's mouth hung open. "Jemma," she said. "What did you do?"

Jemma gulped. "I just thought . . . about freeing Anglavia from the Mist. From *them* . . . "

"See?" said Digby. "Jus' like earlier with that amazin' Light! An' all you did was *think* it?"

Across the square, shouts of "Bless you, Jemma!" started rising into the clear twilight air. The Mist hung back near the town gate, edging in, then pulling back, as if afraid.

"Well, my child," said Sapphire, "this hubbub will surely have roused your father, and no doubt witnessing this miracle will be the elixir he needs to chase any remaining weariness from his bones! So let us send for him. Ah, Ollie!" A small boy ran from the inn—another of Pedrus' children, by the look of him. "Please, go and fetch my husband, quickly, quickly!"

Ollie darted back inside. The crowd's exuberance grew by the second. "Praise be! The Fire One! The Fire One has returned! Time has started again!"

Their cheers dulled in Jemma's head. The prospect of meeting her father suddenly seized her with the strangest mix of emotions: excitement, curiosity . . . and then a sense of foreboding, creeping up from her toes. She pulled up the hood of her cloak, as if it could hide her. The minutes ticked by: six thirty-seven, thirty-eight, thirty-nine, and still the cheers droned on, thick and distant, as if through a lake of syrupwater.

Every face, every tree, and every building in the square was still crystal clear. As crystal clear as the electric sense of someone approaching from behind her. Crystal clear as she turned around. And crystal clear as she saw the unmistakable dark hair and determined stride of Nox Agromond, exiting the inn and heading straight toward her.

CHAPTER THIRTY

Bloodlines

Jemma wheeled around, but there was nowhere to run. The crowd was too thick, and blocked her way. Hands were grabbing her from behind, pulling her back, while Digby, his expression as horrified as she felt, looked on.

"Jem—it's not 'im—not who you think!" Marsh's arms, holding her up, and her mother's, wrapping around her as her legs buckled . . .

He was there. In front of her. The man they dared say was her father. Jemma's vision pulsed, dark, light, dark, and she pushed away, gripped by absolute panic. That face . . . that hair . . . those eyes . . .

Those eyes. They were not black, but blue-green. Like ocean waters.

Like hers.

"Jemma. My daughter." His voice was hoarse, and soft as a breeze. "Please, fear not. . . ."

Jemma fell backward into Marsh and her mother, all the dangers and uncertainty of the past eight days releasing in salty rivers down her cheeks. The tightness in her gut unwound; her heartbeat subsided. It was him who she had seen in her dream that morning, pulling her toward Oakstead— not Nox Agromond! Yes, this man's features were similar to Nox's, but the smile spreading across them hid no trace of deception.

"Father . . . ," she croaked. "Father!"

He reached out, and folded her into his arms.

Eight chimes of the town clock wound through the inn's corridors, up the narrow staircase, and into Jemma's parents' room. Jemma drew her knees up and settled into a cushioned wooden armchair with Noodle and Pie on her shoulders and a mug of burdock tea in her hands. Her parents sat on a rickety sofa at the other side of the small fireplace. Barely two hours had passed since she'd arrived in Oakstead, but she felt as though she had always known them, and the more she looked at her father, the more he seemed illuminated by something other than the firelight, radiating from within—something quite different from what animated Nox Agromond.

"Father," she said, "how is it that you look so like him?"

"We and the Agromonds have an ancestor in common," he said. "One who fled from them some three hundred years ago and married into our family. You know of her already, I believe. She wrote this." He picked up an ancient-looking book from the table next to him and passed it to her.

"*From Darknesse to Light*—Majem's book! Majem Solvay was born an *Agromond*?"

"Indeed she was," said Lumo, "and as cruel as any of them, until, just before she turned thirteen, she had a change of heart. She escaped from the castle and came to Oakstead to seek the help of the Solvays living here at that time. They took her under their wing, gave her a home, and trained her in the Light Arts. Later, she and their son Valior fell in love, and wed."

"That must have angered the Agromonds no end! Is that why they hate us so much?"

"Our emnity goes back hundreds of years before that, but Majem's escape—her betrayal of them, no less—made their hatred more bitter. There was a time, though, long before, when Agromonds and Solvays ruled this land together in harmony and prosperity: the Agromonds in the south, and we, the north." Lumo took a sip of water, and smiled. "Yes! I see your look of astonishment, Jemma, but it is so, and all told in Majem's book. Read it, when you are ready."

Jemma shivered, and turned the book in her hands. "So Majem was one of them! To have been so evil, and become so good. . . ."

"Nobody is evil through and through, Jemma," said Lumo, "or good, for that matter. Each of us has the capacity for both, and for most of us, one wicked act, or even several, does not make us a wicked person. That depends upon how we choose to commit our lives. Yet even good people have the capacity for cruelty, just as evil ones have the capacity for kindness."

Jemma nodded, remembering her harsh words to Nox about his lost twin, and how kind he could be to her. "What caused such a change of heart in her?"

"That too is in the book," said her mother. "Some of it is . . . painful to read. Wait, at least until your ordeal has faded from your mind. Then we shall talk of it, and of the future, and tell you more about your brother, as well."

"My brother . . . What was his name?"

Lumo and Sapphire both drew in a breath, then spoke together. "Jamem."

"Jamem," Jemma repeated. Another anagram . . . The eerie sense of connection she'd felt to Majem threaded through her again. And now there was a third person hooked into the story. Jamem. She wanted to ask more about him, and about his disappearance, but the sorrowful looks on her parents' faces made her think better of it. She'd only found out about his existence a few days ago, after all, while they had endured twelve years of heartache. Her questions could wait.

Running down the crag—her silken dress ripping on branches . . . Screams from the castle—her father, calling her name in a strange, muddled way: "Ma-jemmajemjamem!" Would she ever be free of it all? The dungeons, the small boy's whimpers, her father's fury . . .

Wait—this can't be *my* dream! I don't *know* any small boy, and my father is Lumo, Lumo Solvay! He's never even *been* to the castle! *And yet, it* must *be her—the rats were in a pouch around her shoulders, and she could see the Stone's aqua glow. The bell began tolling, once, twice. . . .*

"Enough! I'm free now, free!" Jemma woke on the last strike of three, the dream details vivid in her head. The silk dress, the small boy—they weren't her memories! They belonged to someone else. Someone long ago. Someone who, like her, had broken free.

"Majem," she whispered. "It was her I was dreaming about."

Outside, it was still dark, but a candle stub burned by Jemma's bedside, next to the book and crystals. Noodle and Pie were fast asleep on her pillow, their tiny snores purring like mothwings. She took stock of the patched cotton gown she was wearing, and remembered her mother bathing her just before bedtime, then bringing her here and tucking her in.

She closed her eyes. But the evening's events kept churning through her head: more stories she'd exchanged with her parents, then going down to the kitchen with them for a nightcap of camomile tea with Marsh and Digby. Her parents had given Digby a pony to thank him for bringing her home. Then, since he had to leave early in the morning and return to Hazebury to help his father with deliveries, Jemma had said goodbye to him.

That had been harder than she'd expected, and she felt sad now, thinking about him. She would miss him. Her friend. Her rescuer. Her rescuee. For more than four years, they'd seen each other every Tuesday at dawn, and the past two days' adventures had driven him deeper into her heart. He'd stood by his word to Marsh, and brought her here despite the dangers. And after all her dreaming, here she was at last, miles from Agromond Castle—but there he would be, still living in its shadow, making the weekly trudge up the crag with Gordo and Pepper to deliver the Agromonds' supplies. Even though he'd promised to visit as soon as he could—being careful to avoid Blackwater—there was a hollow in her, a piece missing. A piece labeled "Digby."

Candlelight danced around the room. Jemma's churning thoughts were turning into a thick butter, threatening to keep her awake all night. Sleep was a hopeless cause.

"No point just lying here like a log," she mumbled, pulling herself to sit. Settling cross-legged on the bed, she picked up Majem's book and opened it. Title. Name. Then she noticed something beneath it, hand-written in faded lettering, which she hadn't seen before. As she looked, the shadow of ink began to sparkle, faint light shining through the words, just as it had shone through the cover when she'd first read it. She tingled with anticipation as the light became brighter, until the words' graceful flourish was clear across the page.

This Book is dedicayted to the Fire One, unto whom I write in this my thirtieth Yeare.

"The Fire One! So Majem knew about the Prophecy . . . and wrote this dedication, all that time ago, to *me?*" The idea felt strange and fascinating. Even though she knew she couldn't be the Fire One without having been Initiated, she felt compelled to read on.

Childe, have Fayth that the Forgotten Song, whose sole purpose it is to help thee in thy Quest, shall come to thee when thou need'st. Trust in this. Blessings of Light be with thee. MS.

"MS. Majem Solvay," Jemma whispered, slightly perturbed by the word *quest* with its capital *Q.* "But what on earth does she mean by the Forgotten Song?" Spurred by curiosity, she turned the page.

CHAPTER THE FIRST: BEGINNINGS

I was born in that most dark of Places, Agromond Castle, at nine in the morn

Nine in the morn! And the date: it was three hundred years to the day before Jemma's birthday. The cord of connection between her and Majem tightened.

At the Moment of my Emergence from my motheres Womb, it is sayd that a grayt Chorus of Owls did set up their mournfulle Song, and black Cats did wail 'neath the Castle walls.

Jemma's gaze sped over the pages, despite the old-fashioned language. She read about Majem's father, Kralyd, marrying a beauty who, though not of sorcerer's blood, brought more wealth into the already-bulging Agromond coffers. She read how Majem, the youngest of two sets of twins—each a boy and girl, as those of healers and sorcerers always were—was the most powerful of their four children. Majem's gruesome Offerings had delighted Kralyd, making her siblings green with envy. She had no remorse. No feeling for others. Jemma skimmed over several pages of details, her stomach now churning as much as her head.

Then she came to a passage that made her throat clench: *The Children imprisonned in the Dungeons*—twins and triplets who were kidnapped and brought to the castle to be dealt with—*in accordance with Twin Lore*, which Majem went on to explain.

There exists between Twins an invisible Bond, she wrote, *the brayking of which by the Deathe of one by whatsoever means, doth release a grayt Force.*

"A bond between twins," Jemma murmured. "When one dies, no matter how, the bond breaks, releasing a great force. Digby mentioned something about that, on our way to Oakstead."

She read on, her patience stretching to grasp the rest of the Lore. But she was determined.

When the twins were from the families of healers and sorcerers and therefore had special Powers, the great force released at one twin's death automatically went to the surviving twin, increasing its strength—and its Powers.

However, when twins from normal families died, since they had no special Powers, the great force simply *flyeth into the Ether,* as Majem put it—unless, at the moment of death, it was harnessed by someone powerful enough to direct it to a place of their choosing.

Which is exactly what the Agromonds did.

Twice a year—though always *at Tymes unpredictable, to avoid Detection,* they took twins and triplets from far and wide, then sacrificed the strongest one, and, using *the proper Rimes and Rituals,* directed the force of its twin bond *into the dark Entity,* which in return gave them Power.

Jemma needed no reminding what that Entity was. "Scagavay," she whispered, her blood running cold. But it got worse. Under the Agromonds' command, not only did the great force go to Scagavay—the slain twin's soul went too. Its body was then locked in the dungeons with the surviving twin, who was simply left there to die.

She choked back tears, utterly nauseated. "Those poor children! Just like that girl ghost in the forest said: swallowed by the monster. . . ." Then a terrifying thought hit her: that was exactly what would have happened to her too. All her dreams, with the dark voice saying *You are mine, all mine!* had been telling her so. And Majem had done such awful things . . . had reveled in them! How could somebody so evil possibly have changed? Despite the horrors of everything she'd just read, Jemma had to find out. She turned the page.

CHAPTER THE SECOND: THE DAYE THAT DID CHANGE ME

Two dayes before our Initiation into the Ways of Mord were my twin Faustus and I in the dungeons, when Faustus did for sport and spite locke me into the smallest Cell.

—Free me, Brother! sayeth I, For thou art naught but the hind quarters of a Hog, green with envy for my Powers! Yet he did taunt me with much Laughter, then walketh away, leaving me with a Boy of four or five yeares, and his dead Twin, who we had put to the Sacrifyce but days before. Deathe now stood nigh to the Boy also, he being scarcely more than skin and bone.

Through many Hours did the Bell toll, and his cryes did beginne to wear me, the stench of Deathe becoming vile to me, and as I saw his lost Sister lying there, his pain moveth me, as though I myself had such Loss and Greyf buryed deep in my Soul.

O, how he did cling to me, and I did speak soothing words to him, my Hearte braykinge more and more open. Then at last with a gentle Smyle, he sayeth—Thank you, deare Ladye, for biding with me and being my Comfort. This say-eth he to me, a chief cause of his suffering! Then did his blue eyes emptye and turn blank, his Spirit floating from him and through the walls, seeking his deare Twin as do they all, yet can they never fynd them, for they are lost to Scagavay, and those remaining banished to the Forest to search for ever more.

Banished to the Forest . . . Seeking his lost twin . . . Jemma's mind spun back to the forest phantoms, pleading for the souls of their trapped brothers and sisters. Perhaps she had even seen this boy among them. . . . It was all so heartbreaking. But the book held her eyes like magnets.

There did I sit four hours more with the Boy's poor empty body, my Greyf and Gilt grayt indeed. But thenne two Creatures did come to me, offering solace. Creatures whych until that daye had I reviled, yet these had golden Pelts and Eyes like rubys. I called them my Rattusses—

"No!" Noodle and Pie woke with a start. "Sprites! I can hardly believe what I'm reading—two rats, just like you . . ." The rats crawled onto her lap.

At day's end, my brother Faustus having plainly forgot me, did my Mother fynde me—

Instantly, Majem's mother had seen the change in her. Majem must flee, she said, for her father would surely kill her if her Powers no longer served his ends. Majem protested: she was not yet Initiated—could not possibly survive the forest! Her mother assured her she had a plan to protect her—a plan that would also ensure her own freedom, for she too could no longer abide the evildoings at the castle.

So be of Courage, my child, and leave this very night, and rest assured that I too shall soon find my release.

Terrified, Majem ran from the castle and down the crag, her Stone around her neck, her two new rat friends in a pouch around her shoulder. Just as Jemma had dreamed. The

Aukron spied her, and attacked. She would die—she knew it! But no . . . A sudden rush of force filled her. The beast lay wounded. In what seemed like no time, Majem was at the bridge, crossing the river into Hazebury—with no Mist around her.

"No Mist," Jemma said. "And two rats. The same color as you." Noodle and Pie blinked at her, and an absurd thought leapt into her head. "You're not *related* to them, are you?" Another blink. "No . . . it's too weird. This whole *thing* is weird. . . . So, what was that force Majem felt? Ah, here we are: *And soon did I surmise what must have come to pass—Oh, no!*"

Majem's mother had murdered Majem's twin. Murdered him, to increase Majem's Powers and give her the strength to defeat the Aukron. Though Majem never went back to the castle, soon the terrible tale rippling through Anglavia confirmed her suspicions: her brother Faustus had indeed been slain by their mother. Kralyd put his wife to death for her treachery.

Rattled by the story, Jemma raced through the rest of the chapter: Majem's journey to Oakstead . . . Healing a sick boy on the way . . . Her thirteenth birthday, alone on the moors . . . Then at last, four dawns after fleeing the castle, she arrived ragged and exhausted at the Solvays' door. Their son Gudred answered it, invited her in. She was taken under their beneficent wing, and trained in the Light Arts. Gudred, though just a year older than Majem, was the family academic, and taught her to read and write. At nineteen, she married his older brother, Valior. Her father's fury was taken out on the whole country: poverty, misery, and Mist spread like disease. On the Solvays, Kralyd placed a particular curse, which Majem and Valior discovered when their son, Ruddeg, was born: he was an only child. This was a shock, for Solvays, like Agromonds, had only ever borne twins. But from now on, the curse decreed, Solvays would only bear single children, so if one died, there was no twin to inherit its Powers, which were therefore lost.

The final blow to Majem and the Solvay family was Gudred's mysterious disappearance. By now, at the age of only twenty-six, he was already beloved as a great warrior and Visionary, and his renown only grew with his absence. At the time of Majem's writing *From Darknesse to Light*, he had not been seen in over four years. *In my Hearte*, the chapter ended, *do I know that never shall we set Eyes on my deare Brother-in-law again*.

"That's so sad, Rattusses!" Jemma closed the book and yawned. Dawn was beginning to break, and at last, weariness weighed down her eyelids.

She blew out the candle and lay down, with Noodle and Pie nestled into her neck. The story wove through her mind. All those twins who had met such a terrible end! The forest phantoms, Majem's brother—and Nox's sister, Malaena, too. It was just as well, she thought, that the Agromonds *had* cursed the Solvay line. Being a twin was obviously far more dangerous than being a single child, as she was.

CHAPTER THIRTY-ONE

Threads

Wakey wakey.

"H'mmm?" Jemma opened one eye and saw four ruby ones staring at her. A gust of wind flapped the curtains, carrying the sound of voices from outside.

Sun! Come, see. Noodle and Pie hopped onto the window ledge. Pale squares of light slanted onto the wall opposite, throwing the rats' whiskered silhouettes against mottled whitewash, but Jemma's heart felt dark and heavy. Remnants of Majem's story flickered through her head, and she tried to breathe away its thick shadows as she slid out of bed and went to the window.

Over the rooftops, the sun was golden, the Mist barely more than a wispy veil pulled across it. Her spirits lifted a little as she leaned out and looked at the cobbled courtyard below. In the center was a circular fire pit, into which a small, barefoot boy was placing kindling. A few feet away, a long table was spread with a patchwork cloth, held down at intervals by thick candles and bowls of nuts. Several other ragged children ran around it, laughing. Then Pedrus staggered out through the kitchen door, puffing under the weight of a pig carcass that he hitched by its hind feet onto a post at one side of the pit. As he crouched to light the tinder, his daughters, Bethany and Moll, walked through an archway into the courtyard, carrying baskets of heather and gorse that they laid along the table. In the light of day, Jemma could see that they were about the same ages as her and Digby. Their dresses were plain and dusty-looking, and she noticed that their hands were swollen and rough: working hands, like Marsh's.

The smaller one, Moll, looked up, and nudged Bethany. Jemma waved at them, and they waved back, then scuttled inside. They seemed happy. What was it like for them, never to have been confined by castle walls, and to have each other's company day after day? She felt a pang of jealousy and sadness. If not for the Agromonds, she and Jamem would have had that kind of companionship. She had missed so much. Him. Her parents—

There was a knock at the door. "Jemma?" The latch lifted, the door creaked open, and her mother peeked in. "Good morning!"

"Good morning, Mother." *I should be as happy as a lark,* she thought, *seeing the sun for the first time. And my mother's here.* But melancholy had her in its clutches, and wouldn't let go.

"I've brought you some tea. Your favorite, Ida tells me." Sapphire walked over and put a steaming mug of mauve liquid on the window ledge, then gave Jemma a hug. "I see heaviness in you today," she said. "Digby's departure, perhaps?"

Jemma shrugged, and took a sip of tea. Its citrus tang did nothing for her nerves.

"Ah, no. It is about your brother. And things you have read . . ." Sapphire glanced at the book on the floor. "How far did you get?"

"Just to where Majem and Valior marry, and the curse Kralyd put on them."

"A fair bit, then. I was afraid it might be too much for you, so soon."

"I couldn't sleep. It was there." Jemma nursed her tea, wondering whether to mention the hand-written dedication. Last night, it had thrilled her to think of her ancestor writing to her across so many generations. Today, it felt empty and pointless.

Sapphire tilted Jemma's head, searching her eyes. "These threads of the past are burdensome indeed, my child," she said. "It's normal that you should feel their weight. Do not fight your heartache, though, for that will only give it more strength. But don't allow it to hold you captive either. There is always balance. Today, the sun is shining for the first time in many years. The air is warm. Oakstead is free of Mist for at least a hundred paces from the walls. We are safer than in many years from the threat of the Agromonds and their supporters, who despise sunlight, and will not venture into it. Everywhere in Oakstead, people are talking about it—about you. For this is your doing, Jemma. How perfect that you returned yesterday, on a Sunday!"

"Sunday? But . . . yesterday was Mord-day." Saying the name sent a chill through her.

"Here, we call it Sunday, in honor of the sun, the bringer of light and life. 'Mord' is everything opposite to that: darkness, and death. Before Mordrake Agromond, there was no Mord-day. Only Sunday. We have always refused to call it otherwise."

"Sunday." Jemma thought of her life's longing. "*Sunday . . .*"

"Our name, too, honors it," Sapphire said. "'Solvay,' in

Lappic, means 'way of the sun'. Today, let us enjoy it, and tonight, we shall celebrate! As you can see, Pedrus is preparing a feast for us. Now, there are clean clothes on the chair—old ones of Bethany's, which should fit you. Oh, and this." She dipped into her pocket and pulled out Jemma's Stone, attached to a new, golden chain. "The chain is special, given to me by Lumo's mother, who trained your father and me, and Marsh before us." She fastened it around Jemma's neck.

"Thank you." Jemma laid her palm over the Stone and felt its familiar comfort.

Her mother stood back. "There. Now, after you're dressed, come down to the kitchen. I see that Noodle and Pie, anyway, are eager for breakfast. They'll have to mind Paws, though—he's the inn's cat. But I'm forgetting, you've probably never seen one. Cats don't like rats."

Jemma smiled, remembering the effect that Noodle and Pie had had on Mowser in the Goodfellows' storehouse. "I don't think Paws will be a problem," she said.

"Good. I'll see you downstairs, then." Sapphire hugged Jemma again, then left the room.

The rest of the morning was a bustle of preparation for the night's feast. Everyone was in good spirits. Her parents were feeling stronger. Marsh's stump, which she proudly displayed, was better—she'd taken the bandage off before sleeping, and the scabs had healed overnight into a healthy pink. Noodle and Pie were perfectly at home, having terrorized Paws into keeping his distance. And although Digby had gone, he'd left a note for her with Marsh. *Gud luk Jema, by by*, it said, his scrawl looking as though someone had dipped a spider in the plum-colored ink and allowed it to crawl across the page. At the bottom was a single X, whose meaning Marsh explained while Bethany and Moll, who were busy chopping beets and parsnips for that night's soup, tittered knowingly. Jemma felt a flush of pride as she folded the note into her pocket. Yet despite all this, she couldn't shake her gloom.

Before lunch, her parents took her for a stroll around Oakstead. They showed her the house where they had lived before she was taken, now empty; the side streets with their mostly deserted shops; the fountain in the square where she'd paddled as a baby. Everywhere they went, people stopped to welcome her home, and talked about the clock, and how the Mist had rolled back as far as the orchards now, the fruit trees were showing buds for the first time in years, and the fountain water looked less green by the hour. It was a miracle! Still, Jemma's spirits kept sinking. She wondered increasingly about Jamem. Had they played here together? What would he have been like now? His absence gnawed deeper into her, and she wished her parents would talk about him. But the two times she mentioned his name, they quickly changed the subject.

After lunch, she was too agitated to rest. Leaving a note for her parents, she went outside with Noodle and Pie and followed a path down to a brook, then wandered alongside it until she came to a willow. She sat beneath it, trying to enjoy its soft shushing, the brook waters' lapping, and the warmth of the Mist-free sun on her skin. This was everything she had longed for, but still, sorrow scraped her heart. She sighed, and closed her eyes.

Black swirled around her. You are mine—all mine! *Screams, the children*—Help us, help! *A tiny shadow reached for her from the darkness, a shadow shot through with flame, whispering, then screaming, "Jem-Jem!" Gray baby fingers stretched toward her—*

"No! Stop it, stop! Enough of these dreams!" Jemma leapt to her feet, grabbed Noodle and Pie, and ran back up the path to Oakstead. A few people were gathered in the square, and looked surprised as she pelted past. She sat on the edge of the fountain to catch her breath. The water was even clearer now, and she set the rats down, then leaned over and dabbled her fingers in it. Suddenly, she saw a flash of flame, like in her dream, rippling on the surface. Her heart punched into her chest. She looked again: it was only her hair, reflected in the water.

"Miss Jemma—are you all right?"

Jemma wheeled around. Bethany, the older of Pedrus's daughters, stood several feet away. "Oh! Bethany . . . Hello. I'm . . . I'm fine, thank you. And please, just call me Jemma."

"Right. Jemma." Bethany edged closer. "You seemed a bit affrighted, if I might say. I would be too, if I was you. Bein' the Fire One an' all."

Jemma shrugged. She didn't feel like the Fire One. More like a soggy mop.

"Mus' be a lot for you to take in all that's happened. I'm jus' glad you didn't get killed, like Jam—" Bethany slapped her hand over her mouth. "Mother of Majem! I'm so stupid."

"You mean my brother?" Jemma's heart flipped. "It's all right, I know about him."

"Thank goodness! I always speak without thinkin'."

"Me too." Jemma smiled. "Actually, I'd like to talk about him."

"Really? I don't know much, though, just what everybody

knows, about him disappearin' an' all. Must be hard for your parents, mustn't it, yesterday bein' his birthday?"

"Whose—Jamem's?"

"Why, yes . . . But surely you knows that, don't you? I mean, you an' him bein' . . ."

"Being what?"

Bethany's eyes widened, and she slapped her hand over her mouth again. "Mord take my tongue! You *don't* know, do yer? Lawks, I'll get skinned alive!" She gathered her skirts and ran across the square toward the inn.

"Bethany, wait! *What* don't I know? Tell me!" Jemma gave chase, the rats skittering after her, but by the time she reached the inn and entered the courtyard, Bethany was nowhere to be seen. Jemma stumbled into the kitchen. Marsh was sitting at the table, frowning at a book.

"Why, Jem," she said, "you're here! Your folks got your note—but what's bitten you? First Bethany charges through here like she was bein' chased by a ghost, and now you—"

"Something she said . . . about me and Jamem . . . What is it I'm not being told?"

Marsh put her book down. "Jem . . . 'taint for me to say. You mus' ask your folks."

"But Bethany said yesterday was his *birthday!*" she said, wondering why it mattered to her so much, "and they didn't even mention it!"

"Why would they? Their focus was on you, an' on seein' you for the first time in twelve years. But if it's any comfort, they had a little ceremony to honor him yesterday mornin', like they done every year, they told me. They done the same on your birthday too."

"Oh." Jemma sat down. "Did they ever find out what happened to him?"

"Jem . . . I . . ."

"He's dead, isn't he?" said Jemma, certainty falling around her like a heavy cloak. "I think I've known that all along." His disappearance needled her again, prodding at thoughts she didn't want to think.

"I'm sorry, Jem." Marsh took Jemma's hand.

Jemma sighed. "How much older than me was he, anyway?"

"Older? I . . . Jem, like I said, you got to talk to your folks 'bout all this. Today, if you must. Jus' . . . maybe think about waitin' a day or so. Give 'em time. An' yourself too."

Jemma nodded. Whatever her feelings, they were nothing compared to what her parents had suffered. She didn't want to spoil her homecoming celebration. Not for them, nor for herself. "You're right, Marsh. I'll ask them tomorrow," she said. "I just wish I didn't feel so *sad*."

"Try the Light Game, Jem. For yourself, an' your own feelin's. It'll be good practice."

"You always told me that before, at the castle. I did use it once," she said, remembering how she had chased Nocturna's rose potion through her veins, "but mostly, I kept forgetting."

"Don't I know it! You was such a flibbertigibbet at times. Ah, Jem. Little did you know how much I used that Light to stop their evil creepin' into you when you was little, an' strengthen you while you was sleepin'." She squeezed Jemma's hand. "I'm here to help you, pet, like I always been. But hows about we put all this aside, hmmm? Jus' for today, anyway.

Now, maybe you can help me with readin' this." She picked up her book: *How to Grow New Limbs*.

Jemma took it, and leafed through it. "Marsh . . . This is about trees. . . ."

"Oh, my! You don't say!" Marsh rocked back in her chair and laughed. Soon Jemma was laughing too. Perhaps, she thought, she was going to enjoy tonight's celebrations, after all.

"And the Earth bathed in Light!" Freddie and Maddie Meadowbanks played the last chord with a flourish, then lay their lutes on the ground behind them. Everyone applauded. Other than in her dreams, the only music Jemma could remember was Marsh singing nursery rhymes to her in a rather off-key croak, and she was amazed at how the glorious rise and fall of a melody carried her along when sung—in tune—by even a small gathering. It had banished her gray mood almost entirely, and she'd only thought of Jamem seven times all evening.

She looked at the people seated around the firelight: her parents; Marsh; Pedrus and his wife, Tess; Bethany—who kept avoiding her gaze—and Moll, and their younger twin brothers, Ollie and Will; Freddie and Maddie; and a handful of her parents' friends. At her feet, Noodle and Pie sat cleaning their muzzles. Every face glowed with the contentment of good company and a full belly. Jemma had never eaten such tasty soup—she'd even liked the parsnips in it—and the pig had been delicious.

Outside the courtyard walls, the town clock chimed once. Eight-thirty.

"Well, my girl," Lumo put his arm around her. "What a night it's been, eh?"

"Mmm." Jemma leaned into him. "It's more wonderful than I could have imagined." *If only you could be here too, Jamem,* she added silently, glad she'd said nothing about him to mar her parents' joy.

"A penny for your thoughts, Jemma?" Lumo whispered.

Jemma smiled and shook her head.

"Ah, secrets already!" He laughed, then started humming Freddie and Maddie's song.

Jemma hummed along with him, pulling Majem's cloak around her knees—it had been carefully washed by her mother, and had quickly dried itself. Despite its ragged state, and the shadow of Majem's story, it felt right to be wearing it tonight. It had helped save her life.

She gazed into the fire, her vision fuzzing. The flames were mesmerizing, taking on the form of mountains, rocks, animals, faces, which separated into multicolored dots, then joined together again. Then three names began weaving through her mind, jumbled together, then dividing, and she sang them under her breath: *Majem. Jemma. Jamem . . .*

Jamem, Jemma. His birthday, hers. Six days apart. With how many years between? *Jemma, Jamem.* What had happened to him? Another song pressed up from her memory, one she'd buried days ago: *Rue, rue, rue the day they took me bonny babe away. . . .* Jemma tried to push it down, but it pushed back louder. *They took me babe, so fair and red, I loved me laddie but now he's dead. . . .* She stood, her blood swimming, and slowly walked toward the fire.

"Jemma?" Her mother, a blur to her left, stood, and stepped up beside her.

His sea-green eyes will see no more, like so many babes before. . . . Majem, Jemma, Jamem . . . The songs interwove. The ground seemed to tilt, throwing her off-balance. And there it was again, her face, in the flames. It split into two faces. Side by side. Two baby faces.

Jemma fell to her knees. *Jemma, Jamem. Marked, unmarked.*

"Jemma!" Sapphire knelt at her side, with Lumo behind her. "What is it?"

"Rue, rue, rue the day . . ." Jemma sang softly. Rue's bonny boy, the boy in her care, taken, then dead and gone. *Your fault! It was you they wanted—not him!* Majem's brother, her twin, slain, to make her stronger. And her own brother . . . ? She thought of the flame-shot shadow she'd dreamed about earlier, and in the forest, with its chubby fingers reaching toward her. . . .

The faces in the fire merged again, then separated, then merged. *Jem-Jem,* an infant's voice surged up, insistent, from her memory, *Jem-Jem!*

Older? No. Jamem was younger than she—younger!

Another whoosh of flame. Her face, his. Two shocks of red hair, then one. Tiny fingers, reaching; two tiny hands, clasping a stuffed rabbit . . . She remembered him! She remembered being with him at the castle, remembered them playing together, laughing, crying—for months, until the day she was taken with him into the Ceremony Chamber . . . blackness all around . . . two screams, then one. Jamem gone. But how could it be? Kralyd's curse made it impossible! And yet the truth shrieked at her, searing under her skin. She stood, and turned to her parents.

"Jamem," she said. "He wasn't just my brother—he was my twin! Born six days after me. . . . And he was murdered—murdered by the Agromonds, to increase my Powers!"

CHAPTER THIRTY-TWO

Jamem's Gift

Silence gripped the gathering.

"Yes," said Lumo, "it is as you say. We were going to tell you, of course, in time. But today, we wished only to celebrate you—"

"Celebrate me? But it's my fault he died!" Jemma shook from head to toe. "If I hadn't been Marked, they might have chosen him!"

"If you hadn't been Marked, Jemma," Sapphire said, rising to her feet, "the Agromonds would have killed you as well. But they undoubtedly saw the Mark as a chance that you might become one of them—an opportunity for them to gain more Power. More so with you alive, than if . . ." Her voice trailed off, and she wrapped her arms tightly around Jemma.

Then Lumo's arms were around her too. "It was not your fault, child," he said. "Don't think it, not for one second! And thank goodness you bear the Mark, for because of it, we still have you. And it bonds you and I, for I too bear it, handed down from Majem. That Jamem was born without it was mere chance."

"Mere chance . . . Poor Jamem!" Jemma buried her head in her mother's shoulder as more memories poured through her—Jamem's laugh, his sea-green eyes, the emptiness of missing him. She heard herself sobbing, heard the mumbled goodbyes of the gathering, and Marsh bustling toward the kitchen, then the rustle of Noodle and Pie at her feet, the cry of a single nightjar, and the steady breath of her parents. Finally, as the town clock chimed its last strike of nine, she pulled away from their embrace. "But how?" she said. "How could we have been twins? What about Kralyd's curse?"

Her mother wiped away Jemma's tears. "Are you sure you want to hear this now?"

Jemma nodded. "Yes! Please . . ."

"Come, then, let us sit," her father said. He rolled a log over to the fire and sat Jemma down on it, then he and Sapphire seated themselves on either side of her. "It is all part of the Prophecy," he said, "that stated that when twins were born once more to the Solvay line, Kralyd's curse would be broken. This was to be a sign, for one of these twins would be the Fire One, destined to bring an end to the Agromond dynasty. Which one, the Prophecy doesn't say. So the Agromonds took you both, not knowing which of you was the danger to them, and no doubt planned to kill you both. But then they found the Mark on you . . ."

"And thought I couldn't be the Fire One. Because the Mark meant I would be evil, like them." Shards of memory shot through Jemma: the circle of black candles . . . Shade and Feo, holding hands and toddling toward the altar . . . Jamem, dropping his stuffed rabbit as Nocturna wrenched him away from her—she clamped the images down. "How did they find out about us?"

Lumo heaved a sigh. "Spies. One of the baker's apprentices and his sister. After Jamem was taken, they acted so distraught that nobody saw through them—and their evil was well disguised, no doubt, by some kind of Agromond sorcery. Then, when the message from Yarville came, begging for our help, we thought it safest to take you, but . . ." He looked at the ground.

"Father, the Agromonds tricked you! I read about it in the articles. If you'd left me behind, they'd have found some other way to get me. That baker's apprentice and his sister, for example."

"Jemma is right," said Sapphire, leaning over and squeezing Lumo's hand. "Now it is you, my dear, who must not give in to self-blame. There's no doubt those two would have acted, had the Agromonds' ambush failed." She looked at Jemma. "They disappeared shortly after you were taken, and we soon discovered they were from Blackwater—their father an Inquisitor, no less. It taught us a bitter lesson, and thanks to our supporters' vigilance, no enemy has been able to enter Oakstead since. But alas, it came too late to protect you."

Jemma ground her teeth. "So they had it all planned. Nothing could have changed it."

The three of them sat and gazed at the embers. A gust blew across the courtyard. The fire flared. Somewhere outside Oakstead's walls, an owl hooted.

"There's one thing I still don't understand," Jemma said. "How could Jamem have been born so much later than me? Six whole days!"

"It is rare, Jemma," said her mother, "but it happens. For years, I wondered if he was reluctant to come into the world, knowing, somehow, what his fate would be. But in these past few days I have found comfort in the possiblility of another purpose: a gift from Jamem to you and your destiny."

"A *gift?*"

"Yes. You see, the time for Initiation is always between the older and younger twins' births. Normally, this is only minutes, or an hour. But Jamem being born six days after you . . ."

"Gave me more time to get home."

"I know, it sounds farfetched," Sapphire said, "but whether by accident or design, it is a gift nonetheless, and I shall always honor him for giving it."

Jemma clenched her jaw, unable to bring herself to say it: she had been too late. Jamem's gift was for nothing. An ember cracked, and leapt out of the fire. She ground it with her heel, then gazed up at the sky. Tiny points of light laced the darkness. So that was what stars looked like. Dots of white fire. They were pretty, she supposed, but her heart was too hollow to feel it.

"You were wrong, Mother, when you said last night that the Agromonds haven't won. They have. Without me being Initiated and fulfilling the Prophecy, how can it be otherwise?"

Her parents exchanged glances.

"The Agromonds have not won," her father said, "because the Prophecy can still come to pass. We were going to wait before talking of this, Jemma, but . . . you have in fact been Initiated."

"What! By whom?"

Her mother smiled. "You Initiated yourself."

"When? How?"

"The night before last, by healing your friend's mother. The same was true for Majem, who, if you recall, ran away from the castle before her Initiation. Do you remember reading in her book that she healed a young boy on her way to Oakstead?"

"Vaguely . . . yes."

Sapphire put her arm around Jemma's shoulders. "It happened between the hours of her twin's birth and hers, and the way she describes it, later in the book, is exactly what I glimpsed when you were working on Alyss: Light pouring through you. And this is exactly what occurs during an Initiation into Light. That Light brings seeds of knowledge from all our lineage who have gone before, and plants them in your very cells. Though of course, for those who choose to be Initiated into Darkness, it is darkness that comes."

"And Majem had chosen the Light," Jemma murmured, remembering Bryn's words: *Magic is what men make it. Ask for bad, get bad. Ask for good, get good.* "So I *am* Initiated, after all."

"Yes. The force of the Light you created yesterday, and your clearing of the Mist last night, proves it," Lumo said. "There is no doubt, Jemma. You are the Fire One, as foreseen by the Prophecy almost three hundred years ago."

Jemma looked at the embers, the eerie feeling she'd had when reading Majem's dedication to her creeping through her again. The parallels between her story and her ancestor's—their escape, their self-Initiation, and the murder of each of their brothers—were uncanny. Majem had even had two *rats,* for goodness' sake.

A lot to take in. Noodle and Pie licked her fingers. *We know.*

A lot. It was. She had known nothing of these things a week ago, yet now they were part of who she was. The Fire One.

"So . . . was it Majem's Prophecy?"

"No," said Lumo, stoking the fire with a branch. "It was Gudred's. Her brother-in-law."

"The Visionary." Jemma breathed in the smoke-tinged air, and pulled Majem's cloak around her. As if reading a dedication to her written three hundred years ago wasn't enough, the idea of actually being *seen* by the supposedly great Gudred made her head swim. It felt spooky.

No. It felt special.

Inevitable.

A spark ignited in her. "So I can avenge Jamem's death," she said, "and everything they did to me. To *us*." The spark flared into a small flame. "And to Marsh . . . Talon and her mother . . . Caleb and Rue . . . the ghost children in the forest . . . Everyone I saw on the way here . . . all that misery, murder, and Mist—" She leapt to her feet, tumbling Noodle and Pie to the ground. Determination blazed through her. "I can—I will! I hate them, *hate* them!"

Quite so. The rats shook themselves. *But please don't toss us around like that.*

"Oh, sorry, Rattusses—"

"Jemma." Lumo stood, his voice firm. "I understand how you feel. But your Powers, though great, are still raw. They need schooling, focusing. You must learn to master and intend their every nuance. Hatred should never be your guiding force; it only creates more of itself. And besides, if you were to move against the Agromonds while blazing with such vengeance, the Mist would read you and strike you down as fast as thought can travel. Outwitting it is no easy task. Only Ida has ever succeeded—"

"Then I shall learn!"

"Indeed. But it took Ida many years. You will require time. And patience."

Jemma gritted her teeth; patience was not one of her gifts, she knew. "I shall learn," she repeated. "Starting tomorrow!"

"Wait!" Sapphire stood. "Let us not get ahead of ourselves! Lumo, training is all very well, but we must also think of Jemma's safety. We cannot talk of such ventures while Majem's other book is still missing! You know she said it was vital for the Fire One to have it—"

"Majem wrote another book?" said Jemma.

"Yes." Sapphire started pacing by the fire. "A single small volume, written by hand. She talked of it to her son, Ruddeg, on her death-bed. She was frantic, telling him it was lost, and must be found, for it contained the key to overcoming the Agromonds and fulfilling the Prophecy. Lumo, I would be loathe to give my blessing to any of this until *The Forgotten Song* is found. . . ."

"*The Forgotten Song*," Jemma murmured, the words nibbling her memory.

"Sapphire," said Lumo, "Majem was old when she died, and as you know, becoming addle-headed. Ruddeg never knew whether she was telling the truth about the book or hallucinating. How many generation of Solvays have searched for it high and low? Yet none have found it. We cannot hold Jemma back for something that may not even exist—"

"But Lumo, please! She's only just arrived home. . . ." Sapphire stopped pacing, her face wan in the firelight.

"Father, Mother!" Jemma grabbed her mother's arm. "*The Forgotten Song* does exist! There's a dedication to me in my copy of *From Darknesse to Light,* and it's mentioned there. I

302

saw it for the first time last night—it looked as though it was written in light. Majem wrote it when she was in her thirtieth year, so a long time before she'd grown old. She said . . ." Jemma knit her brows, trying to recall the words. *"The Forgotten Song* would come to me when I needed it, that was it. I must have faith in that, and trust it."

"But it's such thin assurance!" Sapphire said. "Words, written in light—"

"Sapphire, you of all people, to doubt such a thing!" Lumo put his arm around her. "I know. You are feeling that all of this is happening too fast, too soon. Wanting to wait before watching our daughter embark on such a momentous mission. I confess, I find it hard too. But we must both commend her for her courage, and learn to trust."

Trusssst . . . Jemma thought of Drudge, and smiled.

"But . . . but . . . what if they come looking for her . . . ?"

"Mother," said Jemma, "you said yourself this morning that they won't go far out of the Mist. The sun protects us all. But I've just thought of something else: they think my Powers are gone! It's perfect—I can train and practice in peace!"

Sapphire sighed and leaned into Lumo's shoulder. "Very well then; trust I must. We shall commence your training tomorrow. So let us all get a good night's sleep now."

Well, baby brother, Jemma thought as they walked toward the inn, *I'm ready to take my first steps toward fulfilling this Prophecy. Nothing will bring you back, but I'll do my best to make things right, and show you that your waiting six days to be born wasn't a wasted gift after all.*

CHAPTER THIRTY-THREE

Training

The Mist swirled and whirled, spinning Jemma upward. I have you now! it hissed. You're mine—all mine! Noodle and Pie were whipped up into the vortex above her, their tiny limbs spread-eagled. She grabbed one in each hand and held fast. Strange words began pouring from her mouth, words she hadn't heard in days—"Leth gith bal celde"—followed by new ones: "Cebvasya ag wonn oge . . ." She shot a lifeline of Light down to earth, felt the tug as it anchored to the ground, and the rush as she plummeted earthward.

"Leth gith bal celd-e-e . . ." Her voice trailed into the void.

"Mother of Majem!" Jemma sprang upright, jolting Noodle and Pie out of sleep. "I'm so tired of these dreams—every day since I started training! And now, those words again. What do they *mean?*" She dragged back her sheets and rolled out of bed, pulled on Digby's old clothes—even her mother agreed they suited her better than Bethany's cast-off frock—then stumbled down to the kitchen, the rats scampering close behind.

Marsh was stirring a large pot, and turned as Jemma ran in. "Another dream, eh?" She put her spoon on the stove. Noodle and Pie clambered up and started licking it.

"It was worse than ever! We were being sucked upward—me and the rats—and I kept saying these weird words. Thank goodness you taught me about the grounding cord yesterday!"

"Seems your dreams is testin' you, givin' you the chance to practice what you've learned. When you're in the thick of danger, see, there in't no time to think. Everythin' has to come quick as lightnin'. So goin' over an' over it in your dreams is gettin' it into your bones. That's good."

Jemma groaned and flopped into a chair. "But I wake up more tired than before I went to bed!" The strange words still echoed in her head: *Leth gith bal celde . . .*

"You're learnin' fast, though, Jem. Faster'n your folks an' me did. You've come a long way in less than a week. Your ma tells me you been doin' wonders with the Light Game, controllin' it at will now. An' that healin' you did yesterday on little Boris Trufold's bloated arm . . ." Marsh shook her head in wonderment. "It'll all stand you in good stead, you'll see.

"Now, let's have us some breakfast. There's nothin' like some good nosh to— Oy, scarper, you little rascals!" She laughed, swiping at Noodle and Pie with her stump. They leapt onto Jemma's lap and proceeded to clean their porridge-smeared muzzles.

"These words," Jemma said, "were a kind of chant. I've heard some of them before: *Leth gith bal celde.* I thought they were anagrams, but I've tried working them out at least fifty times. They're just nonsense. Last night, there were different ones. Oh, I wish I could *remember* them!"

"Breathe deep, Jem. It might help."

Jemma inhaled, the cinnamon smell of porridge calming her a little. "*Leth gith bal celde. . . .* Wait—*Cebvasya ag wonn oge*—that was it! What could it *mean?*"

"No use askin' me." Marsh put a bowl of porridge on the table, then a second, and sat down. "I never was that good with words. They sound sort of Celdorian, though, or Russo."

"Good morning!" Sapphire walked in, followed by Lumo, and kissed Jemma on the cheek. "Ah, dreams again, I see."

"With strange-soundin' words," said Marsh.

"Which I can't understand!" Jemma thumped her fist on the table. "I feel so stupid!"

Her father sat beside her. "Remember what we've told you, Jemma," he said. "Self-blame can be the harshest enemy. It undermines you. If you're serious about returning to the castle someday, you must overcome such weaknesses, for the Mist will detect the slightest whiff of them and waste no opportunity to weaken you further."

Jemma poked at her porridge with her spoon. "Stupid Mist," she muttered. But it wasn't the Mist that was annoying her. It was the fact that despite her progress in other ways, her father was right. She was still impatient. Impetuous. Still jumped to conclusions. ("Never assume anything," he kept saying.) And she still got angry with herself when things didn't come easily to her. "I just want to know what those words mean," she muttered, trying to perk up.

"You'll work 'em out in time, pet." Marsh nudged Jemma's bowl toward her. "Now eat up. We've plenty of work cut out for us this mornin'."

* * *

The second and third weeks rolled by. Jemma settled into her routine: mornings, Mist training with Marsh; afternoons, healing and Light Arts with her parents—all of which she enjoyed—and twice a week, what her father called "thought alignment," which she dreaded. It was no fun being reminded about her faults. All three of them stressed that she must keep mindful of what might attack at any moment, especially Mordsprites. "They move so quickly," her father said, "that you may not even have time to put up a shield of Light against them. They're like dark thoughts: once they catch you unawares, they've got you in their clutches." The best defense was positive thoughts and feelings, which created a force field that Mordsprites hated as much as the Agromonds and their followers hated sunlight—but positive thoughts and feelings, he added, would not be so easy to access in the Mist.

It was all exhausting. But Jemma loved evening time, which she often spent with Bethany, Moll, and their brothers. They would wander to the wheat fields and grazing grounds around Oakstead—they were thriving now that the Mist had retreated yet another half mile or so—and her new friends taught her games like tag, hopscotch, skittles, and knuckle-bones. By the end of the third week, Jemma felt she'd known them for years.

On her fourth Sunday in Oakstead, a surprise came: Digby. He'd left Hazebury the previous evening and had ridden all night on his new pony—the one Jemma's parents had given him—finding a long way around Blackwater via the Elm River Pass, to avoid being recognized by any Blackwater hoodlums. Together, he and Jemma strolled for hours by the brook. He was amazed by the sunlight and the cloud-patched blue sky, and wished his family could see it. The idea that the Agromonds and their cronies could be scared of such a thing seemed mad to him. "I'm glad, though," he said, "if it keeps 'em away from you, an' keeps you safe." He was horrified when she told him about Jamem, and didn't like the thought of her training at all—to even *think* of confronting the Agromonds was far too dangerous, he said, Prophecy or not. That had annoyed her, but then he'd grinned, which made her heart flip, and ruffled her hair—it had grown to a thumb's length already, and her mother had leveled out its unruly spikes. He liked it, he told her; she no longer looked like a boy. At one point, sitting by the brook, he held Jemma's hand—just for a moment, but her heart turned several somersaults anyway, and continued fluttering for the rest of the day.

The only blight was the news he brought from the villages. When they were eating dinner in the inn's kitchen with Jemma's parents and Marsh, Lumo asked him how things were in Hazebury. Not good, he said. The Agromonds had cut everyone's rations, including his family's. People were hungrier than ever. In some places there'd even been protests, which had been swiftly squashed by Inquisitors.

"You'd think nervousness an' unrest was a disease," he said, "the way it's spreadin'."

Digby left the next morning. But although Jemma felt sad watching him gallop away, the distance between them seemed less now that he'd visited, and she felt sure he'd be back soon.

Four more days passed. Then, on Thursday evening, came another surprise. Jemma, Ollie, and Will were splashing each other in the fountain, when two figures walked through the town gates, dragging a very tired-looking cow behind them.

"Talon! Alyss!" Jemma ran to them and hugged them both. "And you brought Horn with you!" Although Alyss was clearly still weak, she looked so much better now, with flesh on her bones and color in her cheeks.

They brought more disturbing news from Blackwater. People were angry that they hadn't been given the extra rations Nox had promised. Stealing and random assaults had gone through the roof. As soon as Alyss had felt strong enough, she and Talon had fled, leaving in the dead of Monday night to avoid spies and Inquisitors. They'd walked for almost three days—Alyss often riding on Horn's back—and fed on berries and milk. They were worn out, but after the growing unrest they'd witnessed, coming out of the Mist was nothing short of a miracle. No word of the renewed sunshine at Oakstead had reached Blackwater. Thank goodness, Jemma said. If people there knew, the Agromonds would soon find out, and realize she hadn't lost her Powers after all.

"Well, grisly goblins, Jemma, I think it's amazin'—I love it!" Talon squeaked. "An' if you can get rid of the Mist like that . . . well, look out, Agromonds!"

Jemma laughed, then took Talon and Alyss by the hand and pulled them toward the Heathshire Arms. "I've told my parents all about you. Come and meet everyone! Ollie, Will—run and tell your folks to add to tonight's dinner!"

What a week. First Digby's visit, and now Talon and Alyss were here. The echoes of growing mayhem throughout Anglavia faded in Jemma's mind. In Oakstead, at least, life was looking up.

* * *

In the middle of the following week, Marsh announced that it was time to challenge Jemma's abilities further by venturing deeper into the Mist, where it was thicker. By now, Jemma could easily expand the clear space around her by a good thirty feet, but Marsh had warned her against doing so once they were away from Oakstead and heading toward Hazebury. Instead, she had been teaching Jemma to blank her thoughts so that the Mist couldn't read them.

"This far from the castle, it don't see you as a threat, see," she explained as they rode, "so you can clear the Mist all you like an' it don't pay you much mind. But the closer we get to *them*, the more the Mist'll be on guard. That's its job. You go clearin' it, an' it'll know you're the enemy. But when your mind's blank, it can't see you. It's like you're invisible to it, not there."

"It's the Mist that ought not be there," Jemma grumbled. In the four-and-a-half weeks since she had arrived in Oakstead, she'd grown accustomed to the sun's increasing presence. She loved it. Life in the thick of the Mist was a thing of the past. But coming back into it she felt the pall of it again, dampening her spirits. Accursed Agromonds!

"Blank, Jemma! You're alertin' it."

Jemma imagined drawing a veil across her mind, dissolving every thought. Only a few days ago this had seemed impossible, but had quickly become easier. The Mist swirled around her as if she was no more danger to the Agromonds than a shrub.

Several miles later, Marsh pulled Flashwing to a halt. Jemma drew Grayboy alongside.

"This'll do," said Marsh. "How is it, coming this deep into the Mist again?"

"It definitely felt more threatening as we got farther from Oakstead. But when I blank, it's almost as if the Mist decides it *likes* me. Doesn't it affect you, Marsh?"

"Used to. But I trained to overcome it since I was 'bout your age, Jem. Obsessed, I was." Marsh smiled. "Looks like you're gettin' the hang of it too. That's good! So, let's up the stakes a bit."

They dismounted and tethered the horses to a nearby tree, then walked off the track and into a clearing surrounded by gorse bushes.

"Marsh, the Mist must know I hate it, so why doesn't it attack me?"

"It don't care what you think of *it*, Jem. It's used to people hatin' it—to *you* hatin' it. It's made of hate, so it's like it don't even notice it. Its sole purpose is to defend *them*." Marsh fixed Jemma's gaze. "The Agromonds."

Earlier, when the Mist was thinner, Jemma hadn't reacted at the mention of their name. Now, anger flared through her. The Mist leapt into the clear halo around her, pressing into her.

"Deep breath, Jem. Calm yourself. . . . That's it. Now, still your mind. . . . Blank . . . Good girl."

"Ouff!" Jemma shook herself off. "I wasn't expecting that."

"See? That's what we got to prepare you for. The slightest thought you 'ave against *them*, the Mist'll sense quick as a flash. Then, if you don't know how to stop it, it'll muddle you, an' make anythin' bad feel bigger in your mind till you think you're goin' stark ravin' mad. The more you struggle, the worser it'll get, like you was a fly in a web. You got to keep alert, learn to be stronger than it, an' trick it. Now, let's try the next level. You remember what I taught you, for practicin'?"

"Blank, then intensify, to get the Mist to suspect me, then counter—think of something I love, to confuse it—and blank again."

"That's it. But don't worry, we'll start easy, an' I'll cue you at first. Right: *Blank!*"

Jemma evoked the whiteness more easily than even moments earlier.

"Good." Marsh's voice cut into Jemma's concentration. "Now, intensify. Think of Feo."

Jemma chuckled as she remembered Feo as a chubby little boy, breaking the wings off his toy Mordsprite. He'd thought it looked happier without them.

"Jem, I said *intensify*! You got to rile the Mist, or you won't get any practice. Think of somethin' that gets your dander up about Feo. Somethin' small, mind, to start with."

The spiders, that last Ceremony . . . Disgust at Feo fired up under Jemma's skin. How could he have been so cruel? Mist twined around her neck and tightened like fingers.

"Now, counter!"

Jemma tried to fill her mind with whiteness, but she kept seeing Feo chewing the poor creatures, squashing them on the floor. Her thoughts reeled, panic rising—

"Jem, don't jump ahead!" Marsh yelled. "It's no use tryin' to blank when you're caught up in them feelin's! You got to counter first—think of somethin' you love!"

The spiders . . . The heat . . . What had happened next? Noodle and Pie . . . they'd come to her rescue! Gratitude flooded her. The Mist inched away. But suddenly other images invaded her mind, far worse than the spiders: skeletons, ghosts, their screams filling her head—

The Mist was upon her again.

"Jem, *counter*! Hold your Stone!"

"I'm *trying*!" The Mist was strangling her, choking her thoughts. Her arms felt limp.

"Surprise it—think of the first time you saw your ma!"

Ma—*ma*—*ma*—*ma*— The word caught up with the screams in Jemma's head, becoming harsh and shrill, like a taunt. *Ma—ma—maaaaaAAA!*

"Jemma!" Marsh's voice was barely audible through the screeching, which was like metal on metal, splitting Jemma's brain in two. She began to shake. Standing still was unbearable—she had to escape the sound ripping through her, or she would shatter. . . .

She turned and ran. Past gorse, over heather. Tripping on divots, getting up again. As her feet pounded the ground, the shaking stopped. But the screeching went on . . . and on . . . and now she became vaguely aware of being chased, a large shape speeding from behind—

Something thumped into her back, crashing her to the ground. Marsh's pony sped by. Arms were around her, turning her over. Marsh lay beside her, holding her down.

"*Focus!*" Marsh mouthed frantically, but Jemma still couldn't hear her. "*Mother—*"

Jemma thought of her mother's eyes. Blue points of light, reeling her in, anchoring her. Just like they had in the crystal, in the storm, and then, the first time Jemma had seen Sapphire herself, by the inn's door. Her heart soared. Her terror eased. The Mist loosened its grip. The shriek in her head faded, Marsh's voice buffeting through its echoes.

"Now, think of the river, the sun!" Marsh sat her up, still holding her firmly. "Breathe it in, Jem, deep into you! That's it, that's it. . . . Now, *blank!*"

Jemma's thoughts drained, and whiteness flooded her head. The Mist enveloped her, caressing her in its chill embrace. She gulped down air as the two of them sat holding each other for several minutes more. Then Jemma heaved a huge sigh.

"Ugh!" she said, pulling away. "That was awful!"

"You're tellin' me! Oh Jem, I thought I'd lost you for a moment. . . . I'm so sorry! It was too much, too soon. We'll ease up a bit, slow down your trainin'—"

Jemma shook her head. "No. I'm all right. We can't slow down. Not after what Digby and Talon told us about what's going on. The Agromonds have to be stopped."

"Jem . . . you jus' said their name, here in the Mist, without so much as flinchin'!" Marsh smiled through her tears. "My, you're a brave one, you are. Teach us all a lesson, I reckon. You'll be summonin' Luminals next, just you see. Come on." She stood, and pulled Jemma to her feet. "Let's be gettin' back to Oakstead. I don't know about you, but I could use a good bowl of soup. Then I think you should take the afternoon off."

"Maybe," said Jemma, knowing she wouldn't.

"I don't understand, though," she said, once they were riding back, "why the Mist closes in whether it thinks I'm friend or foe?"

"You feel the difference, though, don't you? One way it's

attackin' you, 'cause it sees you as the enemy; the other, when you blank and see your mind all white, that's what it sees too. Like you're part of it."

A part of it. That was the last thing Jemma wanted to feel, especially after what had just happened. How would she ever master it enough to move against the Agromonds when the time came? Would she ever be ready? Her parents seemed to think so. They were pleased with her progress. Her heal-ings, Light-focusing, and control of the crystals were coming on in leaps and bounds. And she was integrating the Stone's Power beautifully, her father said; soon, it would be so much a part of her that she would hardly need to think of the Stone at all. She'd also been developing something on her own that had begun with Pepper: communicating with animals other than the rats. Bats, birds, and bees now came to her call. Even larger creatures—dogs, goats, and horses—responded to her intentions. (Noodle and Pie, though, were still the only ones who could communicate with *her* in words.)

But however much she learned, it never felt enough. She still couldn't read others' thoughts as her mother could. And her distance viewing was abysmal. Once, when attempting to track Marsh, Jemma had thought she was in the kitchen, whereas in fact she'd been out in the orchard, leaning against a pear tree. As for summoning a Luminal—which nobody, not even her mother, had been able to do for years—there seemed no chance of that. Not the faintest wisp of a Light Being came, no matter how hard she tried. Still, something spurred her on, and wouldn't let her rest. Some compulsion that argued against her parents' worries that she was over-doing it and their concern for her safety, and kept reminding her of her childhood chant: *I am the Fire Warrioress, the fierc-est in the land. . . . Evil, evil, go away, cast out by my hand. . . .*

She gripped the reins and gritted her teeth. Could she really succeed against the Agromonds, when so many had failed? She didn't know. All she knew was that she would keep training until she felt strong enough to go back to Agromond Castle and do what she must. That day, she liked to think, was far in the future. But something kept telling her that it was blowing toward her more quickly than she was ready for, like a black storm gathering on a not-so-distant horizon.

Part Four

RETURN

CHAPTER THIRTY-FOUR

Called

The wind whisked Jemma over heather, moorland, forest. Five times twenty-four have passed, it moaned. Hasten, or they will not last! Agromond Castle loomed above pine tops; three small, luminous orbs pulsed from within. Five times twenty-four . . . they will not last. . . . Three mournful clangs; the three orbs, their light fading . . . "Help us . . ." *Children's voices, keening from the dungeons.* "Help!" *Then one voice rose above the rest:* "Jemma, help!"

Three orbs. Three children. The voice, again—"Help us, Jemma, help!"

"Flora!" Jemma woke in a panic, jumped out of bed, pulled on her clothes, and hurtled downstairs. Sapphire and Marsh were standing in the courtyard, drinking tea by the fire pit. They turned as Jemma ran outside.

"Mother, Marsh! I dreamed . . . the triplets—Digby's sister and brothers, calling for help . . . from the castle . . . taken by the Agromonds!"

"Ah." Sapphire's eyes paled. "I see this was no mere dream."

Marsh turned ashen. "So it's happened, has it?"

"Mother, Marsh—you both sound like you were *expecting* it!"

Sapphire stood and put her arm around Jemma. "My child," she said, "we have foreseen this for a while. It is a dreadful blow indeed. But it was always just a matter of time before the Agromonds reverted to their old ways. Of course, we had no way of knowing their next victims would be Digby's brothers and sister, nor that they would act so soon. The abductions used to be no more than twice yearly, and you've been gone barely five weeks."

"You mean . . . they've done this because they no longer have me?" Jemma pulled away from her mother. "Then it's my fault! If I hadn't escaped, they wouldn't need others!"

"Jemma, that is not what I meant!" Sapphire said. "Stop blaming yourself. Had you stayed—even if you'd gone to their side—do you think they would have given up their quest for more Power? People like them never have enough! They want total dominion, over everything and everyone. So *you* are not to blame, my child. It is they."

Jemma pulled away from her mother. "But why didn't you *tell* me? If I'd only known!"

"If you'd known," Lumo's voice interrupted from the doorway, "you'd have wanted to go and try to prevent the unpreventable."

"It wasn't unpreventable! We could have warned their parents."

"Jemma," Lumo said, sitting by the fire pit, "the Agromonds' force and cunning would have outwitted any amount of vigilance, just as it outwitted ours all those years ago. Nobody has ever been able to predict when they would strike."

"Flora." Jemma slumped onto the bench beside him. "I can't bear it! What can I *do*?"

Her parents and Marsh were motionless, their eyes darting to one another. "You know, don't you?" Jemma sighed. "I have to go and rescue them. I can't let them die."

Sapphire sat beside Lumo. "Yes. You must go. And sooner than I would like, for I cannot help being afraid." She bit her lips, her hands trembling.

Lumo put his arm around her. "I know. We thought there would be at least several weeks more." He looked at Jemma. "But you," he said, "it is as though all your senses were tuned to this event coming to pass now, driving you on. Never wavering. You have a core of fire, my child, that burns strong."

Jemma thought back over her almost five weeks of training. Her father was right. Some part of her had always known that she would return to Agromond Castle sooner rather than later. That was why she had kept pushing herself, at times even rousing from her dreams to work alone at night, or missing meals in order to squeeze in every moment of practice she could.

"Mother, don't worry," she said, her nerves twanging. "I'll be fine."

"But . . . the book . . ." Sapphire muttered. Every day since Jemma had told them that *The Forgotten Song* really existed, Sapphire had left no stone unturned in her search for it.

"It'll come to me when I need," Jemma whispered, "just as Majem said." *I hope,* she thought. Her mother would be up all night, she was sure, having one last frantic rummage through any obscure corner of Oakstead she could think of. Finding the lost volume would surely give them all some comfort.

"Jemma," said Lumo, taking her hand, "I am proud of you, and how quickly you've learned. We all are. However, you are still impetuous, and tend to jump to conclusions too readily. This concerns us, for the Mist will be fiercer once you're moving against those it defends. It will take advantage of the slightest flaw, and . . . well, we hope you are ready."

Jemma gulped, wishing she'd taken her father's thought-alignment classes a little more seriously. "I hope so too," she said. The thought of facing the Agromonds felt like a vise tightening around her. But Flora, Tiny, and Simon didn't deserve to die, let alone in the way the Agromonds planned. She drew in a deep breath. "I *am* ready. I have to be."

Lumo nodded, sighing. "We shall accompany you as far as we can, as will Ida."

Noodle and Pie peeked from Jemma's pockets and crawled onto her lap.

"And you two, of course." Lumo ruffled their fur. "Now, according to Majem, the Agromonds always prepared the children for a week. But we don't know when the triplets were taken. So I think it wise that we leave no later than tomorrow."

"Tomorrow . . ." Jemma's nerves shimmered. "But what do you mean, 'prepared'?"

"Feedin' 'em up, an' givin' 'em potions an' the like," said Marsh. "To prime 'em."

Jemma felt sick. What must the triplets be going through? And Digby, and his parents?

Lumo turned to Marsh. "Ida, for the rest of the morning, some last lessons, if you will, going over everything you can think of. And this afternoon, Jemma, we must do more work to lessen your self-deprecation, and perhaps try another Luminal summoning—" He was interrupted by the sound of hooves clattering from the town square, and a familiar voice yelling.

"Jemma! Where's Jemma? I must find her!"

"Digby!" Jemma sprang to her feet and ran toward the archway as Digby thundered into the courtyard and leapt from his pony.

"Jem! You got to come. The triplets—they—gone, five days ago!"

"Yes, Dig, we know—but five days?" Jemma remembered the words from her dream: *Five times twenty-four have passed....* "Why didn't you come sooner?"

"We din't know. They was stayin' the week at our cousin Smithy's, half a day south of us, an' when Flora an' the boys disappeared, well, Abe Smithy, he's only four, an' thought it was a game.... Din't tell his folks till the end of the day. Soon as they realized, Uncle Smithy tried to come to us, but the Mist kept at him, he was that angered—"

"Oh, Dig . . ." Jemma took his hands and squeezed them, her heart breaking for him.

"Took him more'n two days to reach us. Two days! By then our little 'uns had been gone more'n three. Pa an' me, we went straight up to the castle, an' saw 'em, Flora, Tiny, an' Simon, in the dungeons . . . it was awful, awful! Couldn't unlock 'em, Drudge don't have the keys no more, see—Nocturna took 'em, he said—so we said we'd go an' talk to the Agromonds, bargain with 'em, tell 'em we won't deliver to 'em no more, but Drudge, he talked us out of it, said it wouldn't do no good, they wouldn't care, an' would only kill us too. He kep' sayin' your name, *Jmaaagh, Jmaaagh,* you know, the way he does, *get Jmaaagh.*" Digby was trembling. "Said you was our only hope. I been riding all night . . . I hate to ask you, Jem, after what you been through, only I din't see what else . . . an' Ma n' Pa, they begged me. Please—"

"Dig, of course I'll come!"

Lumo and Sapphire stepped up beside them.

"We were already preparing our journey, Digby," Lumo said.

"But Lumo," Sapphire said, the blue washing almost entirely from her eyes, "if the Agromonds took the triplets five days ago, then . . ."

"Then we must leave now," he said, "since there are just two days left to save them."

The rescue party was soon ready. Pedrus had saddled another pony for Digby—his own was exhausted—while Bethany, Moll, and their mother had hastily packed sandwiches and flasks of mauve tea. Talon had given Jemma a woolen nightcap—it was a good disguise, she said; she couldn't see a single strand of red poking from it—and Pedrus lent her his saddlebags for Noodle and Pie, who settled in with the book, cloak, and crystals. At the last moment, Bethany thrust a shiny golden coin into Jemma's trouser pocket. "I blessed it at your homecoming fire," she said. "You never know, it might come in handy."

Jemma, her parents, Digby, Marsh, and the rats rode out of Oakstead on the stroke of ten.

They cantered along in silence, Marsh leading the way,

with Digby and Jemma close behind her, and Lumo and Sapphire bringing up the rear. The sun became hazier with each mile as the Mist thickened, and the morning air grew chilly and damp. Jemma pulled her cloak from the saddlebags and managed to wrap it around her, glad she'd thought of bringing it. She patted the Stone around her neck for extra reassurance.

Digby rode just ahead of her on Steadfast. How must he be feeling? Surely he must hate the Agromonds, so why didn't the Mist attack him? Poor Flora, Tiny, and Simon! The desire for revenge flared in her. Instantly, something that felt like an icy hand slapped her face, almost knocking her from the saddle. *The Mist is so quick to read me,* she thought. She reeled in her feelings and kept her eyes fixed over Grayboy's ears, until her mind and the white view ahead became one.

Soon they passed the point where she and Digby had been ambushed. Jemma's heartbeat quickened, rousing her from the rhythm of Grayboy's hooves. Noodle and Pie were restless in her pockets.

"What is it, Rattusses? You feel something too?" She looked around, alert to any sign of suspicious-looking strangers. But there were only rocks and heather.

Then came a scream, and a thud behind her.

"Lumo, Ida! Help!" Sapphire gasped. "No—stop!"

Jemma turned. Her mother was writhing on the grass, clutching her head. Her pony stomped the ground several feet away, snorting, its ears flat on its head.

"Never, never!" Sapphire screamed, lashing out at thin air. "Not my daughter, you won't—oh, merrily doth the skylark water on the garthmfflick!"

"Mother!" Jemma leapt off Grayboy.

"Jemma, stay!" Lumo was off his horse, running toward Sapphire. At the same moment, he and Jemma slammed into an invisible shield.

"Sapphire!" yelled Marsh. "Counter—use the Light!"

But Sapphire was rolling around singing at the top of her voice: "Jamemmamememma! Ah, the carbonariforous glug glug glu . . . Wheeeeeorrrrr!"

"Accursed Mist!" yelled Lumo. "Mord take it, it's— Oh! Folderolay flaflafla flombug!"

Marsh was beside Jemma now, pushing against the shield. Marsh's words ran through Jemma's head: *Counter . . . Blank . . .* She closed her eyes and thought of the moment she'd first seen Marsh riding out of the Mist to meet her. Warmth flooded her heart; the shield seemed to give a little. She opened her eyes. Marsh was still pushing frantically. Lumo was spinning in circles, slapping his head and muttering gibberish. But Digby was kneeling by Sapphire. Sapphire clung to him, wild-eyed. Gratitude welled up in Jemma and suddenly she too was through the shield and running toward them, as was Marsh. Seconds later, Lumo joined them, looking disheveled and disoriented.

"Digby! Thank you, my boy," he said. "Sapphire, speak to me!"

"Oh—oh—" Sapphire sputtered as Digby and Lumo helped her to her feet. "I had the merest thought, the merest flicker of worry about Jemma . . . then it grew into hatred for them for taking her. . . . I couldn't counter, couldn't blank . . . Too confused . . ."

"I, too," said Lumo, looking pale, "was taken off guard."

"But how did Digby get through?" Jemma asked. "He must have been thinking of the triplets. Why didn't it stop him?"

"Actually," Digby said, "I wasn't thinkin' of 'em. I just saw she needed help. That sort of took me over."

"An' don't forget," Marsh said. "Digby got through when he was lookin' for you in the forest that night, Jem. P'raps he has some immunity to the Mist from deliverin' to the castle every week."

"Digby," said Lumo. "When you think of your brothers and sister imprisoned at the castle, what is your feeling?"

"I want to help 'em, save 'em. Rips me up, it does."

"No thought of revenge against the Agromonds?"

"Revenge? I'll say. There's times I want to tear 'em limb from limb. But them thoughts is like poison goin' through me, tanglin' in my head till it's a mess an' muddle, an' I can't think straight. I figure that don't help the triplets none. So I jus' focus on 'em being home safe, like it's actually happened, you know? Then anythin' seems possible."

"Extraordinary," Lumo said. "Being able to put aside such anger . . . Your purity of heart is your best defense, Digby. For all our training, it puts us to shame."

Jemma walked over to Grayboy and the other horses, and gathered their reins. Clearly her parents would not be able to go on, vulnerable as they still were to the Mist.

"Jem," Marsh's voice came from behind her. "Your folks is goin' to have to turn back."

"I know." Jemma clenched her fists and tried to quell the hatred rising in her. She wished the Agromonds were dead.

"Their old wound—all that grief—is a sign the Mist recognizes 'em by—"

"Marsh, I'm not *stupid!*" Jemma wheeled round and raised her hand to hit her.

Marsh grabbed her arm. "It's the Mist, Jem, not you. Counter it!"

"Let me *go!*" Jemma struggled to free her arm.

"*Counter!*" Marsh held fast, her expression like steel. Jemma closed her eyes and concentrated. Here was her beloved Marsh, who had risked her life to save her, and was risking her life now to help her rescue children she hadn't even met. . . . Her fury subsided. Marsh let go of her arm.

"I'm so sorry!" Jemma said. "That was awful. . . . I just felt a little annoyed with you, then suddenly I was really furious."

"Don't mind about me, Jem. But you was thinkin' thoughts against *them,* weren't you, jus' before? You got to remember, the Mist'll take the smallest bad feelin' an' make it bigger. It can make enemies of us 'fore you can say 'Mother of Majem.'"

"I know. It won't happen again."

"Let's hope not. Come on, let's get back to the others."

"I see you've surmised our decision," said Sapphire as they approached. She and Lumo hugged Jemma, then Digby gave them each a leg up onto their horses. They looked disheveled and exhausted.

"Would that we could come with you," Sapphire said with a sigh, "but we'd only hinder you. We can help you better from out of the Mist. We shall send out Lightlines to you, and, with the whole of Oakstead, hold the vision for your success."

"Farewell, Jemma," Lumo said. "Nobody could wish for a finer daughter. Please, hurry back to us as fast as you can. . . . And Digby, remember my words to you. Ida, your friendship and love can never be repaid. All of you, we await your safe return: yours, and Digby's brothers and sister. May Light, and our love, be with you."

They turned their horses and trotted away. Jemma watched as their silhouettes were swallowed into the Mist.

CHAPTER THIRTY-FIVE

Mord Defenses

Jemma's energy drained. How quickly she had taken her parents' support for granted! And now, they were gone. She should have anticipated it, should have protected them with a light sphere, should have—

"Jem!" Marsh snapped her fingers. "Counter it, quick, or you'll be on your knees in no time."

"Every little thing! I don't know if I can—"

"You can. You jus' got to keep up your guard. Look, if your ma hadn't gone down, you'd still be managin' all right, hmmm?"

"I suppose." Jemma looked at Digby, who was holding Steadfast's reins as he shuffled from foot to foot. She couldn't let him, or the triplets, down. "All right, then. Let's go."

On they rode at a steady canter, Digby leading the way. His face looked more tense by the moment, but every time Jemma felt his anxiety creeping into her nerves, Noodle or Pie nosed out of the saddlebags and nipped her buttocks, reminding her to keep countering and blanking. She didn't even dare express any sympathy for Digby in case it knotted into anger or thoughts of revenge. Marsh, her expression like a mask, was clearly minding her own advice too, and focusing on shutting out the Mist. It was as though the chilly whiteness had drawn a veil between them all, and the thicker it became, the more their separation increased.

* * *

At the Elm River Pass, Digby steered Steadfast off the main track and headed down the steep path leading to the river. They had decided to take the long way around Blackwater that he had found the previous week; it was worth the extra hour it would take to avoid any Agromond followers, and Flashwing, Steadfast, and Grayboy were agile enough to make up the time once they were on flatter ground again.

They pulled up at the water's edge to eat the packed lunch that Bethany and Moll had prepared. The ground was slushy, and the river rushed by—the result, Digby said, of snow melting farther north. In Hazebury, the waters were even higher than they were here.

Finding a dry patch of moss under a tree, they spread out their meal. Jemma was surprised how hungry she was, and ate her cheese sandwich with gusto. Marsh too was tucking in, and Noodle and Pie were crunching an apple as if there was no tomorrow. Digby sat looking at the ground, tugging distractedly at a blade of grass.

"Chin up, lad." Marsh laid a hand on his arm. The Mist looked thicker around him, Jemma thought, than it did around Marsh.

"Digby," she said, "careful what you feel. I think the Mist is reading you." Her heart went out to what he must be going through. Were the triplets being starved? Tortured? Or both?

"Mind out, Jem," said Marsh. "Watch your own thoughts."

Digby got up and walked toward the bushes where the horses were tethered.

"Well, thanks for the gratitude!" Jemma stood and followed him through the wet grass. "I come out to this sun-forsaken place to help you, and you walk *away* from me?"

"Jem!" Marsh yelled after her. "Counter!"

"Digby, look at me when I'm talking to you!" Jemma caught up with him and grasped his shoulder. He stopped, his back to her, hands in pockets. He was shaking.

"Jemma!" Marsh's footsteps rustled through the leaves behind her. "I said, *counter*!"

"Digby! Can't you even face me?" Jemma yelled, trying to pull him around. "Hazebury dross!"

The force of her disdain shocked her and she dropped her hand. Those awful words—they were Nocturna's, Shade's, not hers! Digby turned, his face a picture of misery.

"Oh, Dig, I'm so sorry. . . ."

Marsh caught up to them. "It's you the Mist reads, Jem, not him! What he feels is normal with what's goin' on. But you . . ." Marsh shook her head. "I don't know what we're goin' to do if you keep lettin' the Mist get to you like this. You *got* to get a faster hold of yourself!"

Jemma bowed her head.

"T'ain't your fault, Jem." Digby wiped his face with the back of his sleeve. "I shouldn't have walked away from you. Your pa warned me to be careful."

"But I'm such a fool! Just an idiotic—" Jemma checked herself and took a deep breath, remembering her father's words about self-deprecation. "Still. I'm sorry."

"We got to stick together, eh, Jem?" said Digby, pulling her into a hug.

She nodded, and hugged him back.

Marsh heaved a sigh of relief. "Come on, you two. We best— Why, Mother of Majem, look at that!"

A sphere of Mist-free air had expanded around them.

Digby backed up, testing. The air around him remained clear. "Well, I'll be," he said. "Why d'you s'pose that is?"

Marsh raised her eyebrows and smiled. "I wouldn't know, I'm sure." She untied Flashwing and sprang into the saddle. "But you feel any trouble comin', you jus' remember the way you felt holdin' her like that. I wager it's as good as any counterin'. Now, best let the Mist back in, or it'll get suspicious. Then let's pack up the rest of lunch, and be off."

In the early afternoon, they came to a wooden bridge, and crossed to the woodlands on the other side of the river. The ponies cantered easily over the fir-needled ground, and soon Jemma heard the faint *whomp, whomp* of the waterwheel through the rush of water, and could just make out the ghostly form of Blackwater's greenhouses beyond the trees on the opposite bank. As they rode on, her nerves unwound slightly. The most dangerous place was now behind them, and there hadn't been a single person in sight.

Digby cantered ahead of Jemma and Marsh, the distance between them growing.

"Not so fast, Digby," Marsh muttered, kicking Flashwing on. Suddenly, she pulled to a halt, and held out her stumped arm, stopping Jemma. "I got a bad feelin'," she whispered.

"Then . . . Digby—we should warn him!"

The snort of a strange horse, ahead of them. The gruff voice, grating through the Mist.

"Oy, who goes there?"

"Jus' a poor traveler." Digby spoke in a dull tone.

"Wot, on a fine pony like that? Don't give me that guff, you lyin'— 'Ere, don't I know yer?"

Jemma went cold. Zeb. Lok's right-hand man.

"Yeh . . . I do know yer—*you're* the one wot escaped! Well, I've got yer now!"

"No—let go!"

The sound of a whip. Steadfast, whinnying. Digby, yelling.

"Jem," said Marsh, "use your animal talents—quick!"

Swift as lightning, Jemma's thoughts sped to the upper branches of the tall pines. *Wings, fly down, surround him, the one in the black coat—go, now! With no harm to anyone, man or beast . . .*

More yelling, whipping, screams of pain. Then, from the canopy above, a whirring sound began. It grew rapidly louder, then exploded into a chorus of caws and a fury of flapping as a mass of wings and feathers swooped down through the branches.

"Oy! What the— Help!" Zeb yelped.

"Come on, Marsh!" Jemma kicked Grayboy, and he lurched forward. Digby was just visible through the Mist, Steadfast backing away from the thick curtain of birds that had dropped around Zeb and his steed. Jemma galloped by, reaching out to smack Steadfast's rump as she passed. Steadfast took off after her with Marsh thundering behind, leaving the panicked screams of Zeb and his horse to be absorbed into the Mist and the trees and the cacophany of wings.

The sun dipped toward the horizon. Once they were well south of Blackwater, they had crossed to the west of the Elm again, just before it branched off into the smaller Stoat River. For several hours, they had kept up an even pace, stopping occasionally to let the ponies drink and. snatch a snack of grass before pressing on.

The air was brisk, a stiff breeze whipping up. Jemma pulled Talon's hat over her ears and huddled into her cloak. The terrain became more hilly, the gray tree silhouettes more frequent. They were entering Agromond territory. Once or twice the Mist investigated her, jumbling words in her head, but she finally had the measure of it, and by focusing on Flora's smile, and envisioning the triplets safely back in Hazebury, she kept it at bay.

Soon, Jemma heard the faint rush of water in the distance: they were back near the Stoat River. Hazebury wasn't far now. Digby and Marsh were practically out of sight, apparently unaware that she'd fallen behind. She kicked Grayboy into a faster canter.

"Dig, Marsh—wait for me."

The wind buffeted Jemma's words into the hillside. Unease bristled her back, and she urged Grayboy on. But Digby and Marsh were also gathering speed. The unease twined around her heart. Something felt very wrong. Grayboy, evidently, felt it too. He laid his ears flat, stretched out his neck, and surged forward, then veered sharply to the left, heading toward the river. Jemma was thrown to the right. The reins snapped from her hands, and her left foot wrenched from the stirrup, leaving her knee hooked over the saddle. She grabbed the pommel and held on for dear life, the rush of the Stoat becoming louder with each stride Grayboy took. Noodle and Pie peeked from the saddlebags, squealing as she'd never heard before. She followed their gaze. A black cloud was approaching, thick and deadly, swifter than Grayboy could bolt.

Mordsprites. Hundreds of them.

Jemma remembered her father's warning: *Once they catch you unawares, they've got you in their clutches. . . .* Thank goodness she had seen them in time! Mustering every ounce of concentration she could, she envisioned a ball of gold Light expanding around her. The first ranks of Mordsprites slammed into it. She managed to grab one of the reins and heave herself back into the saddle. But the saddlebags were slipping sideways. Before she could stop them, they slid from Grayboy's haunches and out of the protective light sphere, with Noodle and Pie inside.

A Mordsprite caught them in midair.

"No—Rattusses!"

The Mordsprite flew upward, lifting saddlebags and rats into the swarming throng.

"Noodle, Pie, jump!" Jemma shot a grounding cord to them as they tried to scramble free, but the Mordsprite swerved, and the cord missed. "Jump—*jump!* I can't keep up—"

She leaned into Grayboy's neck and urged him on. *Faster, boy, faster!* He shot forward. The saddlebags were just ahead now, Noodle and Pie dangling perilously from them.

"Now, Rattusses—*jump!* I'll catch you!"

Suddenly, Grayboy pulled up at the river's edge. Jemma flew over his ears, grasping for the rats, but she landed empty-handed in freezing water. Sputtering to the surface, she slammed into a rock. She clung onto it, looking frantically around. The black trail of Mordsprites turned to the right and disappeared into the Mist, dropping the saddlebags into the torrent below with the rats still dangling from them, and the crystals and book inside.

"Noodle! Pie!" Jemma screamed. She tried to wade farther into the river, but was swept off her feet and slammed into another rock, her cloak ripped from her shoulders by the rush of water. She pulled herself up the muddy bank, then ran in the direction of the flow, but the Mist was so thick that she could only just make out a piece of driftwood being tossed in the swell. Noodle and Pie were nowhere to be seen. *Please, please, let them be safe. . . .* For a split second, she thought she saw a streak of light speeding across the river, but it was swallowed, like the driftwood, into white noise.

"No-o-o-o!" Jemma leaned against a tree and wailed into her hands. "No-oooo—my Rattusses!" The Mist curled around her as if gloating in triumph. The treacherous river rushed by. The thought of never seeing Noodle and Pie again speared through her. How would she manage without them? It was unbearable. As unbearable as if she lost Digby or Marsh.

Digby. Marsh . . .

Suddenly, she realized where the Mordsprites had headed off to. "Oh, no, *no* . . ."

Grayboy nibbled her hair—Talon's hat, she now realized, had also been claimed by the river. She shivered, her muscles like jelly. It was all she could do to climb back into the saddle. The pony set off of his own accord at a rapid trot, weaving between bushes and trees until Jemma could see Flashwing and Steadfast's gray forms through the Mist.

"Marsh!" she cried. "Digby!" Nothing but chilly white. "Where are you? *Digby!*"

"Jem!" Digby leapt up behind a bramble bush. "Over here!"

"Dig, thank goodness!" Jemma slid off Grayboy and stumbled through the heather toward him. Marsh was lying in the mud, rubbing her right calf, groaning. Jemma dropped to her knees beside her. "What happened?"

"Caught me unawares," Marsh growled between gritted teeth. "An' now look at me!"

"A great black cloud it was," Digby croaked, squatting down. "Came right up behind us. Brought Marsh down, an'— Jem, are you all right? You're soaked! An' you look right shook up."

"Thrown into the r-river. Noodle and Pie . . ." Jemma choked on the words. "Swept away."

"No!" Digby gasped.

"Oh, Jem!" Marsh reached up and put her hand to Jemma's face.

Jemma bit back tears. First her parents, then the rats, and now Marsh, who surely couldn't go on in such pain—but at least Jemma could do something about that. Her hand was drawn to Marsh's calf, sensing the jagged fracture beneath the skin. She pinpointed her intention, and drew energy through her Stone, saw the bone mending in her mind's eye—

"Aaaagh—stop!" Marsh yelped and pushed Jemma's hand away. "I can feel it knittin' all wrong. It's no good out here in the Mist, Jem, with you feelin' so upset; an' I'm no help neither, the state I'm in. I'll ride back to Oakstead. Your folks'll fix me up."

"No, no! Let's make a shelter—I'll work all night, and, and . . . tomorrow, you'll see—"

"Jem, there's no time. Here, you two, help me up."

Jemma and Digby lifted Marsh to sit. Her face was tight with pain.

"Listen to me. Jem, I knows you feel the loss of your

338

friends deep in your soul, an' believe me, I knows how guttin' it is. After my Julius was killed . . . Well, you jus' can't let it stop you. Think of the loss of them triplets to Digby and his folks. Think of the Prophecy. You mustn't hold back now, not for a second, least of all to wait for me to heal. You got to go on without me."

Jemma closed her eyes and took a deep breath. The Prophecy. Despite everything, it still burned inside her, driving her. She'd been drawn inexorably to this destiny from the moment she first started having doubts about the Agromonds, and had set it in motion with her first step toward escape. She tilted her face skyward and opened her eyes. How she would ever bring back the sun, she had no idea, but rescuing the triplets was vital. They couldn't wait.

"Right," she said. "We'd better get moving."

With the help of a nearby rock and a great deal of effort, Digby and Jemma lifted Marsh into Flashwing's saddle. Digby padded her wounded leg with Steadfast's saddle rug.

"Well, pet," said Marsh, squeezing Jemma's hand, "it's up to you an' Digby now. Don't forget the Light Game, will you? An' blankin', an' . . ."

"I'll remember, Marsh." Jemma squeezed her hand back, gratitude for her dear ally's years of devotion pouring through her. "Thank you. Be safe, won't you? I— Oh!"

A golden wisp of light whisked out of nowhere and began spiraling around Marsh.

Marsh gasped. "A Luminal—Jem!"

"What? I didn't do that!"

"Yes, you did! It wooshed up from behind you, I seen with my own eyes. Quick as a flash, they come. Whatever you was thinkin' just then is what brought it. Best protection I could wish for!" Marsh's face glowed in the Luminal's golden light.

"Protection?" Jemma thought of the streak she'd seen speeding across the river toward Noodle and Pie not ten minutes earlier. "Oh, I hope so. . . ."

"I know so, Jem. Ain't no more Mordsprites can get me with this for company, even if they do catch me unawares!" She squeezed Jemma's hand again, her expression turning serious. "You can do this, pet. I knows you can. See you soon, eh?"

Jemma nodded, and Marsh rode into the Mist, the Luminal rotating slowly around her.

"A Luminal," said Digby. "After all these years! Not bad, Jem. Reckon I'll be all right with you."

"I don't even know how I did that, Dig. *If* I did. So don't go expecting Luminals at every twist and turn, all right?" She sighed. "I can't believe Marsh didn't sense the Mordsprites coming."

"Ouff, you should've seen 'em! They jus' *went* for her. Din't seem to even notice me."

"Really? Maybe you do have some kind of immunity, Dig, like Marsh said. From Mordsprites, as well as the Mist." She smiled. "Must be that purity of heart of yours."

Digby shrugged and put his hand on her shoulder. "P'raps it's 'cause I wasn't thinkin' of them Agromonds. I was thinkin' of you, an' holdin' you, back there."

Jemma remembered her father's words about positive thoughts keeping Mordsprites at bay. Digby's had probably saved Marsh from a worse assault too.

"How are you now, Jem?" Digby said. "After . . . you know . . ."

Jemma knew what he meant: Noodle and Pie. Sadness clawed at her. "I have to try and believe they'll be safe, somehow."

Digby nodded. "I feel like that about Flora, Tiny, and Simon. Come on, let's get goin'. Ma will cook a good hot meal for us— Hey, I just realized, you're completely dry!"

"So I am! That's odd. . . ." The book and cloak were somewhere at the bottom of the Stoat River, along with the crystals. Had her Stone taken on some of their Power? She put her palm over it, and silently thanked it, grateful for not being soaked through.

They cantered on in silence. It was an effort for Jemma to suppress the image of Noodle and Pie being swept away, but she found that by imagining them surrounded by Light and jumping from the driftwood onto dry land, she could counter the hollow in her heart, and the rest of their journey passed without incident. Dusk brought a sharper breeze to the air, and at last, Hazebury's ragged thatched rooves and gray stone cottages emerged through the Mist. From far above, came a doleful sound that struck doom into her bones:

Clang!

A light drizzle began to fall as they pulled up outside Goodfellow's Grocery, its sign squeaking in the gathering wind.

CHAPTER THIRTY-SIX

Preparing

"I'll stable the horses," Digby said, his teeth chattering. "You go on in."

Jemma opened the door, expecting to find the warmth she remembered, but inside was almost as cold as out, the atmosphere denser than November clouds. Gordo and Berola Goodfellow sat hunched at the kitchen table, a candle stub set between them. They looked up as she walked in.

"Oh," said Berola. "It's you. You've got a nerve, you have."

"Don't know why you're here," Gordo muttered. "You, of all people."

"But Gordo, Mrs. Goodfellow . . ." Jemma was taken aback. This wasn't at all the sort of welcome she'd anticipated. "I don't understand. . . . You asked Digby to fetch me. . . ."

"You? Come off it!" Gordo snapped. "It's your fault this happened! Hadn't been no snatchin's for years, not since they took you. If you hadn't escaped . . ." He lowered his eyes and stared at the candle's wan flame. "An' now, who knows if our babies is still alive, even."

Guilt snapped through Jemma's nerves, but then she remembered what her mother had said: No amount of Power would be enough for the Agromonds. The abductions would have started again, no matter what. Gordo and Berola were desperate. That was why they blamed her. They just needed a little hope.

"Gordo, Mrs. Goodfellow," she said gently, "I understand you thinking it's my fault. But I'm going to do everything I can to get your little ones back. They *are* still alive, I know it. My dreams showed me . . . and my parents said—" Jemma stopped herself before any mention of sacrifice could escape her lips.

"Dreams?" Berola sneered. "An' what do your *parents* know? They din't exactly help you when you was up there, did they, for all their so-called Powers!"

"Please, you must believe me! The more you're behind me, the stronger I'll be, and the better my chances. I need your support, your blessing. We *will* get them back, Digby and I—"

"Digby? You in't takin' him too!" Berola stood, her eyes piercing the gloom.

The door opened, and Digby came in, accompanied by a snap of cold air. His face instantly registered his parents' mood.

"Ma, Pa," he said, "what's goin' on?"

"They blame me for what's happened," said Jemma.

"Jem's come to help us," Digby said, walking to the table. "You know that!"

"An' you think, do you," said Gordo, his voice bristling, "that we'd trust her? She should'a stayed in the castle, where she belonged!"

"But how can you say that? We was agreed—Jemma's our best hope!"

"What do you know, boy?" Gordo leapt to his feet, fists clenched.

"I know you're bein' bull-headed, you and Ma!"

"Us? What about you, bringin' that huffy young miss here?"

Suddenly, Jemma saw in her mind's eye what had happened: the Agromonds, taking a piece of clothing from the triplets and twisting it, to twist the minds of those nearest and dearest to their little victims—an added act of cruelty. It had infected Gordo and his wife—and Digby was in danger of being drawn into it. "Digby," she said, "your folks are under some kind of spell. It's confusing them, making everything worse. Careful . . . It's getting to you too."

"Me?" Digby scratched his head. "Rotten rhubarb! I think you're right. . . ."

"A spell, makin' everything worse?" Berola said, thumping the table. "How dare you! As if anythin' could be worse than losin' our little 'uns! You're a fine one, you are—"

"Ma, stop it!" Digby yelled. "It's not Jemma's fault—this in't like you!"

Jemma drew in her breath as Digby and his parents stood glaring at each other. How could she break the sorcery? How was it connecting to them? She narrowed her eyes. Something that looked like thin dark strands of smoke was snaking between the three Goodfellows, dividing and tightening into a finer web. Remembering her parents' instruction, she focused hard, and imagined golden Light infusing the strands, dissolving them and banishing the soupy gray.

"Let no more come without permission!" she proclaimed. "So be it!"

The room seemed to exhale, as if even the furniture were

relaxing. Digby shook himself, and Gordo and Berola blinked as if they'd just awoken.

"Why, Jemma, lass—you're here!" said Berola. "When did you arrive?"

Jemma heaved a sigh of relief. "A few moments ago."

"Bless you, bless you!" Berola waddled over and gave her a hug. "Thank you for comin', an' so fast! We been at our wits' end these past days, haven't we, Gordo?"

"That we have." The furrows on Gordo's face seemed to have deepened since Jemma had last seen him, drawing his normally jovial expression downward. "Any ideas, about, you know . . . gettin' 'em back?"

Jemma shook her head. "We couldn't plan when we were coming through the Mist. It would have read our intentions."

"Well, here's a thought," said Digby. "Tomorrow's delivery day. We can take you in the cart with us, Jem—"

"You're still going to make deliveries, even though they took the triplets?"

"Why, yes," said Berola, sitting again. "First off, they prob'ly don't even know they's our little 'uns, since they took 'em from a diff'rent village. Second, if the Agromonds don't get food, neither does Flora, Simon, an' Tiny."

"Oh. Of course." Jemma felt her face flush. "Sorry, Mrs. Goodfellow. I wasn't thinking."

"S'all right," Berola said. "An' it's Berola to you, lass."

"So," Digby continued, "we get you into the yard, then once Pa an' me finish our deliverin', I'll stay behind with you an' hide out—"

"No, no, no!" Berola interrupted. "Not you too! What if you was to get caught? To lose all four of you—"

"Ma, them's our little 'uns, an' if Jem is good enough to rescue 'em for us, then I'm stickin' by her. It's only right!"

"But Digby, I couldn't bear it if . . ." Berola bit her lip.

"I can help, Ma! We have a better chance of gettin' the squibs back with two of us than if it's just Jemma. I know it."

"They're right, Berola, love," Gordo said. "It's all or nothin'. We must give 'em both our blessin'."

Berola hung her head for a second, then attempted a smile. "Right, then. You'd best get on with plannin', hadn't you? I'll get the stove goin' an' make us some soup."

"Thanks, Ma." Digby squeezed her shoulder, then turned to Jemma. "So, like I was sayin' . . ."

They planned as Berola cooked. Though hiding out in the stables was safe enough for Digby, it would be too dangerous for her, Jemma said; what if Rue was at the Dwellings, and saw her, or even just *sensed* her, as she'd said she could? It would be best if she waited in the castle. ("That means smugglin' you in," Digby said, "'cause that Shade creature's been there the last few times, bossin' us around.") They agreed that, after an hour or so, Digby would join Jemma in the Vat Room, where they'd stay until after dark. Then Jemma could sneak upstairs and take the keys from Nocturna's room.

"It won't be the first time I've stolen from her while she was asleep," Jemma said, flinching as she remembered. "I've done it once, I can do it again."

"That's the girl! Then Pa comes back with the cart . . . we free the little 'uns . . . and away we go! Sounds simple enough, don't it?"

"It does, lad, it does." Gordo nodded in agreement. "We'll soon have our babies back, Berola, love, you'll see."

346

"I hope you're right." Berola sighed, stirring the pot. "I hope you're right."

Jemma snuggled into Flora's bed, her stomach pleasantly warmed by Berola's soup. She was grateful to be facing this rescue with Digby, but the thought of being back at the castle without Noodle and Pie weighed heavy in her heart. Majem's missing book niggled in the back of her mind too. Even without the cloak, crystals, and book, which the Stoat River had claimed, she would have felt more confident with *The Forgotten Song* in her pocket.

She clutched her Stone for reassurance, but trepidation wove through her. The Prophecy felt like a heavy wagon poised at the top of a steep hill with her on it, and any moment now it would start rolling downward, gathering speed as it went, with no way to stop it.

The night hours dragged by, marked by the distant toll from Agromond Castle. Jemma drifted in and out of a restless doze. Images tumbled through her head: the rats, floating in nothingness; voices fragmenting, echoing; Agromond faces, looming and receding; three luminous orbs, being swallowed into Mist and darkness. Three orbs. Flora, Simon, Tiny. Finally, five distant clangs roused her, and she dragged herself out of bed.

She pulled on Digby's old brown breeches and off-white shirt, then stumbled down to the kitchen and gobbled half a bowl of porridge before following Berola and Gordo out into the gray dawn and across the yard to the stables. Digby was adjusting Pepper's harness, having already loaded the cart with supplies. Dark circles ringed his eyes.

"Dig, you look exhausted," said Jemma. "Did you sleep at all?"

"I'll be fine. How 'bout you, though? You look a bit rough."

"I'm all right. Just . . ."

"It's the Prophecy, in't it?"

Jemma nodded. "It scares the daylights out of me, Dig. But even after we've rescued the triplets"—*If we do,* she thought—"the Agromonds won't stop at this. There'll be others . . . and I'm the one who's supposed to put an end to their tyranny, but I don't have a clue how."

"One step at a time, eh?" he said. "We'll cross other bridges when we come to 'em. Let's jus' keep seein' the outcome in our minds. Reckon that's what Marsh'd say, don't you?"

"I reckon," said Jemma, feeling comforted by his saying "we." She pulled a carrot from her pocket and fed it to Pepper, who snorted and tossed her head.

Berola waddled over and hugged Jemma. "You jus' come back to us safe an' sound, you hear?" she said. "All of you."

"We'll do our best," said Jemma.

"Aye," said Berola, wiping a tear from her cheek. "You'll do your best, I know."

Gordo held out a sack. "Get in, lass," he said. "You ready for this?"

"Ready as I'll ever be."

Jemma curled into the sack and crouched down. Gordo and Berola packed tufts of wormwort around her and stuffed potatoes around the outside of it. Gordo shoved the drawstring into the opening for Jemma to tie, so that she could free herself once inside the castle. Then Digby hoisted her onto the cart and slammed the tailgate shut.

"See you later," he said.

Jemma heard him clamber up into the driver's seat beside Gordo. The cart trundled into the street, wheels rattling over cobblestones. She imagined the small Hazebury cottages and wondered about the people inside. Did they know that Flora, Simon, and Tiny were missing? They must do, surely. And like centuries of villagers before them, they must also know where the children had gone. Perhaps they were peering out through inched-back curtains, feeling sorry for the Good-fellows' plight, relieved that it wasn't their own. What did they think of Gordo and Digby, taking supplies to the castle nonetheless? Perhaps their senses were too dulled by eons of Mist to question it, or they were simply too afraid.

The road rose as they crossed the bridge. The river's babble gradually dwindled. Soon, Jemma felt the jiggle of unpaved track heading up Mordwin's Crag. Five-thirty tolled. The day stretched endlessly ahead like a thick, dark corridor teeming with unseen dangers, with tonight's rescue the dimmest light at the end of it. One wrong move, and that light could go out forever. But she knew she must counter all her fears this instant, and blank out, or the Mist would quickly detect her presence. Closing her eyes, she inhaled the thick worm-wort scent and imagined it veiling her thoughts as it filled her lungs, relaxing her. Her limbs sank into the wooden floor, becoming one with it. A bright light spread in her mind's eye, expanding until it became her entire inner vision, white and impenetrable, indistinguishable from the Mist.

Now, it would not be able to find her.

CHAPTER THIRTY-SEVEN

Closing In

"I'll get this one, Pa," said Digby. "Can you manage them jars?"

"Righto, lad."

Jemma heard Gordo walk across the yard and into the castle.

"Here we go, Jem," Digby whispered, pulling her to the tailgate. "Shade's there, like we thought she'd be. Sorry if treatin' you like a sack of spuds gets a bit rough." He lifted her onto the ground and bumped her across the cobbles. As he dragged her over the threshold, darkness pressed into her bones, as if the castle were goading her, threatening.

"Well, *Mister* Drudge," Shade's voice sliced down the corridor, "what have I told you about mauve tea? It is to be reserved for us, not wasted on the likes of Mr. Goodbellows here."

"Goodfellow, if you please, Miss." Gordo's voice sounded tight.

"And make haste with those pancakes, stupid old man!"

Jemma heard Drudge's wheeze as the oven door opened, his "Gnnn . . ." as he slapped pancakes onto plates. The scratchy tone that had once filled her with disgust was now music to her ears.

"Phew!" Digby hoisted Jemma's sack against a wall. "Them spuds is heavy."

"*Potatoes*, you ignoramus." Shade snorted. "You do *know* that, don't you? Or are you simply too idiotic?"

"I . . . I . . ." Digby was bristling, Jemma could tell, and she willed him to keep calm. "I'm sure I don't have your sharp wit and intelligence, Miss."

"Ha! Nobody in this Mordforsaken place does." Shade was clearly in her element. Jemma could just imagine her, head thrown back, dark hair shining in the kitchen lamplight, black eyes flashing like her mother's. "I don't know why you're bringing that despicable vegetable here anyway. Potatoes indeed! Common fodder, fit only for pigs or the likes of you. Good day to you both, Mr. Goodfallow."

"Goodfellow, Miss."

"Good-for-nothing! Be on your way."

"Let's go, Pa. Good day to you, Miss. Oops, my shoelace." Digby's breath came close to Jemma's face. "See you soon," he whispered, then his footsteps and Gordo's faded away.

"Hazebury dross! Now, old man"—Shade picked up a tray—"when I return from delivering Mama's breakfast, I expect mine and Feo's to be ready." Her shoes clicked across the floor, then down the Pickle Corridor toward the stairs.

"Gnnnasssty!" Drudge clunked the oven door shut and shuffled over to Jemma. "Ssso they, good!" He patted the sack. "Jmmaaah, good!" His acrid breath bit into her nostrils.

Jemma puckered her face. "Drudge!" she said. "It's so good to hear you!"

"Me . . . Help?" He tugged the top of the sack.

"I'll wait till Shade's fetched the last tray, then let myself out."

"Ssso they . . . Good!" Drudge's voice was almost animated

as he went about preparing the next two trays, muttering all the while, "Ssso they, good!"

Seven o'clock struck. Before long, Shade's crisp footsteps approached again. She picked up another tray and minced out of the kitchen without a word. Drudge's slow shuffle followed, his old bones cracking under the weight of Nox's tray.

"Latrrr, Jmmmaaah," he wheezed. Then he was gone.

Jemma waited a safe amount of time before freeing herself from the sack, which she bundled up and stuffed behind the others Digby had left. Brushing wormwort from her hair and clothes, she looked around the kitchen. It was deathly quiet. Its stone walls and ceiling still glistened with grease and damp, the air still breathed contempt, yet everything seemed to have become smaller and more decayed, even in the few weeks since she had escaped.

She glanced at the Corridor of Dungeons. Which cell were the triplets in? Her stomach knotted. Five days already since they'd been taken! It was tempting to go to them now and tell them about the rescue, but she and Digby had agreed it would be too risky: Under pressure from the Agromonds, any of them—especially Tiny—might talk. She must resist, and wait for Digby in the Vat Room, as they'd planned.

She moved toward the West Corridor, then heard a heart-rending cry.

"Help us . . . help!"

Flora! The terror in her voice jarred through Jemma. Without a second thought, she turned and pelted past Drudge's sleeping nook, and down the corridor.

"Help us—help!" Two small arms strained through the bars of the littlest dungeon at the end.

"I'm coming! Hold on." Jemma reached the cell and grasped Flora's hands. Two boys, one tall, with sandy hair like Digby, the smaller one hugging a worn teddy bear, scrambled to the bars. They thrust their hands through, snatching at Jemma's clothes.

"You've come, you've really come!" Their voices jumbled together. "Flora said you would, she said—"

"Tiny, Simon—hello! Yes, yes, I'm here. . . ." The stench of urine made Jemma reel. Flora, Tiny, and Simon were shivering, fear hollowing their small faces.

"Where's Digby?" said the taller boy, who Jemma guessed must be Simon.

"He's coming later," Jemma said, releasing Flora's hands. "Tonight. Then we'll get you out of here. But now, you must listen very carefully. Don't let *anybody* know you've seen me, or that Digby will be here. If they catch us, we'll be locked up too, and there'll be no way for any of us to escape. Do you understand?"

Three heads nodded.

"Now tell me, do they know you're Goodfellows?"

Three heads shook.

"Good. No matter what, don't let them know, or they'll think it's odd that your pa and Digby didn't say anything this morning, and will suspect something's up. Have you got all that?"

"Don't tell 'em you're here—" said Simon.

"Or Digby," added Tiny, putting his thumb in his mouth and clutching his bear.

"And don't tell 'em we're Goodfellows," said Flora, "so's they don't suspect."

"Right." Jemma glanced around the cell. Her escape hole, of course, had been plastered over. The air was as dank and chilly as when she'd been captive, but there were no blankets or extra clothing to keep the triplets warm. A chamber pot, half-full, was close to the door, and crumbs were scattered in the dust. "Mord take them," she muttered between clenched teeth, "keeping you all in here—"

"I'm hungry," Tiny said.

"So am I," said Flora and Simon in unison. "Can we have some food?"

"Haven't they fed you?" Jemma was shocked. So much for preparing them!

"The horrid girl said we couldn't have food," said Flora. "The smelly old man sometimes brings us bread, though, and some yucky purple stuff to drink."

"And stew with slimy bits in," added Simon. "But it makes us feel sick. We haven't eaten hardly anythin' since the honeyeyed bees the nice man gave us. Only he wasn't so nice. . . ."

"He said there'd be more," said Tiny, his thumb-sucking becoming louder, "if we went with him in his shiny carriage. But there wasn't." He wiped a tear from one eye with the back of his dust-caked sleeve. "An' then he brought us here, an' wouldn't let us go."

Jemma's blood boiled. "Hang on," she said. "I'll see if I can find you something."

She sped back to the kitchen, ears alert as she skittered to the oven and opened the door. There were a few pancakes on a baking tray, still warm. Just then she heard Drudge's shuffle approaching down the Pickle Corridor, closely followed by keys rattling and the familiar clicking of black patent leather shoes. Shade! Jemma quickly closed the oven door and ducked into Drudge's sleeping alcove as Shade's acid voice cut through the air.

" . . . the little brats, since we must test them for tomorrow's Ceremony."

"Gnnnnn . . ."

Jemma peeked into the kitchen.

"Here," said Shade, handing Drudge the huge bunch of keys as they appeared. "You unlock them. I'm not going down that corridor if I can help it. It stinks."

Jemma eyed the chamber pot beneath Drudge's pallet. How she would love to empty its contents over Shade's head! But she pulled back, holding her breath as Drudge creaked past. Then she peered into the kitchen again. Shade paced in and out of view between the door frame, muttering to herself.

"Stupid, stupid . . . accursed girl! If only Mama . . . *me*! They're all so *weak*." A clump of plaster fell from the ceiling, narrowly missing the back of her head. "Wretched decay!" She kicked the fallen plaster, which shattered into dust. "It's all *their* fault!"

So there was conflict in the Agromond camp! That could be useful . . . Jemma strained to hear more of Shade's muted ranting, but it was drowned out by a mishmash of frightened voices drifting up the corridor—"*Why? Where are you taking us?*" She could just make out Drudge's silhouette, and three smaller ones being ushered out of the dungeon.

"Gnnnn . . . You poor child'nnn . . ."

"But we have to wait here for Jemma!" said Tiny's voice.

Drudge, Simon, and Flora shushed him in unison.

"Shut up, Tiny!" said Simon. "We promised—"

Jemma's heart missed a beat. Had Shade heard? But Shade was evidently too intent on her private monologue to have noticed. Jemma pulled back into the shadows as Drudge and the triplets passed by.

"So this is the mealy bunch, is it?" Shade sneered. "Well, I suppose they'll have to do. We'll soon find out which is the strongest." Her heels clicked toward Drudge. "The keys, if you please, *Mister* Drudge. If you think you can get away with keeping them from me, think again."

"Gnnnn . . . aa . . ."

"And don't *gnnaaaa* me, you miserable old bag of bones. I'm running this castle now, and don't you forget it! See?" Shade rattled the keys at him. "I'm not giving these back to Mama, oh, no! I should have taken them weeks ago, after that lowborn chit escaped. Now, you three, stop trembling, and—" Shade stopped. "Wait a minute, wasn't there another sack this morning?"

You could have heard a mouse blink.

"Yes . . . ," Shade said slowly. "The *spuds*, wasn't it? What happened to them?"

Jemma's heart was in her mouth.

"Well, fool, I'm waiting for an explanation!"

"Gnnn . . . missstake." Drudge inhaled with a great wheeze. "You, Missss, no like . . . Boy, came back."

Clang! The single toll of seven-thirty rang out.

"Is that so? Well, in that case I shall dock their pay for their idiocy in bringing them in the first place. Come, you little squirts. We're late."

Finally, Shade was gone, and the triplets with her. Jemma came out of her hiding place.

"Drudge," she said. "I'm going to follow them."

Drudge grabbed her arm and shook his head.

"I have to, Drudge! Mord knows what those monsters have in store for them! But I need to get a message to Digby. He's in the stables. Please, will you go and tell him the plan's changed? Tell him to wait out there, then I'll meet him tonight, here in the kitchen. At ten o'clock, after Gordo comes back."

Drudge nodded. Jemma ran into the Pickle Corridor and toward the stairway in pursuit of the triplets and whatever atrocious ordeal awaited them.

CHAPTER THIRTY-EIGHT

Back in the Fold

The Ceremony Chamber door was closed. Jemma crouched by one of the suits of armor, whose halberd looked perilously ready to fall on her, and listened.

"You three, cease sniveling," Nocturna said. "This is just a little test."

"Mama," said Shade. "Allow me. Here, you!"

"Ow!" Tiny yelped. "My arm . . . Oooooooow!"

"Feeble!" Feo's voice was deeper than a month ago.

"Shut up, Feo," said Shade. "Now, boy, what's this raggy thing you're clinging onto? Give it to me."

"No! Give him back—Bruno!"

"Bruno, is it? Aaah, poor ickle thing. Does he like having *his* arm twisted, I wonder? Oh, dear, it's come off. Ha ha ha!"

"Noooo!" Tiny started crying. "You're hurtin' him!"

"Shade!" Nox's voice. "Was that entirely necessary?"

"Perhaps you'd like to bungle this whole thing as well, would you, Papa?" Shade's voice was drenched in disgust. "Hmmph. As I thought. Here, boy, take your stupid Bruno thing. You, other boy. Come here."

Tentative footsteps. Flames crackling. Jemma heard groans, and panting, then Simon cried out in pain. She clenched her fists.

"Ha!" said Shade. "Both boys are utter weaklings, as I expected. You, girl. Your turn."

Flora gasped. The boys whimpered. Fury shot through Jemma's veins. It was all she could do not to intervene—but captured, she'd be in no position to help them.

"Shade," Nox said, "enough! It's obvious she's the strongest one. You don't need to—"

"Why, Papa? Do you not have the stomach for it?"

Flora screamed. Jemma's hand leapt to the doorknob, her heart ripping into pieces.

"Stop it!" Tiny cried out. "Jemma—help us, help!"

"Shut up, Tiny!" Flora sobbed. "Shut up!"

"Oh, Jem-*mah*, is it?" Shade's voice rippled with danger. "And why would you call for *her*, may I ask?"

"'Cause . . . 'cause . . . ," Tiny whimpered, "sh-she's the Fire One! Flora s-said."

"Fire One? Ha! Fables and lies! And how could she possibly help you, even if she was here? She has no more Powers now than a dead dormouse!"

"Yes she has! An' . . . an' . . . she's not dead, or a d-dormouse. She's alive, an' she's here!"

"Tiny!" Flora yelled. "Shut *up*!"

"What do you mean, she's here?" said Shade. "Talk, little blabbermouth! No? Then give me your stupid rag-bear thing. There!" Jemma heard a soft thud, and a fizzling sound.

"Bruno!" Tiny cried. "No! He's burnin'—you're killin' him!"

"You'll be next, if you don't talk!"

"Oooow, s-stop h-hurtin' me! I told you, Jemma's here, we saw her—"

"It's not possible!" Shade's voice was like shards of ice. "She would not have been able to get through the Mist!"

"When did you see her?" said Nocturna.

"Where?" said Feo.

"Feo, you idiot!" Shade snapped. "Where have these brats been, but in the dungeons?"

"Tell us more!" said Nocturna. Jemma heard a slap and clutched the doorknob, trembling with rage.

"There's nothin' more to tell," Flora sobbed. "She jus' . . . looked at us . . . then left."

"We must search the castle!" Nocturna shouted. "Find her—find Jemma! *Jem*-maaah!"

Wherever Jemma hid, they were bound to find her now. There was only one thing for it. She rose to her feet and threw open the Ceremony Chamber doors.

Seven fire-lit faces turned to her and froze. Dust motes seemed to halt in mid-air.

"Jemma!" Flora ran to her. "You're here—"

"Shut up, child." Jemma mustered her hardest tone. "And don't paw me like that."

"But . . . but . . ." Flora's eyes filled with tears. Jemma's heart squeezed, but she steeled her gaze, clasped Flora's shoulder, and marched her back into the room.

"Back to your mewling brothers, girl." Jemma halted by the front pew and shoved Flora toward Tiny and Simon, who sat quivering at the foot of Mordrake's statue. Rook was perched on Mordrake's head, as if on guard. To the right of the fireplace, by Mordana's statue, the four Agromonds stood open-mouthed. Feo and Shade had grown markedly in the past month; Shade was now at least a head taller than Jemma. All of their faces were pinched, and tension crackled between the four of them like water on a red-hot skillet.

Make the most of that, said a voice in her head. *Play them against each other. Play on their weaknesses. Keep on the offense.*

Jemma pulled herself to her full height and put her hands on her hips.

"Well," she said, "as you can see, I'm back."

"Jemma . . ." Nox took a step toward her, then stopped.

"Your hair!" Feo exclaimed. "It's so short!"

"What," said Nocturna as the weasels squirmed around the hem of her dress, "is the meaning of this?"

Shade's diamond birthmark darkened on her cheek. "It's a ruse—it must be! How did you get through the Mist and sneak your way in here, you sly cur?"

"I have my ways, Shade," Jemma said, holding Shade's stare and hoping fervently that the right words would come to her. "You all believe I have no Powers now, since I didn't reach Oakstead in time to be Initiated. But I assure you, I do. They will grow to be greater than you ever dreamed— and I've brought them in service to you and the great Mord ancestors. Why else do you think the Mist let me through? If I'd come here to oppose you, it would have stopped me. You know that."

"Well, Jem-*mah*, if you *do* have Powers, as you claim," said Shade, quick as a whip, "then it might be possible for you to get through the Mist, mightn't it?"

"Quite," said Nocturna, her eyes narrowing. "Marsh managed, all those years ago. Why should we suppose that you were not trained to get through it, just as she must have been—trained by Marsh herself, even?"

"Ah, yes, Marsh," Jemma said, seeing her first chance to stir things up between them. She sauntered deliberately to

Nocturna, certain that Nocturna wouldn't be able to resist a jibe at Nox. "I see in your eyes," she said, "that you thought Marsh was a spy sent by my parents. You were not believed. But you were right."

"What? You admit it?" Nocturna was taken off guard, then swung around to Nox, scattering the weasels from her hem. "You see? And you denied my suspicions!"

"I admit it," Jemma barreled on, "because it's the truth! Marsh was supposed to help me escape. But she couldn't have helped me through the Mist, because"—she paused for effect—"because she's dead! I found her in the forest, her flesh ripped to shreds, one hand torn from her."

Nox and Nocturna exchanged knowing glances.

"The Aukron got her!" Feo's eyes widened. "Yes! Tell us more, Jemma!"

"There's so much to tell, Feo, about the days that followed, and my terror of you finding me—that is, until I met my so-called *real* parents." She affected a sneer, praying that her thumping heart wasn't audible. "They're so weak! And so are their pathetic followers. The Outside is not at all what I thought it would be. . . . I found that I missed you. You're what I know . . . what I *am*. So, as I was saying, Mama—I may call you Mama, mayn't I? And Papa?"

Nocturna inhaled, her nostrils flaring. Nox's head gave an almost imperceptible nod.

"I return with my Gifts. For you—for us! Mama, Papa, just imagine: the crag's magic restored to it; the wealth that the quarry will bring again; the castle brought back to its former glory—better, even! Together, we can do this, and so much more! If you don't believe me"—Jemma's heart was

362

hammering, on the edge of her greatest bluff—"then capture me now!"

She spread out her arms. Nobody moved. "Well?"

Feo beamed. Nox's eyes crinkled. Shade's were full of hatred. The triplets looked horrified.

"The crag's magic restored, you say?" Nocturna stepped up to Jemma, her Eau de Magot perfume like a toxic aura. "And how do you know about the crag and the quarry?"

"My dreams," Jemma said. "I saw it all. The quarry closing down, the fortune ending—"

"Oh, please! Any fool could have told you that!" Shade pushed her mother aside and shoved her face inches from Jemma's. "*They* might want to believe you," she hissed, "Papa with his simpering eyes, just look at him! He still can't take them off you, his dear little Jem-*mah*. Neither can Feo, mesmerized by a pretty face, if you can call it that. As for Mama, she's so desperate for Power, she'd believe anything. But you can't make an ass of *me*!"

"Are you suggesting, Shade," Nocturna growled, "that I'm so easily taken in?"

"Well, Mama, she escaped on your watch, if I may remind you—"

"As you have reminded me a thousand times since!"

"I would never have let her go! And as for you, Papa, you always were the biggest fool for her. Who's to say she's not tricking you, even now? We should lock her up!"

"You're just jealous!" Feo said, evidently delighted to be able to take a shot at his twin. "Lock her up? She's not exactly trying to escape, having walked in under our very noses!"

"You're all idiots!" Shade stamped her foot. "I'm the only one who sees what she really is!"

"Oh, so we're *all* idiots now, are we?" Nocturna shouted. "You insolent child!"

Jemma watched as they continued arguing and pacing, their arms flailing. Jagged, blood-red strands of energy emanated from them, becoming thick and entangled. The weasels took refuge under the front pew. Flora, Simon, and Tiny looked on, their expressions a mixture of fear and disbelief as the bizarre drama unfolded. The chaos couldn't have worked better if Jemma had planned it. Now, if she could just get some decent food in the triplets' bellies. . . .

"She hasn't changed!" Shade shrieked. "She's just putting on a damn fine show!"

"And you're such a good judge, are you?" Nocturna wagged a red-nailed finger at Shade. The wide sleeve of her dress fell back to reveal her alabaster-white wrist. Shade grabbed it.

"Better than you, Mama!" she said, twisting Nocturna's arm.

"Ow!" said Nocturna. "Unhand me, you fiendish child!"

"*Caw!*" Rook, perched on Mordrake's head, fluffed up his feathers, his jet eyes piercing Shade with malice. "*Caw caaaAAW!*"

The triplets shrank back. But Nocturna's precious bird had given Jemma an idea.

"Oh, poor Rook!" She walked toward Mordrake's statue, kicking Simon—as gently as she dared—out of the way. "So brave, wanting to defend Mama! There now. Jemma's here." She reached up and held her wrist under Rook's chin, spearing a thought into his dull brain: *You are in my power.* . . .

Come to me. . . . His eyes glazed, and he stepped onto her hand. She turned to face the family. "You don't mind, do you, Mama?"

The four of them looked stunned. Nocturna yanked her arm away from Shade. "I . . . No . . . ," she said. "But . . . he's never allowed anyone but me to touch him before. . . ."

"Well, we're friends now, aren't we, Rook?" Jemma kissed his beak, stroking his feathers as she walked across the room and placed him on Nocturna's shoulder. He sat there, dazed.

"There, Shade!" cried Feo. "Jemma must be changed! Rook always hated her the most."

"Anyone could hypnotize that squawking idiot!" Shade stamped her foot. "I want *proof* of these supposed Powers! Besides, why has she come back today of all days? It's too much of a coincidence, with the Sacrifice tomorrow!"

"That is exactly why I returned now!" Jemma said, surprised by the force of her own words. "My dreams showed me what you were planning. We all know how important it is for you—for *us*—that the Ceremony goes well. But I also saw that you were in danger of failing. Yes, failing! So I hurried home to help, and when I went to check on these whelps in their cell"—she gestured at the triplets huddled at Mordrake's feet—"I found to my horror that I was right to be afraid. You know how vital it is for the victims to be strong, and primed for the Ceremony—yet you've been starving them! How could you?" Her fury at the Agromonds' abduction and treatment of the triplets came through full force. "To risk so much with such negligence!"

"But . . . I did not command this," Nocturna said. "Who . . . ?"

"If not you, Mama"—Jemma could almost taste victory—"then who indeed?"

"You . . . you . . ." Shade scowled daggers at Jemma.

"But it isn't too late," Jemma barreled on, "if we hasten, and feed the brats immediately. And we must keep them comfortable for as long as possible before tomorrow morning—"

"Indeed, let us do so, this instant!" said Nocturna. "Feo, ring for Drudge!"

"Yes, Mama." Feo strode to the fireplace and yanked the tattered bell-pull hanging to the right of it. Hope flickered on the triplets' faces.

Nocturna turned to Shade, her face red with fury. "Shade, you will pay dearly—"

"No, no, Mama, please!" said Jemma. "No recriminations. Don't you agree, Shade?"

Shade screwed up her face in disgust. "I'll show you!" she sneered, flames from the fire sharpening her eyes. "Waltzing in here like Madem'selle Muck! Well, if you're so powerful, let's see how you deal with *this!*" She flicked her right arm toward Jemma, and a bolt of pure blackness shot from her fingers. Jemma raised one hand instinctively, stopping the bolt, which fell to the ground. She felt as astounded as Shade looked.

"Good one, Jemma!" said Feo. "Parrying a Dromfell like that. Shade, you always think you're the best, but Jemma's got more in her little finger than you—"

"Shut up, Feo!" Shade slapped the back of his head, then minced up to Jemma, her Mark turning a deeper purple. "Dreams, fancies, stopping Dromfells . . . I need more than party tricks to convince *me*. I. Want. *Proof!*"

"All right, Shade, you asked for it," Jemma blurted before she could stop herself. "I can read your mind!"

"Don't talk such rubbish!" Shade grabbed the neck of Jemma's shirt. "You accursed impostor. I'll show you—"

"Shade!" Nox took three paces and grabbed Shade from behind. "You'll choke her!"

"It's all she deserves," said Shade, writhing in her father's grasp, "for all her lies!"

Jemma rubbed her throat, panic gripping her. Why in Majem's name had she said she could read Shade's mind? She'd never been able to do that! But suddenly a horrific image leapt into her head, and words were gathering in her mouth again. Words she didn't want the triplets to hear, but which she couldn't prevent from pouring out.

"If it's such lies, Shade," she said, "then why don't you tell Mama and Papa about those bodies you've been hiding under your bed?"

Shade froze.

"What?" Nocturna cried. "What bodies?"

"A boy," said Jemma, nauseated at the sight in her mind's eye, "and a girl. Twins. Six years old. She rode Mephisto to get them, and practice on them. Just three weeks ago."

"Is this true?" Nox snarled into Shade's ear.

"What if it is? *You've* not killed any children since you took *her*." Shade spat at Jemma. "Mord forbid you make a mess of the first Sacrifice in years. I had to practice, to be sure it would be done properly!"

"Properly?" Nocturna marched over and slapped Shade's face. "Reckless girl! What have we always taught you? This kind of Sacrifice must be done with the correct rituals, the force be honored, or it can turn horribly against us! I trust at least *one* of their souls went to Scagavay . . . ? But I see from your expression that it did not. Oh, this is insufferable! And *you* talk of 'properly'?"

Shade glared at Jemma and Nocturna, her eyes oozing hatred. Then all malice seemed to drain from her. She went limp in Nox's grasp and burst into tears.

"Mama, you think Jemma's better than I!" she wailed. "And Papa has always preferred her to *me*, his own flesh and blood! Mama, please, I'm sorry—I know I shouldn't have killed those children. . . . I . . . just wanted you to be proud of me again! Oh, to think I used to be your pride and joy!" Shade wrenched free of Nox's hold and threw herself at Nocturna's feet. "Mama-a-a-a, forgive me, *ple-e-ease!* You don't know how miserable I've been since falling from your favor!"

"I . . . well . . ." Nocturna looked taken aback. "Perhaps I did react harshly . . . but you must see, Shade, that you— we—cannot turn away this opportunity for more Power. Just give Jemma a chance, and we shall know tomorrow. . . ."

"Yes, yes, anything you say, Mama!" Shade clutched the skirt of Nocturna's dress. "Oh, I'm so unhappy! I just want you to love me as much as you love her—"

"I do, I do. More!" Nocturna pulled Shade to her feet and stroked her hair awkwardly. "You're my little Shadowkins! Hush, now. It will all come out right—"

"But what if it doesn't, Mama?" Shade sobbed. "What if Jemma *is* lying? Surely, to be on the safe side, we should keep her locked up, just for tonight? If you *really* love me, you'll do that for me, won't you? Mord forbid she should try to steal something from us in the dead of night, as she did before!"

Shade grabbed the keys tied to her waist and rattled them at Jemma. "*These*, for instance."

"Oh, Shade, Shade!" Nox sighed, looking weary. "You really are overreaching yourself."

Overreaching yourself . . . The phrase echoed in Jemma's mind from the conversation she had overheard all those weeks ago. Nocturna, too, evidently remembered. She turned to Nox slowly, ire scudding across her face.

"I heard those very words from you before, Nox," she said, "the night I voiced my suspicions about Marsh. And I was right, was I not? Jemma herself said so. But you let Marsh go, instead of killing her as I decreed. What if Shade is right?"

"But if she is wrong," he retorted, "and Jemma has indeed returned in fealty to us?"

"Then I'm sure she won't mind," said Nocturna, turning her coal-hard eyes on Jemma, "spending this one night in the dungeons. Will you, my dear?"

CHAPTER THIRTY-NINE

Secrets in Vellum

Victory flashed through Shade's tears.

Jemma felt the blood draining to her feet. Locked away, how would she be able to retrieve the keys, much less rescue the triplets? "I confess I'm disappointed in my sister's mistrust of me," she said, trying to prevent her voice from wavering, "but of course, if that is what you wish, Mama . . ."

"Go-o-o-od!" Nocturna's face reconfigured into its habitual angular certitude.

Eight o'clock began tolling from the Bell Tower. The door creaked open and Drudge appeared.

"Ah, Drudge," said Nox. He waved toward the triplets. "Take these three to the kitchen and feed them, if you will."

"It would be best if it was something they like, Drudge," added Jemma, affecting her brittlest tone of voice.

"And put them in a larger dunge—er, room," Nocturna added, "with warm blankets, if you will. A little Slumber Potion in syrupwater will keep them relaxed and well-rested too."

Flora, Simon, and Tiny cowered as Drudge shuffled toward them. Jemma's heart was breaking for them. She hated the idea of them being drugged, but at least it would dull their terror. Besides, it would stretch her hand to protest. She hardened her face as they traipsed out of the room, Tiny casting a forelorn glance at the fireplace for his lost bear. All that remained of it was the lone arm that Shade had ripped off, lying near the hearth.

Drudge herded the triplets out, and closed the door.

"Now that is taken care of," said Nocturna, "let us repair to the Lush Chamber and hear of your adventures, Jemma. But first, we must get you out of those vile rags. We burned all your attire after you left, so you'll have to wear something of Shade's. Shade, your black-on-black stripe, I think. You've outgrown it, have you not? Feo, while Jemma is changing, go and tell Drudge to add extra pancreas to today's luncheon stew—Jemma's favorite, to honor her return."

"Thank you, Mama," Jemma said.

The rest of the morning dragged by. The family gathered around the fireplace in the Lush Chamber, Nocturna, Nox, and Feo entreating Jemma for stories of her adventures. Nocturna's mother scowled down from her portrait above the mantel as a mix of truth and fiction flowed easily from Jemma's mouth—Feo being especially delighted by her gory description of Marsh's remains. Once out of the forest, still afraid that her family ("I mean, you," she said) would be looking for her, she'd cut and dyed her hair. (Feo complimented her, telling her it made her look more fierce, "Though I'm glad it's your normal color now," he added.) Jemma was careful to mention the boy she'd been traveling with ("A common lad I met on the road. He had food, and seemed to like me"), knowing that Digby had been seen with her by the Widow Strickner and again on the road to Oakstead. This, Nox said, was indeed just as the Widow and two spies had reported—proof that Jemma wasn't lying to them. Thankfully, none of them realized that the boy with her had been Digby. For a moment, Jemma's heart was in her mouth as she wondered whether word about the gang who had ambushed them had reached Nox, but he said nothing of it, and something told her they'd been too ashamed to boast of such a crushing failure.

All the while, Shade's cast-off Mord-day dress clung uneasily to her, as though atoms of Shade still inhabited its fabric and were seeping into her skin. At least she still had Digby's old boots on; all of Shade's were too big for her, and wearing something of his was comforting. She'd also made sure to put Bethany's golden coin in the dress pocket—luckily, it had buried itself deep in her trouser pocket, and was the one thing that hadn't been ripped away by the river. She kept fingering it to remind her of her roots, but still, she couldn't help feeling nervous.

Eventually the questions ebbed. Nox stared into the fire. Feo picked at his fingernails. Shade slumped back in her armchair. Nocturna's eyes closed, her crimson mouth spreading into a contented smirk. Jemma could almost see the scene unfolding in those twisted reveries. The Mist spreading, bringing more of Anglavia under Agromond suppression. The crag's magic strong again, and the renewed riches that would come from the sale of its rock. The rewards of finally having won Jemma over to their side.

Noon struck. Shade's head lolled forward, her eyelids flickering shut. The keys dangled from her belt, tantalizingly close to Jemma's grasp. But now, it would be up to Digby to steal them while Shade slept. She mulled over the night's plan. *Imagine it, like it's already happened,* Marsh would say, *like you're already holdin' them keys . . . unlockin' the cell door . . .*

"Dreaming again, Jem-*mah?*" Shade opened one eye. "I see those schemes you're hatching, don't think I don't."

"I don't know what you're talking about, sister dear."

"*Sis*-ter, is it? Ha!" Shade closed her eye again.

Everyone dozed. Only Grandmama Mallentent seemed to be awake, her crazed paint-cracked eyes staring from her portrait as if they saw into Jemma's duplicity. Jemma fixed her gaze on the fire, and on the family motto glaring at her from the mantelpiece: *Mordus Aderit.* She tried re-ordering the letters to make pleasant words, but it only yielded ones that seemed to taunt her: *Ruse. Dare. Dread.* Dread. The word slithered into Jemma's head, then wormed into her bones, where it curled up and tightened like a noose.

Jemma mopped her mouth with a napkin, her stomach in revolt. The stew had been vile. The silkiness of the pancreas made her retch, and how could she have ever liked the bitter taste of spleen, with its crumbly texture? Even the crunch of the bees-in-syrupwater dessert was disgusting to her now.

"Thank you, Mama," she said. "That was delicious."

"You're welcome, my dear. Now, let us retire for Repose."

"Where will Jemma rest, Mama?" asked Shade.

"Why, in her old room, I suppose."

Jemma's heart skipped. Good! That meant she could retrieve her journal from under the mattress—

"But, Mama," Shade said, tapping her black-varnished fingernails on the table, "should we not lock her up this afternoon, as well as tonight?"

"For Mord's sake, Shade." Nox sighed. "I object!"

"And who are you to object?" Nocturna snapped back at him.

"A mere precaution, Papa," said Shade sweetly, making no attempt to conceal the smugness on her face.

And so, on the toll of two, Jemma was marched downstairs by Shade and locked in the cell closest to the kitchen, next to Drudge's sleeping alcove. He was napping, his bony form rising and falling gently. Shade strutted away with a satisfied sneer on her face, leaving Jemma to Drudge's snores and the drug-induced breaths of the three Goodfellow children that echoed from the end of the Corridor of Dungeons.

Three tolls of the bell. Three luminous orbs, spiraling above her head. The castle walls undulated, their gray stones crumbling inward into a cloudy mass that swirled her upward. She tried to yell—Leth gith bal celde!—but the cloudy mass sucked the words from her throat and spun them into the air. Their letters separated, rearranged themselves: Leth gith bal celde . . . eth lithg . . . the light . . . the light be . . .

"The Light be called!" Jemma woke with a gasp, feeling as though fire was pumping into her muscles. Shade's old dress was drenched in sweat. She leapt from the pallet. "So those words *were* anagrams," she muttered as she began pacing, "but of two words jumbled at a time, instead of just one!" She thought of when she'd first heard them in Bryn's cave, and the times after that. "But why all mixed up, and not in plain Anglavian?" If only Noodle and Pie were there! Talking to them always helped her to think more clearly. She gazed at the pallet, remembering how they used to sit on her pillow, waiting for her to wake. "I mustn't think of you, Rattusses." She sighed. "I have to stay strong." Then she noticed something sticking out from under the straw.

The corner of a thin, fragile-looking book.

She pulled it out. Its cover was made of the softest mole-skin she'd ever felt, bound around seven or eight sheets of cracked, yellowed vellum. Slowly, she opened it, hardly daring to hope what it might be. In the middle of the first page, hand-written in scrolled capitals, she read:

ETH GROEFNOTT GNOS

The elegant slant, the graceful flourish . . . Jemma recognized the writing immediately. The letters needed no coaxing: they were simple anagrams. Her skin tingled as she read.

"*The Forgotten Song.* This is it—Majem's missing book!" Beneath the title, other words shone from the page. "*Rof het Rien Foe. Yam ey valprie* . . . For the Fire One. May ye prevail . . ."

Heart thumping, Jemma paced again as she sped through the following page.

The purpose of this Booke knowest thou already, else would it not be in thy Handes. Heere is writ the Guydance thou shalt need. Learne it well and in strict order, for thou must know it by Heart till it be a part of thee.

First be the Opening Call.

Second be the Song itself, writ herein for the remynding of the One who shall teach it to thee. Joyne with it wenne the Tyme cometh, for it is thy voice whych is awaited.

Thyrd be the Releasing Rime of Saeweldar, whych thou must say as the Song is sunge by Others who shall also joyn with it.

Last be the Words to be spoke on the clearinge of all else.

All Rimes herein are for thine eyes only, writ in Code to conceal them from the Evil Ones. Discover the Code, and unlocke the Secrets herein.

Guidance. A song. Rhymes and secrets. A code she had to decipher. For her eyes only . . . It was thrilling. And ominous. There were two more lines, and she read them slowly, a strange sense of destiny creeping under her skin.

Thanks be to thee, Rien Foe. May your Heart shine, and your Courage burn through Doubt and Despair like a Flame in the Mist, hidden and quiet, yet fierce as the Sunne. Yours, MS.

"A flame in the mist . . ." Jemma's entire body tingled. "Fierce as the sun . . ." Majem's words sank into her like a solemn oath, and she turned the page, prepared to take that oath.

The Opening Call, she read at the top. She was getting used to the archaic language, and swiftly interpreted the instructions. She had to be ready, then focus, then say what was written below with force, three times. In Anglavian, not in its jumbled form.

"I can do that," she said. "So, let's see what this Opening Call is."

The next words made her stop in her tracks.

Leth gith bal celde!
Cebvasya ag wonn oge

The words she had pulled from thin air. Had dreamed, over and over. They were here. Majem had written them, almost three hundred years ago! How was that possible? Had her ancestor somehow been speaking to her across time, and through the ether, as well as through her book? Whatever the case, the result was that Jemma had already deciphered the Code. She had the key to unlocking the rest of the Releasing Rime's meanings—now, just when she needed it.

"The Light be called," she whispered, her nerves shimmering as she reread the words that had just revealed themselves. Then she took a breath and drank in the second line:

Cebvasya ag wonn oge . . . Cebvasya ag wonn oge . . .

Magically, the letters unraveled. She went cold.

"Scagavay." The name barely croaked past her lips. "Be gone now." Jemma felt as though spiders were crawling under her skin. She began pacing again, drumming the two lines into her mind with each step until she was sure of them, then turned the page, hoping that what she'd find there would somehow calm the spiders down. It didn't.

It made no sense at all.

Drawn across each page were four series of five straight lines spattered with black-tailed dots, like tadpoles sitting on a fence. The following pages were the same. The spiders were running amock now, turning agitation into desperation. How would she find guidance, if she couldn't even begin to understand this?

"Trusssst!"

Jemma wheeled around. "Drudge! You startled me—"

"You . . . learn Opnn Call . . . Good!" The old man

377

beckoned to her, and she went to the door. He reached through the bars, took the book from her, then tapped on the offending page. "Thisss," he said, "fffrrgot . . . Frrrgotn sss-sss . . ."

"*That's* the Forgotten Song? But it looks like rubbish— pages of it!"

"Mew," Drudge wheezed. "Mew . . ."

"Mew? Like a cat?"

"Gnaaaaaa! Mew . . . Mew . . . sick."

"Sick cats?" Jemma frowned. "Drudge, I don't— Oh! You mean, this is *music*?"

Drudge's face cracked into a smile, and he nodded fervently as he scanned over the next pages. Then he handed the book back to her. "Me, teach you," he mumbled. "Sssong."

"*You*? But . . . how do you know it?"

"Me, good . . . read—"

"You mean, you've read the book? Was it you who put it under the straw? Of course, it must have been! But where did you find it, and how did you know I'd be here, not upstairs?"

"No quessssstnnnss! No time! Trusssst, Jmmmaaaah, trussst!" Drudge grabbed Jemma's forearms and closed his eyes, swaying slightly. Then she heard the strangest sound, like the keening of the wind, but softer, soothing, its rhythmic pitch flowing in waves from Drudge's hands, through her body. It was not audible in the dungeons, but somehow filled her head, a melody that contained fragments of Marsh's nursery rhymes, of the song she'd heard her mother sing in her dreams, and the song Freddie and Maddie Meadowbanks had sung the night of her welcome-home feast in Oakstead. Every note of it seemed to resonate in every cell of her body. She felt as though she'd known it forever.

378

Drudge released her forearms, and the sound stopped.

"That was beautiful!" Jemma tingled from head to toe; she felt full, and light. "But I don't know how I'll ever remember— Drudge, are you all right?"

He looked deathly pale. "Show," he rasped, pointing at his head, then hers, "efffrrrrt." He heaved several breaths, and his face started returning to its normal sallowness. Then he touched Jemma's sternum with a bony finger. "Remmmemmb, here. Song here."

"Oh!" A bolt of energy shot from his finger through Jemma's chest and down to her toes. She almost dropped the book. Drudge took it from her, turned several leaves, and handed it back. At the end of the music symbols, the text resumed:

"The Song doth open Portals to the Angelic Realms," she read aloud. *"Once hearde by the Fire One it shall be remembered always. . . ."*

Drudge was breathing more easily now, and he patted the book. "Finishhh."

Jemma read out the remaining text on the page. *"Scagavay being thus weakened shoulde thenne be assailed with the Releasinge Rime of Saeweldar, whych is the opposite of Scagavay.* Saeweldar. The opposite of Scagavay. So . . . Saeweldar is some sort of Entity as well?"

Drudge nodded, his silken hair wisping across his face. "Scagaaav—baaad! Saewldrrr—good!" He nudged the book. "Reeead, quick!"

Clang! The clock tower tolled out. One . . . two . . . three . . .

"Four, already! There's no time now, Drudge. Shade will be here any minute. But Drudge, if you know it, why can't you just tell me?"

"Wrrrds, not remembrrr. You . . . musssst learn . . . by heart. Finissssh. Tonigh. Promisss!"

"I promise. Tonight." Tonight, she, Digby, and the triplets would be leaving here. Suddenly it hit her: that would also mean leaving Drudge. Again. Her heart sank to her stomach.

"Gnnnn . . ." Drudge patted her hand. "No, sssad."

"Drudge, come with us! Gordo will have the cart, and—"

"Gnnnnaa!" He shook his head and smiled. "Me ssstay. Trusssst, Jmaaah!"

"But, Drudge—"

"Trussst! You, your path. Me, mine. Remembr. The ligh . . . be . . ."

"The Light be Called. I'll remember."

Drudge teetered into the kitchen, and Jemma gazed after him. A faint blue aura seemed to be outlining him—the same as she thought she'd seen emanating from him the night she escaped. She blinked, and it was gone. Then she tucked the book back beneath the straw. It was such a small, shabby volume, but it breathed the wisdom of her ancestor, and gave her enormous hope.

CHAPTER FORTY

The Eve of Destruction

The Light be called . . . The words spun through Jemma's head, buoying her for the rest of the day. Even when discussion turned to the next day's ritual, she was able to smile through Shade's eager anticipation of it and ignore the pit in her stomach. At nine-thirty, after a light supper of weasel-milk cheese and pancreas paté, Shade led her once more down to the dungeons.

"Clothing a lamb in wolf hide doesn't make it a wolf," Shade sneered, looking Jemma up and down. "Tomorrow, we'll see what you're really made of."

"Speaking of tomorrow," Jemma said as they crossed the kitchen, "I think it would be wise to make sure that Drudge has done as we instructed with those three brats, don't you?"

Shade scowled at Jemma, but nevertheless walked with her down to the larger dungeon second from the end. The triplets were huddled together on a pile of fresh straw, the blankets heaped on top of them rising and falling with the deep breaths of Slumber Potion–induced sleep.

"Satisfied, Jem-*mah?*"

Jemma nodded, steeling her expression against the heartache she felt for Flora, Simon, and Tiny as Shade marched her back to her cell.

Shade clanged the door shut, and locked it. "Breakfast at

seven. Ceremony at seven-thirty sharp. I trust that you will be *ready* for it. Good night to you."

"And to you, sister dear."

Shade's footsteps echoed into the distance. Condensation dripped. The almost-half hour until Digby's arrival yawned ahead of her. Remembering her promise to Drudge, Jemma sat on the pallet and tried to decipher the remaining lines at the end of Majem's book.

"The Releasing Rime of Saeweldar," she read. *"Bal sorl heerd hel vitaepi nicet . . . Lyre easeth ben bedows foure het.* Bal sorl . . . Robs all? Slob lar?" Too agitated to concentrate, she tossed the book onto the bed, then lay down and tried to relax. Breathe. That was no use, so she stood and walked in small circles. First clockwise. Then reversed. Then clockwise again. At last ten o'clock tolled, and she heard footsteps running from the covered yard. Lamplight approached, and two silhouettes stumbled into view.

Jemma's heart leapt. "Digby, Gordo! Over here— behind you!"

"Jem!" Digby ran to her cell. "Look at you, locked up like this! Are you all right?"

"Yes, yes—but thank goodness you're here! It seems like weeks since this morning."

"I know. I been worried sick since Drudge told me the plan had changed. But now Pa's arrived with the cart, I feel better. We're ready— Oh my, Jem, what's that you're wearin'?"

."I know." Jemma tugged at the thick black fabric of Shade's old dress. "It's vile."

"Where's my little 'uns?" Gordo walked up behind Digby, holding the lamp. "I want to see 'em!"

"Down the corridor," Jemma said. "Second cell from the end. Please be quick though, Gordo, we can't waste—"

Gordo was already gone.

"Me too," said Digby. "Just be a mo'." He ran after his father. Jemma paced nervously until they returned, just as Drudge shuffled in from his lamp-extinguishing rounds.

"Sleepin' like angels, thanks be," said Gordo. "Ah, Mr. Drudge, good evenin' to you."

"So," said Digby, "the keys. With you locked up, Jem, who's going to get 'em?"

"It'll have to be you, Dig."

"But I don't know where Shade's room is! Can't Drudge go?"

"He'd be too slow," said Jemma. "But her room is easy to find. Just be careful not to wake her, though; she's got the strength of an ogress."

"Oh, nothin' to it, then." Digby attempted a grin.

"You'll be fine, lad," said Gordo, his voice trembling. "We'll have 'em out of here in no time, just you see." Digby set his mouth and nodded.

Jemma described how to find Shade's room. Digby took a deep breath, then sped off. Gordo went to the door to the Pickle Corridor and shifted from foot to foot as he stood staring after Digby.

Drudge took Jemma's hands. Calm washed through her as once again, blue light flickered around him. This time, it was undeniable.

"Ligh game," he said. "See boy . . . Make sssafe."

"Is there anything you don't know, Drudge?" said Jemma. "You're amazing!" She closed her eyes, and saw the vision that was running through Drudge's head. Together, they projected a protective sphere of Light around Digby as he ran, lamp in hand, through the hall, up the main stairway to the Bed-Chamber level—avoiding the third and seventh steps, which creaked—and rounded the corner to the West Corridor. He crept along it until he was outside Shade's room, then slowly turned the handle and eased the door open.

"Wait—his lamplight will wake her!" Jemma opened her eyes. Drudge was deep in concentration. Suddenly his mouth fell and his body started twitching.

"Gnnn . . . gnaaaa," he wheezed, gripping Jemma's hands. "Ssstop!"

"What? What's happening?" Jemma closed her eyes again, and suddenly she saw it too: Digby, his hand over his face, retching at the stench of rotting flesh . . . tripping over a leg protruding from under Shade's bed . . . dropping his lamp . . . Shade, waking. Jemma frantically envisioned the light sphere around Digby again and tried to strengthen it, but Shade leapt into full swing, lashing out at him, screaming, forcing him back into the corridor as Nox, Feo, and Nocturna rushed into the fray. Nox grabbed Digby by his collar. Feo picked up Digby's lamp, and the whole family marched toward the stairs, while Digby, still retching, struggled in their grasp.

"Oh, no!" Jemma gasped. "It's my fault! I stopped concentrating on the Light!"

"Shshshsgnnnnaaa!" Drudge opened his eyes and pulled his hands from hers. The calm blue around him fragmented, and disappeared.

"What is it?" Gordo trotted over. "What's happening?"

"They've caught him—they've caught Digby!"

Voices were rapidly approaching.

"Gordo," said Jemma, "you must hide."

"But, my boy—"

"Quickly, Gordo! Go with Drudge—and stay out of sight, or they'll capture you, too!"

"Book. Stone," said Drudge. "Give."

Jemma grabbed Majem's book from the pallet and handed it to him with her amulet. Then, remembering Bethany's coin, she dug that from her pocket too, just in case, and pressed it into Drudge's palm. He scuttled across the kitchen, Gordo in tow, and slipped into the scullery.

"If you don't talk, boy, you'll regret it." Nocturna's voice cut through the darkness.

"I tell you, Mama, he's in league with Jemma! He's exuding guilt like steam off a dungheap. They've probably been plotting to free those three miserable wretches—why else would he want to steal the keys in the middle of the night? That's really why she came back, I'd wager!"

"You can't know that, Shade," said Nox, but doubt edged his voice.

Jemma threw herself onto her pallet and closed her eyes tight. Every nerve in her body jangled.

Something slammed against her cell door.

"Wakey wakey, Jem-*mah*," said Shade. "We've brought someone to see you."

Jemma opened her eyes. Digby was pressed against the bars, his arms held behind his back by Nox. A large bruise was spreading across one cheek.

"What's the meaning of this?" Jemma tried to feign

indignance as she stood, and pulled herself tall, but Digby's bruise tugged at her heart.

"You tell us, Jem-*mah*," Shade growled. "You know this creature, I believe?"

Nox's face flickered between hope and anger.

"He . . . Haze . . . Hazebury dross . . ." The words barely croaked past Jemma's throat.

"Very convincing, I'm sure," Shade sneered. "So, perhaps you'd like to be the one to punish him for trespassing?"

Jemma began to tremble, all pretense draining from her.

"I thought not. Then I shall have to." Shade grabbed the back of Digby's hair, wrenched his face around, and gashed his bruised cheek with her nails. He yelled out in pain.

"No!" Jemma lurched instinctively toward him.

"Finally, we have the truth!" said Shade. "Mama, Papa, you must agree with me now. Why, those were probably his disgusting hand-me-downs she was wearing yesterday!"

"Jemma—you wretched girl!" said Nox, through gritted teeth. "You deceived me!" He tightened his grip on Digby and pinned him more firmly against the cold steel of her cell door.

"She deceived us all," said Nocturna calmly. "Quite a feat, I must say."

"Not I, Mama," said Shade. "I tried to tell you."

"I'm sorry, Jem." Digby whispered, his bottom lip quivering. "I failed 'em . . . them poor little 'uns. . . ."

"You see?" Shade yelped. "I was right! How noble he is! Or is he? Perhaps he's their big bwuvver, and being a good boy, rescuing them for Mama and Papa Gutbellows—"

"Shut up, Shade!" Jemma reached through the bars and laid her palm against Digby's ravaged cheek. The bruise faded slightly with her touch. "Dig . . . it's my fault, not yours."

"No!" Feo, who until now had stood back in the shadows, took a step forward and wrenched Jemma's hand away from Digby's face. He shot a look of pure hatred at Digby, then turned away.

Bitter wrath spread across Nox's face. "I gave you a second chance, Jemma," he said. "I fought for you! But Shade was right—"

"We must search her, in case she's hiding any kind of weapon!" said Shade. "Out of my way, Papa. Feo, hold the lamp higher, so we can see."

Nox yanked Digby away. Shade unlocked the door, then she and Nocturna whipped through Jemma's cell, turning over the straw on the pallet and strewing it across the floor. Shade pressed Jemma against the wall and rifled through her dress pockets.

"Nothing!" she hissed, then fingered Jemma's throat. "Where's your Stone? You were wearing it earlier—"

"It . . . I made it disappear, to protect it from you."

"Lies, more lies!" Shade pulled on the neckline of her old dress, ripping it across one shoulder.

"Shade, Jemma's Stone is of little consequence now," said Nocturna. She waved an arm at Digby. "Go with your father to lock this treacherous ruffian in the dungeon at the end, next to our other visitors, so these two can't communicate."

"With pleasure, Mama." Shade strutted out of Jemma's cell, and Digby was dragged away. Nocturna turned to Jemma, her black eyes flecked green with regret.

"A commendable show, Jemma," she said, "to have so artfully beguiled us. I admire you, really I do. You have always had a certain something about you, and it seems your new Gifts are indeed genuine. Such a pity they will go to waste."

She stroked Jemma's cheek, one corner of her mouth turned upward in a half-smile, then let her hand drop with a sigh. "Well, so be it. We shall at least be rid of the danger you pose to us. We shall decide your fate tomorrow, when our minds are fresh. Now, where's my dear son?" Nocturna turned to where Feo was slouched against the opposite wall, the light from his lamp etching sharp shadows on his face. "Ah, there you are. Guard the door until your sister returns with the keys. I shall retire now for my beauty sleep. I bid you both good night."

Nocturna walked out of the cell, glided away across the kitchen, and was gone.

Feo closed Jemma's cell door and leaned against it with his back to her, arms crossed. Seconds later, Shade returned, closely followed by Nox, who walked past without a word. Shade rattled the keys at her waist and selected the brightest one. "You have all night to dwell on your demise, Jem-*mah*," she said, locking the cell door. "Yours, and your precious sweetheart's. Ha! We shall think of how best to dispose of you both after we've dealt with those other three brats. Come on, Feo, and stop trying to look so ferocious. It's pathetic."

Feo cast a sullen glance at Jemma, then followed his sister into the gloom.

CHAPTER FORTY-ONE

Feo

Jemma clutched the bars of her cell and wept. In her mind's eye, she could see Digby slumped against the back wall of the littlest dungeon, his ripped and bruised face set in pained disbelief. The triplets, in the cell next to him, were still as corpses under the effect of Slumber Potion. Her tears splattered to the floor.

"Jmmaaah . . . Shshshush." Drudge was standing outside the door, holding Majem's book in one hand and a stub of candle in the other. "Take!" He shoved the shabby volume at her. "Now!"

His vehemence surprised her, and she took the book.

"The Ligh . . . be . . . ," he said. "Sssay!"

"It's no use, Drudge." Jemma heaved a sigh. "I'm never going to get out of here."

"Trusssst!" His voice was firmer than Jemma had ever heard it. "Now. The Ligh. Be. *Sssay*."

"The Light be called."

"Loud!" he said. "Mean it! Wordsss . . . have powerrr!"

"The Light be called!" Hope glimmered in her bones. "The Light be called, the Light be called!"

"Next . . . Sssay!"

"Scagavay, be gone now!"

Drudge rested his palm against her face. The glimmer of

hope expanded. "Trusssst, book," he said, setting the candle stub on one of the cross-bars of her door. "Finisssh. Now! Thisss too. Take." He pulled her Stone and Bethany's gold coin from his breast pocket and handed them to her. "Me, go. Mussst, strongfff, tmorrrow." He turned and slunk toward the scullery.

The book pulsed in her hand. "The Light be called," she whispered, her hope growing more. Drudge was right: those words *did* seem to have power. Besides, as he said, it was better to trust than to be defeated by despair. Dropping her Stone and Bethany's coin into her own pocket, she settled cross-legged on the pile of straw and flicked to the pages of music. The Forgotten Song. How did the dots correspond to the fantastic sound that Drudge had transmitted to her? Reminded of the force of it, the horrors of her situation receded slightly. Carefully, she turned to the final page and murmured the lines that had defeated her earlier.

> *"Bal sorl heerd hel vitaepi nicet,*
> *Lyre easeth ben bedows foure het."*

She drank in the words, determined to be more patient this time.

> *"Thus shall Saeweldar be summoned. And wenne all be still*
> *shall the last Incantation to fulfil the Prophecy be spoken:*

> > *"Si ti neto di od nise,*
> > *Wom styn ob nege,*
> > *Rel tethe es nubne."*

There, the book ended.

She took a deep breath, relaxing her gaze, and looked at the first line again.

Bal sorl heerd hel vitaepi nicet . . .

The letters floated in her mind and began to settle into their true order. "All orbs . . . held here . . . in captivitee . . ."

Orbs. Like the three she'd seen in her dreams. They represented the triplets, she was sure—but *all* orbs? What did that mean? Perhaps the next line would clarify it.

"*Lyre easeth ben bedows foure het.* Rely . . . No. Release . . . thy . . . thy bondes . . ."

"What's that you're muttering, Jemma? Some sweet candlelight invocation, perhaps?"

Startled, she looked up. Feo stood at the cell door, holding a candle that he set down next to the stub Drudge had left.

"Feo!" Jemma hastily tucked the book under the straw. "I . . . didn't hear you coming."

"Perhaps if you weren't so engrossed in whatever it is you're trying to hide, you would have." He looked strangely calm, his features soft in the candlelight. "You look nice in my sister's dress," he said. "It suits you. What a pity she had to go and tear it." He reached through the bars and brushed his fingers along Jemma's bare shoulder.

Jemma shrugged off his hand, struck by how much he now resembled Nox, as well as her own father. "What are you doing here, Feo?"

"How about you show me what you were reading? Then I'll tell you."

"It's nothing."

"Nothing? And it came from where? Mama and Shade just searched your cell. I saw with my own eyes."

"It's . . . just . . . something I found upstairs in the Lush Chamber. I hid it. By magic."

"Is that so? Well, show it to me. If you don't, I may just have to alert my dear sister, who will pry the information from you. But if you do"—he smiled—"perhaps I'll help you."

The diamond Mark on his cheek flared. He was exuding deviousness, but Jemma saw no alternative. She picked up the book and gave it to him.

"*Eth Groethnott Gnos*. What the . . . ?" Feo flipped it open, his roughness loosening the book from its binding. "*Calling Rime of Sae . . . Saewel . . .*" He tutted in exasperation and turned the page, tearing it. "Nothing but dots and lines! Looks like a load of old codswallop to me."

"No. I mean, yes. It is. Codswallop." Jemma bit her lips as another page ripped.

"Why would you want to read it, then?" Feo snapped the book shut and shoved it into his pocket. "So. My side of the bargain. Why I'm here. There's something I need to tell you, Jemma, before it's too late. You see, I always liked you, the way you were so different, so dreamy and independent. Even when they all thought you were airy-headed, I didn't. I could never have had the guts to be like you, refusing to do cruel things in the Ceremonies."

"But . . . I thought you loved the Offerings!"

Feo laughed and tossed his head. "I wanted their approval," he said. "What was I to do? Mama and Papa have always thought I was weak. You looked down on me. Even my own twin despises me! If I'd stood up to them and been like I

392

wanted to be—more like you—it would've been worse, don't you see? So I played along, while hoping, like Papa did, that somehow, miraculously, you'd come over to our side, and that someday . . ." He blushed, his diamond Mark darkening. "I knew you weren't really my sister, you see, but until you knew the truth, I had to hide my feelings for you, and play along with them. But oh, Jemma, how I detested it, detested!"

"Then why did you want to hear all those gory details about Marsh this morning?" she said. "You acted as though you believed my story—"

"I did believe it! I thought you really had changed. But it was perfect, don't you see?" His black eyes blazed in the candlelight. "You'd come back—I was so happy! I thought all I had to do for you to like me, just a little—while still keeping in Mama and Papa's favor, which Shade was so conveniently destroying for herself—was to pretend I was relishing it all."

Jemma was flabbergasted by his lucidity. He'd rarely strung more than a few words together before, much less expressed any emotion. "If that's really true" she said, "you're a better liar than either Shade or me—"

"Yes, it's true!" Feo fixed Jemma's gaze. Darkness seemed to deepen around him. He stepped closer and sighed. "Your eyes are amazing, Jemma, do you know that?" A smooth pinkish hue appeared around him, then floated toward her and engulfed her in its silky embrace. It made her skin crawl, yet she was transfixed, and Feo looked so hungry for affection that she felt almost sorry for him.

"Feo," she said, clutching the bars, "it must have been awful for you—"

"Jemma!" Feo grabbed her hands and held them to his chest, pulling her up against the bars. His face was inches from hers, the scent of wolfmint sweet on his breath. "So you *do* care! Oh, Jemma, we're so alike, really." His eyes misted. "I could help you, you know. . . ." He twined his fingers through hers.

Jemma's heart raced. "Would you, Feo? I mean, help?"

"Yes," he whispered, "yes! At least, I would have, before. . . . But it's too late, isn't it? Unless . . . unless you give me a reason to persuade them, convince them . . ." His fingers twined more fervently. "You could, couldn't you? Stay. With me . . ."

"Oh!" The full force of Feo's meaning finally hit Jemma, and she quickly changed the subject. "But you're not really like them, Feo, are you? Everything you've said—how you hate the Ceremonies, and can't be yourself—shows that. So why stay here? You could get the keys from Shade! And then come with us—"

"With *us?*" Feo's expression suddenly changed. The pinkish hue shrank back around him, turning jagged and muddy, but his fingers kept twining around hers. "Oh, no, no, no! Not after seeing you with . . . that . . ." His eyes flickered down the corridor toward Digby's cell. His top lip curled back. "For years, I've allowed myself to hope that you and I . . . Still, I was glad for you when you escaped. Glad, do you hear? Mord knows what I was thinking! But when you returned, I felt sure my time had come. And now you dare suggest that I'd help you—and *him*? Oh, Jemma, Jemma! The way you touched his face . . . In one fell action, you killed all my hope. You and that Hazebury dross!" He gripped her fingers, hard.

"Ouch! Feo—"

"That's what I came to tell you, Jemma. I'm over it, over you!" Feo snatched his hands away. "You've taught me what I needed to know: how to harden my heart and really be like them. At last, I belong!"

"Feo, no! Think about it: years ahead of cruelty, brutal Ceremonies—is that what you want?"

"Yes, it's what I want! It's all that's left to me now."

"Feo, please!" Jemma lunged through the bars and tried to grab Majem's book.

"Oh, so you *do* want this!" He sneered and backed away, yanking the book from his pocket and waving it in the air. "Then it's not such nonsense, after all . . . some formula to destroy us, perhaps? Or do you expect me to just let you go? Oh Jemma, how blind you can be! You see, my family is all I have now. I can't let you escape, my little vixen, for their disdain of me would turn to hatred. Besides, the end of you will bring an end to the longing I've suffered. At last, I shall be free of you, free of this constant pain in my heart!" His black eyes flashed at her; then he opened the book and shot a fuming gaze at it. The pages burst into flames, and he flung the book's blazing remains down the corridor.

"There! You didn't know I could do that, did you?" Feo laughed at Jemma's gasp of horror. "It may not be much compared to your powers, Jemma, but if I've upset you then so much the better!" He turned abruptly and strode away as the flames sputtered into darkness.

"No!" Jemma yelled into the gloom, rattling the cell door. "Noooooo!"

"Jem!" Digby's voice drifted up the corridor. "Jem, don't. You'll only make it worse."

His voice was joined by the triplets' drowsy chorus.

"Digby, Jemma, what's happenin'? Where are you? What's that burnin' smell?"

"It's nothin'," Digby said cheerily, "an' I'm next door to you. Can't see you at the moment, though. Me and Jem, we're playin' a game. Hidin', in't we, Jem?"

Jemma put her hand over her mouth to stifle her sobs.

"I'm scared," Tiny said. "Will you tell us a story?"

Digby's voice fell to a murmur. Jemma guessed from his tone that this was a familiar tale, one he knew would calm his brothers and sister and lull them back to sleep. She curled up in the straw. Soon his voice trailed off. Where were Gordo and Drudge? Gordo must be frantic, his worst fear, and Berola's, about to become reality.

She had failed them. Failed them all. Her last shred of hope flickered and died.

Jemma yearned for Drudge's company, even though he couldn't possibly help her now. She thought of the silky white strands of hair, his ancient face, his yellow eyes and teeth, and his wisdom, his extraordinary Vision. The love she felt for him lifted her spirits slightly, and all at once, the elusive few words of the Releasing Rime tumbled into her head: *All Orbs held here in Captivitee . . . Release thy Bondes—be thou free!*

Free. There was no chance of that now. Like Majem's book, her life and theirs would soon be nothing but ashes. She may as well give in and let herself drift away now, steeped in the dungeons' dark silence . . . drift, as if on a river, dissolving into nothing. Was this what it was like to die—light, bodiless, at the end of everything? She was becoming the water, like the Stoat River winding its way around Mordwin's Crag and down the valley, toward an endless ocean.

CHAPTER FORTY-TWO

Turning Tides

Away down the valley Jemma flowed, far from Agromond Castle and into a world of peace. A tiny point of light appeared like a star in the center of her vision. It rose upward, drawing her with it, separating her from the waters, then expanded around her into an evanescent blue sphere. The sphere flattened and elongated, transforming into a tube, and she was pulled into it, falling like quicksilver, images flashing by of her childhood, other childhoods, other ages, faster and faster, until she flew through a small window into an attic room where a dark-haired young woman, dressed in the full-skirted clothing of long ago, was sitting at a small desk, quill in hand.

The woman was writing. A man stood behind her, his long, flame-red hair falling around his shoulders. Then Jemma was dissolving into him, merging with him. *I feel you here,* he said, wordlessly. *Now take heed, and remember well the words you see.*

She looked down billowing white shirtsleeves to long delicate hands that were resting on the woman's wooden chair back, and watched as words flowed from her quill: *Si ti neto di od nise. Wom styn ob nege. . . . Rel tethe es nubne . . .*

The words Jemma had read not an hour before—the final words of Majem's book.

"Now is it complete," the woman said, "and I trust that the Fire One will understand it, for thou hast Seen that she shall be as adept at the unraveling of anagrams as I. Thus may she reveal the Truth hid in the confusion of appearances, and fulfill the Prophecy you have dreamed." She blotted the ink, then closed the notebook she was writing in. The man picked it up, and Jemma felt its moleskin cover as though it was in her own hand.

A rustling sound distracted the woman. Two golden-furred rats with ruby eyes appeared on her writing table, and she picked them up. "Ah, my Rattusses," she murmured.

Then Jemma was flooded with sorrow; the sorrow of parting, never to return. "My dearest," rumbled a low voice in her chest, the chest of the man she was inhabiting, "I shall go forthwith, and await the time."

"I shall miss thy works and thy wisdom, Gudred," the woman said, "as well as thy love. Would that thou could'st go when thou art old, and not have to wait such long years in that dark place! To think of thee, witnessing the horrors, without being able to prevent them. . . ."

"It must be now"—Jemma felt the rumbling again—"for the magic of Mordwin's Crag will sustain me better if I go while I am yet young. Besides, when I am old, I shall not have the strength to withstand the Mist, nor the wits to fool it. As for the horrors, you know it must be so, for if I intervene, I shall be discovered. And I must survive, for the child. The Fire One."

"Then go," the woman's voice quavered, and she handed him a note. "Take this too, to remind you how well that I love you, Gudred Solvay, and shall always remember thee."

"I too shall remember. . . ." His voice trailed into echo: *Remember . . . remember . . .*

The room shimmered and went dark. Jemma felt as though she was being sucked out of the window, speeding back up through the tube, the wind whispering, *Si ti neto . . . Remember . . .* as seasons rushed by. Another sound began thrumming through her—the castle bell, tolling. One, two . . . *Remember . . .* three, four, five . . . The spicy smell of Drudge's porridge wafted to meet her. Six . . . a rustling sound, nearby. Seven . . . seven, already? Jemma was freefalling through the castle roof, past Nocturna's room, down to the dungeons, touching the edge of Digby's dream of open fields and the confusion of monsters and fire swimming through the triplets' young minds.

More rustling. Straw scratched her face, the flagstones cold and hard beneath her. The rustling got louder. Something small, cold, and damp nudged her cheek. Nudge. Nudge. A cold, damp . . . *snout?* Jemma's heart leapt against her sternum. Her eyes shot open and were met by four rubyred dots blazing at her in the pale dawn light, interspersed by two small noses and whiskers, attached to two golden-furred bodies—

"Noodle, Pie!" Jemma sat up. "My Rattusses, you're alive!" Images flashed into her mind's eye: driftwood buffeting the river's edge; Noodle and Pie leaping ashore, then scurrying up Mordwin's Crag, focused, like two homing pigeons, intent on finding her.

The rats hurled themselves into Jemma's arms and nuzzled into her neck as she held them to her, tears of joy streaming down her face. For several moments more they ran over her, up to her shoulders, through her hair, and down to her lap, rolling around and squealing with glee. Then they lay on their backs, tiny paws in the air, ears alert as she garbled about all that had happened, and the disastrous predicament they were in now.

"But with you back again, Rattusses," she said, rubbing their tummies, "I feel as though anything can happen!"

Just then Drudge shuffled into view through the kitchen door, carrying a tray of the Agromonds' empty porridge bowls. He clattered them down onto the table.

"Drudge!" Jemma stood and went to the door, a rat in each hand. "Look who's here!"

Drudge nodded as if it was no surprise to him, then hobbled over. "Gorrrd . . . plan—"

"Gordo! Where is he? Is he all right?"

"Ysssss! Trusssst." He gesticulated toward the Pickle Corridor. "Agrmm . . . zzz . . . Come. Sssoon." He paused for breath. "Lissssn. You, dream. Mjjjm. *Si . . . ti neto . . .*"

"Yes! But . . . Drudge, how do you know about it?"

"Rememm . . . ," he said, "Rememmbr." He fixed his eyes on Jemma and suddenly she was looking through them at the quill moving over the page, the words taking form.

"Mother of Majem!" she gasped, realization surging through her as the letters of Drudge's name reordered in her head. "*Me . . . Good . . . red. . . .* How many times have you tried to tell me? You're Gudred—the Visionary who disappeared! It was *you* in my dream just now . . . and, and, it was you I dreamed of all those weeks ago—you, when you were a young man, coming through the Mist to the castle, almost three hundred years ago! It wasn't somebody who was out to get me at all . . . but *you!* Oh, Drudge, if only I'd realized!"

Drudge's eyes filled with tears, like an old mariner who's finally been recognized and pulled ashore after centuries of being adrift. "Came . . . for her. To help . . . you," he whispered.

"And the crag's magic kept you alive for all that time," she said, remembering what he'd said to Majem in her dream. Suddenly another memory came to her, of being small, inconsolable, a terrible loss ripping through her; then an old man was rocking her in his arms, his silver hair shining. . . . "You comforted me," she whispered, "after what they did to Jamem."

A tear trickled down Drudge's face and he stroked her hand, a smile flickering across his cracked lips. Then his expression steeled. "Time," he said, turning toward the kitchen. "Ratsssses, come." Noodle and Pie hopped from Jemma's hands and scuttled after him.

"Hey! Rattusses, why are you going too?"

"Trusssst!" Drudge said, and melted into the scullery. Seconds later, Nocturna swept into the kitchen dressed in her crimson Ceremony-Day velvet, Rook on her shoulder, weasels circling her feet. Shade, Nox, and Feo were close on her heels.

Jemma thrust her hands into her pockets and stood as tall as she could as the group began their silent, funereal march toward her. None of them would meet her gaze. The words from her dream began circling her head: *Si ti neto di od nise* . . . The fingers of her right hand touched her Stone, then beneath it, Bethany's gold coin. *Blessed it in the fire,* Bethany had said. An idea took root.

Nocturna walked slowly past Jemma's cell, proud and erect. Shade tossed her raven hair, brandishing the bunch of keys at her waist. Nox and Feo looked staunchly ahead as the eight Agromond feet stepped in time down the corridor. Keys chinked . . . the triplets moaned . . . Digby yelled . . . and all the while, Jemma turned Bethany's coin over and over, letting her thoughts float and expand. In her mind's eye, she could see Drudge in the scullery, his hand resting on the flagon of syrupwater. Gordo was there too, with Noodle and Pie on his shoulders. *Hold Shade back,* she heard in her head. *We'll do the rest.*

"Digby, help!" The triplets' screams melded into one.

"Leave 'em be—take me instead!"

Jemma took a deep breath, her fingers working the coin. Her plan became a single point in her mind, a crystal thought that she directed toward Shade: *Stay behind, Shade! Taste your triumph over me, just for a moment. . . .*

"It's to no avail, snivelers." Shade's sneer whined through Digby's cries and the triplets' sobs. "So you may as well stop grizzling."

Jemma took another deep breath and focused her intention, slicing it like a blade down the corridor and into Shade's head: *Taste your triumph, Shade. Think of the satisfaction! After years of hating me . . .* The group emerged from the shadows with Nocturna at the helm, her weasels forming a wave of fur along the floor. Just behind her were the ashen-faced triplets, flanked by Nox and Feo. Shade brought up the rear. *Oh, how you hate me—you always have! So gloat a little. Gloat! You've earned it.* They walked solemnly into the kitchen. *Shade— your triumph. Gloat!* They were almost at the door to the Pickle Corridor, and still Jemma kept spearing her thoughts into Shade's mind. *You've won. Finally, you've won—rub it in!*

Nocturna had just stepped into the corridor, when Shade stopped.

"Indulge me if you will, Mama," she said, "while I enjoy a moment with Jemma?"

"Very well, my dear. But dally not. We have but a few minutes until the appointed hour." Nocturna, Nox, and Feo herded their terrified victims away as Shade strutted to Jemma's cell. She stood a safe distance from the bars, arms crossed.

"Fool!" she said. "To think you could get the better of me! Soon, the Ceremony will begin, the girl will be sacrificed, and the boys will go to the dungeon of bones where we shall not be bothered by their whimperings. But rest assured, you and their brother will not live long to hear it."

"So, I've lost the battle for their lives." Jemma sighed. "But you'll never kill me. I have protection."

"Protection? Besides your Stone, which you so conveniently made disappear last night? What rubbish!"

"Rubbish? I think not." Jemma pulled the coin from her pocket and held it up between her thumb and forefinger. Even in the dank corridor, it shone. "This talisman," she said, waving it close to the bars, "holds the Power of my entire lineage. Whoever possesses it is immortal."

"Is that so?" Shade's eyes settled on the coin and widened with greed. "Then why aren't any of your ancestors still alive?"

"Because only one at a time may command the talisman, and it was always meant to come to me. As long as I guard it well, I can live forever." Jemma began to close her fingers around the coin. Shade made a grab for it. Jemma dropped it to the floor, then clasped Shade's wrist with both hands and pulled her toward the bars.

"Let go!" Shade twisted and writhed, pounding Jemma's arms with her free fist.

Jemma held fast. At any moment Shade's strength would overpower hers. Only one thing could weaken her. . . . From the corner of her eye, she could see Gordo and Drudge coming out of the scullery, Gordo staggering under the weight of the syrupwater flagon, which was balanced against his chest. Noodle and Pie clung to his jacket, grossly magnified by the liquid in the jar.

"I said, let me *go*!" Shade yelled, pounding harder.

Gordo, Drudge, and the rats were halfway across the kitchen. . . .

"Ow!" Jemma feigned pain, and released Shade's hand. Shade dived for the coin and her fingers closed around it.

"Mine!" she crowed, holding up the gold disc. "Now we shall see who's immortal—ha!"

And now we shall see who's weakened by her greatest fear, Jemma thought.

"Shade!" she yelled. "Look out, behind you—in the kitchen!"

Shade looked over her shoulder. Gordo was teetering toward her; Noodle and Pie, through the syrupwater, looked enormous and grotesque. She shrieked and froze.

"I can't hold it no more!" Gordo slid the flagon to the floor. The rats launched themselves from his shoulders and landed on Shade.

"Get them off me!" Shade dropped the coin and backed against Jemma's cell door.

"Gladly!" Jemma grabbed the keys hanging from Shade's waist, her fingers scrabbling at the knot tying them there as the rats bounded all over their trembling victim.

"Aaaagh—stop, stop! Drudge, you old fool, help me, for Mord's sake!"

"Gnnnnaaa!" Drudge snarled, pulling a small knife from his pocket and handing it to Jemma. She cut the keys free, then pocketed the knife, unlocked the door, pushed it open against Shade's weight, and stepped into the corridor.

"Mama!" Shade yelled. "Hellmmmmfff!"

Gordo slapped his hand across Shade's mouth to stifle her screams. "Off you go, lass, and get Digby," he said. "I'll hold this she-devil."

Jemma sped down the corridor with the keys. Moments later, she and Digby were pelting back to the kitchen. Shade, still weakened by her terror of the rats, was safely in Gordo's grasp.

"Digby, lad," said Gordo. "Your face! That bruise—them scratches—"

"I'm fine, Pa. Let's get this harpy locked up." Digby grasped Shade's arm, shoved her into the cell, and slammed the door. "There! Enjoy a taste of your own medicine!"

"Please . . ." Shade was quaking under the rats' scampering paws. "Take them with you."

"Fat chance!" Digby's face reddened with rage. "After what you done to my little brothers an' sister, you're lucky I don't come in there an' skin you alive."

"Come on, Dig, we'll deal with her later." Jemma locked Shade's cell. "Stay with her, Rattusses, just until we're upstairs. Gordo, Drudge—" She spun around. "Where *is* Drudge?"

Gordo shrugged. "Dunno. One minute he was behind me, next he was gone."

Jemma's heart sank. Frail though he was, she wanted the old man by her side. "Let's go," she said, pocketing the keys.

"You'll r-regret this," Shade growled. "Just you see!"

Jemma and Digby took off across the kitchen, Gordo

trailing behind. As they reached the door to the Pickle Corridor, Gordo yelled out. They turned. He was on the floor, clutching his calf, blood dribbling from the bottom of his trouser leg.

"You go on," he said, wincing in pain. "Somethin' hit me . . . like a bolt of black lightnin', it was. Came straight from her hand. . . ."

"A Dromfell!" Jemma said. "If she hadn't been weakened by the rats, it could have killed you!"

Shade was leaning against the bars of the cell door, one arm stretched toward Gordo. Noodle and Pie lay belly-up on the floor by her feet, stunned. They shook themselves, clambered up her legs, and clawed at her other hand, which was clutching something at her neck.

"Ow! You little beasts!" She released her fingers, revealing a black stone hanging there.

"Her amulet!" Jemma ran over, reached through the bars, grabbed Shade's pendant, and yanked. A wave of nausea hit her. The reason was obvious. She hurled the pendant toward the scullery and shot a beam of Light at it. It exploded in a rain of black dust.

"I'll get you for this, J-Jem-*mah*!" Shade squirmed, trying to beat off Noodle and Pie. "You'll see!"

Digby had rolled up Gordo's trouser leg, revealing a deep black-edged gash on his calf that was bleeding badly. Jemma crouched down and lay her hands on it. Seconds later, the blood stopped, and she and Digby helped Gordo to his feet.

"That should hold for now," she said. "Gordo, do you think you can get to the cart?" Gordo nodded.

"Good. Bring it around to the front and wait for us there."

Jemma glanced at Shade's cell. Though Noodle and Pie were still keeping Shade in check, her dark aura was strengthening. Even without her amulet, she seemed to be growing rapidly immune to the rats, her phobia of them dwindling. "Leave her, Rattusses!" Jemma pulled her Stone from her pocket and fastened it around her neck. "Quickly, before she can harm you. Come on, Dig. They'll be starting the Ceremony any moment."

Jemma, Digby, and the rats ran along the Pickle Corridor and up the stairs. Jemma repeated Majem's instructions as they went, as much to drum them into herself as to tell Digby: Opening Call, Song, Releasing Rhyme. Call. Song. Rhyme.

They tumbled into the cavernous hall. The Ceremony Chamber doors were closed. Pale smoke seeped underneath them and curled upward, like wispy talons ready for the kill.

CHAPTER FORTY-THREE

The Darkest Hour

"Where is Shade?" Nocturna's voice was sharp as a sword edge. "Nox, fetch her!"

"Dig, grab that," Jemma whispered, pointing to one of the halberds. "Stop him!"

"Right." Digby wrenched the long handle from its suit of armor. Jemma quickly threw a protective sphere of Light around him and the rats, and then herself.

"Shade!" Nox bellowed. The doors flew open. "Where— What the devil is this?"

"Out of our way!" Digby jabbed the halberd's curved blade at him.

"Don't try anything with me, boy," Nox snarled, backing into the Ceremony Chamber.

Jemma and Digby followed him in. Through the pale smoke, Jemma could see that the pews had been cleared to the far side of the room. A large circle of black candles glittered in their place, surrounding the two front pillars. Simon and Tiny were lashed to Mordrake's statue, Flora to Mordana's, looking petrified. In the middle of the mantel-altar, surrounded by smoldering willow branches, sat the black globe. Nocturna stood in front of it with Rook on her right shoulder, the weasels coiled around her hemline. Feo, stiff as a board, stood beside her. The flames behind them flashed off the sword Nocturna was clutching with both hands.

"Jemmahhh!" she hissed. "Even now you seek to thwart us! Whatever you have done with Shade, we shall not be stopped!"

"We'll see about that!" Jemma ran toward Flora; the rats pelted over to Simon and Tiny. Nox shot a Dromfell at Digby, disintegrating his protective light shield, and he fell to the flagstones, the halberd clattering beside him. Jemma threw another protective shield around him: Nox wouldn't be able to produce another Dromfell so soon, but Nocturna or Feo might try.

Nox strode to Nocturna and Feo, turned, and raised his arms. "Mordsprites!" he boomed. "I summon you!"

"Dig!" Jemma yelled as she reached Flora, "think positive thoughts!" Arming herself with memories of her parents, Marsh, and sunshine, she pulled out her knife and began hacking at Flora's binds. Already, shadows were swarming in the vaulted ceiling. "Above you, Dig!"

Digby struggled to his feet as the heaving mass swooped down on him. His eyes steeled with determination; his light shield intensified. Inches away from him, the Mordsprites stopped dead, then turned and fled.

"Nox!" Nocturna shrieked. "Stop wasting time on secondary sorcery! We must hasten!" Her eyes, and Nox's, rolled back in their heads until only the whites showed.

Jemma went cold. They hadn't even said the Opening Invocation, but were going straight into a trance . . . ? That could only mean one thing: they were about to summon an Entity. Already. And not just any Entity . . . Her small knife no match for Flora's ropes, she pocketed it and began tearing at the impossible-looking knot and willing it to untie.

"*Morda-Morda-Morda-lay* . . ." Nocturna, Nox, and Feo started the slow, deliberate chant. The black candles flared.

"Morda-nothin'!" Digby charged toward them, halberd in hand like a lance, but was thrown to the ground again by a force surrounding them, visible only as a gray aura that had expanded around the black globe, pulsing in time with their words.

"You who keep'st the Light at bay . . ."

The candles flared again, more strongly.

"Dig, leave them!" Jemma yelled, realizing with a jolt of horrific memory what the black candles were: a sacrificial circle. "The candles, Dig—put them out!"

"Right!" Digby stood and swiped several over with his halberd. They sprang back into place, still lit.

Come on, knot, come on! Jemma pulsed Light through her fingers as they worked. The rope shifted slightly.

"Hurry, Jemma." Flora's voice was barely a squeak.

"Bring to us on this Your day . . ." Nox and Nocturna's expressions were like stone, their white eyes unseeing. But Feo was staring at Jemma, a look of intense anguish on his face. Suddenly, he broke out of the Agromonds' gray force-field.

"I'll get you, common dross!" He lurched toward Digby, his eyes blazing with hatred. Flames leapt into life around Digby's light sphere. Jemma quickly reinforced it, and the flames went out.

"Keep back, you!" Digby jabbed the halberd at Feo, while veering from side to side and kicking over a few candles. They snapped upright again, burning brightly.

"Your darkest demon—Scagavay!"

Darkest demon? Jemma gulped. Last time, it had been "favored phantom," and that had been terrifying enough.

Untie, knot—please! At last, the rope slithered undone.

"Come on, Flora." Jemma pulled the quivering girl over to Simon and Tiny. Noodle and Pie were just gnawing through the last strands of their ropes, and the boys shook themselves free.

"*Morda-Morda-Morda-lay* . . ."

Jemma grabbed their hands and dragged all three triplets toward the door, kicking at as many candles as she could on the way. But the candles remained standing, as if attached to the flagstones by springs, their flames still strong.

"*You who keep'st the Light at bay* . . ." Nox and Nocturna droned on. Smoke belched into the room.

"Flora, Simon, Tiny," said Jemma, "hurry outside! Your pa will be there any minute."

The triplets bolted for the door, and Jemma ran toward Digby, who was swinging the halberd at Feo. Feo shot another Fire gaze at him, but the light sphere around Digby was strong, and the flames instantly died.

"Hazebury muck!" Feo snatched at the halberd's handle.

"Agromond menace!" Digby dodged Feo's grasp.

"*Bring to us on this Your day* . . ."

Jemma stood by Digby's side. For a split second, Feo's eyes wavered to her and flashed with sadness. Then he fixed them on Digby again, his expression hardening. Behind him, smoke curled around Nox and Nocturna as if embracing them. Jemma gathered her focus and took a deep breath.

"The Opening Call, Digby," she said. "I'll say it three times. Join in when you can—"

Screams from the hall split the air. She wheeled around. Shade stood in the doorway, clutching Simon and Tiny by the collar in one hand, Flora in the other.

"Did you really think a mere lock could hold me, Jem-mah?" she sneered. She kicked the door shut behind her and marched into the Chamber, adding her banshee-shrill voice to the Agromond chant.

"Your darkest demon—Scagavay!"

Jemma hurled herself at Shade. Noodle and Pie were ahead of her, running up Shade's legs. For a second, Shade flinched. Simon and Tiny wriggled free and ran for the door, but it was shut fast. Gripping Flora's hair with one hand, Shade hurled a Dromfell at Jemma with the other. Jemma ducked, and it exploded against one of the pillars.

"You coward, Shade. Let her go!"

"And *why* exactly would I do that, Jem-*mah*?" said Shade, sweeping Noodle from her shoulder as if he were a speck of dust, and sending him flying.

The Agromond chant droned on.

"Jem—help!" Digby yelled. "I can't hold him!" His light sphere was flickering, choked by the smoke now surrounding him and Feo. Feo was choking too, and apparently unable to summon more flames. Red with rage, he finally managed to grab the halberd's handle. He and Digby were now face-to-face, deadlocked, the handle horizontal between them.

"Dig, hold on!" Jemma shot reinforcing Light at him.

"Oh no you don't, you she-devil!" Shade snarled. "We can't have you helping him, now can we?" She caught Jemma's wrist with her free hand and twisted, forcing her to the floor. "I'll teach you to destroy my amulet!" Even without it, her strength was immense. She flung Flora to the flagstones, then straddled Jemma, pinning Jemma's arms with her knees and closing her fingers around Jemma's throat. Noodle and

Pie scratched and bit, but Shade was oblivious to them now, and to Flora and the boys, who had thrown themselves on her and were pulling at her dress, her hair, anything their small hands could grasp, yelling *Get off her! Leave her alone!* at the top of their small voices.

Choking for breath, Jemma called upon her Stone's Power and managed to pry Shade's hands apart.

"Very well, have it your way, Jem-*mah!*" Shade's diamond birthmark was almost black with rage. "Revenge can still be sweet!" She ripped Jemma's Stone from her throat, then dropped it with a roar of pain, her hand red and blistered. She blew on her palm, and the red faded. Then she blew on Jemma's face. Jemma felt her whole body freeze.

"And that," said Shade, "is the last breath I'll ever waste on you!" She stood, shaking off the triplets and rats, then kicked Jemma hard, in the stomach. Jemma doubled up, groaning, and reached for her Stone, but Shade kicked it away as she grabbed Flora by the hair and hauled her toward the fireplace.

"Let me go! Pleeeeease! Jemma—help!" Flora's cries ripped Jemma's heart. Simon and Tiny lay on the floor, trembling. Digby was on his back now, with Feo on top of him, holding the halberd's handle across his throat.

The Agromonds were winning.

Don't despair. Two snouts nudged Jemma's hand, and dropped her Stone into her palm. Warmth trickled through her.

"*Morda, Morda, Mordalay* . . ." Shade's strident voice now joined with her parents'.

"Feo!" Shade yelled, holding Flora around the neck with one arm. "Stop squandering precious energy on that scab and get over here! It's time for the Sacrifice!"

Flora screamed. Digby roared, held down by Feo. Simon and Tiny wailed.

"No . . ." Jemma clasped her Stone and struggled to her knees. Noodle and Pie leapt onto her shoulders and rippled energy into her, but still the pain from Shade's kick was intense, and she let out a moan, clutching her belly.

Feo looked at her. His face softened. He loosened his hold on Digby and mouthed her name. *Jemma . . .* The pinkish aura she had seen the night before flared around him.

"It's not too late, Feo," Jemma rasped. "You can still change your mind." The aura moved toward her, hesitated, then moved again. "Please, Feo, think of what you said last night."

"Bring to us on this your day—"

"Feo!" Shade shrieked. "Your family needs you—*now!*"

Suddenly, Feo's pink aura withered and disappeared. His mouth set. He spat at Digby and released the halberd, then stood and backed away. The Agromonds' protective shield shimmered like dark water as he stepped back into it and took his place next to Shade. Both his eyes and Shade's glazed, and they joined in the chant.

"Your darkest demon, Scagavay!"

Flora, still gripped by Shade, was choking on the smoke, tears streaming down her face. Digby hauled himself to his feet and charged toward her, but the force field around the Agromonds was even stronger now, and he slashed and clawed at it in vain. Jemma crawled over to him, clutching her Stone, the rats on her shoulders. Tiny and Simon followed close behind. Her lungs seared from the stinking black cloud spewing from the fireplace. Her light shield was all but gone. Digby helped her stand, the light around him strong again now that Feo was no longer attacking him.

"Morda-Morda-Mordalay . . ." Nocturna slowly stepped away from the group and turned to face Flora. Wind whisked from the fireplace, spiraling all the grayness in the room into one dense mass above her head, where it hovered, pulsing like a monstrous dark heart. Nocturna gripped the sword with both hands and slowly began to raise it.

Jemma summoned all her strength and concentration. "The Light be called," she yelled. "Scagavay, be gone, now!"

Nocturna wavered; the sword wobbled. Scagavay's dark mass shrank slightly.

"The Light be called!" Jemma shouted a second time, as loudly as she could. "Scagavay, be gone—now!"

Scagavay shrank again. The black candles sputtered. Nocturna's sword clanged to the ground. Nox and Feo stopped chanting. For a second, their gray protective shield wavered. Seizing his chance, Digby rushed into it and wrenched Flora from Shade's grip.

"Got you!" He picked her up and carried her back to Jemma's side.

"The Light be called!" Jemma yelled as Noodle and Pie sent a burst of energy through her shoulders. "Scagavay, be—"

An arrow of blackness shot out from Scagavay, puncturing her light shield and twining around her throat. Her words choked. Noodle and Pie fell to the ground.

"Bring to us on this Your day . . ." The Agromond voices strengthened again. The ever-growing mass above their heads swelled. "Your darkest demon—SCAGAVAY!"

The candles in the circle flared. Flames in the fireplace

leapt up. Scagavay started to emit a sound, high at first, like a distant scream, which rapidly crescendoed as a deep roar rose up behind it, overpowering it and filling the room with one deafening howl. The wind renewed its assault, whipping up the debris around Jemma, Digby, and the triplets. Noodle and Pie clawed their way up to her pockets.

"Come on, Jem," Digby yelled. "We can do it!" He took her hand. Her light shield intensified. The strand around her throat fell to the floor in sooty fragments, and together, they shouted at the top of their lungs:

"SCAGAVAY, BE GONE NOW!"

The flagstones around their feet seemed to melt. Wisps of light, hundreds of them, gold, green, pink, and blue, poured up from below and swirled toward Scagavay.

"Jem!" Digby gasped. "Look—Luminals!" The Luminals wove through Scagavay's thick mass, separating it into strands, which began to shrink and dissipate. Several candles went out.

"No!" Nocturna shrieked. She picked up the sword and grabbed one of her weasels by the scruff of its neck. "Mord Ancestors," she shouted, holding up the writhing creature, "witness my Offering!" With one deft move, she sliced its throat and dropped it, then snatched up a second one and repeated the slaughter. Scagavay dipped smoky tendrils through the sacrificial blood pooling at Nocturna's feet, and expanded again.

The triplets screamed. Luminals kept coming, but as fast as they materialized, they were absorbed by Scagavay's darkness. The surviving two weasels slithered toward Jemma, teeth bared, then leapt for her throat. But Digby was quick.

He grabbed them by their tails and flung them, screeching, into a pillar.

"Jem!" he yelled. "The Song!"

The Song. Jemma fought to remember its melody, but it muddled in her mind. Then she heard it—the heavenly sound that had poured into her through Drudge's arms the day before, winding through her head, gathering force.

"Jem—that's beautiful!"

"It's not me, Dig—"

The melody was coming from the back of the room. Jemma wheeled around, and there, emerging from the shadows, was Drudge. He stood for a second, teetering. A blue aura flickered around him, stronger than Jemma had seen surrounding him before; and then a younger, luminous body began shimmering through his wizened exterior as he walked slowly toward them. The song flowed from his mouth, but seemed to be swirling around him also, growing louder with every step he took.

The Agromonds' voices trailed off. Clumps of ceiling plaster rained around them. One of the pews cracked. In a far corner of the room, a beam crashed to the floor.

Drudge's hair blew back in the wind, his gait steady and purposeful. Layers of aging dissolved, as if being peeled away by his warrior spirit. It was Gudred who stepped up beside Jemma.

"Three hundred years I have tarried," he said, his voice strong and clear. "Now it is your voice they await. Sing, Jemma. Sing with me, and with the Song!"

He took her hand. Suddenly, the glorious sound was somehow rising from the ground, rushing up through her feet and out of her mouth with a crystal clarity that felt utterly new and familiar at the same time. It was as if a whole choir was pouring out from her and into the room. *The voices of Majem, and all my ancestors,* she thought. But it was so much more: an army of Light Beings, of souls who had come to add their voices to the Song. They *were* the Song. And as they sang, Luminals appeared again, increasing in number and intensity. Scagavay pulled back, fragmenting, then coalesced again into a trembling cloud above the Agromonds' heads. Stunned into silence, Nox and Feo were ashen. Shade clamped onto Nocturna, whose sword now hung limp in her hand as Luminals came thick and fast, flying through Scagavay's cloudy sinews, breaking them apart.

"Jem," said Digby, "it's working! Scagavay's shrinking!"

Jemma's heart lifted, then fell again when she turned to Gudred. His light was dimming.

"You must go on," he rasped. "Finish it. . . ."

She held his hand tighter, as if doing so could keep him there, and continued to sing. The glorious chorus grew. Scagavay's roar died down; the wind dropped. The black globe was shrinking. The Agromonds stood stupefied, their protective shield gone. A stone arm fell from Mordana's statue. With a loud *crack!* a fissure zigzagged across the hearth.

The invisible choir stopped its melody, hanging on one heavenly chord as if every note in the universe were hovering on the edge of some momentous event.

"Now," Gudred whispered, "the Releasing Rime . . . Say it!"

But before Jemma could take a breath, Nocturna's voice pierced the Ceremony Chamber. "Mordrake, Mordana," she shrieked. "I hear your promise and accept your demand!" She grabbed Feo, threw him onto the hearth, stomped one foot onto his neck, and raised her sword.

"Mama, no!" Feo screamed. "Please, no!"

Nox stepped toward them, but Shade pushed him back and wrapped him in dark energy bands, holding him fast. Her face quivered with glee. Scagavay hovered above them, taking the form of a huge open mouth, ready, waiting. . . .

"Stop!" Jemma shrieked. She leapt forward and shot out a light sphere to protect Feo, but Nocturna parried it and swung her sword at her, forcing her back. Shade shot a Dromfell at her. She ducked, but it grazed her shoulder, its impact knocking her backward to the floor. "Stop—you can't! He has the Mark—he's one of you!"

"Yes, he has the Mark," Shade sneered, "just as you do! It seems meaningless, does it not, Jem-*mah*?" She turned to her mother. "Do it, Mama—do it!"

Nocturna raised her sword again, and drove its long blade into Feo's heart. He shuddered, groaned once, and was still.

CHAPTER FORTY-FOUR

Saeweldar

A silver-gray wisp rose from Feo's body and was sucked into Scagavay. The triplets' screams melded with Scagavay's roar, with Nox's cries of disbelief, and with Shade's banshee whoop of victory, drowning out the thin thread of song still trickling from Gudred's mouth.

"And now, in accordance with Twin Lore," Shade cried, grabbing Feo's amulet from around his neck, "I take possession of my full Powers!" Darkness thickened around her as if paying her homage, then Scagavay's murky grayness leapt outward again, filling the room.

Jemma crawled toward Gudred. He was aging with every second, lines gathering on his face, his body shrinking.

"The Releasing Rime," he wheezed. "Sssay!"

She opened her mouth. But Scagavay was upon her again, spinning mercilessly, and she was lifted off the ground, spiraling upward with the dust and debris. The Bell Tower began booming, each toll juddering through her as she was engulfed in a demonic hiss: *At last, I have you! You are mine, all mine!*

Jemma sent a grounding cord earthward, which steadied her slightly. Fighting for breath, she tried to utter the Rime, but the words buffeted back into her throat. Claws of wind whipped into her pockets, siphoning out Noodle and Pie and whisking them beyond her reach. They slammed against the ceiling, their tiny limbs spreadeagled, her amulet wrapped around Noodle's neck. She shot a beam of Light around them just in time to prevent them being pulverized by a carved demon head that had been ripped from the vaulting. Then, with a sharp jerk, the grounding cord broke, and she was whisked up and pinned against the ceiling next to the rats, the breath being sucked from her lungs.

You're mine! The hiss crescendoed to a roar. *Mine, my sweet thirteen!*

Jemma's thoughts sputtered as her lungs strained for air. *Releasing Rhyme . . . must say it . . .*

Far below, through Scagavay's swirling gray, the black globe pulsed back to life. Firelight leapt up, illuminating Shade and Nocturna, who were waving the black altar cloth like a victory flag and dancing together on a lake of red, Rook's dark wings sailing above them. Nox was lying face-down across Feo's blood-soaked chest. Digby was holding the triplets' faces to him so that they shouldn't see the horror unfolding. Gudred, years galloping upon him again, was on all fours, any remains of the Song coming from him inaudible above Scagavay's roar. Every word of the Releasing Rime was obliterated from Jemma's head, whirled and deafened into oblivion, and at any moment she, the rats, Digby, and the triplets would all be whirled into oblivion with it.

Help me, Majem, she pleaded. *What am I to do?*

A soundless voice welled up from the depths of her being. *Scagavay is like the Mist. You know what to do. Blank . . . counter. . . . Blank.* For the Mist, that had meant embodying its dampness, its whiteness, to become one with it, but this . . .

Summoning every ounce of concentration, Jemma closed

her eyes, filling her mind with Scagavay's tarry evil. Every foul thought she had ever had flooded her, every word of anger, every judgment, and she embraced them all until she was one with the darkness. A vile stillness settled around her. Into it, she threw the full force of her intent. The words of the Rime unjumbled from the chaos, merging with the Song's Power as she shouted with all her might—

"All Orbs held here in Captivitee,
Release thy Bondes, be thou free!"

The black globe pulsed once, twice, and then shattered, scattering gray ash everywhere. Scagavay's howl ceased. For a split second, Jemma heard the celestial chord of voices ringing out again. Then everything went silent in her head.

She was suspended in mid-air, the scene below her slowing as if immersed in syrupwater. The candles went out. Nocturna and Shade released hands and circled to a halt. Digby let go of the triplets. Nox, still lying on Feo's chest, was shaking with sobs. Gudred, his light now a mere flicker, looked up at her. *Again!* said the voice from within, so again she yelled the words at the top of her lungs, though she couldn't hear them. All around, the blackness separated into strands, then into particles, releasing hundreds of light orbs as it did so—golden orbs and silver-blue, pink-tinged ones, all sailing through the Ceremony Chamber air and sprinkling the silence with children's voices, whispering, chattering, laughing. Then one small, particularly bright orb appeared in front of Jemma's eyes.

Jem-Jem, said a tiny voice in her head, *Jem-Jem*—

"Jamem . . ." She reached out and touched the orb. It lingered for several seconds, sparkling with the color of flame, and she felt as though it were dissolving her palm, flowing into her with an airy rush that made her gasp. "Jamem!" she said again. Then the orb spun away and joined the others. They began to combine into larger orbs, and larger still, prismatic colors glinting off them as they rose and gathered into one breathtaking sphere of shimmering, multicolored fire. In an explosion of light, Scagavay was sucked into it.

The darkness was gone.

Jemma felt a surge of pure joy. The celestial voices rang out again, hanging in mid-chord as a cushion of warm air floated her down through tumbling dust motes. Noodle and Pie were floating down too, her Stone scintillating around Noodle's neck. The three of them were gently deposited next to Digby. His face was ecstatic and he was saying something, but all she could hear was the crystal choir. Slowly, it faded, and other sounds began filtering through, Digby's words mixing with the triplets' excited babble and the rats' squeals.

"Jem!" He let go of the triplets and threw his arms around her. "You done it—look!"

Translucent light filled the room. The triplets, standing behind Digby, stood in wide-eyed amazement. Behind them, Nocturna and Shade cowered into the altar cloth, shielding themselves from the brightness. Nox, now kneeling next to Feo's body, gaped. And containing them all, almost filling the room, was one enormous Luminal, throbbing gently like a giant heartbeat. Its brilliance sparkled off the walls in all colors of the rainbow, and reflected in the faces it illuminated.

"*We've* done it, Dig," Jemma whispered, vaguely aware of small paws clambering up her leg and a small muzzle nudging something smooth and cool into her hand. She opened her palm. Her Stone lay there, its aquamarine glow pulsing in time with the Luminal. She tied it around her neck by its broken chain.

"Sssae . . . Sssaewel . . . ," a voice croaked behind her. She turned. Drudge was on the floor, reaching for her. She ran to him and knelt by his side.

"Oh, Drudge . . . Gudred . . . Thank you."

He smiled his yellow-toothed smile and laid a chilly hand against her cheek. His touch communicated what his voice no longer had strength for: this was Saeweldar, the combined soul of every child who had been slain at Agromond Castle. Including Jamem. And Feo. And Nox's sister, Malaena. Each was now released from the darkness—the monster—and united in one glorious sphere of Light, one powerful Luminal. Scagavay was gone. Forever.

The flow of images ebbed from Drudge's hand. He touched Jemma's Stone. "Mjjjem," he muttered. "Hers. Yours." The furrows on his face softened. "You . . . ssso like her . . ."

Jemma could feel Drudge's heart—Gudred's—straining toward the one it had missed for all these years. Love welled up in her: hers, Drudge's, Gudred's, and Majem's. "But she was married to your brother," she whispered, blinking back tears, "so you made this your mission. To come here. For her. For me. For all of Anglavia—"

"Jem!" Digby yelled. "Watch out!"

Jemma looked up. Nox was lunging toward her, his face and clothes streaked with Feo's blood. Digby tried to grab him but missed. Nox threw his full weight against her, propelling her backward. As she landed, one end of a huge beam crashed onto his back, pinning him to the flagstones and knocking him unconscious. If he hadn't pushed her, she would have been crushed beneath it. He had saved her—

Then she saw that the other end of the beam had landed on Drudge's legs.

"No!" Jemma scrambled to where he lay and grabbed his hand. Digby was there too, struggling to remove the beam, but it was too heavy. He knelt next to Drudge, biting his lips. Flora, Simon, and Tiny, standing behind their brother, clung nervously to one another.

"No pain." Drudge patted Digby's knee, then turned to Jemma. "Rime," he said. "Finishshsh."

Si ti neto di od nise . . . Wom styn ob nege . . . The Rime instantly unscrambled in Jemma's head. She tried to speak, but couldn't.

"Ssssay!" He stroked her hand. "Mussst . . . mean it . . ."

"It is done . . . It is done. . . ." The words felt empty. "I can't. Not now . . ."

"Then sssoon. Loud. Promisss!"

Jemma nodded. "I promise," she whispered.

"Gooood! My work . . . over . . ." Drudge smiled, his cracked old voice becoming soft and clear. "One . . . more tasssk . . . Farewell, Jmmmaaah . . ." He closed his eyes and breathed his last.

Jemma lay across his chest and sobbed. To have lost him now—just when everything he had waited for had come to pass! Why couldn't he have lived to enjoy it? After three hundred years!

Meant to be. Noodle and Pie nudged her cheeks. *You'll see.*

Then Jemma felt the oddest sensation, as if liquid air were

425

flowing through her from below. She looked up. Light was shining from Drudge's body, separating from it, rising, and as it rose, Saeweldar began dividing again into thousands of orbs. She, Digby, and the triplets stared, awe-struck, as the orbs followed Drudge's light-form upward until it stopped just below the vaults. Then two bright new globes shimmered through the broken wall, glinting pink and blue rays around the room as they spun toward the others, as if magnetized by them.

"The two that Shade killed," Jemma murmured. "Drudge is taking them too. . . ."

There was a flash; all the orbs merged again into one brilliant sphere, and with a final swoosh, vanished through the ceiling.

A shaft of dawn angled onto the spot where Drudge's body, now empty of his spirit, lay. He had gone.

"Jemma . . . Flamehead . . ." Nox groaned, coming back to consciousness. She looked at him, trapped under the other end of the beam, his arms outstretched where he had pushed her.

"You saved me," she said. "Why?"

"Feo . . ." His face was tight with agony. "Didn't want you to die too. I always loved you, you know."

Jemma reached over and took his hand. "We'll get you out, somehow."

Nox laughed softly. "Don't bother. All . . . pointless . . ."

Jemma looked around the room. Its walls were ripped open, piles of beams and plaster everywhere. The pews were smashed. Nocturna and Shade were on their knees, clinging to the altar cloth. Feo's body lay behind them, the two blood-soaked weasel corpses nearby. Rook and the surviving weasels

426

had vanished. Mordrake's scythe lay on the floor, shattered; both he and Mordana were split from head to toe. The altar was in smithereens, the fire barely smoldering. And Drudge, the wizened old warrior who had dedicated his life to this moment, was gone, the empty shell of his body crumpled like a handless glove, with Noodle and Pie sitting on either side of his head as if keeping vigil. Nox was right. It was all pitifully, murderously pointless.

Jemma let go of his hand and stood. "I hope this satisfies you, Nocturna Agromond!" she yelled across the room. "Was it worth all this death and destruction, and all those poor children's lives, to get more Power? Sacrificing your own son, even! Tell me, you who thought nothing of killing my brother!"

Nocturna raised her head slowly, her crimson lips spreading into a sneer. "I?" she said. "I? Foolish child, still you do not know! Oh, yes, little Jamem was slaughtered in cold blood, the poor lamb so helpless, screaming out for you, his precious Jem-Jem, the sister he knew and loved so well while you were both here at the castle! Oh, the pity of it! But it was not I who murdered your brother, Jemma. No, it was he!" Nocturna's long-nailed finger pointed straight at Nox.

"You!" Jemma took a step back.

"Jemma . . . Flamehead . . . I . . ."

"Ha!" Shade chimed in. "And you thought he cared about you! But what kind of caring is it that kills one while it coddles the other?"

"Jem," said Digby, stepping toward her. "Don't listen—"

Nox looked up at her, imploring. There it was in his eyes, what she had never allowed herself to see before: the bloody deed, the guilt, the greed, his duplicity, his knowledge of the pain he had caused, all twisted up with the love he felt for her, and for his own dead sister.

"Think of your twin, Jemma!" Nocturna stood, pulling Shade up with her. "Your twin, and the loss your parents suffered for all those years!" Black diaphanous strands of energy began emanating from them and moving toward Nox.

"Jemma," Nox whispered hoarsely, the black strands snaking around him. "Forgive me."

Anger and sorrow flooded under Jemma's skin. She saw the knife nearby, where she'd dropped it, and picked it up.

"Jem!" Digby stepped in front of her and took hold of her shoulders. "Jem, don't listen to 'em! It's like when we was in the Mist—if you get caught up in their hatred, you'll only strengthen 'em again. Look, you can see it already."

Nocturna and Shade's mouths were curled into matching snarls. Their dark auras expanded.

"Hold your tongue, boy," Shade hissed. "Worthless piece of Hazebury dro—"

"Shut up, you!" Digby barked. He turned back to Jemma. "Jem, remember who you is. You've waited your whole life for this! Yes, it's a Mordawful mess. But think what it means: the end of their reign, Jem. A thousand years of it, over!"

"It's all right, Dig," Jemma said calmly. The black strands oozing from Nocturna and Shade tightened around Nox, then started making their way toward her. She clenched the knife's handle.

"Yes, Jemma, yes!" Nocturna shouted. "Avenge your little brother's horrible death. You can, you must!"

"Jem, don't!" Digby grabbed her arm. Behind him, Flora and the boys' eyes flared with alarm.

"Out of my way!" Jemma pushed Digby aside and leapt forward, infusing the blade with Light as she sliced the air, severing the shadowy web entangling Nox. Its sticky sinews snapped back into Nocturna and Shade. Jemma opened her hand, and the knife fell to the ground.

"Whoa, Jem!" Digby said. "I thought—"

"I know you did, Dig." Jemma glanced at Nocturna and Shade, who looked deflated again, then turned to Nox. "Forgive you?" she said. "I don't even know how to make sense of that idea, after all you've done. But revenge would only keep the evil going, and then all of this would have been for nothing." She knelt and stroked Drudge's silky hair. "And you didn't wait here three hundred years for that, did you?"

Noodle and Pie licked her hand, then burrowed into the hollow of Drudge's neck.

Digby knelt beside her. "What is it he wanted you to say?" he asked. "Don't forget. You promised."

"Yes, I did." Jemma sat back on her heels and took a deep breath, knowing that despite the horror and sorrow of all that had happened, she must mean the words with all her heart. She thought of her parents and Marsh, of Drudge's sacrifice and centuries of waiting, of Majem, the Prophecy, and Jamem, of all the help that had brought her to this point, and of those with her now: Digby, Noodle, and Pie. Even the triplets, with all the terrors they had suffered, had contributed to this moment. Every one of them had played a part. And so too, she realized, had her years at Agromond Castle, and her escape from it. If she hadn't been abducted, she would never have known Drudge, would never have learned to *Trussst*, never have become as determined as she needed to be to fulfill Gudred's Prophecy. It was all meant to be. All of it.

Thank you, she muttered under her breath, rising to her feet. *Thank you.* And all at once the longing she'd harbored since the first stories Marsh had told her all those years ago seemed to well up from the ground, rushing through her and pouring out on the tide of her voice.

"It is done, it is done!" she shouted.

"Now, Myst, be gone,

Let there be Sunne!"

CHAPTER FORTY-FIVE

Dawn

"What's happening?" Tiny squealed, his eyes like saucers. "The light!"

Through every crack in the outside walls, dawn was finding its way in, seeking out the musty corners of the Ceremony Chamber and illuminating places that had only ever seen darkness. Gray granite paled, gargoyles' faces grimaced, and spiders ran for cover, leaving their prey quivering on sparkling webs.

"Look!" Flora pointed to where Shade and Nocturna were backed against the fireplace, the altar cloth pulled around them like a shroud. "They're scared!"

"Well, I'll be, so they are!" said Digby. "Afraid of daylight. Imagine that."

Just then there was banging on the door behind them, and yelling.

"Digby, Jemma—let me in!"

"It's Pa!" Simon, Tiny, and Flora hurtled toward the door. It creaked and strained, then splintered off its hinges as Gordo burst into the room.

"Oh, my little 'uns, my little 'uns—Digby—all of yer—"

"Pa, Pa! You should've seen—it was all dark—everythin' shakin'—"

"I know, I know." Gordo knelt and scooped them into his

arms. "Me n' Pepper, we couldn't get near, with stones crashin' down everywhere. Then a big light went up. . . ." He looked at Jemma and Digby. "Soon as I saw it, don't ask me how, I knew you was all safe— Oh, my! Mr. Drudge . . . Poor ol' fellow." He let out a long whistle.

"He's at peace," said Jemma, knowing as she spoke that the words came from Drudge. "He says . . . it was a strain for him to be alive, after so long." Her heart lifted. "He's meeting his loved ones."

"Who'da thought he was so . . . so special, eh?" Gordo said, shaking his head. "Las' night, y'know, when him an' me was hidin', I was beside myself about the five of you. But he jus' laid a hand on me, an' the way it calmed me, an' kep' me strong . . . like magic, it was." He stood, then winced, his hand going to the Dromfell wound on his calf.

"Oh, Gordo," said Jemma, going over to him. "Let's see what I can do about that." She squatted down and placed her hand on the wound.

"I'm fine, lass. It'll wait." Gordo held the triplets close. "You don't need to bother with— Why, young Jemma! How're you doin' that?" The gash on his leg scabbed over, then vanished.

"I had the best teachers." Jemma stood again, and smiled. "Besides, it's not me who heals you," she added, remembering Bryn's words. "I just help."

"Oh. Right." Gordo scratched his head. "But 'ow are *you*, lass? I mean, Mr. Drudge, an' everythin' you been through . . ."

"I'm all right, thanks." Jemma looked across at Drudge's frail form. It seemed to have shrunk, the face strangely empty without his spirit to animate the beaked nose and cracked lips. But his love and dedication, and all she knew of him, lived inside her now. Little more than five weeks ago she would never have thought it possible, but almost everything she had believed about her life had been turned on its head since then, and everything she'd hated or feared no longer had power over her. Nocturna and Shade seemed little more than terrified wraiths. Even her anger toward Nox was rapidly dissipating; all she saw was a broken man. The worst thing was how shaken the triplets still looked, though Gordo's arrival had cheered them up. *And you too can help to clear those horrors from their eyes,* said a new voice in her head—a voice that was clear and ageless, no longer cracked and worn, *and I, and all of us who are part of you, will help as well.*

Jemma smiled at Gordo. "Yes," she said. "I'm all right. I really am."

"Well then," said Digby, pointing at Nox. "Let's get this beam off him. Noodle, Pie, mind yourselves."

The rats hopped off Drudge's body and scuttled up onto Jemma's shoulders while she, Gordo, and Digby hoisted the beam to one side. Nox groaned, coming to, his face a picture of agony.

"Thank you," he said, then passed out again.

"Don't mention it," Digby said, gritting his teeth. "Come on, Jem, let's go and deal with them other two, make sure they don't escape. Flora, Tiny, Simon, stand back, just in case."

Noodle's and Pie's tails lashed across Jemma's neck as she, Digby, and Gordo approached Nocturna and Shade. The two stood in statuesque silence, apparently oblivious to Nox and to Feo's blood-soaked body lying in front of them. But the fire had gone from their eyes, leaving only four hollow, burned-out coals. Digby and Gordo knotted together the ropes with which Flora and the boys had been tied, and wound it tightly around their prisoners. Bound from shoulder to thigh, Nocturna and Shade looked like two giant grubs. Digby secured the ends of the rope around one of the remaining pillars, making sure that they were directly in a beam of light just for good measure.

"There," he said, grinning. "Fear has its uses, eh, Jem? Should keep 'em nice an' meek for a while. Now, let's get out of here!"

"Yes," she said. "Let's go."

"Us too!" Flora, Simon, and Tiny skittered up to them.

"Aye." Gordo picked Tiny up. "We'll all go."

Jemma felt a tug at her sleeve. Flora was beaming up at her.

"Thank you for savin' us, Jemma," she said.

"You're welcome." Jemma smoothed down Flora's matted hair. "I'm sorry I had to be so nasty yesterday."

"That's all right," Flora said. Jemma could see the shadow of Nocturna's sword scudding across Flora's eyes, and shuddered. Then Noodle and Pie hopped onto Flora's shoulders. Her face lit up, and she turned and skipped after Gordo, Simon, and Tiny. Jemma and Digby walked slowly behind.

"Just a minute, Dig." Jemma stopped by Drudge's body and knelt down, laying her hand gently on his chest. With a slight crackle, what was left of him collapsed into a golden puff of dust, his clothes deflating onto the flagstones. One lapel of his jacket wafted back, revealing an inside pocket from which a corner of parchment was showing. Jemma pulled it out and unfolded it. Its edges were tattered, and it was worn along the folds, barely holding together. Most of the scrolled handwriting was obliterated by holes and dried rivulets where the ink had run, but she instantly recognized whose it was.

"My *dearest* G," she read, whispering, "*with heavy heart . . . your leaving. Should I depart this life before thee . . . shall ever watch over . . . I remain, your M.*"

Jemma folded the note as carefully as she could and replaced it. "Ever watch over," she repeated, in awe at the endurance of such love. "But you're reunited now." She stood, and with a last sideways glance at the still-unconscious Nox, walked with Digby out of the Ceremony Chamber and into the hallway.

Gordo and the triplets were standing in the middle of the hall, open-mouthed. The stairway's curved balustrade lay in pieces on the floor, daylight slicing in through the ripped ceiling. The huge oak front door hung off its hinges as if begging for mercy from the chaos outside.

"Blimey!" said Digby, taking Jemma's hand as they picked their way across the dust and rubble. "What a mess!"

"Look—the Mist!" said Simon. "It's going away!"

They all stopped by the entrance and watched the whiteness folding back, revealing granite blocks and broken gargoyles everywhere. To the left, toward the sheer edge of Mordwin's Crag, the grass was covered with shards of glass from the Repast Room window. Straight ahead, fragments of battlements were embedded in the earth. To the right, hewn boulders littered the ground up to where Pepper stood waiting with the cart. Beyond, the forest looked as though it were waking from a long sleep, the pines' dark arms stretching outward. Above their gently swaying tops, a golden disc hovered low in the sky, shining through the merest veil of gray, which was decreasing every moment.

"The sun," whispered Jemma. "Flora, Tiny, Simon, look— that's the sun!"

The triplets, Digby, and Gordo were already squinting at it, shading their eyes from the unaccustomed brightness.

"Go on, Jem," said Digby, nudging her. "You first."

Jemma let go of his hand and stepped outside.

The air was balmy, the scent of firs and pines strong in the clearing air. She breathed it in, then turned and looked up at the hulking shell of the Ceremony Chamber, the spiky ruins behind it where the Bell Tower used to be, and the white sky above. Even what remained of the castle looked less heavy, glints of crystal blinking off it in the dawn light.

"It's glorious!" she said. "Come on out, all of you!"

Noodle and Pie sprang from Flora's shoulders and streaked toward Jemma like two golden arrows. Digby followed, grinning from ear to ear. Gordo and the triplets stepped onto the grass, then started laughing as they experienced the soft glow of sunlight for the first time. Flora and the boys scampered to and fro, the terrors of the last few days seeming to ebb from them as they rolled onto the ground, pulling Gordo with them.

"Ooh, me back. Ouch!" Gordo said, laughing. "Careful, now. Your pa's gettin' a bit cronky."

"Shush everyone!" Jemma said. "What's that?"

They stopped and listened. Voices, hundreds of them, were rising up from the forest, getting louder by the second.

"Sounds like an army," said Digby, "coming up the road."

They waited, ears alert. A bead of sweat dribbled down

Jemma's forehead, and she realized how warm she was. Apparently, they were all feeling it. Gordo mopped his brow. He and Digby removed their jackets, Simon and Tiny pulled off their jerkins, and Flora rolled up her sleeves. Noodle and Pie, perched on a boulder, were licking their fur. The golden disc of sun was now higher above the treetops, brighter, more defined. All around, the sky was changing, turning blue. It seemed to go on forever.

The last wisp of Mist melted, and the mass of approaching voices erupted into a cheer.

"It's over!" One voice soared above the rest. "Praise be! It's over!"

Jemma touched the Stone around her neck and smiled.

CHAPTER FORTY-SIX

Let There Be Sun

"It's over—down with the Agromonds!"

"Down with the Agromonds!" the chant began. "Down with the Agromonds!"

A phalanx of people rounded the corner from behind the trees, headed by Berola.

"Ma, Ma!" Flora, Tiny, and Simon ran toward her.

"My babies!" she cried, breaking away from the crowd and rushing forward. "My babies! I been so worried—" The triplets flew into her open arms.

Behind Berola, the crowd was gathering: men, women, children, even pony traps carrying elderly folk and infants. There were far more than the population of Hazebury could possibly be; everyone from the surrounding villages, it seemed, had come along. They gathered around Jemma in a large crescent, jostling and chattering. Noodle and Pie clambered onto her shoulders, and she couldn't help smiling, thinking what an odd group they must appear to be.

Voices petered out as stunned faces took in the ruins around them. Then one voice shouted, "She done it—the Fire One!"

Jemma recognized the man from the group she and Digby had seen after leaving the storehouse, weeks ago. A cheer rose, and she noticed several other people who had been on the path that morning: Mrs. Scragg, Mrs. Jenkin, and the boy Ned. All trace of grayness had vanished from them, and their faces were animated as they joined in the general chatter.

"*Heard this commotion . . . looked up . . . castle, starting to crumble . . . Berola says, It's the Prophecy come to pass . . . Mist thinning . . . sky, getting brighter . . . word got about fast . . . folks from everywhere: Dingleborough, Oxton—*"

"Jemma, lass!" Berola elbowed her way to the front with the triplets and threw her arms around Jemma, almost dislodging Noodle and Pie from her shoulders. "Thank you, thank you!"

"Ouff!" Jemma gasped, winded by Berola's hug. The rats scuttled into the safety of her pockets. "You're welcome. . . . I couldn't have done it without Digby, though."

"So where's them Agromonds?" a woman yelled. "The monsters!"

Jemma pointed to the ruins. "In there. Three of them are alive. The fourth, their son, is dead." She felt a pang of sadness, especially thinking about how Feo must have felt when he saw his mother about to slaughter him.

"Then let's get 'em!" the man yelled. "Death to the Agromonds!"

"Aye!" said another, red-faced. "They took my wee twins, just weeks ago. Death to 'em!"

"An' so say I!" A young woman was clinging to his arm, her face puckered with grief. Jemma thought of the two small bodies under Shade's bed: this must be their parents. Their anguish tore through her.

"I'm so sorry . . . I . . ." She was at a loss for words.

"I'm with Murwyn an' Vi!" came a voice from the crowd.

"Revenge for their babies—for all of 'em! Death to those monsters!" Others joined in: "Death to the Agromonds!"

"No, please!" Jemma looked at Digby in alarm. "No more bloodshed!"

A group of men and women surged toward the castle, taking up the cry for vengeance. Jemma and Digby tried to hold them back but were swept aside. Jemma ran after them, pulling at their shirts and jackets.

"Stop!" she shouted. "Stop, please!"

Digby raced ahead and stood in the doorway, his fists clenched.

"You heard her!" he yelled above the crowd. "Toby, Pete—listen to me. Jemma ain't been through all she's been through just for us to be as murderous as that lot!"

"Out of the way, Digby," growled Pete. "Let us pass."

The crowd pressed forward, fists and voices raised. "Let's get 'em! Revenge!"

Jemma ran to Digby's side and let out a scream at the top of her lungs. It cut through the rising pandemonium, the force of it stunning them into silence.

"STOP!" she yelled. "Look at you, even turning against Digby—against your own kind! I know as well as anybody what the Agromonds are, and understand how you feel. They murdered my brother, and put my parents through years of suffering, keeping me here. But please, please, think! If you act like them, what makes you different from them?"

A few people blushed and murmured, and shifted from foot to foot.

"She's right!" Berola barreled up and turned to face the throng, hands on hips, feet planted squarely on the ground.

"An' if you don' stop this, Toby Weatherill and Pete McCloud you'll have my rollin' pin to answer to—an' no more of my meat pies, to boot!"

The crowd tittered. Toby and Pete stepped back.

"Well said, love," said Gordo, striding up next to her with the triplets. Tiny nestled next to Jemma and stroked Pie's head, which was peeking out from one pocket.

"Then how do we avenge our babies?" shouted a woman near the front. "Tell us that!"

"I don't know, Mrs. Duff," Digby said. "We can't stop feelin' what we feel. But I seen from them Agromonds what it does when you act from hatred, killin' for what you want without a thought for what's right an' wrong. In the end, it kills you too. Makes you soulless, just like them, till there's barely nothin' left that's human."

"An' what of our little 'uns' souls, trapped for eternity in that pile o' rubble?"

"No, they're not!" Jemma said. "They're free now, all of them. They were led to the Light by Gudred—though we knew him as Drudge—"

"Gudred?" said Pete. "You mean the famous Solvay Visionary? Come off it! He died hundreds of years ago."

"That's what everyone thought," said Jemma, "but he came here, to wait for this to happen, and help fulfill the Prophecy. His love, and the crag's magic, kept him alive—"

"Sounds like rubbish to me!" said Toby.

"But it's true, Toby!" Digby said. "Jemma should know! He was her great-great . . . well, I don't know how many greats, but her great-somethin'-uncle, anyway. He gave his life, almost three hundred years of it, for this. For all of us! An' now, at last, we're rid of these tyrants, we can live in peace. So let's honor all them little 'uns, an' mourn 'em, an' let 'em rest in peace."

"Aye, rest in peace!" Berola said, still standing firm, Gordo and the triplets beside her.

"Well then, what do we do with them evil fiends?"

"I got an idea!" A burly, leather-aproned man shoved from the middle of the crowd and strode up to them. "Griff Barton at your service," he said. "Blacksmith, an' mayor of Oxton, for what it's worth. We got Inquisitors' holdin' cells wot are built to keep in an army, with locks the same. Made the locks meself, I'm ashamed to say." He reddened, then smiled. "I kep' duplicate keys, though. Put them Agromonds in there an' they won't get out in a hurry, I can tell you."

"Aye," said Gordo. "Let's put their so-called justice to good use!"

"It's a start," Jemma said. "Thank you, Griff."

"My pleasure." Griff smiled. "An' I say we round up all them others wot have followed 'em all these years, too— Blackwater folk an' the like. Come one an' all to the Inquisitors' Inn!"

Most people were quieting down, but Murwyn and Vi, whose children Shade had so recently abducted, pushed to the front. They were trembling with rage and sorrow.

"An' what of our two," said Murwyn, "crushed under all that rubble, their souls gone goodness only knows where?"

"I'm so sorry," Jemma said softly. "We can dig for them if you like. . . . But their souls have gone. Into Light . . . We saw them both, they joined all the others near the end. It was beautiful, it really was."

Tiny reached out and took Murwyn's hand. "Yes, it was," he said. "All pink an' blue they was, them two wot flew in last, an' it was like they felt *happy*, an' it made me feel happy. Mr. Drudge, he was all sort of bright an' airy too, then floated up an' led 'em away—all together, jus' like Digby said, flyin' through the roof like one great big, bright balloon."

Vi gasped. "I saw that," she said, wiping away a tear. "You did too, Murwyn, love. You even remarked on it, remember?"

"Aye—we all saw it, not half an hour ago," said a tall man at the back. "Gold, pink, an' blue, like the lad said, an' so bright we could even see it through the Mist, risin' up from the castle. In't that right, Amelia?"

"That's right!" said an equally tall woman next to him. "Then it moved over the forest an' sort of hovered there for a minute, liftin' light from the trees, an' getting' bigger an' brighter. Quite lovely, it was."

"Lifting light from the trees?" Jemma gasped. "The forest phantoms! Drudge has taken them, as well." Of course. He wouldn't have left a single lost soul behind. All those twins and triplets were reunited at last, and free.

"Y'know," said an older man near the back, "I feel as though the heaviness I've carried since they took our Clodagh and Clodwin has sort o' lifted. . . . Twenty years of sorrow, gone!"

"Me too, I feel that," several voices joined in.

"An' . . . that was their souls, you reckon, goin' up like that?" said Murwyn. "If I knew at least their souls was safe, p'raps I could start to be at peace with it."

"Look!" Tiny yelped, pointing at the sky. Every eye followed his finger. In the middle of the blue, a large, bright

443

patch had appeared. It grew brighter still, like a white lake reflecting every color of the rainbow in pale, luminous hues. It pulsed once, twice, three times. Then slowly, it faded away

The crowd stood in awed silence. Then murmurs began again, swelling into chatter about that light in the sky, how intense it was, and how colorful everything looked now that all those poor children's souls had been saved at last. Murwyn turned to Vi. The two held each other and dissolved into tears.

"Let's let 'em be, love," Vi sobbed. "I'd rather remember 'em as they was."

Jemma heaved a sigh of relief. "Oh, my," she said, turning to Digby. "For a moment I thought we were going to have more violence on our hands."

"So did I, Jem. Got to say, though, I knows how they feel. I wanted to rip them harpies to shreds. Him too, even though he did save you from that beam."

"S'cuse, Miss Jemma." Jemma felt a tap on her shoulder. She turned. Ned stood next to her, his eyes bright and alert. What a difference from the ghost-like boy she'd seen when she and Digby left the storehouse! "Thank you for bringin' back the sun," he said, then darted away into the bustling crowd. It was as though they had all been under a spell, but now it was broken.

Jemma was never sure how much time passed in the whirl that followed. Question after question; person after person coming up to her and thanking her; snippets of Scagavay's dramatic end chattering their way through the crowd; the surge to the door as Pete and Toby carried Nox out, still unconscious. Soon after, Nocturna and Shade were led out by

Griff. They were deathly pale under the glare of sun and the hundreds of eyes watching them. The crowd fell back, creating a passage several people thick. The relief was palpable when the two were herded, bound in their coils of rope, onto a cart. They stood there, as stiff as mummies, as they were trundled away to meet their fate.

Last to be brought out was Feo's body, covered in Griff's apron to hide his wounds. The story of his murder had circulated like wildfire, and a shocked gasp went up. There were even a few whispers of sympathy for the lad whose own mother had slain him in cold blood.

"He was the only one of them who didn't kill anyone," Jemma said, her heart twinging as Griff and Murwyn carried him past. "He was so close to breaking away from them, Dig. Just couldn't quite do it."

"Yeah, well," Digby said, "I didn't much care for him, 'specially when he was tryin' to strangle me. But I s'pose his folks was as much of a magnet for him as mine is for me."

The crowd began to disperse, bidding Jemma goodbye and thanking her again before setting off. Carts rattled away down the rough track toward Hazebury, until only Jemma and the Goodfellows remained—and two other people, a woman and a boy, who hung back behind the Goodfellows' cart.

Rue and Caleb.

Even from a distance, Jemma could see that Caleb looked taller, his back straighter; and Rue's eyes were soft and sane. As soon as they knew they'd been seen, they turned and began to walk down the road to Hazebury—shy, Jemma guessed, after living in isolation for so long. They were about to disappear into the trees, when Caleb stopped and waved. Jemma waved back, and he paused for a moment, then smiled. In her mind's eye, she saw him in a year's time, walking taller than she. Saw him working as a baker in Hazebury, and Rue gathering crops in the fields. Whatever curse they'd been under had lifted. It would take them a while to adjust, but in time, she knew, the effects of it would also fade. Perhaps she could even help with that. . . .

With a final wave, the two of them disappeared from view.

"Rue an' Caleb?" Digby said.

Jemma nodded, and thought of the other person she'd met in the forest. Bryn. What did he think about the sun? He'd been content without it, but she felt sure he'd like the plants and flowers that would now flourish. She would visit him soon and find out.

"There's prob'ly a lot of folks who'll take time getting' used to this," Digby said, turning his face up to the sun. "Me, I love it!" He grinned, then broke into laughter. "Hey, Jem, what d'you reckon Lok an' his cronies are thinkin' right now? I bet they're none too pleased!"

"No, I bet they're not!" Jemma chuckled.

"Unless they've all been under some kind of spell, of course," he added. "Who knows? Maybe they's as happy as skylarks."

Happy . . . Jemma looked at him, and the joy in his blue eyes, and realized that was what she felt—probably for the first time in her life. Happy, and free.

"Time we was goin' now," said Berola, chivying Simon, Tiny, and Flora onto the cart.

"Hop aboard, Jemma lass," said Gordo. "We've plenty of room."

"Thank you," said Jemma, "but I'd like to stay for a while with Noodle and Pie. Sort of . . . take it all in. And make a new kind of Offering. In honor of Drudge." One was already taking shape in her mind, using sprigs of fresh greenery and some of the small white flowers that were springing up at her feet, as well as Bethany's gold coin, if she could find it in the rubble of the dungeons.

"I understand." Berola hugged her, then climbed up next to the triplets. "Come by later, then, hmmm?"

"I will. And . . . would you do something for me, and ask those two that just left if they'd like a ride down the hill? They might feel a bit lost. The boy's lived around here his whole life, and it's probably years since his mother left the forest."

"Course, lass," said Gordo. "We'll help 'em any way we can." He pecked her awkwardly on the cheek before heaving himself into the driver's seat. "Thank you again, Jemma Solvay. You're welcome to stop with us as long as you like, y'know. Though I 'spect you'll be wantin' to get back to your folks as soon as you can."

"Yes," said Jemma. An image flickered into her head: her parents, galloping over the moors with no Mist to stop them, heather and gorse vividly purple and yellow in the morning sun. Her heart leapt. "Yes! They're on their way. . . . Marsh, too—her leg is already healed enough to ride. They'll be here by nightfall."

"Then I'll make a slap-up feast," Berola said. "We'll have a right proper celebration! I'll tell Coral and Joe to make up beds at the Hazebury Inn for you all. You'll be their first guests in goodness knows how long! Come on, Digby lad, let's be off, eh?"

Digby put his arm around Jemma. "Shall I come back later and fetch you in the cart?"

She shook her head. "I'll walk. Only this time, we'll take the road." Noodle and Pie squeaked their approval.

"See you later, then," said Digby.

"See you later." Jemma wrapped her arms around him. "Thank you. For everything."

"Don't mention it." Digby held her for a moment, then kissed her softly on the lips. Her head felt full of light as he pulled away and then hopped up into the seat beside Gordo. He was grinning from ear to ear. So was she.

"Bye, Jemma, bye!" Flora, Simon, and Tiny waved from the cart as Pepper plodded toward the road to Hazebury. "Bye, Noodle, Pie!" Flora chimed in. "See you later!"

Jemma watched them and waved back. A warm gust of wind fluffed Noodle and Pie's fur, tickling Jemma's ears and flapping a short lock of flame-red hair across her eyes. As the cart reached the bend in the road, Digby looked up. The sun was now high overhead. He stood, turned, and waved again.

"Hey, Jem!" he yelled. "You noticed anythin' odd these last few hours?"

"You mean, besides the sun, the blue sky, the lack of Mist . . . ?"

"No bell!" he shouted. "There's been no bell!"

No bell, Jemma thought as Pepper carried the Good-fellows out of sight. Time was no longer marked by that dark, heavy sound. Centuries of Agromond tyranny were over. No more Mord-days. From now on, it would be Sunday again.

"It is done, it is done," she whispered to herself, to the whishing trees, to Drudge's spirit, to Majem's, and to Jamem's. *"Now, Myst, be gone. Let there be Sunne. . . ."*

Beneath her feet, the ground trembled. But it was the tremble of awakening, not of cold or fear. The crag, shedding its deep slumber, was already stretching and yawning under the sunlight it had missed for so long. Coming back to life. And Jemma knew that its power would soon be available again, offered to anyone who needed it. It could nourish the fields, the crops. Be used for healing. For the benefit of all, rather than hoarded by the few for their own evil ends. And from now on, its gifts would be received with gratitude and respect. She would make sure of that.

"*It is done,*" she said again, scratching Noodle's and Pie's chins.

Before her, Anglavia stretched out for miles, its hills and villages sparkling under clear midday sun and sky.

ACKNOWLEDGMENTS

With deep gratitude to everyone whose support and encouragement helped bring Jemma's story into the open. Special thanks to my husband Jon, for his insights, tireless fielding of questions, and patience while I was glued to my laptop; my family in England, for their love and enthusiasm (and I hope the little ones will have as much fun finding their names tucked in these pages as I did writing them there); Roger Weinreich, for cheering me to the finish line on the first draft and beyond; Karen Deaver and Cynthia Paces, for invaluable early-draft feedback; Dana Friis and Ann de Forest, for invaluable later-draft feedback; Susan Reiner, Tim Morgan, and David Gollancz, for incisive comments and ideas; and Nikki Gregoroff, Deb Chamberlin, Jamie Danek, and teen beta readers Isabel Cleff and Logan Danek, as well as Nichola Perks, Jade Danek, Kimberly Jones, Kolter Erickson, Mariel Carter, and Cianna Wynn. There are many others—dear friends, fellow authors, and writing group mates—whose comments and excitement also spurred me on. You all fueled the fire. And this list would not be complete without loving remembrance of Billie, the original Solvay, whose name inspired a dynasty.

A big thank you to Gotham Writers Workshop in New York, especially Alex Steele; Kathy Temean at the NJ SCBWI; and Tisha Bender.

I'm indebted also to Delacorte Press and the amazing team who worked so hard to make this book what it is: Colleen Fellingham and Jody Revenson, copy editors extraordinaires (with extra thanks to Colleen for extra questions along the way!); Tamar Schwartz, for eagle-eyed proofreading; Melissa Greenberg, for fabulous cover/chapter fonts, section motifs, and overall design; Rebecca Short, assistant editor, for such a thorough and thoughtful first read; and Chris Rahn, for such beautiful jacket artwork.

Last but by no means least, to my wonderful editor at Delacorte Press, Michelle Poploff, who saw the potential, and whose careful guidance has brought this book to life.

ABOUT THE AUTHOR

Kit Grindstaff was born near London and grew up in the rolling countryside of England, a country which is curiously similar to Anglavia. After a brush with pop stardom (under her maiden name of Hain), she moved to New York and embarked on her still-thriving career as a pop songwriter. Kit now lives with her husband in the rolling countryside of Pennsylvania. *The Flame in the Mist* is her first novel. You can find her on the Web at kitgrindstaff.com and theflameinthemist.com.